THE ARROW THAT

FLIETH BY DAY

BY

ERIN RAINWATER

The Arrow That Flieth By Day
© 2006 Erin Rainwater

For Him

There is no fear in love;
but perfect love casteth out fear.
~John

*M*andy's sleep-laden eyes revolted against the spears of sunbeams shooting down from the tepee's open flaps nearly fifteen feet above her. An awful smell assaulted her nostrils. Recognition of where she struck. A sickening knot formed once again in her stomach.

She lay on a mat in the dwelling into which she had been forcibly shoved two days earlier. Judging by the amount of light coming through the top opening, it was late morning.

She did not chide herself for sleeping so late. She had spent most of the night crying. And praying.

Glancing toward the back of the tepee, she noticed the empty mat of the middle-aged woman whose lodge she shared. Mandy presumed the woman was also a white captive but from long ago. Her eyes were blue, her hair light brown, but she wore it braided and tied with beaded string. Her dress was hide, and she wore a necklace made of some poor animal's teeth. Though she was kind, and her expression sympathetic, she strictly held to Indian ways.

She obviously did not feel so imprisoned as Mandy, who had several times taken a stab at conversation. She had tried especially to get through the idea of escaping, but the woman apparently spoke no English. At their first meeting Mandy pointed to herself and said, "Mandy," then pointed to the woman. She touched her chest with her finger and spoke a foreign name. Mandy shook her head. "English name." The woman appeared to think hard for a moment, then said, "Vi...Vic...tor...i...a."

"Victoria! You do speak English!"

"English," the woman replied. But it wasn't long before Mandy realized that the woman's name was about all she recalled of what had once been her primary tongue.

Rising from her mat, Mandy went to the "door" of the tepee, which was merely a flap in the hide, and peeked out to survey the camp as she had done several times in the preceding days. The smell that her nostrils repelled came from a pot of...whatever...left simmering over the fire just outside the lodge. Though she was hungry, she was certain her stomach would not keep down food similar to what it had summarily rejected the day before.

The inhabitants of the camp were about their daily

routines, it seemed, and paid no attention to the lodge that held the white woman. She would need to familiarize herself with those routines, along with the layout of the village. She had no intention of becoming like the woman in her lodge. She would have to figure out a plan of escape.

Returning inside, she picked up the brush Victoria had offered her the morning before when her hair had a kidnapping's worth of gnarls. As she brushed out her long blond tresses, she recalled with disquietude the events of the past two days.

* * *

Cheeks flushed, Mandy boosted herself from the lap of her fellow passenger on the Concord stage and reseated herself in proper form.

"I'm sorry, Jim, but that one was a rather sizeable rut."

"Don't apologize." The redheaded lad of twenty wore an impish smile. "I'm rather enjoying the ride."

She glanced at the Russian couple sitting across from her and her seatmate, Jim Fletcher. Although they spoke no English, it was obvious they were amused by her predicament.

She gazed again out the window as the setting mid-June sun emblazoned the sky with streaks of scarlet and orange. She recalled the fearful and exacting five-month trip she had taken along a similar westward route four years earlier when her father, mother and siblings had pulled up roots in Pennsylvania and migrated to Colorado Territory in 1861. Her family had found their niche in the growing community of Denver near the foothills of the Rocky Mountains. Mandy served as legal assistant to her father, James Berringer, just as she had in his law office in Pittsburgh. It was legal business that had taken her to St. Joseph in Missouri Territory on her father's behalf. Now, just twenty-four hours from home, she was anxious for the trip to be behind her.

"Way station ahead!" shouted the driver from his loft.

"And not a mile too soon," Jim said.

The wheels of the stage were scarcely stopped when Jim had the door open and one leg out. He helped Mandy alight, and she brushed a fine layer of trail dust off her lavender calico dress.

They entered the "home station" where supper and a bed awaited them. Mandy knew the food would be hot, the coffee strong, the company talkative.

"Welcome, welcome," the stationmaster shouted as he shook the men's hands. "I'm Josh Magruder. Y'all are right on time. The missus'll serve up supper whilst I unhitch the team."

The venison, beans and baked potatoes were on the table when the passengers finished washing up. These were rare delicacies on a trip such as this. To expect other than salt pork, greasy fried potatoes and dry cornbread was presumptuous. The meal was topped off with a large slice of hot dried-apple pie and coffee.

"All we need now is a piano," Jim said. "Mandy here tells me she plays up a storm after supper back home in Denver. Sure would go nice right about now." He rubbed his bulging midsection. Then, straightening abruptly, he turned an ear towards the door.

A moment later they all heard it—faint at first, then the clear, undeniable sound of a child crying hard.

The faces at the table exchanged confounded glances. The plaintive cry repeated. Mr. Magruder sprang to his feet, snatched up his rifle and sprinted to the window. He squinted into the thick darkness of the prairie whose sole source of light on this cloudy night was that cast from the cabin. Then he moved to the door and inched it open.

"Heaven help us! How in tarnation...?"

Jim and Mandy raced to join him. "Y'all stay put," he ordered. "Let me see to this."

They watched as the stationmaster slipped out and, after peering in every direction, lifted an Indian child into his arms. His eyes still searching the blackness, he backed hastily into the cabin, closing and bolting the door behind him.

"Where on earth could he have come from?" Mandy asked as she took the child from him.

"I didn't see no one else out there. But this kid didn't just wander all the way out here by hisself. Did y'all see any sign of Arapaho along the route? The kid's outfit looks t' be Arapaho."

"There's ones northa here near the border, and there's been raidin' up there since spring," the stage driver said. "Separate tribes some miles south, too, but it's been a while since I've had trouble from any of 'em along my route. But just cause I didn't see hide nor hair of anyone, forty-five years on the stage line has taught me t' not assume no one was watchin' us."

"This child is sick," Mandy said, her hand pressed to the boy's feverish face. He looked to be about three years old. Each exhaled breath produced a croupy sound. He was filthy, his cheeks were streaked with dirt mixed with tears, and his feet were bloody. His sole piece of clothing was a thigh-length buckskin shirt.

Mandy held him and soothed him while Mrs. Magruder gathered cloths and a basin of cool water. The men, including the Russian, took up their weapons and stood guard at every window. The immigrant didn't need to speak the language to understand the danger. Pistols and rifles were aimed out but in no particular direction. There was nothing to sight on—yet.

Throughout the night, every animal noise, every shift in the wind, every distant roll of thunder had the inhabitants jolting. Those whose turn it was to sleep were hard pressed to find it.

The child slept restlessly alongside Mandy on her cot. She had soothed him with a lullaby and rocked him to sleep, then laid him down next to her so she could be watchful of his breathing and his fever. She tried not to let him sense her apprehension. Some Indians were superstitious and got weak-kneed at the thought of bumping into roving spirits in the night, but some laid claim to no such beliefs, and those were the dangerous ones. She could almost feel their breath on the back of her neck.

Her eyes lifted to the window next to her cot and took in the rectangular patch of night sky. The moon struggled to peek from between silvery edges of cloven clouds. That same moon was suspended over an Indian lodge where the child must belong. It hung, too, over the two-story white frame house where her parents and brother and sister would be sleeping peacefully now.

She thought back on the evening before she left for St. Joe, when her father had bid her a private farewell on their front porch. He prayed for her safety from Psalm 91: "Thou shalt not be afraid for the terror by night; nor for the arrow that flieth by day; nor for the pestilence that walketh at noonday. A thousand shall fall at thy side, and ten thousand at thy right hand; but it shall not come nigh thee."

Then he put his arm around her and pressed his cheek against her head. "Now don't you go running off with the first handsome young lawyer or riverboat pilot you encounter on this trip. At least give me fair warning if I'm going to lose my very best legal assistant."

Mandy laughed. "Pa, I'm twenty-eight years old, am not the spectacle of beauty you say I am, and despite your optimism, am long past hope for marriage." They embraced, her heart full of love for her father.

Now, after several more moments of sky gazing and reminiscing, Mandy settled beneath the blankets. The Indian boy cuddled close to her, his arms curled into his chest, his breathing less labored. She stroked thick wafts of black hair from his bronze face and whispered, "Don't worry, little one, it shall not come nigh thee, either."

Early the next morning, the driver held the stage door open for his passengers while speaking to the one who would not be boarding.

"Are yeh sure yeh know what you're doin', missy? It just don't set right with me, leavin' one o' my passengers behind. Not for any reason."

"Quite sure, Mort," Mandy answered. "The little one needs another day to recuperate before such a taxing journey. The next stage comes again this evening, and we'll be on our way tomorrow morning, just one day behind you." She looked down into the wide brown eyes of the mystery child whose hand had buried itself in hers and whose fate was now in the care of white-skinned strangers.

Jim asked, "Why can't you just leave him with the Magruders and let them put him on the stage like they offered?"

"I'll feel better if I can take him myself rather than forcing him on a load of passengers who may not want anything to do with him."

"Here's a note tellin' the driver you're paid in full through to Denver." Mort said. "You'll have to pay extra for the kid, though."

"Thank you, Mort. See you there sometime when you're passing through."

"I'll look forward to it, missy."

5

Mandy turned to Jim. "Listen, someone in my family will be awaiting my arrival. I've spoken before about the twins, Julie and Jeffrey. My father is fifty-five, has silver hair and moustache, and will probably have on a white, wide-brimmed straw hat. My mother is about my height and has light brown hair she sweeps up into a large braid on top of her head. Please explain the circumstances to them, and put their minds at ease, will you?"

"That ain't gonna be too easy, seein's how my own thinkin' ain't exactly leanin' that way."

He climbed into the coach and stuck his head and elbow out the window. "I'm still afraid those redskins'll come around here lookin' for that kid."

"Or...they could attack the stage looking for him."

Jim hesitated. "As your pa might say, your point's well taken, counselor. Now, you take care."

Mandy and her hosts waved and watched the stage race away in swirls of dust.

"Well, it's time I got to work," Mr. Magruder said. "Storm's acomin', a supply wagon is due this afternoon, I got horses to feed and some repairs to make on the stable roof. That last hailstorm dropped some real cannonballs. But at least I can keep an eye out from up there. Somebody *must* be lookin' for that kid. Keep the guns handy, Mable."

"Sure thing, Josh." The stationmistress turned to Mandy. "I've got to haul some water up from the creek. Mind giving me a hand?"

"Not at all."

Mrs. Magruder fetched two revolvers and handed one to Mandy. She secured it in her wide purple belt. She picked up a bucket from beneath the bench outside the front door of the station house and started for the creek, the Indian child clinging to her hand. She picked him up and carried him when she saw his feet were still sore. He stayed at her side the rest of the morning while the two women cooked, cleaned, and did the kitchen chores.

Mrs. Magruder was about to call her husband in for the noon meal when a shout followed by a crashing sound came from the stable area. The women ran out and found Mr. Magruder on the ground writhing and gripping his knee. The stable door was swung wide open, and six horses were heading

6

onto the prairie.

"Josh! Are you all right? What happened?"

"Aww, a ladder rung gave way as I was comin' down from the roof," he answered through gritted teeth. "I fell against the door and knocked it open, then the horses spooked and ran out. I think I mighta busted my knee cap."

"Oh, dear, we've got to get you inside."

The women helped him to his feet. Each provided a shoulder for him to lean on as he hobbled back to the cabin.

"I gotta get those horses back."

"Don't fret now, Josh."

"How am I supposed to not fret? The supply wagon'll be here any time now. Those horses were to be rested and exchanged for the ones pullin' the wagon. It's my job to have 'em ready when…" A piercing cry of pain ended his sentence.

"You just set tight, Josh. I'll get 'em back."

"With my help," Mandy said.

"But you two can't—"

"We two can manage it just fine," his wife stated. "And right now, there ain't much choice, is there?"

"But those Indians could still be out there."

"We got our guns and will use them if needs be. Right, Mandy?"

She hesitated but a moment. Yes, she'd protect herself if the need arose. But she could be firing on the child's kin. Her voice subdued, she answered, "Right."

As much as it insulted his pride, Mr. Magruder conceded to the women's plan to recapture the horses while he sat and did nothing.

They saddled Mrs. Magruder's mare and her husband's bay gelding. The wind was rising and the temperature falling as dark clouds moved in, so Mandy went back to the cabin and donned her royal blue cloak. She tried to instruct the boy to remain inside, holding her hand up to signal him to stay, but found him running out to her by the time she was mounting.

"I'll take him in to Josh," said Mrs. Magruder, "and he'll just have to hold on to him till you're gone. I doubt the horses've gone far. They're herd animals and don't take a shine to bein' off by themselves for long. You go after the one that headed straight east. Approach him gently and speak softly. No sudden movements."

"Understood."

"And Mandy?"

She looked down from the back of the bay.

"You *would* use that gun." Her brow lifted, making the statement a question.

"If needs be." She patted the revolver that was tucked in her belt.

As Mrs. Magruder predicted, the horse Mandy chased hadn't gone much more than a mile before stopping to graze. She slowed the gelding and moved toward the stage horse slowly, speaking in gentle tones. He didn't seem to mind her approach. The two horses touched noses and both heads jerked slightly.

"Easy, boy. Easy." She reached and stroked his neck, then slipped the clasp of the lead onto his rope halter. She headed back toward the station.

Halfway there she saw the Indian boy running trippingly toward her. "Oh, no!" She trotted over to him, dismounted and lowered herself to one knee. He ran into her arms.

"You shouldn't be out here. Just look at you." Holding him at arm's length, she noted the scratches on his hands and legs and face that belied the many times he had fallen on his trek to find her. "I was coming back." She wished he could understand.

He began to shiver. She removed her cloak and draped it around him. As she did so she was struck by a sound, one she not only heard but actually felt. It was like thunder, rolling ever closer. Had the storm arrived already? Yet there was more to it...a vibration, that penetrated to the marrow.

An ominous sense overtook her.

She rose and turned slowly.

Fear struck with a scorpion-like sting.

A band of eight to ten Indians raced toward her, their horses' unshod hooves pounding the earth.

Her hand flew to her belt and withdrew the revolver. Racing thoughts collided within her. Stand and fight, or flee? There were more attackers than there were bullets. But was there time to make a run for the station?

Fight? Or *flee*?

She raised the revolver and took aim.

The boy bolted forward, shedding the cloak and racing

past her toward the fast-approaching braves. She reached for him but missed, dashed after him, finally snatched him up and ran furiously back to the bay.

He spooked and reared.

The stage horse ran off into the open plain.

Panic-stricken, she reseated the gun in her belt and grabbed repeatedly at the reins before taking a firm hold of them. She tossed the child onto the saddle and climbed up behind him. Clutching him tightly, she dug her heels into the muscular horse and ran him hard.

The shrieking warriors spread out to surround her. She found herself being steered away from the station, but continued to kick the sides of the sprinting steed. But the swifter Indian ponies soon encompassed her and tightened their circle.

The boy cried out and reached toward a brave who was overtaking them. The gesture nearly sent the child tumbling. As Mandy restrained him, she inadvertently pulled on the reins. The horse slowed; the warriors hedged about her. Her heart pounded. Her throat tightened.

One brave rode next to her, grabbed the rein and pulled her horse to a stop. He then reached out to the child, who anxiously took hold of the man's arm and was swung onto the pony. Stunned that the boy was plucked from her grasp, she reached after him. The brave shouted at her and knocked her arm away.

Another menacing, muscular brave drew alongside her as she gripped the handle of the revolver. He grabbed her wrist and snatched the gun from her hand. The rage in his threatening black eyes paralyzed her. He motioned to the brave who held the boy, and they immediately galloped away heading south. Mandy's little charge never once looked back.

The remaining braves began shouting and shaking fists in her face. Her breath came fast and deep.

The one who had taken her gun leapt from his horse, seized her around the waist and pulled her to the ground. His stormy eyes remained riveted on hers, intensifying her terror. Verbal assaults penetrated her ears. His powerful hand bit into her arm and he dragged her to his horse. She resisted when he started to lift her onto its back. "No! Let go of me!"

He spun her around and raised his hand above him. She

cowered, ducking her head to the side, awaiting the blow.

It did not come.

She lifted her eyes and guardedly glimpsed her assailant. His dark eyes were glacially cold, his hand still upraised.

One of the braves spoke and pointed to the west from where a dozen more Indians rode.

The enraged warrior eyed Mandy again and cocked his head toward his horse.

Surrendering to a crushing feeling of hopelessness, Mandy condescended.

The warrior lifted her onto the back of his paint and mounted behind her. His burly arms enclosed her, sending frost through her veins.

Taking hold of the rope bridle, he urged his horse south with a pounding of his heels.

CHAPTER 2

*E*merging timidly through the tepee opening, Mandy surveyed the area surrounding the lodge. The men and women of the camp were immersed in their work. Little boys ran and played chase games. Little girls carried dolls dressed in Indian costumes. Some of the dolls were secured in miniature cradleboards like the ones in which the women carried their babies.

A couple of curious girls who looked to be about eight years old ran up to her. They spoke to her without compunction as if she understood their every word. She let them feel her lavender cloth dress and brush their fingers along her white skin. They walked around her, studying her from all angles, stroking her yellow hair. She was a lover of children, and engaging with these little ones brought a smile for the first time since she arrived. The girls giggled, spun on their heels and ran away.

As she watched them leave, her eye caught sight of the little boy from the way station. He stopped when he saw her and regarded her for a moment. She waved at him, but he didn't return one. He was with a young woman—his mother, most likely. Mandy was happy for their reunion, but now must be about accomplishing her own with her family.

A tall, lean brave appeared at her side. She shrieked and outstretched her arm to keep him at bay. He did not speak and made no motion toward her. He just…*stood* there.

She sprang back into the lodge and waited for him to go away. A quarter of an hour must have passed, yet he was still standing outside. She assumed he was her guard and was there to stay. But there were essential things she needed to learn, and this man did not, at least at first glance, seem as intimidating as the vicious one who had pirated her off to this place. Gathering her courage, she stepped outside and, after a side glance at him, began to walk. He followed.

Everywhere she ventured, he shadowed her. He began speaking to her like the young girls had—friendly, non-threatening, and undaunted by the decidedly one-sided conversation. Still, she feared him, and hated his attendance, yet continued her reconnaissance, trying to sight the least busy places of the camp, the best hiding places, the areas with the fewest lodges. All the while, her guard chattered.

Some women standing at a ring of cook fires smiled and signaled her to come closer. With a bit of reluctance, she complied. They seemed as excited about having her there as the children had been. She observed how they cooked their meat on skewers that hung from ropes fastened at the tops of tripods. The skewers dangled at an angle over the fires. Her family had used similar means while traveling west with the wagon train.

The women refueled the fire by placing hard brown clumps on it, and these made it burn higher. Mandy picked one up and fingered it curiously, wondering what form of fuel this could be. She may need to use such a fuel once she was out on her own, on her way home.

One of the women gestured toward the land beyond the camp, then held both of her hands to the sides of her head and raised curved index fingers. *"Heneecee."*

"What is that? An elk? A deer? A buffalo?" At that instant she realized what the woman was telling her. This was a clump of dried buffalo dung. It was, she remembered hearing on her journey west, a very good fuel.

"Eeeeewwww!" She threw it to the ground.

The women laughed as Mandy stood with fingers spread, trying to decide what to do with her hands. She supposed she must look quite the sight and began to join in their laughter.

Struck with an uneasiness, her smile disappeared and she backed away from the women. Was this how it started with Victoria? Laughing a little here and there, feeling a kinship with the natives, then ultimately losing her identity? The women looked puzzled by her sudden change in mood. She nodded to let them know she appreciated their friendliness, then turned to leave. There stood the omnipresent brave.

"Get away from me!" she shouted, and headed back toward her dwelling. "Do you understand? Leave me alone!"

He outpaced her, then turned and walked backward before her, chatting all the while.

Her steps halted. She pointed to herself and then to her lodge. Then she pointed to him and to the prairie beyond. "Do you get my meaning, whatever your name is? It's got to be something like Oh Great Warrior Who Never Stops Chattering. Let's just simplify it to Jackass Jaws. J.J. for short. Please just leave me alone!"

She spun and crashed into the solid, buckskinned-clad chest of another brave who had slipped unnoticed from around a horse tethered nearby. His appearance was strikingly different from the other braves. His skin was a somewhat lighter bronze. His honey-colored hair was cut to just below his shoulders—comparatively short for an Indian. And those eyes—were they green?

"What are you, some kind of mutation?

The second brave's green eyes scrutinized Mandy as he spoke to his friend. J.J. looked discouraged. He nodded his head in reluctant agreement, and the two Indians left.

Left on her own at last, she continued to survey the camp, seeking the most expedient exits and taking note of the areas where the horses were kept. On the way back to her lodge, she scuttled around a crowd of excited men apparently involved in some sort of game of chance. J.J. was among them and caught sight of her, flashing a broad smile. She offered a scornful glare in return.

The persistent brave grabbed the mutant's arm and drug him along to cut across her path. J.J. looked at her optimistically and spoke a few more enthusiastic words.

"Stay away from me!" she shouted and followed up with a shove to his chest.

Her message was clear to him now. His expression fell; his smile dissolved.

She whirled and tramped away, but after a few steps she slowed, stabbed by a twinge of guilt. He hadn't been at all threatening and didn't deserve such rancor.

Turning to face him, she sighed. "The truth is, you *scare* me, J.J. I just don't know what to make of you. But somehow I feel like I owe you an apology. So, for what it's worth, I'm sorry for the wisecracks. I'm sure you have an honorable name."

She glanced over his shoulder at the second brave's impassive face. "You, too. For the mutant thing. After all, you're really not that bad looking. Quite nice looking, actually. To be perfectly honest, you're downright eye-filling. So, no offense intended."

She gingerly took a few backward steps, then turned and headed for her lodge.

"None taken."

CHAPTER 3

*M*andy froze. When she finally turned, the two braves were propelling their way back into the crowd of men involved in the game.

"Wait!" She started after them. "Wait, please!"

It had to have been the mutant who spoke. J.J. would have used English earlier if he could have. Edging her way amidst the mass of shirtless bodies, her eyes darted in search of the one whose hair and eyes were lighter than the others. He could be her passage out of here.

It was difficult to see around men of such tall stature with arms flailing as they cheered their friends on. She was bumped in the face and shoulders more than once.

One of the braves grabbed her arm and drew her to the center of the circle. The men cheered wildly. Humiliated, scared and near to tears, her eyes cut from one bronze face to another as they took measure of her.

"They do not mean to ill-treat you, woman," came a voice from behind her.

Taking hold of her wrist, the man she had sought spoke in his native tongue to the gathering. A few smiling braves stepped aside for them, and he led her out of the circle. The laughter continued as the game resumed.

Her rescuer stopped and turned to her but didn't speak.

"I-I guess I should first thank you for getting me out of there. I don't ever remember feeling so humiliated."

"They meant you no harm, nor shame, which is more than I can say for your intentions with White Fox."

Mandy glanced down at the hand that still held her wrist. The man released it.

"White Fox?"

"The one you christened 'J.J.' He is an honorable young man who for some reason, perhaps his lack of maturity, or good taste, wanted to get to know you."

"Well, I...I tried to apologize for that. Forgive me if my disposition is a little off, what with being kidnapped and held prisoner and all."

"You're not a prisoner."

"Then why—"

"Would your name happen to be Mandy?"

Stunned, she asked, "How did you know that?"

His eyes cast down under a wrinkled brow.

"Oh, I know, Victoria told you."

"Victoria?"

"The white lady they have me bunking in with."

"She is called Swift Legged Woman. And by the way, the people here are calling you Woman Shot With Sun's Arrow, because of that hair."

"And what do the people call you?"

His weighty gaze held hers. "Mutant."

She flushed and looked away. "I, uh, apologized for *that* once already, too."

His features softened. "For a fact, you did. And I believe it's time I offered an apology to you for trifling with you in return instead of just telling you…"

"Just tell me how I get out of here."

With an outstretched arm he gestured away from the crowd. "Let's walk."

"You haven't yet told me your name," she said as they headed toward a cluster of lodges.

"I am called Dakota."

"How is it that you're so fluent in the Queen's English, Dakota? And *where* did you get those green eyes?"

"From my mother."

"She's white?"

"She was."

His tepee was not far, and upon reaching it he stepped aside to allow her to enter first. She peered in, and to her relief, noticeably absent from this one were scalps hanging from the poles like she had seen in other lodges she had peeked into. She entered and stood near the center lodge pole.

"Dakota, I need you to help me get out of here."

"That's not possible right now." He stepped to the rear of the lodge.

"It's *essential*. My family will be worried sick about me. They'll have soldiers out looking for me, and it could cause a lot of trouble between our peoples. There's been enough of that the last few years, has there not?"

He came to her and held out a blue bundle. "I found this

16

out on the plain. Would it be yours?"

"My cloak!" She took it from him, held it against herself, and tried to smooth out the wrinkles.

"It's because of that kind of trouble that it's unsafe for you to leave here now. There are bands of marauders all around. Chances of a white woman getting ten miles are slim. You're fortunate that warriors from this tribe found you out there before others did."

"*Fortunate*? Your pals chased me down, surrounded me, bellowed at me, one drug me from my horse, and under threat of a beating made me ride here with him, and now I'm kept here against my will. That's not my definition of fortunate."

"I heard about what happened from Thunder Cloud, the warrior who brought you here. The boy they found with you, Little Dog, is somehow the only survivor of an assault on his and other families while they were on a hunting and foraging expedition. There was much evidence that the attackers were white, and finding you with the boy made the warriors assume you had something to do with it. I'm not offering that as an excuse for how you were treated, just an explanation. When Little Dog was finally able to speak of what happened, it was clear that you had only cared for him in the aftermath.

"So you're not a prisoner, Mandy. No one else has been unkind to you, have they?" She shook her head. "You're free to move about at will, aren't you?"

"Being hounded by a six-foot-plus brave at every turn, guarding my every move, is hardly what I call freedom."

Dakota chuckled. "You mean White Fox? He hasn't been guarding you. He's been courting you."

Her eyes widened and her jaw fell.

"You've got to give him credit for taking on such a colossal task, considering the language barrier."

Mandy's hand flew to her cheek. "Oh, no! You didn't tell him what I called him, did you?"

"Of course not, just that you didn't understand what was going on."

"Why would he want to court me? He doesn't even know me, and he can't be more than twenty years old."

"Age doesn't matter so much here. And you're…"

His eyes traced her form and wavy blond hair. Despite her present circumstances, her face held a tenderness that a man longs to see in a woman's countenance. Her eyes were green like his and looked back at him from over the soft curves of her cheeks.

"…you're not unattractive. And with that yellow hair…why, some might consider you prime pickin's."

"As flattering as that sounds, I won't be sticking around to see who wins me. I'm getting out with or without your help." She headed for the opening of the tepee.

"Mandy, you can't."

"You said I'm free."

"I'm telling you there were Kiowa raiders out there and they had you in their sights. If they had gotten to you first they would've killed you, but not before… You don't need the details, do you?"

She didn't need the details.

"God sure must've been watching over you out there."

She lowered her eyes. These past few days she'd been entertaining notions of abandonment by God. But He had been protecting her all along, through the most unlikely of circumstances, and even provided a haven for her in this place.

"I was shielded from the arrow that flieth by day," she whispered.

"I'm sorry, what did you say?"

"Dakota, if I could just get back to the stage route. There's a way station an hour or so north of here."

"There's no station there."

"Yes, there is. I was only a half-mile from it when your warrior-friends trounced on me. You had to have seen it yourself when you found my cape. It's where—"

"*There's no station.*" His gaze fell; his voice lowered. "Not anymore."

She stared at him, not daring to ask what he meant.

"I'm sorry to have to tell you. It's been burned out. The people who ran it…are dead."

She clutched her cloak to her abdomen. "No, you're mistaken. That can't be true."

"I came upon it this morning on my way home. Investigators from the stage line were digging through the rubble. After they left, I took a closer look for myself. The Kiowa left sign."

She shook her head in disbelief. "It was just the two of

them. And Mr. Magruder's knee was injured. He couldn't even walk. They were nearly defenseless."

She looked despairingly into his eyes. "My family will have heard by now and be wondering what became of me."

Dakota moved closer and took a breath before continuing. "You need to know that...the remains of *three* bodies were found there. Perhaps a youth in the raiding party stormed the cabin, took a bullet, and was burned up with the station operators. But...everyone is assuming that third person was a Denver woman named Mandy who stayed behind an extra day to care for an Indian child."

She sucked in her breath.

"I'm so sorry. I know how you must—"

She spun and started for the opening of the tepee. He took a firm hold of her arm. "Mandy, wait."

"I can't wait! I can't allow my family to mourn over me needlessly!"

"It won't be needless if you get yourself killed trying to get back to them."

Desperation filled her eyes. "Please, Dakota. Will you help me?"

His gaze held hers for several seconds, then shifted to a spot behind her on the tepee hide. Releasing her arm, he stepped across the lodge to one of the numerous colorful drawings of Indian life sewn into the wall.

"Your torment strikes a familiar chord in me." His fingers moved along the images. "I have known your anguish."

"How could you know?"

He stopped and caressed one of the figures. "My mother was captured by renegade Indians as a young teen and eventually ended up out here with this tribe. After a few years she fell in love with and married my father, Wild Eagle, and they were happy together. But even at a young age I was aware of how sad she got when she spoke of her parents, and how much they must miss her and worry about her."

He took a step sideways, focusing on another figure.

"When I was five, my mother and I were permitted to go to Indianapolis to try to find them. She loved my father and promised we'd come back. She found her parents, but their joy in discovering their daughter was alive was tempered by the news of her Indian husband and half-breed son. Soon after, she was killed by a runaway team of horses. My grandparents never would claim me as kin and readily sent me east with a missionary couple who adopted me."

He turned to face her. "In time I grew to love my new family very much, but like my mother, I found it unsettling throughout the years to think of my father forever wondering what had become of us. I could barely remember him, but clearly recalled my mother's promise to return."

"But you *did* return."

He motioned for her to come closer to the hide wall. "When I was seventeen my parents drowned in a river crossing," he said as he pointed to a pair of wavy blue lines. As he continued speaking, he passed his hand over scenes along a timeline. "Without a home or family, I returned west to find Wild Eagle, and to claim the heritage that was mine through him. It was no small task considering how little I remembered, and how the tribes move about, sometimes on the plains and sometimes nearer the mountains. But I *had* to find him. Wild Eagle never knew if we were dead, or had just deserted him, until the day I found him twelve years after leaving."

"How terribly tragic for him."

Here he caressed a drawing of two men facing each other with their arms outstretched toward one another. "This is where tragedy turned into rejoicing."

Mandy read the gentle reverie in his countenance and realized he truly could empathize with what now confronted her.

"He had remarried, but..." He stroked the depictive figures on the tepee hide again, then faced her.

"I'll round up some men, and first thing tomorrow morning we'll escort you south to Fort Lyon. You can send a message from there and obtain safe passage home."

She smiled in relief. "How can I ever repay your benevolence?"

Tender green eyes settled on hers. "When I heard the story of how a lawyer's daughter from Denver delayed her homecoming to tend to a sick Indian child despite being coaxed not to, and died because of it, I felt that the world had lost a good woman. You cared for Little Dog and have paid a high price. Let's just consider my...benevolence...as repayment for your watchfulness of him."

Their eyes remained fixed on one another's for several heartbeats. Dakota finally broke the silence.

"I have to go meet with my father and some of the elders. Be ready at dawn tomorrow."

"You know where to find me." With a measure of reluctance, she headed for the tepee opening.

"Mandy?"

She turned.

He lifted her cloak off the ground and held it out to her.

"Oh, I hadn't realized I dropped it. Thank you...again."

She stepped out of the tepee under a cloudless, deep blue sky. The warm breeze seemed to carry a breath of new life, assuring her that tomorrow she would be on her way home.

Yet her soul was heavy from the loss of her friends from the stage station. And she knew she would not soon forget the handsome brave who would help her return to her family.

Having witnessed how much the painted and sewn drawings inside Dakota's lodge meant to him, she more keenly noticed the ones on the outside of the tepee hides all around her. There were stick people, triangles, more of those wavy lines, and other designs she couldn't decipher. Each, she now knew, told a story.

She passed a corral where several dozen horses were enclosed by a fence of cottonwood branches bound tightly together. From among the browns and blacks and sorrels and paints, she took notice of a grand, flaxen-maned palomino. She had always been partial to them, and this one was magnificent.

But then her eye caught something that arrested her stride—a brown horse, taller and more muscular than the Indian ponies.

Not one, but six of them.

The stage horses from the Magruders' station.

CHAPTER 4

There was little doubt these were the horses that had drawn Mandy's stage and escaped from the barn, including the one she had chased and caught. But even if they were, what would it prove? That the raiders responsible for the killings were not Kiowa but were from this camp after all? That the man called Dakota had lied to her?

The threat of roving marauders. The tragic story of his father's great loss. He had seemed so genuine. But she certainly had been duped before by charm, good looks, and feigned sincerity.

The palomino pawed the ground and snorted. Mandy momentarily envisioned herself jumping onto its back, clearing the fence and heading for open prairie. If the killers were here, she would be safer on the run, contrary to what Dakota told her. He could be lying about the dangers out there, and about helping her get home.

Yet she wouldn't have even known about the murders if he hadn't told her. And the Magruders were still alive when that warrior—what was his name? Thunder Cloud?— came upon her from the opposite direction as the station.

But he could have been part of that other group she'd seen approaching, and those may have been the ones who had gone to the station and massacred her friends. How else would the horses end up here?

She must not jump to conclusions. *We must take each morsel of evidence as it comes in our collective search for the truth,* her father often reminded her when they worked on criminal cases in which the facts were not soon forthcoming. *Suspicions will either be verified or found to be without merit. But the truth...it will prevail.*

The only way to know for sure if these even were the stage horses was to find the steed she believed was the one she caught. He had a bare spot on his neck beneath his mane, probably from a poorly fitted harness, she had reasoned at the time she apprehended him.

Thus, her first morsel of evidence was in this corral.

Glancing over her shoulders, she studied the people

nearby. All were involved in their own activities. She walked closer to the gate, checking continually for a set of eyes that may take notice of her.

She lifted the rope off the gate and slowly opened it. It made no creaking sound like the gates at home. Moisture formed on her brow as she bent low and moved in among the horses. Maneuvering through the manes and masses of muscle, she occasionally was squished as they shifted their weight. This stranger in their midst made them skittish.

Moving slowly so as to keep them from spooking, she worked her way toward the horse she suspected was the one she had chased at the station.

"Easy, boy. Remember me? I'll not hurt you." She rubbed his neck with a light hand, then reached up to his mane and brushed it aside, exposing the patch of bare skin she had seen two days earlier out on the plain. She let out a nervous breath.

Rising by degrees, she looked about the corral and the camp beyond. Terror crowded inside her chest when she sighted the malevolent warrior who had forced her here enter through the still open gate and look about the corral. She instantly ducked down. Bent over, she scurried to the back of the corral. Her fear was sensed by the horses, who whinnied and moved about. She stopped for a moment—or what seemed like an eon—to calm them.

A powerful bronze arm encircled her waist and jerked her off the ground. She screamed. The warrior held her so tightly she could not draw another breath, but she kicked and twisted with all her might. The horses grew wide-eyed and jolted, some of them bumping into the warrior. He lost his grip and she dropped to the ground face down. Surrounded by a dozen powerful legs and jittery hooves, she rolled over and lifted her eyes to meet the dreadful glare of the ghastly warrior standing over her. His bare chest and arms bore the scars of fierce fighting. A necklace of bear claws hung from his neck, and eagle feathers dangled from his long black hair. And those intense black eyes!

The Indian reached down for her. She smacked his hand away. "You *were* part of the band who killed my friends!"

He let out a guttural groan as he reached for her again. Ignoring her blows, he caught a firm hold of her wrist and pulled her to her feet. He faced her away from him and pinned

23

her arms to her sides.

He shouted something to the gathering crowd outside the corral. Dakota was among them, looking as confounded as the others. He entered through the half-opened gate.

"Mandy!" he called over the backs of the restive horses. "What on earth are you doing?"

She stood confined by a savage, his warm breath on the side of her face, his powerful hands strangling her arms and causing her hands to grow numb and cold. The sharp, jagged claws of his necklace penetrated her back. The notion of her friends being slaughtered flashed in her mind, followed by the memory of her forced journey here with this brutal warrior's bloodthirsty arms around her. A fury quickened within her like none she had ever known in all of her twenty-eight years.

"You deceived to me!" she screamed with all the emotion that raged within her. "You knew all along who killed them. You lied about everything! You two-faced *half-breed*!"

In that instant of terror and loathing, Mandy kicked back hard into the warrior's shin, ran the heel of her shoe down the length of it and came down violently on his instep. He lifted his head and cried out, loosening his grip on her arms. She thrust her elbow into the hollow of his gut, which bent him in half.

She dashed to the closest horse, the palomino, and tried to swing onto his back. He spun into her, hurling her sidelong to the ground. Her head smacked the earth and her lungs emptied of air.

The horse reared above her. She never felt the pain, nor heard the sharp crack of her bones splitting as the steed's hoof came down on her left ankle.

Dakota and the others heard it. He called her name and cautiously walked toward where she lay, fearful of causing the horses to trample her further. Her captor was recovered enough to help herd them toward the opposite end of the corral.

The palomino stood next to Mandy, eyes wide and nostrils flared. "Easy, Chief. Take it easy. That's right." The horse's head jerked up when Dakota reached out his hand, but the animal otherwise remained still. He petted him and nudged him away from Mandy. Finally, the horse turned and trotted away.

Dakota fell to one knee beside the woman who had stood in his lodge with pain in her eyes and a desperate plea on her lips. What he saw in her eyes and heard from her lips a moment ago did not seem to come from the same woman. Turning her onto her back, he wiped the hair and dirt from her face.

She was taking shallow breaths, but full consciousness eluded her. He called her name. She opened her eyes, but they did not focus.

He carefully lifted her, instructing a brave to raise her leg and keep it immobile as he carried her to Swift Legged Woman's lodge. Two women adjusted the top opening with long poles, allowing more sunlight to enter as he laid Mandy on her mat.

He began to unlace her high-buttoned shoe. She cried out at every movement of her foot, the searing pain having gripped her when consciousness returned. The warrior was there now, too, drawing a knife from its leather sheath on his belt. She screamed when she saw the razor edge of the eight-inch blade glimmering in a sunbeam above her.

Dakota took her face in his hands. "Mandy, hold still. Thunder Cloud has to cut it off."

"No!"

He placed his hands on her legs just above her knees so it was impossible for her to move them. She could feel the smooth, cold metal slide down her leg. Every jerk of the knife made the pain more excruciating.

She heard the murmurs of many voices and saw the disturbed looks on the faces surrounding her. She lifted her head and peered down at her feet. She could see the right one but not the left. The warrior *had* cut if off!

She strained to lift herself onto her elbows. It was her shoe that had been sliced away, not her foot, but what she saw sickened her. Her ankle was bent inward and her foot lay sideways a full ninety degrees out of alignment.

She threw back her head and screamed.

Victoria rushed to her with a stone cup and offered its contents. Mandy shook her head and refused to drink.

"Mandy, listen to me," Dakota told her, his tone urgent but void of compassion. "Your ankle looks very bad. We have to try to set the bones back into place. Then we are going to wrap your limb in damp herbs and splint it. It's going to cause even more pain than you already feel, so you've got to drink this and anything else they give you."

He placed his hand at the back of her neck, took the cup

from Victoria and held it to Mandy's lips.

Even swallowing was difficult with her body tense from the trauma. She didn't want to accept anything these people had to offer but was unable to further resist. And wanting more than anything to be rid of the pain, she submitted to drinking the potion he served her.

Within ten minutes the pain had lessened to a degree, but the medicine also made her delirious. Voices seemed distant. She felt as if she were floating, spinning. She heard the mirthful voice of her older brother Gregg, whom she loved so much. But that could not be. Gregg was dead.

Her foot was being manipulated. It felt like it weighed a hundred pounds. There was a deep, sharp pain, then a tremendous burning. She cried out. Someone was pressing on her legs again. She felt hot, wet cloths being wrapped around her ankle, then pieces of hard wood being tied to her leg.

For several hours she slipped in and out of consciousness. The lodge had cleared except for Victoria, one other woman, Dakota, and another brave. It was White Fox.

Poor J.J. He surely must have second thoughts about courtshipping me now.

And Dakota…she need not wonder how he now perceived that "good woman" he thought the world had lost.

Victoria offered her something new to drink. One whiff of it and she crinkled her nose and turned her head away.

"I told you," Dakota demanded, "to take whatever they give you."

Mandy returned his cold stare but gave in to his logic and reluctantly accepted the brew.

He raked his fingers through his hair, then let his hand fall to his side. He walked to her mat and glared down.

"I never lied to you, Mandy."

He turned on his heels and left the lodge.

That was the vision that remained until the drug claimed her.

CHAPTER 5

*T*wo days later Mandy awoke with a clear head for the first time since the accident. Her memories of the event and the days that followed were hazy, having spent them alternating between pain and stupor.

Victoria had mastered a few more words of the English language. "Drink this." "Sleep now." "Eat it." It would not take much evidence gathering to conclude from whom she had learned it.

What troubled Mandy most was that no matter how hard she tried, she could not discern if she had dreamed or actually saw Dakota standing over her and telling her he had not lied.

Peering out from under a buffalo robe, she watched as Victoria prepared a meal. Mandy had to smile as the woman scuttled about the lodge, fueled the fire, stirred the broth. She was not unlike Mandy's own mother when she hustled through her kitchen chores. Her heart ached for her mother now, and for the grief she would be feeling over her daughter's "death."

"Is that why they call you Swift Legged Woman—because of the way you scurry around here so efficiently?"

Victoria had not noticed her patient was awake. "Mandy!" She crossed to where her charge was lying, speaking with great earnest in her Indian tongue.

"Thank you for taking care of me, Victoria. You are very kind."

"Thank you. Welcome."

"I wish you could tell me what's happened to me, and what's *going* to happen."

Dakota was the only one who could explain, and Mandy still wasn't sure she could trust him. And after the cruel and cutting things she said to him in the corral...

Reluctantly she asked, "Where is Dakota?"

"Dakota. No come."

"And he probably never will." Mandy released a heavy sigh.

It was time to do the inevitable. She must look at her foot, if she still had one. She lifted her head and cast her eyes across the buffalo robe. Thankfully, her foot was still attached. It was raised on blankets, still wrapped and splinted. Only her toes were visible outside the wrap. They were swollen and dusky, and she could not move them. She had to find out if any sensation had returned.

It took some effort to boost herself up first to her elbows, then to her hands, and finally upright. As she did so, the robe dropped to her waist. She quickly lay back down and drew the cover up to her chin.

"Where are my clothes?"

Victoria pointed outside.

"What did you do, burn them?"

The woman made motions of rubbing her hands together, then raised and lowered them in front of herself. Mandy hoped it meant the clothes were being washed.

Holding the robe in place this time, she raised herself up and studied her left foot. She tried unsuccessfully to wiggle her toes. Their color frightened her. She reached down and gently squeezed each one. Nothing. She dug her fingernail into them. Still nothing.

Victoria brought her some broth and soft food. She had no appetite but knew she needed the nourishment to heal. She was also offered some type of tea. The pain began to subside and she grew woozy again.

Later that day, Victoria brought her lavender dress, snow-white petticoats and undergarments as clean as when they were brand new. They felt warm and smelled fresh, having been spread out in the grass to dry in the sun.

Victoria left the lodge that evening and had not returned by the time a storm blew in. Huge raindrops fell heavily on the hide dwelling, some falling through the top opening and sizzling on the dying embers of the fire. The orange glow from what was left of them cast the only light. Mandy lay down and wished for sleep, but the crushing pain in her ankle precluded any such hopes.

Suddenly the door flap opened, and the figure of a man covered with a blanket entered, then turned to replace the flap.

"Dakota, I've been hoping you'd come by. I...need to talk to you."

He did not answer, only removed the blanket, shook off the water and went to the small woodpile. He picked up some kindling and placed it on the fire, then squatted to stir the embers. Only when the fire's enhancing light shone on the man's face did Mandy recognize him.

Thunder Cloud!

His eyes lifted and burned into hers. Her pulses hammered. He rose and took slow, deliberate steps toward her. Her breath held. His gaze moved to her leg, then he lowered himself next to her, threw back the robe that covered her leg and began untying the thongs that held the splint in place.

"Don't touch it!" She leaned forward and pounded her fist into his hard, muscular shoulder. His stormy eyes penetrated her. He moved to the bottom of her mat to work from there.

"I said *don't touch it!*"

He kept at his task and finally removed the splint. She was afraid to move for fear of further damaging her ankle but was equally afraid of what this warrior would do to her. He slowly—and seemingly with great care—removed the cloths and studied her foot. He glanced up at her. She stared back in fright, trembling. He examined her foot again and gently touched it in various places. Parts of it were painful, parts were numb, and parts had no feeling at all.

The door flap opened again, and Dakota jumped in, replaced the flap and removed the fur robe that covered him.

"Dakota! Make him stop!"

He joined the other man, and the two braves conversed for several minutes. It appeared that Dakota was asking the questions, not making the demands.

"Tell me what's going on!"

Dakota removed some clean cloths from under his shirt. They rewrapped her foot and replaced the splint.

Their task completed, the men rose. Dakota covered his friend with a blanket and watched him leave. Only then did he give Mandy his attention.

He went to her mat and looked down at her. "Your foot is bad but may not be hopeless."

"Meaning, I may get to keep it?"

He shrugged. "Perhaps."

His indifference was wounding.

"I'm so confused about everything."

"You didn't seem confused when you left my lodge."

"I recognized the horses from the stage station in the corral."

29

He looked at her as if waiting for her to finish the explanation. Then his shoulders sank. "So, you assumed that *we* burned the station, killed the couple, and stole the horses?"

"I didn't *assume* it. I had to investigate it though."

"And what did your investigation turn up?"

"A crazed Indian who once again assailed me and tried to stop me from getting away and telling anyone."

"You still think that these people were party to a murderous raid, and that I lied to you about it? After everything I explained to you, and promised to do for you?"

"Why should I believe you? I don't even *know* you."

"Obviously you don't." He retrieved another piece of firewood and added it to the fire. "Would you care to know the truth about those horses? Would you even believe me now?"

She still wasn't sure she would.

"They herded themselves and wandered south, were rounded up and brought here. It's that simple. You can choose to believe that or not. It's of no consequence to me."

"Then why did that barbarian attack me when he saw me in the corral with them?"

"He's not a barbarian. And he went in to see why the gate had been left open. He only grabbed you when he saw you skulking around like a thief."

"I'm no thief!"

"So, you weren't attempting to mount my horse and ride off with him?"

She looked away from his accusing gaze, but felt it nonetheless.

"They'd hang you in Denver for such an act, you know."

Crushed beneath the weight of her circumstances and his scorn, she wrapped her arms around herself. "Then *do it*, and get it over with."

He let out a long breath. Moving to the side of her mat, he crossed his moccasins and lowered himself to the ground. She still could not look at him.

His voice softened, shed of its rancor. "You have suffered unfairly, and *I* have been unfair to you. I was raised better than these past few minutes would suggest, and am truly sorry."

Shame overtook her at the memory of her accusations.

"I, too, have much to atone for. What I said to you that day…"

He had heard that pernicious expression concerning his mixed parentage from many people over the years, but for some reason it had never been as penetrating as when it spewed from her mouth. She was obviously grieved by it, and he had no desire to make it worse.

"I don't know many women who would take all that has happened to you and turn it into an apology for saying something rash in a moment of terror."

Like salve on a wound, his graciousness eased her discomfort. Only now could she bear to look at him. His expression was as kind as his words.

"I suppose I owe your compadre, Thunder Cloud, an apology as well for beating him off tonight when he was only trying to help me. He is by any measure the most fear-inspiring man I have ever seen. But, considering what he had to go on when he found me in the corral, and out there with Little Dog, I can hardly fault him for his suspicions. But he truly needs to work on improving his deportment."

The corners of his mouth turned up. "I'll advise him of that. And he's not my compadre only. He's my brother."

Her eyes widened.

"Half-brother, actually. His mother, Long Hair, is the woman my father married the year after my mother and I failed to return from Indianapolis."

"It must have been quite the shock for them all when you did finally return."

"For a fact. I was seventeen, and our reunion was heartwarming to be sure, but I hardly knew what to expect from his son who was seven years younger than me. By rights I was once again the firstborn son of Wild Eagle."

"I'd expect he'd be jealous and angry."

"Believe it or not, though, he showed me nothing but the respect due the eldest son of the chief. No hostility. No suspicions. No competition. He taught me the things I needed to catch up on to be one of my father's people—their traditions, their habits, and even the language, which had been lost to me. And the little guy has proven more than once I can trust him with my life."

"The *little guy*?"

"He's no more than six feet tall—a full inch shorter than me."

31

Mandy grinned. "No competition, huh?"

He smiled in return. "None whatsoever."

Mistrust and animosity forsaken, their conversation went on for hours into the night. Mandy spoke of her life growing up in Pennsylvania, and her family's move west at the start of the War Between the States. Dakota's life seemed intensely more interesting. His adoptive mother was half-French and his father half-German, though their common language had been English. He had learned both of their foreign tongues, thus he was now fluent in four languages. And he had been to *Europe.* When he was ten, his parents had a furlough from their missionary duties and took him there—compliments of one of his grandfathers— to meet his adoptive relatives and experience the culture. One of those cultural experiences was contracting cowpox, and his most vivid memory of the journey was that of the bluish pustules on his hands.

After being reunited with Wild Eagle's people sixteen years ago, he had not stayed permanently with this tribe but had moved back and forth between his two cultures, able to pass unquestionably as a white man whenever he chose. Sometimes he would reveal his dual heritage, being proud of both, but it usually was not well received.

When he was "being white," he frequently was employed as a blacksmith, the type of work he loved most—work in which he could use his strength and his hands to fix and create things. In those times he went by the name bestowed on him by his adoptive parents—John Starbuck.

"But at some point, I always end up shedding my city clothes, slipping back into buckskins, letting my hair grow, and coming home."

"So, you've experienced the rewards—and sorrows—of both cultures, unlike many of your kind who can't seem to find their place in either."

His brows lifted. "What? No criticism of my wandering lifestyle? Most white women I've met consider my life too unsettled to be productive."

"With all your diverse talents, I consider you anything but unproductive."

He smiled at her, more with his eyes than his mouth.

"What brought you back here this time?"

"The tribe is facing turbulent times. Treaties have been

made and broken, and now another is in the planning stages. The younger warriors are likely to rebel against the tribal leaders and opt for all-out war if pressed to relocate again. My father needs me in the capacity of interpreter and negotiator."

She learned more about his brother Thunder Cloud, too. He'd been married once, but she died of cholera. He'd had plans to marry again, but Little Fawn, Little Dog's sister, was killed with the rest of her family on the day the boy wandered into the way station. Thunder Cloud blamed the white man for bringing the disease as well as the massacre.

"He spoke of finding Little Fawn, of cradling her lifeless body in his arms. His grief turned into consuming rage. Shortly thereafter, he encountered you with Little Dog."

"Please tell him that I am deeply sorry for his loss."

The storm was letting up. Dakota leaned forward, resting his elbows on his knees.

"Mandy, tomorrow will tell whether your foot is going to improve or not."

She knew the moment would arrive when the decision would have to be made.

"Dakota," she said softly, "would you pray for me?"

He held the gaze of the woman with whom he had spent the evening revealing more about himself than he ever had to any other. The fire lit her face and played upon her hair, reflecting the color of autumn aspens.

"I've been praying for you since the moment I found that cape out on the plain."

He rose, picked up his robe, threw it over his arm and turned for the door. Almost under his breath he added, "Maybe even longer."

CHAPTER 6

Seven women entered Mandy's lodge unannounced and laid out the contents of long hide pouches.

Two of the women took to the task of removing her splint and unwrapping the herb-soaked cloths. As taken unawares and apprehensive as she was, she didn't protest, trusting they were there to help. When her foot was finally exposed, the women studied it carefully, and debated among themselves.

Dakota and Thunder Cloud entered and began examining the foot as the others had. Her heart pounding, Mandy waited in subdued silence. Waited for her fate to be determined.

"Well?" she finally asked when she could endure the unknown no longer.

"It's undecided," Dakota said. "Most of the women think it's too badly infected to survive."

"I know about gangrene, Dakota. Is that what they're saying? Is it gangrenous?"

He nodded. "Thunder Cloud disagrees, however."

"How does he know about such things? And who are these others?"

"They are the Seven Old Women, the tribe's medicine people. They have a great deal of knowledge in matters of healing. As does Thunder Cloud, not from having it passed down like the women have, but from his own encounters with such injuries when he's been on the long hunts."

"And he thinks it's salvageable?"

"He *thinks* it *may* be. But if he's wrong, you know it could spread and…"

And she could die.

She studied the faces surrounding her, including that of the man she had known only as a savage until her conversation with Dakota the previous night. Should she trust the women with their generational knowledge? Or a man who had fixed a couple of broken bones while hunting? She wanted to believe he was right. But how could she know?

To Dakota she said, "You told me you trust him with your life."

He nodded.

Her racing heart worked its way into her throat. "Then I will trust him with mine. You tell him, tell them all, that I will go along with whatever Thunder Cloud decides. No one else."

"Mandy, be very, *very* sure about this."

"I'm not *sure* about anything. Now, tell them."

Dakota moved to the circle of women and explained Mandy's decision. Thunder Cloud overheard and was visibly stunned when he heard his brother's statements.

"Caught you off guard, did I, little guy?"

One of the women administered some of the potion that had kept Mandy's pain—which never abated entirely—tolerable. The remaining women gathered their items, replaced them in their pouches and left. The two brothers redressed and resplinted Mandy's leg. Thunder Cloud gave her one last prolonged look that expressed the wonder in him, and then he too left.

The drug soon took its effect on her pain and her brain.

At one point she dozed off for a couple of minutes, then woke up startled and looked at a blurry face beside her. "Gregg?"

"No, Mandy, I'm sorry. I'm Dakota."

Her vision cleared faster than her brain.

"You two were close, weren't you?" he asked.

She massaged her temples as she spoke. "Yes, even as youngsters. He was two years older than me, and we grew up best friends. The fondest memories I have all involve him. One of the things I loved most about him was his sense of responsibility. That's how he ended up in the Union army as a signalman. I still miss him terribly."

"You'll never stop missing him," he said faintly.

Dakota remained throughout the afternoon, leaving only to get food. When he returned, they nibbled on pemmican and wild fruits. He also brought her royal blue cloak.

"Fairweather found it in the corral and washed it for you."

"This is becoming quite a habit for us, isn't it? Thank her for me. And thank *you...again*. By the way, how do you say 'thank you' in Arapaho?"

"I say '*hahou*'. You would say '*hahoukac*' since you're a woman."

"You have different words for men and women?"

"Sometimes we do."

35

Mandy's mental fog lifted but left her scatterbrained and giddy. They made a game of tossing nuts in the air and trying to catch them in their mouths. He succeeded most of the time; she blamed her lack of success on the medicine. Their laughter filled the small lodge and overflowed outside, and curious glances came through the opening. When one wayward nut bounced off Mandy's nose and dropped to the ground, they both reached frantically for it and knocked their heads together. He winced and blurted out some expression in Arapaho, and in Mandy's frivolous state she laughed so hard tears streamed from her eyes.

She finally regained command of herself, and he reached to wipe the streak of a tear from her face. His fingers moved across her cheek and caressed a wisp of golden hair that framed her face. His eyes took their time in studying her features, and she felt herself blush as his hand completed its journey along the wavy strand of her hair.

"Perhaps I, uh...I should let you get some rest."

Her eyes held his gaze. "I'm not tired."

"Even so..."

Dakota rose and left her lodge with a promise to return the next day. Mandy laid down and settled on her buffalo robe and wondered what on earth was going on inside her. And it had nothing to do with her foot.

* * *

Mercifully, Thunder Cloud's analysis of the condition of Mandy's foot turned out to be the right one. Many prayers of thanksgiving were raised from that little lodge. Every day the color improved as circulation was restored. But the return of sensation meant increased pain to those areas that had once been numb. Her anguish over her family's pain grew as well, but there was no potion to ease that torment.

Dakota had much to do in these summer weeks. Finding game was becoming increasingly difficult, and many more hours than usual were spent on the hunt. When in camp he visited her often, but always with another person present. It was considered improper for an unmarried man and woman to be alone, although allowances had been made when Mandy was acutely injured. Being chaperoned felt funny, even though

36

their conversations in English were private. Yet at the same time it was a relief of sorts. The ripening attraction between them was more easily put under restraint this way, as it must be. Their relationship was temporary and therefore unsustainable.

On occasion Dakota would carry her outside and seat her on a blanket where the sun's rays warmed and colored her paling skin. The people in the camp were friendly and helpful, watchful of running children and errant horses. They shared food and conversation with her, uninhibited by the language barrier. She had even begun to learn some simple phrases and signs. She was grateful for their companionship, but it was Dakota her eyes sought as the afternoon sun moved west across the sky and the men returned from hunting.

Five weeks into her stay, Dakota informed her he must leave the next day for Kansas Territory and may be gone for a couple of weeks.

"Why must you go?"

"The government is holding a council with some of the Plains tribes, including the Arapaho, attempting to negotiate another treaty. Wild Eagle fears that if he leaves now, the young warriors he and the other council members have thus far been able to restrain will carry out their threats to wage war with the whites, and that could lead to further indiscriminate killing on both sides. He wishes for me to go, so I can give him a firsthand account of what is said instead of it being passed down through many levels of interpreters." He paused before adding, "Your ankle should be well enough for you to ride by the time I return. It's time I kept my promise to take you to Fort Lyon."

For all the joy that prospect brought to Mandy, alongside it was a turbulence the keeping of that promise now brought to her soul.

"In the meantime, I have a surprise for you." He stepped outside the lodge and retrieved a pair of rough-hewn crutches he'd made from cottonwood. The armrests were padded with several layers of deer hide.

"Oh, Dakota, do you think I'm ready for these?"

"Only way to know is to try them out." He lifted her slowly to her feet, then placed first one crutch and then the other under her arms. "Don't bear any weight on that foot yet."

37

She was upright at long last, but unpleasantly surprised to discover how weak even her good leg had become from non-use. Gravity was wreaking havoc as well. The downward rush of blood set her foot to throbbing and made her dizzy. One trek across the lodge and back carrying her weight on the crutches, though no more than a dozen steps, had her ready to lie down again.

Later that afternoon they made another attempt, and she was able to walk outside. They navigated slowly through the camp as they spoke of his upcoming journey and of her upcoming communication hurdles without him there to interpret.

A light rain shower came upon them, and as often happens on the plains, the pleasant shower soon turned into a cloudburst, and they were caught in a downpour.

"I knew I shouldn't have let you stay out here," he shouted above the drumbeat of the pounding rain. "C'mon, lets go to my lodge. It's closer."

Once inside, they stood near the center lodge pole and shook out their wet clothes. He draped a red Mackinaw blanket around her and helped lower her onto a mat. Before long a fire was going, and she scooted closer to it, deeply chilled. He checked her splint and found it intact and dry.

He saw her shivering and felt blameworthy for having kept her out too long.

"I'd sure like to get you out of those clothes," he said.

Her eyes went wide.

His face turned crimson. "I—I only meant…"

Her laughter filled the lodge. "You should've seen your expression!"

He felt grossly embarrassed, but only deserved so much hilarity at his expense, and when her chuckling did not subside, he thought he might end it another way.

"Well, I think I'll get out of mine."

It subsided instantly.

He went to the rear of the lodge. Mandy caught his movements out of the corner of her eye, and somehow her respectfully diverted focus strayed in that direction. With his back to her, he removed the buckskin shirt over his head and shook out his long wet hair. He ran his fingers through the length of it several times, his motions defining the curves of his back and arms. She was transfixed.

Her ingrained sense of propriety took over, and she stared hard into the fire. The gooseflesh on her skin was, she persuaded herself, simply a result of the damp chill.

In a minute Dakota returned to the fire and sat next to her. "Didn't peek, did yeh?"

Fully demoralized by her behavior—her *mis*behavior— and especially by getting caught at it, she kept her eyes lowered. "I'm not going to dignify that outlandish idea with a response."

It was his turn to chuckle. Mandy glared at him with forced indignation. But when his smile widened, she nearly laughed out loud at her predicament. She tried to maintain the appearance of consternation. Her eyes, however, were a dead giveaway.

A crash of thunder gave them both a start.

"Looks like we're stuck here for a while," he said.

She didn't consider it being stuck.

"Well, since we're *stuck* here," she said, "tell me more about these symbols on the hide. They tell stories, right? Some of the symbols are self-explanatory, like your reunion with Wild Eagle. But some aren't as easy to figure out."

"You're right about them depicting memorable scenes in one's life, such as a battle, a special event or a wonder of nature. But they don't always mean the same thing. You see those rows of triangles with the line across the bottom? They represent mountains, but can also mean plenty of game, since the mountains are where you'd find big game. The backwards Z with the arrow at the end of it can represent lightning, or it can be used to denote swiftness, depending on the tale. The half-circle with the lines coming out means the sun, but can also mean constancy. And that line of circles, with every other one colored in, means day and night, or just time."

"So you need someone to interpret their story for you?"

"Yes." And that's just what he did. Many of the stories he had told her over the weeks were immortalized on the walls of this dwelling.

There was even more for the city girl to marvel at. He showed her a belt buckle he had made from shed elk antlers, and a flute he had fashioned from a soft, straight-grained wood. Its music was enchanting, and Mandy was tranquilly entertained as he played "Greensleeves." The most fascinating of all was a rose—complete with leaves and a long stem—he had forged out of steel while working as a blacksmith.

"It's simply *exquisite*." She fondled the lines and curves of the black metal flower.

It pleased him that she valued the articles made by the work of his hands.

"I had no idea such things could be made in a simple smithy."

"It just goes to show what a man can do with a good fire, the right tools, and two strong arms."

He spoke of his future dream of running his own smithy. A dream thus far unfulfilled in large part due to his deeply felt responsibilities to his tribesmen.

"Simply exquisite," she repeated as she passed the rose back to him.

"I want you to keep it." He placed his hand over hers. "To remember me."

He should have avoided even so innocent a touch. Like the dream of his own smithy, this new one building inside him was to go unfulfilled. She had a world to return to, and his was here. But his hand was where it was, and he took no initiative to remove it.

"I'll remember you," she promised breathily.

He leaned toward her and whispered her name as his lips moved to unite with hers. Parting briefly, he studied her to make sure he was judging rightly, and that it was in her heart to continue.

What was in her heart was an earth-shattering longing to continue.

His hand moved to caress her cheek. His finger traced the contour of her lips.

She leaned into his kiss, desirous of suspending this moment in time.

But time cannot be suspended, nor destinies changed, for the sake of a kiss.

Their lips parted, but their eyes could not. There could be no denial of the compelling bond between them. It had hinted of its existence that first day in this lodge. It summoned him again that first night in her lodge, when he realized her words in the corral had cut into him so much more deeply than ever before because for some reason it mattered more what she thought of him. For her it was that same night, when she knew she was forgiven.

But prolonging their time together only delayed the death blow.

The rain had long since let up. He helped her to stand and to set her crutches in place. He held steadying hands on her arms.

"Dakota, while you're gone, could you possibly—"

"I'll write your father, explain everything that's happened, and tell him you'll be contacting him from Fort Lyon in a few weeks. I'll ask one of the government officials to post it as soon as humanly possible."

She wasn't at all surprised that he knew exactly what was on her mind.

CHAPTER 7

The dozen or so Arapaho words and phrases Mandy had learned over the weeks were put to good use with Dakota gone, but were nowhere close to being adequate to communicate as she longed to with his people. He had tutored her in sign language as well and explained that sign was a universal language among the western tribes and could be used to communicate with any Plains Indian one might encounter.

Long Hair was her closest companion. The woman had grown fond of this unwitting captive of her son Thunder Cloud, this source of her stepson Dakota's alternating moods of exuberance and melancholy.

The two women sat outside the elder's lodge working jointly on making a buckskin shirt for Dakota. Long Hair demonstrated how to sew fringe on the sleeve. Mandy envisioned him wearing it on some future day and took satisfaction in knowing that whenever and wherever he wore this shirt, a little bit of her would be with him. When it was finished, she signed the word Dakota had taught her for "beautiful." Long Hair nodded in agreement.

Long Hair's husband and sons were, in Mandy's opinion, the best-dressed men in the camp. The exception was when Thunder Cloud chose to chuck the beaded and fringed outfits his mother made for him and attire himself in bones, feathers, claws and a simple breechcloth. Mandy much preferred the look of buckskin.

When the men of the camp returned from hunting with what little game they had caught, Mandy was invited to stay and eat with Long Hair and Wild Eagle. Thunder Cloud was there also. He and his father smoked a pipe, then conversed with apparent disagreement. Mandy could see a growing sense of frustration and anxiety in the son. As best as she could decipher, he was wrought up about the land...moving across the land, perhaps?...going east...no, *not* wanting to go east...going north. Wild Eagle frequently mentioned Dakota's name.

Upon rising to leave, Thunder Cloud turned and looked down at Mandy's leg. He stooped to examine it more closely, then adjusted the splint and tightened the thongs. He said something to her in a still irritable tone. His penetrating eyes never ceased from making her uneasy. Nevertheless, she said, "*Hahoukac.*" She thought she saw a hint of a crease at the corners of his mouth. Would he smile? He got up quickly and went out.

In the days that followed, Mandy learned much about the way of life in the camp. It was essentially one of constant hard work, yet their tasks seemed to be carried out with joy. Women forayed together for berries, nuts, roots and herbs, and made quite a happy time of it. It was the women who butchered the meat their husbands brought in, and they taught Mandy several ways of preparing it. They dried some of the meat, pounded it fine with stone mortars, and mixed it with melted fat and a paste made from wild chokecherries to make pemmican. It was the women who made the pottery, wove baskets, made tepee linings, and raised and lowered the lodges. She wished she could have participated more in some of these activities but moving about still induced considerable pain. She knew it would certainly be a long time before she could walk unassisted and pain free again, if ever.

One afternoon as she and Long Hair shared a meal in front of the chief's lodge, a brave strode over and began to speak to the Indian woman in a raised and fiery voice. She replied with a calmness that exemplified the controlled and dignified woman she was. Mandy could make out that this discussion was also regarding the land. The chief and most of the men were away hunting, and this warrior was apparently taking advantage of their absence by harassing, even threatening, Wild Eagle's wife.

She stood and confronted him. He jabbed her in the chest as he made his points with her. She slapped his hand away. It infuriated him, and he shoved her backward against the lodge.

Mandy struggled to her feet, leaned on one crutch, and with the other smacked him on the side of his head. He was dazed only momentarily. He turned on her with eyes of rage. Long Hair regained her balance and tried to push him aside. The warrior slapped her with the back of his hand, knocking her to the ground.

As Mandy stared in shock at her friend's form, her head was jarred backward by a hard tug on her hair. The remaining crutch was forced from under her arm, and the face of this "brave" was inches from hers. He spoke harshly through clenched teeth, then threw her down in the dirt beside Long Hair. The man stormed away, shouting at anyone who crossed his path.

Other women who witnessed the scene rushed to help them. Long Hair was uninjured. Mandy's foot bore some of the trauma of her fall, and the pain that had been continual was now intensified. Inside Long Hair's lodge, two of the Seven Old Women rewrapped and resplinted her leg, and gave her some of the analgesic drink.

When the pain subsided to a degree, Mandy returned to her lodge. Victoria arrived at the same time and helped her lie down and situate as comfortably as possible. She offered Mandy some wild fruits she'd been given as a token of appreciation for helping deliver a baby.

"*Neiha*? *Natane*?" Mandy queried.

"*Neiha*."

A boy. Another young brave added to a determined band of people whose future was filled with uncertainty. No name as yet, Victoria said, but Mandy understood that a paternal male relative would bestow one on him soon, just as Dakota's great-uncle had named him after the land in which the Arapaho once dwelt.

The tepee flap remained open throughout the day, thus when Wild Eagle and Thunder Cloud came they entered, as was the custom, without announcing themselves first. They went straightway to where Mandy sat. The chief gently felt around the back of her head and squeezed along the length of her arm. His son removed the splint and examined her leg. He pressed an area above her ankle, then lifted his chilling dark eyes toward hers. Through a strained expression she nodded her head, understanding that he was assessing her level of feeling. He did this in several places, his fingers deeply palpating at times, which caused her to moan, although she tried her best to govern her reaction as would be expected by a warrior such as him.

He replaced the wrap and splint while apparently speaking his diagnosis. From his tone and the look of relief on Wild Eagle's face, she presumed he was saying there was no additional damage done by the ruffian, for which she was intensely grateful.

When he completed the task, his eyes raised to hers again. For the first time since she had known him, she was able to look solidly back into his without uneasiness. She smiled at him and slowly nodded her head once. He nodded once in return.

She watched in pleasant surprise as a smile formed and slowly spread across his face.

By golly, he had dimples.

* * *

Mandy's eyes scanned the eastern horizon searching for the golden horse that carried the man she longed to see. Her yearning for him could not be subdued by the lectures she'd given herself on the illogic of their situation, nor by the knowledge it could not last beyond their parting at Fort Lyon.

She walked to Dakota's lodge and longed to go in, but the flap was closed and she had no right. She fingered the hide and the perfect stitching that held it together. It brought him closer. She pictured the inside: the drawings, the flute, the items he had forged. She remembered the man: his integrity, his wit, his sense of duty to his people.

The low, groaning lament of drums started up again. For several days they had pounded out calls for warriors to gather with faces painted and to dance in circles, yelling out what she was sure were war cries. The very sound of it sent chills up her spine, and she feared what was to come. Returning to her lodge, she hesitated at the opening, glanced back at the gathering twenty yards from her lodge, and shuddered.

Peering down at the pot of food left simmering for her, she shrank from the thought of eating it. Despite her hunger, her stomach still managed to reject in one way or another much of what she put in it.

She entered her lodge and thought of Dakota. She lay down and thought of Dakota. She sat up again and thought of Dakota, increasingly anxious about his whereabouts and his safety. It was exactly two weeks since he had left. He wasn't late, but there was so much that could go wrong. Indian raiders who might mistake him for a white man. Army soldiers who might mistake him for an Indian. She prayed for his safety once

45

again, as she had dozens of times in the past fortnight.

Working her way up to standing again, she turned, and he was there.

He came to her swiftly and snatched her into his arms. She gazed into his loving eyes. "Didn't miss me, did yeh?"

With a smile he answered, "Not so much."

He helped her onto her mat and sat beside her, drawing his crossed legs beneath him. Each told the other of what had taken place during his mission to the government council.

"Something frightening is brewing here, Dakota. There is tension, your father looks pensive all the time, and he and your brother argue about moving…I think. And, if you can believe this, a man actually attacked Long Hair."

"I heard about it from a hunting party while I was still a couple of miles out. I also heard about your valiant effort to defend her."

"What will happen to the brute who did that?"

"He was mean enough to do that but not dumb enough to stick around. Official punishment would've been banishment. But you're right, there is much dissension regarding the treaty. Some of the men didn't want anything to do with another treaty even before this one was called. But now the chiefs think it may be best to comply and go to the new reservation in Kansas."

"But there is reservation land here. Why can't they stay?"

"The government wants Colorado free to settle up. They offer the tribes compensation if they comply."

"And Wild Eagle may agree to that?"

"He and the other chiefs have to consider it."

The paradox was one she had struggled with before. Like many who had moved west, she was anxious to see it settled up and growing. During the four years she had been in Colorado, she had developed a passion for this land and the new way of life that went with it, a life that was sometimes terribly hard. Since living in Denver, her family had faced a major fire that destroyed many homes and half of the business establishments, including her father's law office. It was followed the next year by a ravaging flash flood that struck at midnight and wreaked similar havoc. Each time the Berringers had repaired and rebuilt, determined to strengthen their roots in this territory. Mandy could not imagine how the members of this tribe, some of whom had spent their entire lives on this land sustaining themselves from its riches, could ever give it up.

"The food supply here is nearly depleted," Dakota continued. "We hunt farther and farther every day only to find less and less, so a relocation would be imminent anyway. And on the reservation the Indians will be supplied with food, clothes and other provisions, and given monetary compensation. Complying may be the only way to keep the tribe from starving to death."

Mandy spoke of the months just after she moved to Denver when many Indians came into town begging for food. "Several times they showed up at my pa's office, and at our house. They were so pitiable."

"Spotted Wolf and his people were stranded there that spring. But they were only a fraction of the once proud people who had possessed the land only years before, then had to resort to begging. They suffered great shame. And bitterness. The food the government promised that year didn't materialize, and many Indians revolted."

"What about Thunder Cloud? I see a rage building inside him, too."

"The little guy won't be forced to any reservation. He and others like him would rather fight, even die, than let someone else dictate how and where he must live his life."

Mandy couldn't hide her dejection.

Dakota reached over and stroked her soft blond hair. "I wanted this to be a happy reunion. Maybe this will help."

Reaching into his *parfleche,* the hide bag in which he carried necessary provisions, he retrieved three books and presented them to her. "I traded for these."

She ran her hand over the red leather book containing a work of her favorite poet, Longfellow. It was his long poem, *Evangeline.* Another book of his shorter works delighted her as well. Lastly there was a book with a black leather cover and gilt-edged pages. On the cover in gold lettering were the words, *Holy Bible.*

"I'm at a loss to know what to say. *Hahoukac* hardly seems enough."

"Hold it until I show you the one last gift I brought you." He started to rise, but Mandy placed a hand on his arm.

"I've accepted too much already. I hate to even think of

47

what my ma will say when she finds out her daughter has accepted favors from a man she is not betrothed to."

Innocent as the statement was, it obliged reality to face off against desire. The time for procrastination was ended and the question must be answered.

"What are we to do about us, Dakota?"

A sepulchral silence surrounded them.

He ultimately broke it saying, "If you had come during any of my previous stays here when things weren't so unsettled…"

"Or if you had come through Denver to work as a smith… But we didn't have a say in how we met. As things are, I understand how great is the privation in this place, and what your being here means to these people. I've witnessed the considerable void your absence creates. I am aware of the dangerous times they are facing. Mine is not the desire to take you from those who need you, perhaps for their very survival."

"And mine is not to take you from the happiness of your home and family, offering in return an empty life on an Indian reservation."

Mandy could not restrain her tears. He moved to her and held her close.

In a week's time she would be recovered enough to travel, and he would take her to the safety of the fort where they would part forever.

CHAPTER 8

*T*he day was bright and clear—perfect for a wedding. The groom's mother took six horses to the lodge of the prospective bride to propose the marriage. The girl's older brother decided it could be so, for the groom was a respected warrior and a good provider. The girl agreed to the marriage.

The bride's mother and other female relatives raised a new tepee next to her parents'. There the newlyweds would live. Many gifts were placed in the bridal tepee. When all was ready, the bride's family went to the groom's lodge and escorted him and his relatives to the new lodge. The moment the groom entered, the marriage was sealed.

A celebration took place in the couple's new home that evening. Several of the elder men spoke of the life ahead. The warrior and his bride were admonished to be faithful to each other, forsaking all others, and to always honor and trust each other. The festivities would continue until the last guest decided to leave.

Mandy was unaware that any of these plans had been in the works, although much of the camp had been speculating for some time. Dakota came by for her and was surprised to learn she did not even know she had been invited to a wedding.

"How was I to know? No one sent me an invitation."

"Long Hair said she hoped she'd made it clear to you, but I guess that didn't quite happen."

"Who do I know that's getting married, anyway?"

"Thunder Cloud."

Mandy stared, slack-jawed. "Are you serious? Who would ever...I mean..."

"You mean...who's the lucky girl?"

She smiled. "You know what I mean."

"Blue Flower Woman's family considers it an honor that he chose her."

"No doubt. But you told me the woman he loved and planned to marry died only a couple of months ago, the day Little Dog wandered into the stage station."

"He needs a wife. Now he has one. She's very nice, and proficient, not to mention pretty. I have no doubt they'll grow close and be happy. Their union is a fitting one."

It all seemed logical enough, but Mandy wasn't used to thinking of marriage in such terms.

They walked toward the bridal lodge where laughter and song from the merrymaking could be heard quite a distance away. It lifted Mandy's low spirits, and with eagerness she quickened her pace.

"Slow down, Mandy, before you fall. We need not hurry. There's no such thing as being late for these things."

"I'm being careful. Just don't trip me with those big feet of yours."

"Ha! At least both of mine point in the same direction when I walk."

Her eyes narrowed. "O-o-o, that was low-down and high-smellin'."

As they continued on their way, Mandy noticed some Indians she had never seen before. Their dress was unfamiliar, too.

"They are Cheyenne," Dakota explained. "Our bands often get together for intertribal celebrations. Several of our people attended a wedding of theirs a couple of weeks ago. Thunder Cloud is well-known and respected among them, and they are happy to be reciprocating for this occasion."

The women from both tribes were well dressed for the gala, wearing long-fringed dresses and leggings and brightly colored feathers in their hair. Many of them wore deer hide dresses that were whiter than any material Mandy had ever seen. Long Hair had shown her how animal brain fluid was used to soften and whiten them. Their festive and elegant clothing made Mandy feel underdressed in the unadorned doeskin dress she had made with Long Hair's help.

Drawing closer to the bridal lodge, Dakota reminded her of certain points of etiquette she must follow, this being her first formal affair.

"And remember, when we enter the lodge, I move to the right and you—"

"I know, I know. I go to the left."

"Right."

"I go to the right?"

"No, you go to the left."

"You said *right*."

"I meant, *right*, you go to the *left*."

"You meant, *correct*, I go to the left."

"Right."

She glared out of the corner of her eye. "You're *trying* to madden me, right?"

"Correct."

She stopped and began to wield one crutch like a broadsword, repeatedly swinging it wildly at him. He dodged it adeptly, all except for the last swing. By mischance it struck him hard on the side of the head. He dropped to his knees, his eyes rolled, and he fell face down.

"Oh, Dakota! Are you all right?"

She lowered herself and turned him over. His head fell limp to the side. She shook his shoulders and called his name. He did not respond.

"Dakota, please, wake up!" She put her ear to his chest. His heart was still beating, thank God. Panic gripped her. She cried out for help.

His eyes popped open and he bolted upright, grabbing her and growling like a wolf. She screamed, at the same time realizing she had been had.

"You beast! You scared me to death!"

"You hit me with the very crutch I made for you. If I'd known what you intended to use it for, I'd have let you crawl."

"I mean it, Dakota. I was really scared."

"I'm sorry," he said, laughing. "I had no idea you'd fall for it so completely."

Several curious Indians came toward them, mostly Cheyenne. The Arapaho of the camp had grown accustomed to seeing Dakota and Mandy in their horseplay, but the Cheyenne were inquisitive regarding this yellow-haired white woman. Mandy underwent close inspection like when she first arrived. Dakota explained her situation using sign language. They started again for the wedding feast as a group.

"And finally," he continued with last minute instructions, "never walk between the fire and anyone sitting around it. Always walk behind the person."

"Don't worry. I won't embarrass you."

He stopped at the lodge and took her by the arm. "It's not that I'm worried you'll embarrass me. I just don't want *you* to be embarrassed by unknowingly breaking some long-honored

51

tradition."

Everything this man did endeared him to her all the more. "*Hahoukac*, Dakota. It's very thoughtful of you." Smiling, she added, "But I won't forget the crack about my feet."

He laughed. "I didn't expect you would."

Dakota helped her enter the lodge, then they went their opposite ways. She took a space next to Victoria. Thunder Cloud and his bride sat at the rear of their new dwelling. He laughed freely and looked happier than Mandy would have guessed, having only recently lost his true love, Little Fawn. Some undesirable trait within made her resent him a little for his rapid recovery. She wondered if Dakota would one day settle for a "fitting union" with some "nice, proficient and pretty" woman whom he would grow close to over the years.

The bride, Blue Flower Woman, was adorned with blue and red feathers in her hair, foot-long fringe hanging from the sleeves and sash of her white doeskin dress, and a necklace with large turquoise stones. She was lovely but looked younger than her husband's twenty-six years.

Mandy signed to Victoria, "How many summers does the woman of Thunder Cloud have?"

"Sixteen," was the reply.

Sixteen! Mandy had not judged her to be *that* young. Sixteen was not an exceptionally young age to be married, but to be chosen as the wife of such a one as Thunder Cloud was a distinction she thought would have befallen a more mature woman.

Some of the Seven Old Women present were called away, and Victoria appeared concerned. Mandy looked at her questioningly. As Victoria spoke she put her hand to her back, then her head, and made the sign for "hot." Someone had a fever? Those seven women were enlightened when it came to many illnesses, and Mandy was confident that if anyone could help the sick person, it was them.

When the festivities began to wind down, Mandy decided to take her leave. She certainly didn't want to be that last guest who determined when it was all over and the honeymoon could begin. Making her way toward the opening, she tried to catch Thunder Cloud's eye. She wanted him to know she wished him and his bride happiness and a long future together, something she and Dakota could never have.

52

Thunder Cloud did take notice of her and left a conversation with a friend to take his bride's arm and make his way to her. It reinforced her notion that despite their shaky beginnings, they had truly formed a sort of kinship.

For lack of knowing what else to do, she congratulated the couple and bid them a happy life in her own tongue while making her best attempt to sign the same message. They looked confused; she was embarrassed.

"You just told them you hope they have many bear's eyes together," came Dakota's voice from over her shoulder. He translated her true regards to his brother and sister-in-law. Thunder Cloud touched Mandy's arm and slowly nodded his head once. She smiled and nodded in return. The couple returned to their guests, and Mandy turned to face the man who had once again been her rescuer.

What was to be a joyous occasion produced a disconsolate feeling in her heart. She coveted what the Indian couple had. She desired the freedom to love this man. She longed for a future with him.

But their futures were worlds apart.

CHAPTER 9

*M*andy awoke to the sound of women wailing. She looked outside in the early morning light and saw several people converged around the huge lodge of one of the chiefs. She feared this woeful forgathering meant the person taken ill the night of the wedding had not survived.

Dakota and most of the men had gone hunting, and Victoria, who had left the evening before, had not returned. It was not like her. Mandy walked about and found there was illness in many lodges, but explanations were not forthcoming in any form of communication she could understand. Long Hair denied her admission to her lodge, shooing her away frantically. Others did the same.

By nightfall Victoria was still gone, and there were apparently more deaths in the camp. Dakota had not come by, and she feared for his safety.

Sleep came only after hours of lying awake in the darkness listening to the baleful moans of the Arapaho people she had come to love, her stomach twisted into knots. Some time later she heard her name being called. A hand was shaking her.

Her eyes opened. "Dakota?"

"Get dressed. We're leaving now for Fort Lyon."

He had already placed tinder on the embers of her fire and had gathered her books, her steel rose, and other things she had accumulated in the past two months. He opened a large *parfleche* and shoved the items into it on top of her lavender dress and her blue cape.

"What's going on?" she asked in a voice still raspy from interrupted sleep.

"Just do as I tell you." He went outside.

Once she recovered her faculties, she hastily donned her doeskin dress, finished packing the *parfleche* and set her crutches in place. As soon as she threw back the tepee flap, Dakota reached in for the bag and helped her out. His horse was tethered just outside, and standing next to it was another palomino.

He hurriedly tied the bag behind the saddle of the smaller

horse.

"This mare is the gift I brought back from the government council but you wouldn't accept because we weren't betrothed. She has an easy gait and will carry you to Fort Lyon comfortably." He turned to her and set his hands on her waist to lift her onto the horse.

"Tell me what's going on."

"Later."

"Now!" She took a step back. "Dakota, I must know what's happening."

He snatched the crutches from beneath her arms and bound them to the saddle. "I have no patience with your obstinate side right now."

"I'm not the obstinate one, and I'm not a child. Tell me!"

He looked at her, his eyes sated with apprehension.

"What is it?" she pleaded.

A long moment passed. "Smallpox."

Her breath left her. She could not have imagined anything so ominous. The disease had taken the lives of thousands of people, Indian and white, in her lifetime.

"You've got to leave here *now*. I just pray it's not too late."

"But Dakota—"

"Don't argue with me!" He went to lift her again, but she pushed at his shoulders.

"I've been inoculated," she declared before he could interrupt again. "Shortly before leaving Pennsylvania."

He exhaled heavily and enveloped her in his arms, not easily shedding the panic he had known for even so brief a time. He pressed his face against her hair. "I was in such a frenzy over you that I didn't even stop to consider you might be."

She pulled back and looked into his eyes. "What about you?"

"I had cowpox, remember?"

"You were ten. How can you be sure the protection has lasted this long?"

His gaze shifted and took in the surrounding camp. The lodges all had fires burning even though it was the middle of a summer night. The wailing continued to escape from many of the dwellings.

"I *won't* leave them."

She could only pray that his childhood bout of cowpox would still defend him against its more ravaging cousin now.

"I already explained to many of them the need to isolate the sick ones, but they refuse. And I don't know how I'll ever…" His voice trailed off in desperation.

"I'll help you. Whatever has to be done, we'll do together."

"But your family…by now they're expecting you to contact them from Fort Lyon."

"I hate making them wait to hear from me, but they know at least that I'm alive. Nothing will be as hard for them as believing I was dead."

His arms surrounded her again, thankful for her presence yet still concerned for her welfare. "Mandy, you're so thin. Another day in this place and there'll be nothing left of you."

"I'll eat better, I promise. Whatever you provide."

He sent up a quick prayer for help in providing for her, and for the strength and wisdom to face the hideous task ahead. And for her presence, for he truly drew strength from her.

As they started for the lodges, Mandy asked, "How did this happen, Dakota?"

"There's word that the Cheyenne are sick as well, and farther along in the illness. As best as I can figure, their village must've already been exposed at the time of that wedding at their camp two weeks ago. Some of the Cheyenne were complaining of aches and fevers and coughs then. The people from here who attended that celebration came down with headaches and back pains and high fevers a few days ago. Now they are breaking out in a rash, while others are just beginning to come down with the fever. It will continue to spread, and there's nothing anyone can do. Even the Seven Old Women can only treat the symptoms and not offer a cure."

They went first to his parents' lodge. Long Hair was aching and burning with fever. Wild Eagle, looking frightened as a cornered animal, was wetting a cloth to wipe her face. Dakota placed a steadying hand on his shoulder and took the cloth from him. "Allow me, Father." He went to Long Hair and spoke gently as he stroked her cheek and wiped the sweat-soaked hair from her face. She spoke Mandy's name.

"What is she saying?"

"She fears for your safety. I told her you cannot get the sickness, just as I cannot. But she doesn't understand."

"Tell them that for Wild Eagle's sake they must separate. We will care for her."

"I have told them, but he won't leave her."

Mandy went to Wild Eagle's side. "Listen to your son," she told him in his own tongue. His reply was a resolute shaking of his head.

Dakota said, "All we can do is try and make them comfortable, control their fevers, and get rid of their contaminated clothing. I'll keep trying to get them to quarantine, but I doubt they'll listen."

Mandy could envision nothing but doom, helpless to do much more than watch these people she loved die a horrid death.

That night they checked every lodge in the camp. The faces were different but the scene was the same in so many of them—thus far healthy loved ones caring for the feverish or rash-ridden victim of smallpox. Swift Legged Woman was in the lodge of Fairweather and Red Horse, a survivor of a previous epidemic. Both women were stricken. Swift Legged Woman reached out to Mandy, who crossed the tepee, set her crutches down, and sat next to the woman she had only called Victoria. The white Indian woman lifted her head and spoke in disjointed phrases.

"Dakota!" Mandy called frantically.

He came to her side and translated for her. "She says that you have been a wonderful companion. You have returned to her, with your English voice and ways, memories long since forgotten to her." He paused and listened as the woman spoke further. "She is grateful that you have brought back traces of her other heritage."

Her head fell back on the mat.

"No!" Mandy cried.

"It's all right," he assured her as he watched the movements of the woman's chest. "She's just too sick to even speak anymore."

Tears formed in Mandy's eyes. "At the beginning, I couldn't accept how easily she took on the Indian ways. I thought she was weak. I refused to use her Arapaho name."

"It made her happy hearing her English name again, and

57

you gave that gift to her."

He would not explain to her now how Swift Legged Woman acquired her name. How at the tender age of seven, this fiery, agile girl named Victoria made a score of attempts to escape her captors. She continued to run every chance she had until she finally accepted her fate with the westward moving tribe, settled into their lifestyle, and took a husband. She was given the name Swift Legged Girl, and later Woman, because of her incredible speed, especially for a female.

"Red Horse can see to them," he said. "I want to go back and check on Thunder Cloud and Blue Flower again. I'd like to think they'll be spared, but they were both at that Cheyenne marriage feast. And her backache concerns me."

They entered his brother's dwelling in time to see Blue Flower collapse into her husband's arms. He lowered her gently onto their bed of buffalo robes.

He looked up at Dakota and Mandy, his face hiding none of the concern he felt for his bride. Her eyes were open but were glazed and unfocused.

Mandy sat at her side and wiped the face of the feverish, semiconscious girl. Dakota took Thunder Cloud aside, and they carried on a heated conversation. They were talking too fast for Mandy to understand much of it, but she knew Dakota was trying to convince his brother, who was heavily resisting, to stay away from his wife and the others until the danger of spreading the disease was past.

The warrior shook his head adamantly and started back toward the women. Dakota grabbed his arm and spun him around, urging him to listen to reason. He jerked his arm out of Dakota's grasp and moved to stand next to his wife. Mandy looked up at him. She knew that he, like his brother, was not one to be swayed by pleas for his own safety.

Summoning all of her courage and conviction, she held up her hand to him, and with his assistance raised from the ground. Staring directly into the warrior's penetrating eyes, she forced steadiness into her voice.

"Tell him, Dakota, that he *must* quarantine. Others will follow his lead, and lives will be saved."

"I already—"

"Remind him of the time not very long ago when I placed my fate in his hands above all others. If he had been wrong, I could've died. But I trusted him with my life. Tell him he now owes me *his* trust."

Dakota hesitated before stepping to his brother's side, and once there, hesitated to speak. Such a challenge coming from a woman—a white woman—would only fuel the warrior's already fiery anger.

"*Tell* him."

Against his better judgment, Dakota spoke for her.

Thunder Cloud raised himself to his full height, tilted back his head and stared down at Mandy through piercing dark eyes. Her gaze held steadfastly on his, never even blinking. Dakota didn't stir, save for his eyes cutting back and forth between his brother and the woman who dared to challenge him. Finally, Thunder Cloud spoke in a low, granular voice.

"I will go."

Mandy comprehended his words. She breathed again, and slowly nodded her head once. Without removing his eyes from hers, he nodded once in return.

To Dakota he said, "If you and your woman, who are shielded from this curse by a great spirit, will care for my woman and the others, I will hunt and provide your food."

He lowered himself on one knee next to Blue Flower. Leaning close to her ear, he whispered something. Then with one last sigh of anguish, he rose and left the lodge.

Dakota turned to Mandy. "I can't believe what I just witnessed. You charged him with indebtedness to you. I thought it would enrage him, but it swayed him. No one else could have convinced him to change his mind."

She smiled. "I guess he and I just speak the same language."

He smiled, too.

It was the last time they would have reason to smile for many weeks to come.

CHAPTER 10

*A*s hoped, many of the tribespeople eventually followed Thunder Cloud's example, reluctantly agreeing to allow Dakota and Mandy, along with a few survivors of previous smallpox outbreaks, to care for the sick and dispose of clothing, blankets, hides and even entire dwellings. The family of the chief who succumbed gave their large tepee—thirty feet in diameter and thirty feet high at the peak—as a sick lodge. Dakota dismantled it and reconstructed it a hundred yards from the outskirts of the camp. But the quarantine came too late for the many already exposed, and they soon fell victim to fever, chills, body aches and weepy sores that covered their bodies.

The couple labored vigorously at fighting what often seemed a losing battle. Several new victims were brought to them every day. Clothing, blankets and furs were soiled with infected drainage from the sores and from body wastes no longer under the control of the sickly Indians. Dakota not only nursed the sick but also took part in the gruesome task of burying the numerous dead and burning the clothing and hides.

The unrelenting flow of new sick ones, the lack of sleep, and the pervasive atmosphere of death all set the stage for fatigue and exasperation.

One afternoon, Mandy left the sick lodge to go to her own, saying only that she would return shortly. Dakota followed her out.

"Wait, Mandy, I need to ask…"

"What?" she asked impatiently.

"Does this have to do with…is it…the time in your cycle?"

Her suddenly scarlet face turned away from him.

"I'm sorry, but you need to know…you can't come back here until it's passed. It's taboo for a woman to care for the sick during that time. I guess I should have warned you earlier."

"*Taboo?* That's preposterous!"

"It is their way, and we need to respect that."

"Respect their ways, even if it means letting them die because of it?"

"No one is going to die because you're staying away for a few days."

"No, they won't, because you don't even need me here, do you? You can handle everything."

"You know full well how much I need you. But we *will* respect their rules. Why the big cactus in your craw?"

She didn't have an answer. She spun around on her crutches and hobbled away.

In the days that followed, her solitary confinement nearly drove her to the trail edge of her capacity to cope. Her family was never out of her mind. She brooded continually over the man she loved, over the circumstances and timing of their meeting. If only he had come to Denver years ago. They would've been free to court, to walk arm in arm to Cibola Hall for an evening of musical entertainment, or to attend the elegant Denver Theatre to enjoy a drama or light comedy. Free to fall in love and have a future together. Right now she could not see a future beyond watching people suffer and die daily.

Red Horse brought her food every day. When her time was over, she was sorely pressed to return to the sick lodge. She missed Dakota desperately but was grieved over the harsh sentiments that had passed between them.

On one starry autumn night she timidly approached the sick lodge. The flap was open. She peered inside. It was dimly lit by a dying fire. The disease's pungent odor assaulted her nostrils anew. All was quiet.

"Welcome back," came Dakota's voice from the darkness. She turned to face him. The low light from the lodge revealed a tender gaze, reassuring her that their last conversation had done nothing to hinder his longing for her.

"I was just out for my customary two a.m. constitutional."

He looked up and studied the night sky. "You're late. I'd say it's closer to four."

She followed his gaze toward the diamond-studded firmament blanketing them. A few wisps of clouds passed in front of the quarter moon. A shooting star whipped by.

"That's sure some timepiece you have there."

His gaze fell on her again. "Are you…?"

"Yes, I'm ready to return. But I need to tell you how sorry I am for how I acted the other day. I can't explain all that's inside of me."

61

A cry came from inside the lodge. They both glanced in, then looked long at each other.

"Are you up for this?" he asked quietly.

She nodded. It was not a question of being prepared; it was what needed to be done.

He took hold of her arm and assisted her into the lodge.

* * *

Weeks wove into months. The weather turned cold and the days grew shorter. Mandy's doeskin dress was replaced by a long-sleeved elk hide dress given her by one of the women. It went to mid-calf, and she wore leggings from ankle to knee for added warmth. Plain but sturdy moccasins Dakota had made covered her feet.

Throughout this time, he tutored her in sign and the Arapaho language. Motivated by being better able to communicate with her charges, she grew proficient in both.

Although Dakota spoke not a word about it, Mandy noticed one day that his skin was hot and she observed his stilted movements. He was in pain, and she feared he was coming down with the disease. When he broke out in a mild rash, she was terrified, but he insisted he was all right, and never relinquished his duties. She thanked God for having ordained that episode of cowpox all those years ago. He survived this brush with smallpox with only a couple of pockmarks on his chin to show for it.

The stricken Indians, who had often seemed impervious to the cold—the men often shirtless on sunny winter days—now were huddled together on fur robes, thin, shivering, sometimes in agonizing pain. Mouth boils made it difficult to swallow. Observing the pustules on each other's faces, they often would dab at their own.

True to his word, Thunder Cloud brought meals for them every day as well as broth for the sick ones, laying all in the dry grass twenty yards from the sick lodge. And true to her word, Mandy ate all that was provided for her. Usually it was a rabbit or a lean stray antelope. Occasionally they would not mention what it was, and she was sure it was something more domesticated. She ate it, though, it being their only staple.

After a long and painful struggle, Swift Legged Woman

lost her battle to live. Mandy's grief deepened. Long Hair and Wild Eagle were among the few couples in which both husband and wife survived. Thunder Cloud was one of the rare individuals who was miraculously spared the disease to any degree. Blue Flower Woman recovered slowly. Her eyelids had shed their long lashes, and her body, like most of the survivors', was left with deep pockmarks—the price many were required to pay in conquering smallpox. Thunder Cloud was grateful just to have her returned to him.

The time came when no new cases were being brought to the sick lodge, but there were still six victims who teetered between life and death. Little Dog was among them, and Mandy gave him much of her attention.

But on one dreadful morning, Little Dog succumbed. When Dakota returned from burying him, he found Mandy standing at the center lodge pole, staring at the space of ground where the little one had lain.

"The pestilence at noonday," she said spiritlessly. "'It shall not come nigh thee,' I promised him that night at the way station. But I couldn't keep that promise."

Dakota moved next to her, his heart aching with hers.

"How many have died thus far?" she asked.

He remained silent.

"How many?"

His head lowered. "Nearly a hundred."

"Out of a hundred and fifty in this village." Never had she felt so defeated.

He stroked her hair. "Remember the biblical story of Jacob's son, Joseph, and how his jealous brothers had him enslaved and sent to a strange and distant place?"

She nodded. "I've often prayed that God would turn things around here as He did for Joseph, and make some good come out of all this."

"God didn't just turn things around for Joseph. He had plans for him from the beginning. Joseph told his brothers it wasn't *them* who sent him to Egypt, but *God*, remember? And he told them that even though they meant evil against him, God meant it for good, in order to bring about the saving of many lives."

He turned her to face him. "Mandy, the circumstances of your coming here were truly foul, but without your help these

63

past months, and especially your little talk with Thunder Cloud, this entire band could easily have been wiped out as others have been. You helped *save* one-third of the tribe. I hate that you are separated from your family, and that you were injured, yet still thank God you're here. It's hard to make sense of it all. But I just know He means it for good."

Her tear-filled eyes looked into his, revealing the first sign of hope he had seen in them in far too long a time.

CHAPTER 11

The last of the smallpox victims recovered, but the tribe as a whole never would. Fifty-two people remained alive to face whatever the future held for them.

Mandy was as uncertain about her future as she was about the Indians'.

She walked along a snowy bank by the creek, now able to get by with one crutch. How many months had it been since her family received Dakota's letter with news of her survival, only to have no further word of her whereabouts? Pa and Jeffrey might have gone looking for her, could have traveled to Fort Lyon and found out she never made it there. Would they think her dead again? How was Ma coping with all of the mysteries of her daughter's disappearance? Her heart was not strong, and Mandy worried most about her.

Hearing the *crunch-crunch* of footsteps in the snow behind her, she stopped and turned to see Dakota approaching. He was carrying her cloak.

"I thought Indians were supposed to be silent and stealthy. I heard you from fifty paces back."

"I try to give you fair warning nowadays. I wouldn't want to startle you and have you slug me with that crutch."

"Sure, sure."

"Put this on, will you?" He draped the cloak around her.

"*Hahoukac.* It didn't seem so cold when I set out."

They walked together in shared silence. The backs of their hands brushed, and her small one melted into his large, strong one, his fingers closing securely around hers.

"So, have Wild Eagle and the others decided what they are going to do?"

"My parents and eighteen others are going to the reservation. They really can't survive any other way now. Twenty more are heading north to Wyoming with some Cheyenne to join with the Northern Arapaho and the Oglala Sioux. They are just not willing to give in to reservation life."

"And the rest?"

"There are a dozen who are just heading out for the plains, refusing to be confined or made to change their lifestyle."

"Thunder Cloud is among the last group, right?"

"He and his wife, plus White Fox and his two brothers, three other couples, and Sky."

"Sky! But she's only eight years old."

"You know how independent she is. If her parents had survived, I believe they would have been among those going north. But she won't go. She's quite attached to my brother, and he's agreed to look after her."

The time had come for the question that burned in her soul. "What about you?"

Dakota released her hand and walked a few steps toward the eastern horizon, running his fingers through his hair. "Twenty are going to the reservation now instead of a hundred and twenty. A part of me says they won't need me as much, but the truth is, they're mostly the sick and elderly, as well as the two blinded by the smallpox, and they are left with even less of a sense of community now."

His eyes took in the seemingly endless prairie before him. "Every time I've left here it's been with the knowledge that I could come back at any time and find things just as I left them. Oh, everyone would be a little older, and there were always some brand-new shiny faces. The band may have even changed locations, but I'd always find them. This time when I leave there will be no coming back—nothing to come home to."

Mandy moved to his side, her heart bound to his. "When are they all leaving?"

"My father's group wishes to leave as soon as possible. Those bound for the north are leaving next week. Thunder Cloud will move out whenever it pleases him."

He lifted her chin with his finger. The sunlight danced in her enchanting green eyes. "You've asked about everyone but yourself."

Her eyes misted. "I know where I must go."

He enfolded her in his arms and held her close. "I love you so much, Mandy. You are the life running through my veins now."

They remained in a silent embrace for several minutes. Finally Mandy said, "We don't have to make it permanent. You could come to Denver from time to time and—"

"And what?" He stepped away from her. "Shall I visit you for a week or two in the summers? Take you to the theater? Or out riding? Have supper with your family? Then wave good-bye and say 'See you next year?' Mandy, I want to be with you *every day*, providing for you, sleeping next to you every night. I want us to have children together. But if that is not to be, I can't just visit you for a holiday, go on a picnic in the meadow and leave it that incomplete. I *can't*."

Her head lowered. "But I cannot bear the thought of *never* seeing you again. I would rather live at the reservation than live without you."

Neither could he conceive of how he would live without her. She was the summation of everything he ever desired in a woman. The woman he had long prayed would come into his life. The woman he had almost come to believe did not exist.

"My parents and the others have no choice. But I will not offer you such a home. Once I've seen them safely to the reservation, I'll come back here and get you on your way to where you belong. Then I must return to them."

With their arms around each other they walked back to the devastated camp that was soon to be a bare spot on the prairie.

Early the next morning, Mandy wandered among the families who were preparing to depart. She had come to know all of them well when she cared for them or their loved ones who had been lost in the epidemic. The survivors, most of whom had cut their hair short and wore old clothes to express their mourning, knew none of the usual joy that accompanied preparation for migration.

Despite the activity of gathering and packing belongings, the camp was essentially quiet. The women's task was to unfasten and remove the heavy hides from the lodge poles, then fold and pack them for travel. The poles were bound together by the men and tied to both sides of wooden Indian saddles so that the poles dragged on the ground behind the horses. Large pieces of sturdy hide were suspended between the poles to form a *travois*—a sling on which the household goods were secured.

Emotions were brittle and tears silently shed as the women hugged each other good-bye. Mandy's heart was breaking as she bid farewell to the people whose lives were changing forever, and who had changed hers.

Long Hair found Mandy and took her aside, speaking slowly so she could understand the Indian tongue. She had learned it well enough that even though she may not understand every word that was spoken, or correctly say what she intended, she and the Arapaho were usually able to grasp one another's meaning.

"We do not want you to be sad for us," the chief's wife told her. "You helped save our lives, and we are grateful."

Wild Eagle also came and took her hand in his. "Woman Shot With Sun's Arrow, we thank Man-Above for sending you to us. We will greatly miss having you at our fireside."

Long Hair added, "We have told Dakota he should not leave you to be with us. He is a noble son, but the price he pays is too great."

"No," Mandy answered, "he does right in watching over you and your people."

She hugged each of them, grieving the fact she would never see them again.

When they left to mount their horses, Dakota came to her and they held each other close. "I'll be back before the full moon." His gentle kiss lingered. But the exodus had begun.

A sorrowful band was left behind, one that would be reliving the same scene when the northbound group moved out the next week. They watched soberly as their friends and family headed toward the home of the morning sun.

Mandy did not take her eyes off the form on the palomino until it was too far away to distinguish.

* * *

Sitting on a large rock on the creek bank, Mandy stared into the frozen water below. It was snowing again, and very cold, but she disliked the loneliness of her empty lodge. Her soul was careworn with concern for her family and her life without the man she loved.

Thud! A smacking pain in the middle of her back shattered her thoughts. She turned to see Thunder Cloud standing thirty feet behind her, smirking as he rounded out another snowball. Despite the cold, he was clothed only from the waist down.

Mandy glowered at him, furious that he chose such a sorrowful time—only a day after his own parents left—to amuse himself by making sport of her. She turned her back to him again.

Thud! This one whacked her shoulder. She glared back at him. He stood with feet apart, left fist on his hip, right hand tossing another snowball up and down.

"Go away!" she shouted in her own language and turned from him.

The third ball left her ear stinging with cold. She stood up and spun around. "Dadburnit! That one really hurt!"

The smug warrior pointed first to her, then to his own bare chest. Exasperated, she accepted the dare. Keeping her eyes steadily on him, she bent over, scooped up a handful of snow and formed a nice round ball. "C'mon, Mandy," she said aloud to herself, "make this one count."

She fired. Her aim was low. The snowball exploded below his belly button. A naughty gratification seized her as he yelped from the impact.

Thus the battle began.

Mandy had the advantage of cover, ducking behind the rock for protection. But Thunder Cloud's ammunition came fast and hard, the brave showing no mercy despite the fact she was a mere woman, and a handicapped one at that.

The skirmish was nearly over shortly after it began. Mandy was getting battered. She again took cover behind the rock and, while catching her breath, formed a stockpile of snowballs at a furious pace. She carefully piled them in the crook of her arm, waited for a snowball to go whizzing over her head, then rose and hurled them rapid-fire them at her oppressor. She caught him off guard, and he cowered under the attack. She laughed until her sides hurt.

Reinforcements rushed to the aid of both sides. Blue Flower sided with Mandy against her own husband. The teams were fairly evenly matched, and the battle raged for thirty more minutes until both armies were too exhausted, mostly from laughing, to continue. A truce was called, and as a sign of peace, all remaining snowballs were tossed into the middle of the two lines. All of the "warriors" walked together back to the camp area to resume their prewar activities, laughing as they recalled and embellished the best parts of the battle.

Thunder Cloud slipped his arm around his wife's shoulder. "I did not know my Flower was so skilled in battle!"

When they reached the couple's lodge, he opened the flap and stepped aside. "Come and eat with us, Man-dee." He always called her by her English name, but the accent fell on the second syllable.

Mandy looked up at him. The lightheartedness he had imposed on them all was a welcome relief from the sadness they had felt for the last twenty-four hours, and beyond.

She smiled and said, "*Hahoukac.*"

It didn't seem like enough, but he let her know that it was. He slowly nodded his head once.

* * *

Five days later the second group moved out on their journey north. It was a repeat of the first event: packing up, removing tepee hides, securing goods onto the *travois* behind the horses.

After their departure, there were only thirteen people left in the camp, including Mandy. All of the children were gone except for Sky. It was a solemn, empty place.

Mandy spent most of the days with Blue Flower Woman and her sister, returning to her own lodge only at night. There were numerous chores to be done: repairing clothes and furs, cleaning hides, making preparations not only for one move but for nomadic life on the plains.

Frequently she went to Dakota's lodge, studying again the imprints of his life on the hide, handling and smelling his clothing, lying on his bed of buffalo robes.

One day a band of eight Cheyenne rode into the camp. Their faces, arms, even their horses, were painted in bizarre patterns of bright colors. Thunder Cloud went to greet them, then stood speaking to them in his limited Cheyenne and in sign language. Mandy and Blue Flower looked on from their cooking fire outside the couple's lodge. The warrior's back was to them, so Mandy understood little of what was being communicated.

Thunder Cloud invited the visitors into his home along with the other men of the camp. They smoked a pipe and held a discussion about the news the Cheyenne brought.

Mandy was not only suffering from curiosity but from the cold. She said to Blue Flower, "I am going inside."

"No, you cannot until the men say we may go in."

"But I am cold."

70

"If you are cold, go to your own lodge."

She hated going to her lodge, but she truly was cold, so she went there and worked up a fire. A short time later, the sound of drums and howls came from outside. She went out and halted in alarm as she watched the Cheyenne and Arapaho men dancing and shrieking, their skin painted, their hair adorned with bright feathers, their quivers filled with arrows.

"What is happening?" she asked the women standing nearby. But all were joining in on the chants, and she received no answer. She went to Blue Flower and repeated her question. The young woman, still attentive to the activity of the warriors and clapping her hands to the drumbeat, answered Mandy between chants.

"The Cheyenne have lost seven of their people by the hands of white men. The Dog Soldiers have come to invite our warriors to join them in getting revenge."

"How will they get revenge?"

Blue Flower chanted along with the others.

"*How will they get revenge?*"

"The score must be settled. Seven whites will die."

The war dance ended. The men went for their horses. Mandy's eyes searched for Thunder Cloud. He could put an end to this calamity just by saying the word. Finally she saw him, his back to her as he stood smearing paint onto his horse's neck. The muscular arms that emerged from his sleeveless buckskin shirt were painted, too. In a frenzy she hobbled over to him and grabbed hold of his arm and the metal band that encircled it below the shoulder.

He half-turned sharply, glaring at her. She sucked in her breath when she beheld his visage. His entire forehead was blood red. The remainder of his face was painted with angular patterns of green, yellow and blue. He looked grotesque, the likes of which she had never seen.

The painted warrior regarded her through narrowed eyes. His gaze fell to the hand that clutched his armband as if it sullied something sacred, then lifted to meet her horror-stricken expression. She withdrew her hand.

He pivoted and tramped away through the snow. She started after him. "Thunder Cloud, where are you going?"

"I believe you already know, even though you ask."

"Do you know who killed those people?"

71

"White men."

"Who are you going to punish for it?" She lagged behind him, unable to keep up his pace.

"Seven whites."

"Which seven? The first seven you come across?"

"Go to your lodge, Man-dee."

"I will not. You must listen to me."

"You do not understand our ways."

"I understand murder. Your act is as evil as the white men's."

He lengthened his stride. She fell further behind.

"Thunder Cloud!"

Visibly irritated, he halted and turned to her. He would settle for no more of this white woman's prattle.

But Mandy spoke first. "You want to kill white people? Why not start with *me*? Then you will only need to find six more."

He stood stock still, jarred by her fit of defiance and her startling challenge.

"Here!" She flung her crutch at him. He caught it mid-air. "Count coup against me, man of courage! Strike me with the stick and show everyone here what a brave warrior you are."

Every eye in the camp was on them.

His eyes filled with rage. He lifted the crutch high above him and hurled it like a spear. Her eyes followed it as it sailed over her head and disappeared into several inches of snow.

Suddenly his powerful grip squeezed her arm and he spun her around. The fury in his black eyes was like that of their first meeting near the stage station, and again in the corral when he thwarted her escape. The terror she knew at those encounters resurfaced, and she shuddered within the confinement of his iron hand.

After a turbulent moment of subdued rage, he lifted her into his sinewy, painted arms and carried her toward her lodge. She resisted him all the way, pummeling his chest and arms with her fist.

"Put me down! I do not want your hands on me—hands that kill innocent people!"

He carried her into her lodge and set her down on her furs. Standing erect, he thrust his arm down, his finger pointed in her face. His bitter words came through clenched teeth. "You must learn your place, woman!" He spun on his heels and stormed out.

Mandy sat trembling in the dim, cold lodge. This man, who only a week before started a snowball battle and reversed the mood of the entire camp, was now going to kill, probably scalp, innocent people. Women, children—it wouldn't matter. He was frighteningly unpredictable, and a chilling shiver came over her when she considered that he might well have taken her up on her challenge.

The rumble of horses' hooves and the *kiyi*-ing of the warriors conveyed that the small war party was on its way. As they rode past her lodge, something struck its hide with considerable force. She hopped over to the flap and peered out. Lying just outside was her crutch.

After composing herself, she went back to the lodge of Blue Flower Woman, unsure of whether she would be welcome. When she entered, Blue Flower looked up at her, then lowered her eyes in obvious disfavor but didn't demand she leave.

Mandy took the liberty of a few more steps. "I am sorry, Blue Flower, if what I said or did brought any shame upon you."

The young woman shook her head. "You have been with us for all these moons, yet you still do not know how to keep your place."

CHAPTER 12

Snow whipped through the air with the fury of a cyclone. The stinging cold even penetrated Dakota's heavy woolen coat. The storm had hit suddenly and with ferocity. Visibility was almost nil, making it the most dangerous time to be out alone on the prairie. Many men, women and children had perished in tempests such as this, some within yards of a haven they could not even see. But he knew he was nearly home, and to stop moving now meant certain death.

Home. The word no longer meant what it once did.

With no sense of bearing, he had to rely on his best judgment, his faithful horse, and most of all, his God.

The faint smell of smoke reached his nostrils. The camp was close. He strained to look in every direction, but he saw only white. He urged his horse in one course, lost the smell of the smoke, so turned back until it was noticeable again. He tried another bearing and again had to return. He called out, but his voice was buried in the storm.

A third try, a third failure. The knowledge of being so close kept his heart pumping furiously and his senses alert to any signal that would tell him where he was.

He nudged his mount's sides and let him have his head. The palomino took a few steps, stopped, then started again, stepping into a solid object. Dakota leaned over and felt around. *The corral.* He offered up a silent prayer of thanksgiving.

He slid off his horse and removed the saddle and bridle as well as the food and other supplies he had bought at an Army post. Feeling for the gate, he slipped the rope over the post, patted the steed on the hindquarters and let him in, then resecured the rope. Now he was only twenty yards from his lodge. Twenty long, blind yards.

Leaving the supplies where they lay, he braced against the wind with body bent and arm outstretched, pausing after each step. He prayed not to get blown off course and walk right past the lodge onto the open prairie. His precautions made it a painfully slow but successful crossing.

74

Upon entering his lodge, he stood still for a moment, taking in its warmth and security, grateful to be safe from the raging storm that now couldn't touch him. Then he noticed the fire.

His eyes still adjusting to the fire's light in the surrounding dimness, he glanced around and squinted at a form standing near the rear of the lodge.

"Thank God, Dakota! I was so afraid for you." She hobbled to him and threw her arms around him, the frozen wet wool of his coat sending shivers through to her bones.

"I'm all right. I'm all right." He said it as much to convince himself his ordeal was over as to assuage her fears. Shedding the hooded coat and gloves, he squatted at the fire and held his hands toward it, but he could not take his eyes from the sight of the woman who was placing the red Mackinaw blanket around his shoulders. "Are *you* all right?" he asked.

"I am now."

As he warmed himself, he spoke of the journey to the reservation and of how each member of the small band bore it. Then he recounted a conversation he had with his parents shortly after arriving there.

"They told me again that I belonged with you and not with them. But I just couldn't see fit to abandon them. The very next day, a load of provisions arrived. There was actually a generous supply of food, as well as clothes and blankets. My parents and the others insisted I leave them for good and remain with you, and said that if I did not, they would convene a council of the few remaining elders and have me banished from the tribe, so I could *not* return there. I'm sure they didn't mean that, but…"

Mandy stared in bewilderment. "Are…are you saying…"

He pulled the blanket off and rose. He held out his hands and she took them. "I am no longer bound by my obligations."

She was slow in allowing herself to be assured of his meaning. His smile convinced her she had interpreted him correctly. Joy filled her soul.

Yet they were not ignorant of the cost. "It is not under the most joyful of circumstances that I say this, since so much suffering has taken place that makes our future possible, but…I love you, Mandy, and I want you to be my wife. Will you

75

marry me?"

Her breath held. What she had desired for so long was now in reach, and she couldn't utter a word.

"Does this mean you're turning me down?" he asked with a knowing grin.

She shook her head.

"Then can I assume you're accepting my proposal?"

She smiled back and replied in his Indian tongue, "I believe you already know, even though you ask."

He enveloped her in his arms. "Mandy, I'd like to ask you something else. Would it be all right if...would you consider having a traditional Arapaho wedding ceremony? Here, before we leave?"

Her eyes went wide.

"Now, I'm not saying I will become your husband when I step into your lodge. That is true for my people here who hold to that custom. It is their way. Our way will be before a preacher in a church. But it would mean a lot to me to have a ceremony that celebrates the heritage passed to me through my father."

Her mouth formed a broad smile. "It would mean much to me as well, my love. Your people have, in great measure, become my people."

He loved her even more at that moment, and felt a joy he had never known. There would be times of grieving yet to come for all that was lost. But for now, they celebrated the blessing bestowed on them by the loved ones for whom they had been willing to sacrifice their futures.

* * *

Dakota spent most of the daylight hours hunting, as did the other three braves who remained in the camp. The women finished making and repairing clothing and blankets they would be taking. They gathered firewood, and when the men came home with what meat they could find, prepared the provisions. Mandy was looking forward to returning to the conveniences and normal routine of town life.

One morning Mandy, Blue Flower and Sky went to the cottonwoods along the creek bank for their supply of firewood. It was a pleasant task on early mornings such as this. The clear sky and dry air were welcome changes from the blizzard of a few days before.

"I hope so much that Thunder Cloud returns soon," Blue Flower said. "I have such happy news for him. Before the next winter comes, he will have a son."

"How…wonderful." Mandy spoke it with forced gaiety. Truth be told, the last thing the world needed was a child growing up under the influence of her unstable future brother-in-law. But her happiness for her friend was genuine.

Mandy added dry branches to her bundle. "If only Wild Eagle and Long Hair knew they have a grandchild on the way, and that Dakota and I are to be married as they wanted, I know they would be pleased. Some day we must go and tell them."

"Yes, I would like to witness the joy of my husband's mother. But Mandy, you and I must never see Wild Eagle again."

"Why do you say that?"

The young woman seemed astonished at Mandy's question. "Because he is the father of our husbands."

"But why can we not see him again?"

"It is forbidden for a woman and the father of her husband to look upon or speak to one another. Is it not so where you come from?"

"No, it is not so. The father of a woman's husband often becomes like a second father to her."

"Oh, that would not be proper! It is not our way."

Mandy was aware she had little chance of seeing Wild Eagle again, but to learn it was taboo…

They walked a half mile farther along the bend in the creek before stopping to pick up kindling from under the sturdy trees. They made a game of it, Mandy feeling as much a kid again as Sky.

Movement in the distance caught Sky's sharp eye as she reached the top of the bank with an armload of wood. "I see horsemen coming! The warriors have returned!"

Blue Flower's hand flew to her chest, and she ran to join Sky. Mandy slowly scaled the bank. There was a fluttering inside her chest, too, but not of a pleasant nature. She was sure Thunder Cloud loathed her after challenging him and affronting his dignity in full view of his peers. This was not a reunion she looked forward to.

The three stood amidst the trees, waiting. Suddenly Sky shouted, "Get down!" and pushed the women farther into the trees and over the bank.

"What is wrong?" Mandy asked.

"Those are not our warriors. They are Pawnee. They must not see us or they will kill us."

"Are you sure?"

"She is right," Blue Flower said. "At least two of them are Pawnee. I could not be sure about the other two."

"What are we going to do?" Sky cried.

"I do not think they can see us here," Blue Flower answered. "But they will soon be able to see the camp. Only the women are there. And when the men return from hunting, they also will be killed."

Peeping over the top of the creek bank, Mandy felt certain that the few lodges still standing would not be visible until the invaders passed the trees along the bend of the creek. She turned again to watch them approach. Within minutes they would sight the camp.

"We must stop them!" Sky cried out in a forced whisper.

"If we try, they will kill us," Blue Flower replied in despair, placing a hand on her not yet swelling abdomen. "But my sister is there."

"If Thunder Cloud was here, *he* would handle these enemies," Sky said.

"He is *not* here, Sky," Mandy said, even more angry with him for having left the camp unprotected.

The riders passed within thirty yards of the hidden women. Aside from the two Pawnee braves there was an Indian woman and a white man. The woman's face was expressionless as she rode. The white man rode tall in the saddle, triumphant-like. He was completely bald, lacking even eyebrows, but had a long brown moustache with ends that hung well past his chin.

Mandy knew the Pawnee were the hated enemies of all the Plains tribes, being noted for their brutality. She wondered aloud about the white man on the Appaloosa.

"He is the one called Headless Jack!" Blue Flower said with increasing panic in her voice. "I recognize him by the description I have heard of him. He is known by my people and yours to be the most vicious of *all* men."

Mandy's heart pounded faster. "Somehow we must stop

78

them from seeing the camp."

"I can run the fastest," Sky said. "I will show myself and let them chase me away from the village."

"No, Sky, not you. You are fast, but not faster than a horse."

"You cannot run at all!" the girl argued, gesturing toward Mandy's foot.

"But I can speak English to the white man. You cannot lead them away with your legs, but perhaps I can lead them away with my words."

"No, Mandy," Blue Flower protested. "You do not know the evil of that man."

"After we leave, you two run back to the camp along the creek beds." She bent over, placing a hand on the little girl's shoulder. "Sky, you must run faster than you ever have in your life. Get someone to find Dakota and the others and tell them which way we go." She gave her shoulder a squeeze. "I am counting on you."

Sky threw her arms around Mandy's neck.

"I must go now," Mandy told her. "Get ready to run!" She turned to Blue Flower. "Be very careful. You bear the son of Thunder Cloud inside you."

Mandy looked up the bank's slope and breathed the quickest yet most fervent petition she had ever prayed. She worked her way up over the edge of the bank. Behind the riders now, she drew in a breath to call to them, but panic muted her.

Her eyes cut back to the creek. It was safe there. She could get back without the riders even knowing of her presence. But her gaze followed the line of trees that curved toward the camp. Within seconds the invaders would see it. Through a throat constricted with fear she shouted to them.

The bald man looked over his shoulder and jerked his horse to a halt. The others followed suit. They turned and rode toward her.

"Well, well, looky at what we got here," the bald man said. "Now what in Lucifer's name are you doin' a way out in this desolate spot, white woman?"

Her throat tightened and she could barely speak. "I'm so glad you came by. I…I thought I'd never see another white man again. I thought I was done for."

"How'd you get here?"

79

"I…was kidnapped by some Kiowa not far from Fort Lyon but managed to escape. I had never been so scared, nor cold and hungry."

He observed her use of her crutch. "How'd you get away, the shape you're in?"

"I…I…" Her concocted tale was crumbling. "I stole a horse while they slept the night before last, but he ran off yesterday."

"Havin' a string of bad luck, are yeh?"

She prayed with all her heart that Dakota would get back from the hunt early and come for her.

"If you got taken by the Kiowas, how come you got on Arapaho 'skins?"

Mandy looked down at her dress, petrified her lie was exposed.

"I…traded for this outfit with some Injuns at the fort—a souvenir to show my friends back East. The officers there said the Kiowa have been like insects around these parts lately."

"Now, that don't square with what I heared. My Pawnee friends here say there's word of an Arapaho camp near here. The Kiowas ain't been around here since—"

"That's what the soldiers thought, too. The *dead* ones."

Headless Jack's steel gray eyes scanned in every direction, carefully seeking for some hint of who might be right. Aside from the trees along the creek, there was only white landscape meeting a blue sky.

"Tell you what, lady. We'll take you along with us back toward the Arkansas. There's troops all up and down that river. They'll see to it you get back to where you came from."

He spoke to one of the Pawnee who then dismounted, went over to Mandy and lifted her onto the horse behind the catatonic woman. He threw her crutch to the ground.

"Give that back! I can't walk without it."

The devil released a vexing laugh through the bald man's mouth. "Then I reckon you can't run without it, neither."

CHAPTER 13

*H*eadless Jack never had any intention of going to the Arkansas River. After an hour's slow ride, he announced they would hole up in a favorite hideout of his.

Seated behind the Indian woman, Mandy asked her if she spoke English or Arapaho. The woman did not respond in any way. It was as if she were in a trance.

"She don't talk at all," Headless Jack said. "Hasn't for some time now. Me, I speak most of the tongues these Plains Indians jabber. I'm sure you 'n me'll have some real nice chats ourselves."

They approached a rock formation, a unique find on the southeastern plains of the territory, and rode single file through a narrow crevice between two straight rising boulders.

"This here's my own personal sanctuary," Jack said. "When the sun ain't shinin' point blank on this spot, this entrance is impossible to find to the untrained eye. And that sun is gonna melt our tracks right inta slush."

Jack led them into a small fortress of surrounding colored rocks. They dismounted, Mandy lowering herself with great care so as not to reinjure her foot. She still wore the splint at all times and had never gone without a crutch.

"Make yerself at home, miss. *Mi casa es su casa.*"

Mandy brushed wet snow from a smooth rock and sat on it. All she could do was wait…and pray.

"Father, help me. Send someone. Let them find this place despite its invisibility." Shivering, she prayed again from Psalm 91: "He that dwelleth in the secret place of the most High shall abide under the shadow of the Almighty. I will say to the Lord, He is my refuge and my fortress, my God, in Him will I trust."

Jack got a fire going and retrieved some supplies he had previously cached there. He and the Indians ate but offered nothing to the Indian woman or Mandy. She had no appetite anyway. She was cold, but moving closer to the fire meant being closer to those people, and she would rather freeze.

Hours went by. Headless Jack fell asleep after gorging himself. The Pawnee wandered about, apparently free from apprehension of being discovered in this place. Mandy feared this hideout was truly as impossible to find as Jack said. She grew more frightened as the sun moved across the sky.

When Jack awoke, he sat up and looked around, rubbing his bald head. "You still over there, blondie? Why don't yeh come sit here next t' me so's I can keep yeh warm?"

Mandy remained as silent as the Indian woman.

"When it goes down to zero tonight you'll be beggin' me to share my blanket and fire. Jist you wait."

He stood and walked to her. Her senses repelled the sight and odor of dirty sweat mixed with old whiskey stains and dried blood.

Jack leaned down. "You ain't half-bad lookin'. I seen better, though. But I know what they say 'bout beauty bein' only skin deep." He ran his finger along her jaw.

She slapped his hand away. "But *ugly* cuts clear to the bone."

He backhanded her across the face, splitting her cheek. "You'll be sorry for that, lady. Jist you wait."

He returned to his blanket and grabbed the Indian woman by the arm. "In the meantime, I believe I've worked up another appetite. C'mon, squaw." He led the woman behind a large rock.

Minutes passed. Mandy sat trembling from the cold and fear. She needed to move to the fire. As she lifted off the rock, an agonizing scream filled the air and resounded off the boulders around them. The Pawnee jumped in surprise. Mandy was consumed with terror.

Moments later, Jack appeared. He approached Mandy, a bloody scalp hanging from his hand.

Her eyes widened in horror; her stomach cramped with nausea.

"What's wrong? She was nothin' to you. Just a Ute squaw."

Mandy leaned to the side and retched. Barely able to catch her breath, she recoiled at the sound of Jack's gruff voice at her ear.

"Are you quite finished?" He yanked on her hair and sat her up straight. His predatory gaze crawled over her body. "I jist want you to know why I did that. You see, I don't need her no more. I got me somethin' better now. Somethin' with yeller hair."

He took a few steps back, then threw the bloody scalp at her feet.

"You're next."

Mandy sprang from the rock in blind panic. Despite the splint, her ankle could not support her weight and her leg collapsed beneath her. Headless Jack's large, calloused hand turned her onto her back, and he lay on top of her. She screamed and scratched against his commanding mass and shook her head violently as he tried to kiss her face. His long, wiry moustache scratched her neck. Guttural sounds filled her ear. His stench assaulted her nostrils.

Of a sudden, he was off her. She rolled over and tried to pull herself up. Once upright, she tried to run.

She stumbled, recovered, then stumbled again. She raised herself with a sizeable stick lying nearby and used it to flee for her life.

The pain in her ankle was unbearable but could not match her terror. She ran through the maze of rocks until the stingingly cold air in her stressed lungs and the pounding in her chest rendered her unable to continue. Leaning against a boulder, she struggled for each breath. With every second that passed she feared the leathery hand would grab her.

His footsteps came from close behind her. She pushed away from the rock and fled. A hand grasped her arm and jerked her to a stop. She pivoted, swinging the stick blindly at him. His free hand caught her wrist, and the stick fell to the ground. Mandy threw back her head and screamed.

"Stop it!"

The words were spoken in Arapaho.

"Man-dee! Look at me!"

As his words registered, she stopped resisting and opened her eyes. It was Thunder Cloud—minus the paint and other symbols he wore on his quest for revenge.

Her legs buckled. He grabbed her around the waist. She rested her head against him, her relief emerging much slower than her terror subsided.

White Fox appeared, dragging a bleeding and limping Headless Jack to where they stood. "The Pawnee are dead." He held out Jack's Dragoon pistol to Mandy.

"Wh—what is that for?"

"He would have killed you," White Fox answered. "You know that."

Mandy stared at the gun. The men stood in silence, waiting.

"But I…I cannot just shoot him."

"Of course yeh can't," Jack said, speaking English but having understood their Arapaho. "That's what makes you civilized, unlike all these heathens."

The images of the aftermath of the Ute woman's horrifying death flashed across her mind. "You really don't deserve to live!"

She grabbed the gun from White Fox's hand. The whites of Jack's eyes appeared for the first time. Using two hands, she pointed the heavy pistol at the bald man's forehead. At this range, the large caliber, soft lead bullet would carry most of his brains out the back of his head.

Jack's confidence returned when he saw the perplexity in her face. "You ain't got it in yeh."

Her eyes flashed and her jaw tensed. She slowly thumbed back the hammer, raising the rear sight. Her hands shook as she took aim at the head of the most depraved man who ever lived.

* * *

After hours of searching, Silent Wolf ran his lathered horse as fast as it would go and rode up next to Dakota.

"What is it, Silent Wolf? What is wrong?"

"It is your woman," he panted.

Dakota's insides lurched, as if he'd been struck by an arrow. "What has happened? Tell me!"

"She was taken by some Pawnee, and the white man known as Headless Jack."

He stared in abject horror.

"Blue Flower Woman can show us which way they went."

The palomino was fast, and he loved to run. But urged now by a tension in his master's legs and hands he had never sensed before in all the years he had carried him, he ran harder.

"She did it to protect us all," Blue Flower told Dakota after explaining what had happened. "They would have ridden into the village and killed the women. They would have laid in wait for all of you men, we were sure. She led them away." She

84

pointed in the direction they had ridden.

Dakota swung onto his horse and jammed his heels into its flanks. Thongsoontorn rode with him, then they split up to cover more ground.

Devoured by fear, Dakota prayed as hard as he rode. Headless Jack's reputation for murder and mutilation was notorious. There was not a more evil man on the face of the earth.

And he had Mandy.

* * *

Every fiber of justice in Mandy, both innate and learned, screamed that Headless Jack should die.

She slowly lowered her hands and passed the gun back to White Fox.

The bald man snickered. "Didn't I tell yeh?"

"Get him away from me!"

White Fox led the fiend away, and Mandy lowered herself to a rock. Thunder Cloud said nothing, his silence splitting the air around them. She could feel his heavy gaze.

Finally, he asked, "Man-dee, if you had the gun in your hand when he came at you, would you have shot him?"

"Yes," she answered without hesitation. "But now I…I cannot do it."

He sat down next to her and drew a breath. "Do you understand what name he is called?" She nodded. "Do you know he was given that name because he has been known to cut off the heads of his victims?"

Mandy turned her head, feeling as if she would be sick again. He let out a sigh of frustration.

"Thunder Cloud, my people have our own ways of seeing to it that bad men are punished for their crimes."

"Yes, Dakota has spoken of your law houses. It would be your word against that of the bald man, would it not? If they believe *him*, he will go free. Tell me, where is the justice in that? If they believe *you*, they will kill him. Why is it not just for you to take his life yourself?"

She stared into his dark eyes, considering the irony of this Indian telling her—a woman widely knowledgeable in legal practices and maneuverings—about the American system of

85

justice. And its shortcomings. Still, she could *not* take the law into her own hands.

Despite his exasperation, Thunder Cloud readjusted and tightened her splint, then helped her back to where White Fox and a smirking Headless Jack stood.

"There ain't no law within a hundred miles of here," Jack said. "And you proved me right—you ain't got it in yah to do nothin' with me."

She faced the bald man and glared into his wicked eyes. "You're right," she said weakly. "I can't. It's not my way." Her next words were in Arapaho and addressed to the warriors.

"I leave him to *your* ways."

Jack paled. "No! You can't do that! You *know* what they'll do to me."

She turned to Thunder Cloud. "Help me onto a horse. I will ride out ahead of you and White Fox. Just promise me two things. Promise you will not scalp his hairless head, and you will never let me know what takes place here. Not ever."

He slowly nodded once.

He led her to the Appaloosa and lifted her onto its back. The whole while Headless Jack was calling out to her, pleading for his life. "At least I deserve a fightin' chance!"

She guided the horse next to where he stood. "You'll get the same chance you gave the Ute woman." Her eyes bore into his. "Jist you wait."

His cries for mercy echoed off the rock walls as she exited this secret lair, blending with the memory of the shrieks of the Ute woman. As she rode, her vision narrowed as if she were entering a dark tunnel. One without a light at the end. She felt excruciating pain in her grossly swollen foot. Saw flashes of Jack striking her, clawing at her. Smelled the putridness of his saddle blanket. Heard the sudden stillness when his screams cut off. Felt only numbness concerning her part in his untried execution.

Within minutes Thunder Cloud and White Fox rode up beside her. "Can you ride faster?" the elder warrior asked.

Barely able to stay on the horse at this point, she shook her head.

He told White Fox to ride ahead quickly to inform those at the camp that Mandy was safe. "Keep your eyes watching for Dakota. He must know she is secure. Tell him we will not make it home tonight."

"No, I need to see him," she insisted.

"At this pace we cannot make it anywhere near the camp by dark. Go, White Fox. Ride like the wind."

At sunset they settled under the protection of a cluster of trees near a creek bank. Mandy finally was warmed by a fire and had something to eat. But it was Headless Jack's food. Thunder Cloud wrapped Jack's buffalo coat about her, and they sat on blankets that had belonged to him. She had ridden his horse. This use of his possessions sickened her, and she vomited what little she had eaten.

Thunder Cloud offered her some water from the creek. She was able to keep it down.

"You need to place your leg in the creek and let the cold water help the swelling go down." As he assisted her in doing that, she asked, "How did you find me?"

"Thongsoontorn had been searching with Dakota. They separated, he met us and told us what happened, then continued his search in a different direction. White Fox and I explored a nearby area, and when we heard a scream, we followed the sound."

Taking notice of the developing bruise on her face, Thunder Cloud studied her cheek. "He did this to you?" She nodded. "He will harm no one else."

The icy water chilled her quickly, and they moved back to the fireside.

"Thunder Cloud, I will be grateful to you forever for saving me from that man. I asked Man-Above to send someone who would find that secret place. He sent you."

He picked up a stick and stirred the kindling in the fire. "I am grateful as well for all the times you have helped save my people. From the smallpox. From Headless Jack today. Both times I would have lost my Blue Flower, her sister, and many others."

He set the stick down and sat beside her. After several minutes of silence, he asked, "Is there something else on your mind?"

There was. But she did not want to darken this day even further.

"We killed no innocent people."

A spark of hope flared. "What did you say?"

"I believe you already know, even though you ask."

"Please, tell me. What do you mean?"

He shifted his weight and rewrapped the blanket around himself.

"Our second day out we came upon a small house. The man was walking from the corral, and when he saw us he ran into the house for his gun. But we were through the door before he could even aim. There were six of them: the man, his wife, and four children. Our task would have been nearly finished with one strike.

"As one of the Cheyenne raised his knife to the man's neck, the woman screamed. It was only then that I observed her well. She stood in a corner with her children huddled behind her skirt. I called to the Cheyenne to wait."

He swung his gaze on her.

"The woman had been shot with the same sun arrow as you, Man-dee. And her eyes…they held that same mixture of fear and defiance I have seen in yours. I walked to her and touched her sun-colored hair. She slapped my hand away. Yes, I thought, this one is as Man-dee. The same hair. The same spirit."

Her throat tight, she sought the answer with her eyes.

"I told the Cheyenne she must not die."

Mandy exhaled sharply, thankful it was his code that perished instead of the woman.

"We took the man's rifle and rode back to the Cheyenne camp where we spoke to the survivor of the attack on their band. She told us what the invaders looked like. Two of them had hair of red, the third wore a patch over his eye. They carried with them the tools of diggers of the yellow rock that is so precious to you whites. We spent four sleeps riding toward the foothills until we came upon the men we sought."

He stopped there. Mandy needed no further details. Except…

"You said there were three of them. Did you not seek four more?"

"We found the ones responsible. I told the others we must be satisfied that the score was now even."

His actions left her in wonder of this man who so tested her equilibrium.

"Thunder Cloud, I have borne much anger toward you. I

shamed you. And now I am in shame. I hope you can forgive me."

"I also was filled with rage, for the words you spoke and the way you acted with no regard for your place."

He rested his dark but now gentle eyes on her.

"But the anger fled from me at the white man's house when I encountered the woman with the sun-colored hair."

CHAPTER 14

Shortly after setting out the next morning, Thunder Cloud's horse stumbled, hurling him to the ground. The horse rolled on top of him, and Mandy was struck with the dreadful impression that he had been crushed to death.

"Thunder Cloud!" She swung her horse around, slid down from its back and hobbled over to the brave.

He lay on his side with his legs drawn up, his arms surrounding his ribcage and his face contorted in pain. His breath came in short gasps. Ribs could be broken, and she hoped his lung hadn't been punctured. He tried to push himself up to sitting, holding his side and grimacing. She placed her hands on his arm and back in an attempt to help him.

"Do not touch me! You make it worse."

"I am sorry. What can I do to help?"

"Get the gun."

"The *gun*?"

"Do as I tell you." He winced from the effort of talking.

She did as he instructed, returning with Jack's Dragoon.

"Shoot the horse."

She glanced toward the horse that lay a few yards from the warrior. It struggled to rise but could not.

"Do not make me repeat every word, woman!" he growled through clenched teeth. "Will you *ever* learn to do as you are told?"

Her face reddened and her jaw set. "Perhaps I should just shoot *you* instead and end *your* suffering."

His shock was great enough to show through his agony. He let out a painful breath, then spoke in a more civil tone. "He will suffer long before he dies, Man-dee."

Unpleasant as the task was, she did what needed to be done.

"I am sorry for what I said," she told him upon returning to his side. "With you, the worst in me often comes out."

With his eyes he directed her toward the Appaloosa. "Lead the horse next to that rock." When she did so, he positioned himself to rise. She wanted to help him, but figured he'd chide her for it. He could barely stand but ordered, "Get up first. I will ride behind you."

"Would it not be better if—"

"Man-dee! Do as you are told one time!"

It took effort for each of them to mount the horse with their injuries. They rode slowly east.

Mandy heard an occasional painful breath escape from Thunder Cloud's otherwise controlled bearing. She knew it would vex him if she made something of it, so she said nothing and kept her eyes straight ahead. But at one point his hand gripped her shoulder and he nearly raised himself off the horse in piercing pain. She turned her head. "Should we stop?"

"No." After another minute, he said, "Dakota comes."

"Where?"

"From the river."

Dakota's feet touched the ground before the palomino came to a stop. He rushed to the Appaloosa as Mandy swung her right leg over the horse's neck. She lowered herself into the arms that surrounded her fiercely.

"Mandy! Thank God you're all right. I was so afraid I'd lost you. Thank God you're safe!" He held her so tightly she could hardly breathe, but she did not want him to let go. She could breathe later.

Then, difficult as it was, she pressed away from him. "Thunder Cloud is hurt. It's pretty bad."

She explained what happened as Dakota went to his brother. He confirmed that some ribs were broken and offered to make a *travois* so Thunder Cloud would not have to ride.

"I will not be dragged into the camp like an old woman." The matter was settled.

It took an hour to reach camp at their pace, Mandy soothed and contented to be nestled in front of Dakota, his arms securely around her.

In Thunder Cloud's lodge, they wrapped strips of hide around his chest to set the rib fractures. There were no signs of serious internal damage. Mandy's leg was also rewrapped and resplinted. It had been a long time since the pain had been so intense. She and Thunder Cloud shared some of the pain-killing herbs offered them.

Blue Flower Woman, who had retrieved Mandy's crutch from where the Pawnee brave had pitched it, helped her back to her lodge. "Where is Dakota?" Mandy asked, thinking he had

91

followed them.

"He will come. He speaks with his brother."

As soon as the women left, Dakota squatted next to his brother, his countenance mirroring the younger brave's name. "Where is he now?"

Thunder Cloud set his eyes on Dakota's. "The vultures have him."

Talking was torturous for Thunder Cloud, but he owed his brother an explanation.

"I do not understand how your white woman perceives things. When White Fox offered her the chance for justice, she could not carry it out. After all that had passed, it still greatly disturbed her that the bald man would be executed outside the judgment of her precious law house. She finally left it to us, and we ended it. It is better this way, Dakota, because although she says she is grateful to me for saving her, I fear she might always harbor an aversion toward the one who executed justice. It is better that it is me, and not you."

A horde of emotions had flooded through Dakota during the last twenty-four hours. There was no way he could adequately thank his brother or repay him for bringing Mandy back safely, and for sparing him the entangling dilemma of Headless Jack's bitter end.

One disturbing question remained, holding Dakota in the warrior's lodge. "There is one more thing…"

"No, Dakota. I got to her in time. But he hit her and terrorized her and pawed her. She ran in panic on her broken foot, which now will probably never heal."

Dakota thanked his brother again for the life and security of his woman.

"She saved my Flower, and her sister, and Sky. And the men who would have been ambushed, including you. Including me. She is…a magnificent woman."

Dakota entered Mandy's lodge and found her sitting near the fire Blue Flower was fueling. The teen wife of Thunder Cloud rose and took her leave, patting Dakota's shoulder as she passed him.

His eyes rested on Mandy's face, her expression reflecting the unspeakable horror of the day before. She had lost none of her beauty, but she looked helpless and spent. They both struggled for something to say. Finally, he merely asked, "Are

92

you warm enough?"

She shook her head.

He retrieved a blanket, and as he placed it around her shoulders, he whispered, "You're safe now."

Tears streamed down her cheeks. She began to sob as emotions released. He held her and stroked her and told her it would be all right. He would make it all right.

The feel of his arms around her, the even rise and fall of his chest where her head rested, the earthy smell of his buckskin shirt—all worked to bring a quiescence to her.

Exhausted to the marrow, she had to sleep. Dakota gently tucked her between the buffalo robes, assuring her he would not leave her. But her sleep was fitful. Once when she opened her eyes, she saw him by the fire, down on one knee, his eyes heavenward. The only sound was the occasional snapping of the fire. She drifted away…

The bald man was coming at her. She tried to get up and run, but her legs would not carry her. He threw himself on top of her. His stench penetrated her nostrils. Sweat from his bald head dripped onto her face. His hands were all over her. She fought back hard, but her blows had no effect. Then he pulled his knife and held it to her throat, intending to live up to his name one more time.

"No-o-o!"

"Mandy, it's all right. It was a dream."

No power on this earth could have restrained him from snatching her into his arms and holding her close. She cried and trembled as her body conformed to his. He cradled her, gently rocking, whispering that he loved her.

Though she now rested safely at his breast, many disquieting stirrings provoked Dakota's soul. Nearly losing her renewed his appreciation of every day he would spend with her. But it was accompanied by the blatant realization that he was not capable of protecting her from all harm as he had arrogantly fooled himself into believing.

It was a gnawing sense of powerlessness he would carry inside for many years to come.

CHAPTER 15

*T*hunder Cloud and Blue Flower Woman came to the lodge of Woman Shot With Sun's Arrow with two palomino horses to propose marriage on behalf of his brother, Dakota, son of Chief Wild Eagle. The proposal was readily accepted. Blue Flower's sister, acting on behalf of Mandy's family, went to Dakota's lodge and escorted him to the bridal tepee. When he entered, he and Mandy became husband and wife as far as all the guests were concerned.

Dakota's eyes immediately sought his bride. They welcomed him with open devotion. She looked beautiful in a long, white doeskin dress. The seams and hem were trimmed in garnet; the sash around her waist was indigo. Beaded earrings dangled at her shoulders, enhancing her silken hair of gold.

Dakota, clad in a rust-colored buckskin outfit, looked strikingly handsome. The sight of him stirred Mandy with excitement.

The celebration lasted several hours, the small band of remaining Arapaho not only delighting in the marriage of Dakota and Mandy but welcoming a time of rejoicing after so much sorrow and trauma. They brought gifts of blankets, pottery, utensils and other practical items that could easily be packed later that day—the day of the final exodus.

Although the gathering was small, the couple felt richly blessed in participating in this tradition with the people they loved. They also shared with them the Christian tradition of exchanging vows to love one another for better or worse, richer or poorer, in sickness and health, till death parted them.

After the last of the guests took leave, the "newlyweds" stepped into each other's arms.

"I'll bet this isn't the kind of wedding you always dreamed of," Dakota said.

"But you surpass any man I ever dreamed of standing with at the altar."

Her hands ran through his long hair and closed behind his neck. He lowered his head, and she welcomed his kiss. It lingered longer than they had allowed themselves before now, and it was with great reluctance that they separated. This was not truly their wedding day, and they must wait to be joined as they yearned.

"We, uh, are gonna have to be careful about that," Dakota warned.

"For now."

Mandy insisted on taking the family items given Dakota by his parents, and he allowed it to the point where it wouldn't burden the horses. In truth, he wanted to take as much as possible, too, knowing he would never be returning. It was impractical for them to take his tepee, but he cut out the giant swatch of the hide where his life was etched so intricately.

"I guess that's it," he said with a sigh. "There's nothing else to do but say our good-byes."

When Sky saw Mandy approach, she ran to her and wrapped her arms around her waist. "I wish you were coming with us instead of going to the white man's village."

"I was never prepared for your kind of life, Sky. I do not think I have the courage you do to face the hardships and the elements."

The Indian girl's eyes grew wide. "Ah, Mandy! There is no woman alive with more courage than you!"

Mandy smiled. "It is because you were so brave and swift that day, Sky. You helped save my life. I will always be thankful to Man-Above for giving you such speed and daring."

Dakota sought out the men and women who had been his friends throughout many years. Some had only been youngsters when he came back to the tribe for the first time at the age of seventeen. Now they were grown into adulthood. Breaking ties with these, the last of his band, meant closing forever a major chapter in his life. His life ahead with Mandy filled the greatest desire of his heart, but that heart also was melancholic over the total loss of this aspect of his heritage. All he had learned and experienced would remain with him, but there would never again be this place, or these people, to come back to. These were sorrowful and painful farewells.

When all other words of parting had been spoken, Dakota and Mandy went to see Thunder Cloud and Blue Flower. Blue Flower went to Mandy and they hugged, their tears flowing freely.

The two brothers placed their hands on each other's shoulders.

"We must meet again one day, Dakota. I do not know when or where or under what circumstances, but we must."

Thunder Cloud went to Mandy. "Walk with me, Man-dee?" She gazed at him tearfully, then nodded. "Leave this," he said, taking the crutch from her and holding out his arm. "Lean on me." She did so, despite the fact he was still dealing with the pain from his fractured ribs. To refuse him on that count would dishonor him.

They walked in silence past some tepee-shaped lodge poles whose covers had been stripped from them. There was an eeriness to them—these skeletal reminders of what once had been the warm and secure homes of active and happy families. Mandy could almost hear the laughter, the singing, the music, and the crying that once filtered through them.

Thunder Cloud led her into one of them. "This was the lodge of my mother's brother who died of the smallpox."

"I am glad your mother met with a happier fate."

"Did she? She survived the disease only to be forced to go to a reservation."

He saw the sadness in her eyes.

"I am sorry, Man-dee. You sacrificed much to save my mother's life and do not deserve to bear any sorrow for how she spends the remainder of that life. For as long as I travel on this side of the spirit world, I will be grateful for all you have done for our tribe. Others, too, will hear of the boldness of the white woman with the yellow hair who gave of herself more than once to save our people."

He smiled at her, his dimples deep in his cheeks. "You are not the same paleface I brought to this camp so long ago."

"And you are not the same warrior who could make me freeze in fear."

"They are quite a peculiar pair, are they not, Dakota?" Blue Flower Woman said as she and her brother-in-law stood watching their spouses work out their parting after such a stormy relationship.

"Peculiar indeed." Dakota grinned as he recalled the times Mandy pummeled the warrior she now strolled with back to where they waited.

"Dakota, do you think Thunder Cloud will ever love me?" The question took him unawares. "Blue Flower, why do you ask such a strange question? He loves you now."

"Not in the way he loved Little Fawn. Not in the way you love Woman Shot With Sun's Arrow."

Taking hold of her shoulders, he turned her to face him. "Blue Flower, you know Thunder Cloud is a man who keeps his feelings buried deep inside. But he chose you, did he not? He had his pick of any of the marriageable maidens in this camp, and he chose *you.*" He kissed her forehead, then whispered in her ear, "And I, for one, am glad he did."

She attempted to smile but fell short. "But...I am not so beautiful as I was." Her fingertips dabbed the pockmarks on her face as they had done so often when she was alone, or at night as she lay next to her sleeping husband.

Dakota lifted her chin. "The loveliness you knew as a young girl pales next to what I see now—what Thunder Cloud sees. Your womanhood has made you into a beauty unadorned, and now you impart the radiance of one who is with child. No scars will take that away from you. *Ever.*"

She searched his face for a hint of pity, or hollowness, or something other than the bare truth. Finding none, she smiled broadly, and the tears that fell were not those of one who grieves but of one whose self-esteem has been raised to the heavens.

"No more tears, my Flower," Thunder Cloud said as he and Mandy approached. He went to his wife and wiped a tear from her scarred cheek. "They hide your beauty." He drew her to him and held her close.

Dakota turned to Mandy. "It's time to go."

The final departure began. They all rode together for a few miles, then halted. Here Dakota and Mandy had to turn west; the rest of the band would continue northeast.

"You all must take great care," Dakota said, his steady voice disguising the sepulchral feeling inside his chest. "We have many enemies on the plains."

"And you will not be far from those dogs, the mountain-dwelling Utes," Thunder Cloud replied. "But I will not fear for you, for you have Woman Shot With Sun's Arrow to protect you." He reached down and rubbed his shin and instep, and they all broke into laughter at the memory of that first day in the corral.

The warrior reined his horse over to hers and scrutinized

97

her splinted leg as he had done so many times in the months past. When he lifted his eyes to hers, they held fast.

She reached over and touched his sleeve. "I will miss you, my brother and my friend."

He studied her misted eyes and slowly nodded once.

CHAPTER 16

The journey across the plains was blessedly uneventful for Dakota and his "bride." The only Indians they encountered were amicable. The only whites were traders, Army scouts and settlers who welcomed them to hot meals and cozy fires.

Their entire trek became one extended lesson in the school of basic survival, the vast prairie serving as the classroom. Dakota instructed Mandy in which plants were edible, which were poisonous, and which were medicinal.

He explained how to recognize the differences between Indian tribes, including whether they were hostiles or friendlies, by their dress, their hair, their paint, and even the way they rode horses.

The same ash tree whose bark could be chewed to relieve a toothache also offered its wood for making a bow. She learned to do so by tying the ends of a branch together with sinew binding. Her first arrows were crooked and inaccurate, but she was learning.

She found shooting the rifle more her style. Her father had taught her to shoot when she was ten years old and had told her she was a natural. But with neither arrow nor bullet would she shoot anything living, except a wild animal that threatened. Dakota insisted her attitude would have to change, that she needed to learn how to live off the land and her own abilities.

"Why are you making me learn all this?" she asked one night as they sat in front of a fire in an abandoned cabin.

He was strangely serious, and drew her closer to him, placing her head in the hollow of his shoulder.

"I'd like to be able to tell you that you'll never need to know these things. I want to promise you that I'll be there for you, every day and every night, that you'll never have a need I can't meet. I want to promise you those things, but I can't. No man can."

He turned her face to his. "But for as long as God gives me breath, I swear I'll provide for you, to the best of my ability. And the best way I know how to provide for you includes seeing to it you can provide for yourself."

99

She sensed how strongly he felt about the matter, but frankly did not share his concern. She concluded it had to do with the experience with Headless Jack. It was something that, in his own way, was as traumatic for him as it had been for her. For the sake of his peace of mind she would be patient and attentive to the things he taught her until this anxiety passed.

They arrived in Colorado City on a dreary, overcast day. As they rode through the snow-laden streets, Mandy felt almost out of her element among the sounds and sights that were familiar to her yet far removed in time. She heeded the goings-on in shops and banks and saloons and a laundry that normally would have gone unnoticed.

In front of a white clapboard church a young couple and a man in a black preacher's coat stood surrounded by happy well-wishers. The couple's wedding day. She glanced at Dakota. He had taken notice as well and smiled at her.

After another block he said, "The bank is just ahead. We'll go there first and get some money out."

"Are we going to rob it?"

He laughed. "Surely I told you I have an account in this bank for when I come here and need to buy supplies for the cabin."

He had spoken before of the cabin he built shortly before the gold rush brought men to Colorado by the tens of thousands. It was nestled in a range west of Colorado City heading up towards Pikes Peak. It had only one room with simple furniture he'd fashioned with his own hands. The floor was made of flat stones, but he said they could put down rugs some day if she liked. He built it near a stream so there was no lack of water or fish or game.

"Are there any other little caches of cash I should know about?"

"Actually, there are two other banks in the territory where I have accounts, in places I've returned to and smithed on occasion."

Her jaw fell. "I had no idea I was engaged to a rich man."

"I didn't say there was a lot in each one. But when we get settled, I'll retrieve those funds and see about setting up a smithy."

Upon checking in at the hotel, Mandy was crushed by the news from the desk clerk. The recent snowstorm left forty-foot drifts between there and Denver, and all roads were impassable. And despite the telegraph lines they had seen nearby, the messages within them were whizzing past them between Pueblo and Denver, and there was no office in town from which to send a message.

"How long before the roads are open again?"

"A week, maybe two."

"A *week!*"

"Lady, there ain't no easy way for the crews to get through."

Mandy well knew the region of land between the two cities often drew the worst of the winter storms. There were times when the skies dropped mere flurries in Denver, but news would arrive that people had been stranded in those higher elevations for days, even weeks. Now it would be that long before she could continue her journey home. And without a telegraph office in town, her family would remain in agony wondering whatever became of her after receiving news of her survival at the stage stop.

At supper that evening in the hotel dining room, Dakota said, "Sweetheart, I'm thinking…if we're stuck here for a week or more, why don't we go up to my cabin and wait out the time there?"

"It sounds like the perfect haven." But her smile turned down as she thought of their situation—their unmarried situation. "Except that…"

He read her rightly. "I've been thinking about that, too. Especially after seeing that wedding party today." Several silent moments passed. "How badly do you want to wait to get married?"

"I don't *want* to wait. It's just how things are working out."

"So, what's to stop us from *re*working them out?"

She peered into his eyes, trying to grasp where he was taking this.

"Mandy, let's go see the preacher tomorrow."

"*Tomorrow?*"

"I understand. You don't want to get married without your family there, right?"

"It's not that. It's just that…tomorrow seems somehow kind of…sudden."

101

"You call eight months 'sudden'?"

"Eight months!"

"I quit counting the moon cycles once the epidemic hit the camp. But I learned from the hotel clerk that tomorrow is Valentine's Day."

She slumped back in her chair. "It's mid-February? That's not possible."

"I know. So much has happened."

"And so much we missed. Even Christmas. My family always decorates a tree, hangs mistletoe, eats a huge Christmas supper and sings carols around the piano. I guess that would have been around the time the epidemic was waning, about the time Little Dog died."

Another family holiday overshadowed by mourning.

"I remember our first Christmas without Gregg. His empty place at the table, and at the piano, his absent voice making the harmony incomplete. With me gone, there was no one even to play for them this year."

He reached across the table and took hold of her hand.

"And not only Christmas," she continued. "It's a new year. 1866. And I...I had a birthday last month. I'm twenty-nine years old and I didn't even know it."

Her appetite gone and exhausted from their journey, they retired early that night. As Mandy lay in bed, sleep was kept at bay by the images of all that had transpired in her time away from home. Eight months! Her family had spent part of that time believing her dead, and the rest of it wondering what had happened to her. They likely concluded she was dead after all.

But it was a night also spent in thoughtful resolution. Her life had been dealt some powerful interruptions, and just when it seemed it was getting back on course, another hindrance was literally blocking her path home. But there were other considerations in life as well, and she determined that it was time to do some "reworking."

When Dakota came to her door the next morning, she grabbed a handful of buckskin and pulled him into her room. She kissed him hard and long.

"Not that I'm complaining, but...what was that all about?"

"Yes!"

His brow furrowed. "Yes...what?"

"Yes, I'll marry you today."

102

His eyes brightened and a smile covered his face. "Are you sure? Positively sure?"

"Never surer." She wrapped her arm around his. "C'mon, let's go find that preacher."

Before going to the church, they went to the mercantile. Mandy did not want her worn out lavender calico that had been rolled up in a bag during the epidemic to serve as her wedding dress. She picked out a blue and white cotton dress with flounced cuffs and a lacy stand-up collar.

Dakota chose a dark brown suit, white shirt and black string tie. He wanted to get a haircut and shave, but she wouldn't allow it. She had taken a shine to his long hair and young beard.

After changing into their new store-bought clothes at the hotel, they proceeded to the church. He would buy her a worthy wedding ring at a jewelry shop in Denver.

They spoke for two hours with the minister who asked them many questions about their backgrounds, their religious beliefs and their story. Satisfied that their love was one of permanence and that they were truly committed to each other for life, he called on his wife and brother to witness. He led Dakota and Mandy in exchanging the vows they recently shared in the bridal tepee before their Arapaho friends and family.

When they kissed for the first time as husband and wife, it was not only deep love that passed between them but also intense thankfulness. The future they had once been willing to commit to others was now to be fulfilled in each other.

Over a late breakfast they discussed whether to spend their wait for the road to open in town or go to his mountain home. When he described again the cabin for her, there was no doubt where she wanted to spend the first week of their marriage.

"But what about the snow up there?"

"I talked to a trapper who came down from that area yesterday. We'd be well south of where the heaviest snow fell recently, although there are several inches on the ground."

"I say let's do it then."

"We'll buy a goodly stock of supplies, and head up there. It's small, but I think you'll feel at home."

"Are you sure there's enough room for me in your bed?" A teasing twinkle flashed in her eye.

"I made it big enough for two, darlin'."

"Oh, really?" She kicked him under the table. "Were you expecting someone?"

He stood up, walked to her side of the table and pulled her to standing. Putting an arm around her waist, he drew her against him and held her there.

"I was expecting—was *waiting*—for *you*, my love."

He kissed her right there in front of the patrons and waiters. She blushed with embarrassment but had no desire to make him stop.

* * *

Their westward journey was a pleasant ride through spectacular scenery. White-trimmed pine trees freely offered their earthy fragrance as well as their deep green complexion against the bluest of skies.

Dakota continued to see every mile as an opportunity for instruction in self-preservation. Mandy rebelled.

"Can't you just enjoy the creation surrounding us without turning everything into a nature lesson? I'm growing weary of it."

"Perseverance builds character."

"Character," she mumbled under her breath. "Hmph. Who needs it?"

"What'd you say?"

She simply had to divert his thinking. "I said, you're going to *keep* it, aren't you? The beard, I mean."

"Well, I often let it grow when I'm not living with my father's people. It seems…*je ne sais quoi*…more natural somehow. I can't recall ever seeing a man up here in the mountains without one. And you seem to have taken to it."

"Once it gets past that scratchy phase, I might even enjoy kissing you again."

"Are you kidding? You won't be able to keep your hands off me."

"Kinda cocky, *n'est-ce pas?*"

"*Tout a fait.*"

"Does that mean you are or you aren't?"

"Thoroughly!"

Darkness began to fall, and the wind whipped snow all

around them. Their course was no longer well defined.

"How far do we have to go? Should we stop and make camp for the night?"

"It's not far. Just stop for a moment and listen." He tilted his head, straining to hear.

"What are we listening for?"

He held up his hand to silence her. "This way." Within minutes the cabin was before them.

"How did you find it?"

"Listen."

Now she could plainly hear what had led him right to the front door. The tinkling of a bell.

"I hang it in case of emergencies such as this, and to let anyone who may be passing through know where there's a refuge from the elements."

"You must be joking. Who would ever pass through here?"

"You'd be surprised. Once I spent a year here, and four people came by."

"Four whole people! Wow! I'll bet you broke out the good stuff and had yourselves a merry ole time."

"For a fact," he said, grinning, "we did."

He dismounted, then lifted her from her horse and carried her to the door where she pulled on the latchstring and pushed the door open. He stepped across the threshold and she reset the latch.

They kissed for a long moment, savoring the feeling of being safe inside, together, married.

He set her down next to the pine table, then reached into a small tray of matches attached to the wall just to the left of the door. He lit the two lanterns that hung on either side of the doorway.

As he retrieved the supplies, Mandy looked around her temporary home. The solitary room, about thirty feet by thirty, had a loft above the bed area. The walls were made of thick logs, the spaces between them chinked solidly to keep out the cold air. Small night tables stood next to each side of the bed. A large trunk set at the foot of the bed.

Built into the wall opposite the door was a stone hearth large enough for cooking with plenty of room to spare. Mandy loved the added touch of a stone mantelpiece above it.

Windows—not glass windows, but holes cut out with tight-fitting shutters on leather hinges—were situated on either side of the fireplace as well as on both sides of the door. Opposite the bed area was a kitchen of sorts. Four cupboards, hand-hewn like everything else, loomed above a large counter containing a sink and drawers for storing flour, potatoes, coffee beans, and the like.

In the center of the room set a square table and four chairs made of pine. Hanging from the ceiling above it was, of all things, a simple chandelier with four small oil lamps secured in a metal frame.

Dakota stopped to watch his bride take in her new surroundings. "Like it?"

In the tongue of her Arapaho family, she answered, "I believe you already know, even though you ask."

He kissed her cheek. "I'll go settle the horses in the shelter out back."

"And I'll get a fire going and start unpacking as soon as my fingers thaw out."

He turned for the door.

"Dakota?"

He looked over his shoulder.

"This is all so…so…"

"Exquisite?"

"It's simple like any mountain cabin would be, yet you've given it a quality that makes it a warm, safe and comfortable *home*." Her eyes reflected the serenity she felt in this place, but then flickered in curiosity. "Why?"

"Because, darlin', I built it with you in mind."

She loved him intensely, and hoped to prove worthy of the love he had manifested for her here so many years ago, before they had met, before he even knew she really existed for him.

"Now, I better get those horses put away. I'll return for *you* soon."

As he turned, his eye caught some further slight inconsistencies he'd noticed about the room. "Whoever he was, he was an honest and respectable man."

"Who are you talking about?"

"Whoever it was that stayed here since I last did."

"Someone was here? Are you sure?"

"There's a buffalo robe missing from the bed."

106

"He stole a robe?"

"Exchanged, looks like." He went to the side of the bed and picked up a pair of fleece-lined deerskin boots with fringed cuffs at the top. "Looks like they'll fit."

"Doesn't it bother you that someone just strode in here and set up housekeeping while you were gone?"

"Honey, whenever I leave here, I always leave a pile of wood inside, the bell hanging outside, and the latchstring out. Not just so I can get back in, but so that anyone else who needs to can get in, too." He held up his new boots. "I've got more robes, but I've never had a pair of boots like these."

Her heart warmed anew for the man before her. "I love you, Dakota."

He raised a brow. "Hold that thought." He went out to complete his chores.

Mandy made a fire in the hearth and hung a basin full of snow over it. She proceeded to search through every nook and cranny of the cabin: each cupboard, each drawer, and the large trunk that contained Indian blankets and some of Dakota's buckskins.

On the mantelpiece she placed the forged steel rose he gave her in his lodge the night of the rainstorm. Next to it she set her Bible and her Longfellow books. This was, after all, their first home as man and wife, as temporary as their stay may be.

Dakota returned and hung his Spencer rifle on the pegs above the door. He removed his coat, hung it on a wall peg and washed up in the basin of melted snow. Then he went straight to her, turned her from her task of putting away the foodstuffs, held her face in his hands and kissed her with the passion of a man who had been waiting too long.

When he lifted his head, she smiled. "But Dakota, I haven't finish—"

He silenced her with an even more passionate kiss. "That can wait." His lips brushed her cheek. "I cannot."

Her arms folded around his neck, and he swept her into his arms.

Between the soft treated fur of two buffalo robes they anticipated making their union complete.

"I couldn't have imagined this to be more perfect," Mandy said between kisses. "You are every bit as wonderful as

Solomon was."

His head shot up. "*Solomon?*"

Mandy laughed at the astonished expression on her husband's face. "*King* Solomon, silly. Your touches make me think of how tender he was with his wife."

He let out a mirthful sigh. "Which wife? There were so many."

"The one from the Song of Songs in the Bible. With her he was a tender, magnificent lover. On their wedding night she said, 'His left hand is under my head, and his right hand doth embrace me.' I used to read that and dream it would be that way for me on my wedding night. And now it is at this very moment. Just like King Solomon and his queen."

"Here in our palace of gold and marble and precious stones?"

"I don't need any of those things."

She luxuriated in the feel of his skin and the contour of the grand muscles she had once naughtily admired in his lodge during a thunderstorm.

"What is it that you need, my love?" His arms tightened around her.

She smiled. "I believe you already know, even though you ask!"

CHAPTER 17

*T*his time spent in their mountain retreat was more peaceful than either had ever known. They reveled in the respite from the hardships they had endured and the death they had witnessed.

During the day they played, sailing down a hill on a toboggan Dakota had made for hauling, or hitching it to Chief and letting him pull them through the woods. At night Dakota played his flute, the music of his Indian forefathers filling the small cabin and escaping into the cold night air, eerily piercing the surrounding forest.

Frequently they stopped by a cabin two miles from theirs that belonged to a friend of Dakota's. Will Bowden was a former doctor who had left medicine—and civilization—five years earlier. He told Dakota he'd seen enough suffering to last three lifetimes and settled into mountain life. But like Dakota he came and went, and they found his cabin empty each time they visited.

There were two flaws in Mandy's otherwise perfect mountain universe: thoughts of her family's loss of her, which would soon be over, and her continued forced indoctrination into the ways of the wilderness, which seemed never ending.

Dakota taught her how to build snares and set them properly. She was coerced into perfecting her arrow making and practiced shooting every day. The tension that had to be applied to the bow for the arrow to travel a decent distance made her arm shake from the strain, and her accuracy was way off.

"My arms are sore," she complained one day, to which he replied, "They'll get stronger."

"Pretty soon they'll be as big as yours. They look great on you but wouldn't look very becoming on me." His usual easy sense of humor did not surface during these times of schooling.

Before the week ended, heavy snows fell making it impossible to leave the mountain. Reality usurped her ideal world.

"We never should've come here. If we'd've just stayed in town—"

"Then we'd be stranded in town along with everyone else. No one is going north for a while to come, Mandy. I'm really sorry. No one knows better than me what you're going through."

"I know you do," she said, grateful for the empathy he offered. She entered his arms and drew comfort from them.

"Let's make the most of the time," he suggested with an insinuating smile.

The situation being out of her control, she forced herself to let go of her apprehension and appreciate what was in front of her. She ran her hand up the front of his shirt. "Yes, let's."

He pressed away from her. "Okay then. Get your coat on. I'll grab some ammunition."

"What?"

"We'll work on your aim today. It's time you shot something moving."

She stood in place as he removed the Spencer from its berth above the door.

"I thought you wanted to do something more… domestic."

"There's not much light left. We'll hunt now and we can be domestic later."

"But I don't want to shoot the animals. If I ever have to I'll hunt and kill for food, but don't make me do it now. Please."

"Have you ever even shot at a moving target?"

"Gregg and I used to toss old pie pans into the air and shoot them. I was pretty good at it."

"Pie pans don't dodge and hide, Mandy. C'mon, get your coat on."

Thus it was settled. Mandy was growing increasingly less tolerant of his dissonant reasoning that seemed to overwhelm him all the more as time wore on. She purposely missed her targets that day even when her aim was dead on. It vexed him, which in turn chafed her. She didn't feel much like being "domestic" later on.

Weeks passed with the weather alternating between warm, clear days and heavy snow. She used to marvel at the sudden, marked changes of weather in this territory. Now it only served to depress her.

One afternoon as they drank coffee, he told her he wanted her to check the snares they set that morning. She kept herself composed, but knew it was time to confront the matter head on.

"Dakota, does all of this have to do with your being gone when Headless Jack came?"

He tensed. She reached across and took his hand. "It's all right."

"It's *not* all right!"

His eyes lowered, and his body sank. His voice became faint, dispirited. "I speak four languages, and I cannot find the words in any one of them that describe the torment I went through in those hours you were gone."

Her heart softened for her husband who was plagued by the retrospection of having been helplessly out of reach when she needed him most. She, too, was not without ongoing vivid recollections of her ordeal. For her it was worse at night, in her dreams. She could only hope that time would play its role in their healing.

She intertwined her fingers with his. "Dakota, we got through that, by God's grace. And we'll get through whatever is to come by the same means. I just need to explain that…the reason I'm finding it more and more difficult to snuff out the lives of the creatures around me is because…I'm almost certain there's a new life growing inside me."

He stared at her, stupified.

She smiled in return.

He jumped up and stepped right across the table. "We're going to have a baby?"

She nodded jubilantly.

He lifted her into his arms and swung her around, laughing. Then he set her down and kissed her richly.

"I love you so much," he told her. "I'm so sorry for how I've let my inner fears take their toll on you."

She pressed her fingers to his lips. "Your love and sense of responsibility are admirable, my dear husband. I hated every minute of those lessons, but respect you all the more for them."

Her pregnancy brought added joy to their small sanctuary of love. It also meant she would have even more glad tidings for her family when she finally reached home, which was soon now, since spring brought fairer weather and melting snow.

On their last full day there, Dakota went out to chop enough wood to leave a stack in the cabin. The sun was shining and the air dry, thus he removed his shirt. He had powerful arms and drew gratification from spending the energy it took to chop then split the logs.

Mandy went out to join him and watched for several minutes as he repeatedly swung the ax high then brought it down with a loud *thunk* into the wood. When he was finished, he slung the ax into a log and wiped the sweat from his brow. She squeezed along his upper arm. "Exquisite!"

He tried to suppress the pride that would swell within him, but delighted in the way she regarded his strength.

"I'm hungry as a griz, darlin'. Is supper ready yet?"

"Not quite." She handed him his shirt. "I thought maybe we could walk for a while. I want to savor every moment of today."

He took her hand and they strolled among the snow-laden pines, absorbing the quiet and the peacefulness of their surroundings.

She shook the branch of a blue spruce and watched the glistening snowflakes silently fall. "What shall we name him, or her?"

"Well, as for a *him*...when I was little, my favorite Bible story was that of David and Jonathan. Those two were more than friends, closer than brothers. I hoped to make a friend like that someday. Then, when I was nine, I met a boy who became that kind of friend to me, and what do you think? His name was David. But six years later he contracted consumption and was sent away. I never saw him again, and never knew another friend like that." He smiled down at her and squeezed her hand. "Til now."

"Then David it shall be."

"What about you? What would you choose?"

She hesitated a moment. "David is a wonderful name. And it has history for you."

He pulled her to a stop and faced her. "Mandy, would you like to name him Gregg?"

Her face shone with bittersweet happiness. "It would mean the world to me."

"I will be proud for my son to carry your brother's name."

Her arms wrapped around his neck. "*Hahoukac.*"

"So, what if it's a girl?" he asked. "How about naming her after you?"

"Oh, no. I'm not sticking any daughter of mine with the

name Amanda. I've always gone by Mandy because I hate the formal name so much. Huh-uh! Any other name, but not Amanda."

"I can see you're undecided about that."

"How about if we name a daughter after someone in your family?"

"Like…Long Hair?"

She laughed and poked his side. "Maybe something a little more conventional. Didn't you tell me the mother who raised you was named Marie?" He nodded. "I think that's a lovely name. But I don't recall you telling me your real ma's name."

"Uh, I don't think you'd want to choose that name."

"Why not? You remember her as being beautiful and loving and tender. I'd be honored to keep her memory alive through our daughter."

"But, Mandy—"

"How bad can it be? Medusa? Jezebel?"

He chuckled. "Nothing like that. It's a beautiful name, really. As beautiful as she was."

Her head crept forward in anticipation.

"It was…Amanda."

She looked at him stupidly. "Oh. I…I didn't…I'm so…"

"Well stated, Mandy." He put his arm around her. "It's okay, really. We'll figure out another girl's name. We've still got plenty of time."

That night Mandy began to feel painful cramping. Dread consumed them the next morning when she began to bleed. She knew of women to whom this had happened, and some of them had miscarried. Dakota wished it were possible to journey down the mountain to fetch a doctor, but there was no way he would leave her alone. He had left her once before…

"What about Will?" she asked. "Have you been by his cabin lately?"

"Two days ago, when I was hunting, but the place is still deserted."

As long as she remained in bed, Mandy's pain and bleeding diminished. That is where she stayed for several weeks, her child being her utmost concern. But her family was never out of her mind.

Spring was nearly passed before she could spend the day out of bed, and then she was weak from inactivity. Although

113

her symptoms had subsided, they feared she could still lose the baby. Dakota worried even more that something could happen to Mandy as well and he wouldn't know how to help her. He never left her alone for more than an hour at a time. Often he'd go by the cabin of his doctor-friend. It was always empty.

As spring yielded to summer, Mandy ventured a short distance outside the cabin. For the first time she could view her surroundings without the cover of snow. Their home was in a small clearing surrounded by pine and aspens. A short path led through a cluster of trees and opened into a large meadow carpeted with tall grass and wildflowers that bloomed pink and gold and lavender and orange. She longed for the day she could walk among them and brighten her supper table with their fragrant beauty. Snow-capped peaks surveyed all, and the splendor of this place stirred her spirit.

But her symptoms returned, and she was confined to the cabin for two more months, much of that time in bed. The unsettling fear of miscarriage combined with the abiding idleness nearly drove her into lunacy.

By the time she was beginning her seventh month of pregnancy, her symptoms had again resolved, but she could never be sure it was permanent. It was with great caution that she performed even the smallest of tasks.

Throughout this time, Dakota diligently tended to her needs and the household chores as well as his own responsibilities. In his spare time, he built a cradle for their coming child.

Mandy's strength slowly returned as did her color and energy. They went walking one day into the meadow she had only viewed from the cabin's periphery, and her spirits lifted. After being shut in for so long, each shape and color and scent was like discovering creation anew. The blue and white spurred blossoms of the columbines. The nodding blue blossoms of the tall chiming bells. The oddly shaped, deep blue monkshood, which Dakota warned was poisonous to the horses. Flowers as purple as robes of royalty, orange as fiery embers, yellow as the summer sun above her. A few of each were selected to adorn their supper table.

There was no further pain or bleeding, but they dared not risk travel down the mountain on horseback and came to the disconcerting conclusion that they must remain until after the

114

baby was born. They prayed that Will would return by then, but Dakota had not known him to be gone for such an extended period and wondered if he had moved on for good.

Often when they went on short excursions Dakota would teach her more stratagems in stealth and reading sign, although he never coerced her into doing something she did not want to do. Under the more relaxed circumstances, Mandy enjoyed learning, and Dakota was pleased at how well she comprehended the potentially lifesaving lessons.

On one particular day, Mandy watched in awe when Dakota pointed out a doe teaching her fawn to hide by pushing him down into the tall grass with her nose and foreleg when she saw the humans approach. Creatures everywhere took seriously the responsibility of teaching their charges to protect themselves.

It was because Dakota was so protective of her and was wont to stay close that Mandy grew concerned when he left one midday to hunt and did not return for several hours. A sudden weather change, so typical of Colorado, brought dark clouds that blotted out the blue sky. A cold tempest came screaming through the pines, beating violently against the safe, snug cabin.

A loud crash from outside startled her. She threw a blanket around herself and went out to investigate. Dakota was nowhere in sight. She fought the wind as she hobbled around the side of the cabin, nearly losing her crutch in the forming mud. The small stable behind the cabin was missing half its gate. Lady, her palomino mare, was jittery but calmed somewhat when Mandy approached and spoke soothingly. The gate would take some major repair, but for now she settled for securing a rope across the opening.

Dripping wet, she hurried back to the cabin and quickly closed the door to shut out the storm. When she turned again, she saw Dakota standing at the hearth, covered with a blanket, shivering off the wet chill.

"Thank God you're back! I was so worried."

She scurried to the trunk, shed the wet blanket and retrieved a dry one. Wrapping herself in it, she joined him at the hearth.

Her steps were arrested when she glanced into his eyes— this stranger warming himself at her fire.

115

CHAPTER 18

*T*he stranger eyed her with curiosity. "Who're you?"
Her eyes darted to the empty pegs above the door. Dakota had taken the rifle.

She looked back at the tall intruder. She remembered Dakota describing Will as being several years older than him and having dark hair and china blue eyes. This man's hair was light-colored, still stringy from the rain's drenching. The firelight shone on large brown eyes set in a bearded face.

Her gaze fell to his Hawken rifle that leaned against the wall next to the fireplace. He stood between her and the rifle. She knew it would be loaded.

Her heart pumped harder. History was repeating itself—an intruder had come while Dakota was gone. He would be tormented again by his failure to protect her.

She *had* to get to the Hawken. The Remington .44 was in its place on the night table, too far behind her. Even if the man hadn't noticed it yet, he surely would if she dashed for it now, and would beat her to it.

She forced a smile. "My name is Mandy. Why don't you sit down, stranger, and I'll pour you some coffee."

"That'd be great, ma'am. The aroma 'bout knocked me off my feet when I came in." He sat down at the table, his back to the fire, and blew warm breath into his cupped hands.

Mandy crossed behind him, set her crutch against the wall, and ever so cautiously lifted the rifle to her shoulder. It was heavy, but she held it firmly and cocked it.

He looked around sharply. His muscles tensed as he found himself looking down the barrel of his Hawken.

"Get up. Slowly."

He obeyed. Not taking his eyes off her trigger finger, he held his hands out in front of himself. "Ma'am, I'm not here to rob you or harm you in any way, if that's what you're thinkin'."

"You're trespassing."

"No, please, hear me out. My friend John—"

"Get out!"

He complied, backing toward the door, his hands still in

front of him.

"Wait a minute." She lowered the rifle to her hip. "What did you say your friend's name is?"

"John. Starbuck."

Her eyes narrowed.

"You know him?" he asked.

"I think I might be married to him."

His brow knotted. He continued to back away from her.

"Wait. I can explain. You see, I've only heard my husband's name a couple of times, and I tend to forget it."

He fumbled behind him for the latch.

She took a breath and tried again. "What I mean is, I've only known him by his Indian name—Dakota."

The stranger relaxed only a little. She still held the rifle, though it was now pointing downward.

"Tell me who you are."

"My name is Haines. Tr-Travis Haines."

"Yes! He's talked about you. You're from Julesburg, right?"

He eased a little more. "That's right."

"Oh, Mr. Haines, please come and sit down and let me get you that coffee. I'm really sorry about this, and so embarrassed. You must think I'm quite confused."

"No, ma'am." He stepped forward only after she set the rifle back against the hearth. "Confused ain't at all what I was thinkin'."

She poured him coffee and herself some tea, and they pulled two chairs near the fire.

Dakota had told her that Travis Haines was one of his closest friends. They had met as teens when Dakota first journeyed west to find his Indian family. He stayed with Travis's family for a while and became as one of their own. Dakota was tempted to accept their invitation to stay on with them, but a deeper yearning called him away.

They remained close over the years, Dakota often visiting Travis and his wife, Becky, in northeast Colorado. The last time the two men were together was just before Dakota arrived at the Arapaho camp and met Mandy. He had spent two months with Travis and his infant daughter, Mollie, following Becky's murder by an Indian raiding party.

Mandy highlighted the events in her and Dakota's lives

117

since that time though leaving out the day spent with Headless Jack. As she listened to him speak of his friendship with Dakota—or John, as Travis called him—her eyes frequently strayed toward the door.

"Don't worry, Mandy. John can take care of himself."

The smile she gave him was a facade. She forced the conversation, not wanting to seem inhospitable. "It's strange to hear him called John."

"Yeah, I'm amazed at how he switches his life back and forth all the time. He's…" He noticed her attention once again fixed on the closed door.

Aware of the abrupt end to his statement, she looked back at him. "I'm sorry, what did you say?"

He leaned back onto the rear legs of the chair and crossed his arms. "You really are her, aren't you?"

"Excuse me?"

"You're the one. The one he waited for all those years."

She smiled, and this time it was genuine.

"He must be very happy."

"I'm really worried about him, Travis. He never stays away this long."

"I'll tell you what." He righted his chair and removed the blanket from his shoulders. "I'll go out and find him for you. I can't stand to see a woman fret so, especially one in your condition."

He winked at her, endearing himself to her forever. Mandy was a sucker for a man who winked.

He stood and reached for his rain poncho that was draped over the back of another chair. His now dry hair was wavy and blond, his beard a couple of shades darker. Though he was around the same age as Dakota, the creases at the corners of his brown eyes made him look a few years older, and a bit sad. His lean form filled out his homespun clothes nicely. The tan shirt and brown pants were tailor-made for him and obviously sewn with pride, probably by his late wife. He slipped into his muddy boots by the door and threw his poncho over his head.

"Hope that dumb horse of mine is still out there. I tied him on the lee side away from the rain and wind."

Mandy went to the door and opened it for him. "I'm really glad you're here, Travis."

"So am I."

118

He felt like he was needed, at least for the moment.

It had been a long time since anyone had needed him.

* * *

It was nearly midnight when the two men returned drenched, cold and weary. Mandy covered them with dry blankets and offered them pemmican since there had been no successful hunt that day. She poured fresh hot coffee.

It wasn't Dakota who had been in trouble but Chief. The horse had gotten bogged down in a flow of mud moving like a current of water. The harder Chief tried to fight his way out, the deeper he was sucked into it. Dakota finally got him out but his legs were shaky, and the steed went down when he slipped on a muddy rock.

"Oh, Dakota, he didn't break his leg, did he?"

"No, but he sure twisted it badly. I couldn't ride him. We were miles away, and I knew you'd be anxious, but I just couldn't leave him." He set the cup of coffee on the table and reached to take her hand. "I'm really sorry I worried you so."

"Me, worried? It never crossed my mind. Just ask Travis here. He insisted on going out to look for you even after I told him you could take care of yourself." She glanced at Travis, who cast her a playful wink. "I'll bet you were surprised to see him out there."

"For a fact! What a scary sight to look up and see his ugly face coming at me through the stormy night." They all laughed, then Dakota added more seriously, "It's sure good to have you here, pal."

The two men locked eyes, silently exchanging the sentiments of many years of friendship.

Mandy went to the trunk and got some dry clothes for both men. "You two slip into these while I put together something more to eat." She busied herself at the baking counter, keeping her back to them.

"Careful, Travis," Dakota warned in a voice he intended Mandy to overhear. "She's been known to sneak peeks at unsuspecting fellas while they changed out of wet clothes."

A scarlet warmth crept up Mandy's neck as she stared wide-eyed at the wall in front of her. "I-I never admitted to any such thing!"

119

"Not in so many words."

Mandy heard the men chuckling and tried to keep her shoulders still as she laughed herself silly inside.

Exhausted though they all were, they talked and laughed into the wee hours of the morning. As their fatigue became acute their mood became more serious, and the men related to Mandy some of their more sober experiences, including the tragic murder of Travis's beloved wife.

He had returned from town to find Becky's body. He ascertained that she had hidden their sleeping infant in the cellar, then tried to hold off the Indians. The pistol and rifle had both been fired until the ammunition was spent. Travis found it amazing that Mollie had slept through it all down below. Otherwise they would have killed her, too, or taken her off with them.

When Dakota came along a few weeks later, he found a man destroyed and an infant neglected.

"John was like a brother to me and a father to Mollie. If he hadn't come when he did, we both would have died from my inattention."

Mandy and Dakota watched in sympathetic silence as their guest's wounds broke open from the recurring memories. Dakota's stomach knotted. His own wife's near fatal experience happened in much the same way as Travis's wife—while he was gone.

"Where is Mollie now?" Dakota asked.

"She's staying with friends. You remember the Hannebaums, don't you, John?"

He nodded. "They're good folks. But Travis, why aren't you with her? What are you *doing* up here?"

The poignant questions stung, but their friendship was solid enough that Dakota could ask.

"I came here to get away and sort things out. There's no place like this haven of yours for working through things, and I had to get far enough from home to get some perspective. You see, I've discovered some things, some facts about..." His eyes lost their focus. His jaw tightened and his neck veins bulged. "I just have some thinking to do before I act on what I know."

"You came here to be alone, didn't you?" Mandy asked. "And our being here ruins that for you."

"No, don't think that. I'm glad you're here. Honest. It's

like…I wanted to be alone, yet I hate it." He shook his head and sighed. "I guess I'm sounding about as addlepated as Mandy did when she found me here." He winked at her.

"You make perfect sense," she said. "When you need to be by yourself, the whole mountain is yours. And when you need your friends, you know where we are."

Travis smiled at her, then cast a sideward glance at Dakota. "She was worth the wait, was she not?"

* * *

Over the next few weeks, Travis did just as Mandy suggested, going off by himself for a few days at a time and returning to the cabin when he felt the need for companionship. He watched them as they worked, talked, played and planned together. And remembered…

Bitterness welled up often in him. His wife's death was violent and had left his life in shards.

There was work to be done on the cabin with the coming of autumn, a season that occasionally felt more like winter up where they were. The men got to work chinking the walls and reinforcing the fireplace and repairing the roof. Travis would put all his restless energy into it then leave for several days to go off by himself.

As Mandy and Dakota lay in bed one night, she asked, "You said you never had another David-Jonathan type relationship with anyone since that boy back East. Don't you feel that kinship with Travis?"

"In most ways I do. But you haven't seen a side of him that I know. He can be an angry, bitter man. And when he is, he's no joy to be around."

"I've seen a hint of it, especially when he's talking about Becky. It's sad to watch him be tossed between his grief and his anger, much like Thunder Cloud was after losing Little Fawn."

Travis again returned from his hermitage on the higher slopes. One day as the men chopped wood, he opened up about his reasons for coming to the mountains.

"I know who did it, John. I found out who killed my Becky. A peddler who was passin' through saw the killers riding away, but it wasn't until he came back through this year that it all came out. Then I got a lead on what area those savages are hiding out in."

He slung his ax forcefully into a log and began to pace.

"My first impulse was to drop everything and go find them. I had to do *some*thing besides stay at home and live with the fact that Becky was gone from my life. But I had Mollie to consider. It was tearing me apart inside. So I took Mollie to the Hannebaums and came up here to get away and try to sort things out."

"What did you decide?"

"I can't live with the fact that those demons in human form are out there, free to kill at their slightest whim, free to take away someone else's wife, someone else's reason for living. It's settled in me what I have to do."

"Travis, you'll only make matters worse for Mollie. Either she'll have a dead father or one who's useless to her, off someplace, eaten up with bitterness—"

"Don't bother lecturing me. I've been over every argument imaginable including the one that insists this won't bring Becky back. But it's what I've got to do. Right or wrong. I don't expect you to understand."

"But I do understand."

Dakota sat down on a fallen tree and leaned his ax against it. "Mandy was taken from me once."

"*What?*"

"She would have been ravaged and killed had it not been for my brother getting to her in time. I was actually angry at him for having executed the man before I could get my hands on him."

"Then you know why I must get the ones responsible for Becky's death."

"I'm saying I *understand* how you feel. I harbored in me what you're feeling now, but it gave me no peace. By the looks of you, I'd say this decision of yours isn't giving you any peace, either."

"I haven't known the meaning of peace since the day I came home to find my wife's body. All I want now is justice."

He retrieved his ax and attacked the wood with the power of an enraged bison, and would listen and speak no further.

Later that night, Mandy sat by the fire reading Longfellow as the two men played checkers on a makeshift game board using swatches of material as playing pieces. They each had won two games and were about to play for their Rocky Mountain Grand Championship. Mandy offered to make them some coffee from the dwindling supply, but Dakota said he'd see to it.

Travis watched as Mandy sat reading, caressing her swollen abdomen. He beheld her for several moments, reminiscing about his own wife in that condition. So lost in his reverie was he that when his eyes moved up to the mother's face he fully expected to see Becky's.

"Here you go." Dakota placed the mug of coffee in front of his friend. "Ready to get whipped?" He set the checker pieces in order.

Travis leaned back from the table. "I've got to leave here soon. As soon as we've cut enough wood for the winter, I'm heading out."

Mandy joined them at the table. "We're going to miss you, Travis. I feel like you're family."

"I've got things to take care of."

Mandy knew of what he spoke. Dakota had told her of Travis's decision.

They put off the checker game. Instead, as the men drank their coffee and Mandy her tea, they talked about better times. The men related some of the boyish pranks they had played as teens when Dakota was staying with the Haines family.

"That sounds a lot like Gregg and me," Mandy said.

"Who's Gregg?"

"My late brother. He had quite a knack for getting me into trouble when we were young. And for getting me out of it when we got older."

Dakota got up to refill his mug. "Brothers are like that. Thunder Cloud saved my hide more than once. But I'd say I've done my share in preserving his as well."

Travis's head jerked up. Mandy noted the movement and studied him from over the rim of her raised cup.

"Thunder Cloud? Is that your brother's name?"

"I've spoken of him in the past, Travis."

"Yes…quite a while back. You called him by some Indian name. I just didn't remember what you said it translated to."

"Well, it suits him perfectly." Dakota returned to the table. "He's a rather tempestuous character. Wouldn't you say,

Mandy?"

"Oh, you just have to know how to speak his language is all."

"Travis, you should've seen how she could stand up to that warrior." He side-glanced his wife. "*And* she lived to tell about it."

Travis's grip tightened around his mug.

* * *

Travis cut his hand while sharpening an ax and came to the cabin to bandage it.

"Let me take care of that for you," Mandy insisted. "We've got salve and some clean cloths. I just hope it doesn't get infected." Her gentle and efficient hands had the wound cleansed and neatly bound in a matter of minutes.

"Thanks, Mandy. This'll do just fine." He studied her handiwork and smiled warmly at her. "You have a nice touch."

He stepped away saying, "I don't know how much help I'll be to John now that I've only got one good hand, but—"

"It's Thunder Cloud you're after, isn't it?"

His steps halted. He turned, and they exchanged a long look.

"You think he killed Becky."

His face revealed the plethora of emotions vying for mastery over him for the past year.

"I *know* he did."

"Because some peddler saw some Indians ride away? How could he know for sure who it was?"

"They were Arapaho. They weren't ashamed to leave tokens of their visit. This fella described the leader, and an old Indian in town said it sounded just like a warrior he knew of named Thunder Cloud."

"*Sounded* like? You're going to kill a man on that kind of evidence?"

"I'm going to bring him to justice, one way or another."

"Travis, I'm sure he was nowhere near Julesburg that spring. He would have been hunting and feeding his people near his village. Even by mid-June when he—" A*bducted me*, is what she almost said. "—when I met him, he was well southwest of there."

124

"Do you know with certainty where he was that spring?"

"I couldn't testify to it, but—"

"Well, I know with certainty it *was* him. Mandy, I didn't even mention to John that they were Arapaho for obvious reasons. But who could've guessed that he and that savage are brothers?"

"You know now. Will it change anything?"

He walked around the table, rubbing his brow with his uninjured hand. "I can't let it. I've made up my mind. Thunder Cloud took my wife's life and—"

"He *saved* my life, Travis."

She never wanted to have to speak of the incident again, but if it could prevent a confrontation between her brother-in-law and her friend...

"A man known as Headless Jack kidnapped me."

"Headless Jack! John told me you were taken from him once but—"

"It was Thunder Cloud who rescued me just as Jack was..." Her eyes fell.

He walked to her and placed his bandaged hand on her shoulder. "I'm genuinely glad he was there to save you. But it doesn't change what he did to Becky."

"If you confront him with force, *you* could be the one who dies."

His hand fell to his side. "I'd be none the worse off."

She studied his brooding countenance. "Is that what this is all about? Making a job of getting yourself killed so you won't have to live out your days in self-pity? And you're still ignoring your daughter. Do you think Becky had that child so she could be raised by neighbors?"

"Don't stand there holding court with me, Mandy. My mind is made up!"

He went to the door and jerked it open, yet hesitated as he looked across the clearing to where Dakota was working vigorously at the chopping block.

"Are you going to tell him?" he asked.

Mandy moved next to him and observed her husband pick up a cloth and wipe the sweat of his labors from his chest. Short of physically harming his friend, Dakota would be powerless to stop him. Nor could he leave her to go and warn his brother.

125

She would have to trust God to intervene somehow and keep Travis from accomplishing his goal.

"How can I?" she said soberly. "It would tear him apart."

* * *

Travis set out one morning saying he was going deep into the hills. When he did not return, they knew he had left for good.

Although he had promised Mandy that whenever he left he would send word to her family regarding her whereabouts and well-being, he departed without acquiring any information about them.

And without saying good-bye.

CHAPTER 19

*I*t was the kind of frigid morning that made a body want to ignore the day's duties and stay put underneath the warm buffalo robes. Snow had fallen and the cold was bitter. But it must be faced and fought and overcome. Especially today.

Mandy nudged Dakota in an effort to wake him, but he only groaned in reply from under the covers. She nudged him again. "Wake up, Injun. You have to get up and get the fire going."

His bearded face inched out from under the robe and felt the chill in the room. "In a minute," he mumbled, and ducked back under the fur cover.

She sneered at his back and ever so reluctantly pushed back the cover. She raised her bulky form off the bed, wrapped a blanket about herself, and took up her crutch. Embers still glowed in the hearth, and she added some of the plentiful supply of wood Dakota and Travis had cut. She shivered by the fireplace as the kindling fed the appetite of the growing fire. The room must be warmed soon. Her baby was on its way.

With cumbersome movements she retrieved the clean blankets and cloths she had prepared weeks before, along with the little deerskin gowns she had made during the summer while bedridden. Removing her clothes, she crawled back into bed.

Half-awakened by the movement of her taking her place beside him, Dakota instinctively reached behind him and rested his hand on her.

"Dakota, it's time."

"Time for what?"

"Time to have a baby."

His hand tensed and his breath held. He spun over and propped up on an elbow. "Are you doing okay?" She nodded. "Why didn't you tell me? You shouldn't have been up running around tending to the fire and everything."

"Believe me, I don't *run* anywhere anymore. And I wanted to move around and see how things were progressing." She winced and placed her hand on her abdomen. "I think I

127

found out."

Knowing this was all part of nature's way, and that women had been delivering babies since Eve birthed Cain, did little to calm Dakota throughout the day. It was difficult to watch his wife in such distress while he stood idly by with only words to offer comfort. He was fearful, too, for he knew his time was coming. There would be no doctor, no midwife, no neighbor ladies, no Swift Legged Woman to assist. He alone had to see Mandy through her travail and receive the baby.

By late afternoon her contractions came in quick succession and her pains were considerably stronger. By evening she was laboring severely, and it was all Dakota could do to keep his wits about him. He spoke gently to her, wiped her forehead with a cool cloth, and prayed.

Mandy involuntarily screamed as another contraction gripped her. After several minutes of unwavering pain, she cried, "They're not going away! I think...*it's coming!*" Overcome by an urge to push, she drew up her legs and did so with all the strength in her.

Dakota positioned himself at her feet, and with a gut-squeezing apprehension waited for his child to come forth. With each push, more of the tiny body came forth into his waiting hands. His eyes were wide with wonderment at the magnificent process that brought his baby into the world.

With one final valiant effort, Mandy was delivered of a son. Her relief was instantaneous. She saw her husband's jubilant expression and was filled with consummate joy. He placed the baby on her chest, and she was in awe of the life that had so tenuously grown within her.

Dakota tied off the cord and with shaking hands cut it with a Bowie knife. Once the afterbirth was delivered, he removed the soiled linen, remade the bed and finally curled up beside his wife and son.

"Oh, Mandy! There is nothing so incredible in all of life. One minute he's inside of you, and the next, he's in my hands"—he snapped his fingers—"just like that!"

"Easy for you to say."

They studied the little bundle the two of them had just brought into the world. He rooted against his mother's warm flesh, his amply padded cheeks sinking in a sucking motion.

"I reckon he knows what he wants," Dakota said,

grinning. "I admire a man who knows what he wants and goes after it."

Mandy swatted him lightly on the cheek. "Such talk, Dakota."

She turned on her side and nursed her son. The ecstatic parents scrutinized him from head to toe.

"Would you look at the size of those hands," the proud papa exclaimed as he slid his little finger into his son's palm. "And feel that grip!"

Mandy and the baby rested while Dakota tended to further cleaning. Hard to believe such a little critter could make such an awful mess. But then, there's bound to be a lot of little messes around here for the next year or so.

That wasn't quite true. They wouldn't really be *here*. As soon as it was safe for Mandy and the baby to travel, the three of them would go to Denver. His plan was to collect the money from his various bank accounts and start up a blacksmith shop. Every detail of the smithy was mapped out in his mind. Every tool he'd need. Every peg they'd hang on. The exact layout of the shop. The work was rigorous and physically demanding, and he loved it. He was created for it. There was nothing left to keep him from finally fulfilling his dream, which had always included providing for a family as a smith.

Later that night, Mandy cuddled close to her husband. The ecstasy of giving birth had not worn off.

"It's been a while since I've been able to hold you this close without your large belly coming between us," Dakota teased.

"I'm enjoying it, too."

He stroked her blond tresses. "Mandy, I'm so proud of you. You came through it all today like a real champion."

"I was so scared. I hardly knew what to expect."

"Being on the receiving end was a little disconcerting, too. But I'd say all in all, our first day of parenthood was a complete success."

She melted into his embrace. "Everything is perfect, Dakota. So utterly and absolutely perfect."

CHAPTER 20

Baby Gregg was a fascinating little fellow who enthralled his parents endlessly. His round little head had silky brown hair, his eyes were thus far dark blue, and his skin—well, he was definitely a paleface.

Mandy became quite adept at managing a crutch under one arm and her son in the other. And of course there were the sturdy arms of his father whose greatest joy was to carry him about as he showed him his new world.

One evening Dakota looked up from his knife-sharpening task and watched Mandy as she sat near the fire nursing their son. He marveled at the sight of the mother and child, and recalled again the wonder of the birth. Mandy noticed him staring and smiled. She often caught him in such contemplation.

"You sitting there, with our baby at your breast, is the most peaceful, yet the most powerful sight I have ever seen."

Their life in the mountains was uncomplicated during those early weeks. They had enough meat in the smokehouse, plenty of fish in the stream, and a large supply of nuts and berries they had gathered and dried in the fall along with roots to make tea and honey to sweeten it. Most of the winter tasks were done indoors.

One afternoon as Mandy was making candles, she was reminded that it must be close to the Christmas and New Years holidays. That meant her thirtieth birthday was approaching as well. Dakota was also born sometime in the winter, so she decided they needed a party. As she poured the molten beeswax into the hollowed-out sections of aspen wood, she told Dakota of her idea.

"It's a great notion. Let's give ourselves a week to come up with a gift for each other."

For a couple of hours each evening they hung a blanket from the chandelier and sat on opposite sides of the table working on their presents.

Dakota whittled a block of Rocky Mountain glow maple, sculpturing it into the shape of a magnificent comb for securing her hair behind her head. He engraved her initials, MS, into the head in a fancy script. He wished for some ingredients with which to stain it—nitric acid with iron filings or steel wool—in order to make it contrast more beautifully with her blond tresses, but that would have to wait until they were in Denver. For now he settled for wetting the wood and then sanding it when it dried. He repeated the process three times until the grain was raised. If he did say so himself, it turned out to be rather exquisite.

Mandy's gift to him was a new *parfleche* since his was quite worn. She cut a pattern with his Bowie knife and took to the tedious and finger-piercing task of sewing the hide pieces together. Employing the techniques she had learned from Long Hair, she designed and sewed a beautiful pattern of beads across the flap.

When the day they had chosen to celebrate their holidays arrived, they were filled with the same enchantment of Christmas as in their youth. While the elk was roasting, they exchanged gifts. Each was delighted with the ingenuity and effort on the part of the other to have produced such lovely handiwork.

Dakota studied the pattern of beads on the flap of his *parfleche*.

"Would you like me to explain the symbols for you?" Mandy asked. "Each design has its own interpretation, you know."

"Why, I didn't know that. Please, interpret for me."

"Well, this jagged line of blue and purple with the line across the bottom represents the mountains—where our first home is, and where Gregg was born. And these three intertwining circles symbolize the three of us. The red one is you since you're part Indian. The white one is me, since I'm the paleface in the family. And the yellow one is Baby Gregg. His is yellow because he's brought such sunshine into our lives."

His smile widened. "This is *exquisite*!"

Gregg began to squawk for his Christmas dinner. While Mandy changed him, Dakota presented him with the rattle he made for his son's first Christmas gift. He had carefully sewn a small piece of deer hide around the seedpod of a yucca plant and secured it to a smoothly shaven stick. It held the infant's attention momentarily, but he had only one thing on his mind.

While Mandy fed the baby, Dakota took the Bible from the mantel and read the story of Christ's birth from the Book of Luke. Afterwards he played carols on his flute.

Later in the evening, he laid Gregg on the bed and rubbed his bearded face into the boy's soft belly and made wild animal sounds. Gregg smiled and kicked his little drumstick legs. Mandy looked on with pleasure as her husband and son wore each other out. Finally Gregg fell asleep in the middle of the bed. They lay beside him and continued to watch him as he slept contentedly.

"He looks like an angel lying there," Mandy said.

"Yeah. It almost makes you forget what a terror he can be in his wakeful hours, like the middle of the night."

"Dakota, do you ever…" She hesitated before continuing. "Do you ever worry about him?"

"In what way?"

"Well, he looks pale to me. And although he has an appetite, he sometimes has trouble nursing, and doesn't seem to be growing much. Maybe I'm expecting too much of such a little one, but I can't help but wonder."

"He's pale because he's three-quarters white and has yet to get out in the sun for any length of time. You saw him playing. He's active and happy. He smiles with his whole body, legs and arms shooting everywhere." He reached over the sleeping infant and took her hand. "Don't worry, when spring comes he'll brown up and start sprouting like a cattail."

But as the weeks passed, Dakota began to share Mandy's concern. Gregg was not only pale but his lips had taken on a bluish tint, as did his tiny nail beds. He also seemed to sleep more and was less active when awake.

Without mentioning it to Mandy, Dakota trekked yet again to the cabin of his friend, the former doctor.

"Hey, Sawbones!" Dakota shouted from horseback when he sighted his friend coming out of his cabin.

"John Starbuck! I didn't know you were in these parts. When did you come up?"

Dakota dismounted and the two men shook hands vigorously. "Nearly a whole year ago. I've been checking in to see if you were around but the place was always deserted. Where have you been?"

"Here and there. Mostly there."

132

"Evasive as usual."

Will Bowden merely grinned.

The austerity of Will's cabin was far more the standard of a mountain man living alone than the one Dakota had built for his future wife. He sat at a crude table while his host poured coffee.

"You've got to come visit us, Will," Dakota told him as he reached for his mug.

"Us?"

"I've got a wife and son now."

"So, you finally found her, eh, John?"

"For a fact, I did." He recounted in brief their story, including the birth of their son. "It was incredible, Will. I delivered him myself! Well, I mean, Mandy helped, too." Will laughed, nearly choking on his coffee. "It was all so miraculous."

"Delivering healthy babies of healthy mothers was one of the good memories I have of being a doctor." His expression grew sober. "It was the other, less miraculous events—the ongoing suffering, the countless deaths when the epidemics struck, the feeble attempts at trying to help people deal with their losses. And then the war came..."

Dakota placed a hand on his friend's shoulder. "Why don't you come home with me now and meet my family. Have supper with us."

"I'd love to, but I'm hardly fit company now. I need time to clean up, and I sure oughta trim this porcupine on my face before meeting the little woman."

"No, you're fine. Come with me now."

"If you're sure…"

"Absolutely. Let's go now."

Mandy was excited to finally meet the elusive Will Bowden. "Welcome to our home, Mr. Bowden." Her fingers fumbled at replanting stray hairs.

"It's an honor, ma'am." He removed his capote coat. "But please, make it Will."

They sat down to hot coffee and tea. "So, where's that bundle of miracles I've heard so much about?"

"He's sleeping in his cradle."

"Then I won't disturb him. I'll meet him when he wakes up."

"That probably won't be for some time. I just put him down, and he takes such long naps."

"Well, he sure *does* sound like a miracle baby."

After a feast of roasted rabbit, Will examined Mandy's ankle. "Based on what you've told me, you're lucky this foot's still attached. It looks as if it's healed as well as can be expected. I'm sorry to say you'll probably never be able to bear full weight on it and will always have some amount of pain."

When Gregg awoke, Mandy changed him and carried him over to show him off to his first company. She studied Will's face as he peeled back the blanket to see the little charmer. His smile waned as he looked at her baby's face. He glanced at Gregg's hands and poked his finger into the tiny palm.

"Good grip," he said, and smiled at Mandy. "You have a beautiful baby."

"If you two will excuse me," she said, daring not to ask any questions, "I need to feed him now."

"We have a lot of catching up to do, Will. Come help me feed the horses."

Mandy sat and nursed her son in solemn apprehension, visualizing Will's expression at the sight of Gregg. She held her infant with an extra measure of tenderness as he nursed contentedly.

As soon as they were out of earshot, Will spun and faced his host. "How dare you!"

"Wha—"

"How dare you bring me here under the pretense of a friendly supper invitation when all you wanted was for me to make a house call on your dying infant son."

Dakota's steps halted and his breath left him.

"You of all people know what facing this kind of thing year after year did to me. I came up here to get away from all of that. You could have at least warned me."

Dakota stared at him. "He...he's not *dying*."

Will's expression softened as realization struck. "You didn't know?"

The vacuum in Dakota's eyes gave him his answer.

He sighed in deep regret. "Of course you didn't know. You and Mandy were too happy." He gripped his friend by the shoulders. "I am *so sorry* to have told you this way."

Dakota shrugged off his hands. "You're wrong, Will. He's

not dying. How could you possibly make a judgment like that with only a glance at him?"

Will had faced this same reaction numerous times when he had borne similar news to parents in the hospital in St. Louis. He spoke now with the compassion he wished he had imparted earlier.

"I'll examine him more thoroughly if you want me to. But his color, his lips and fingers… surely you've noticed."

In a daze Dakota walked to a tree stump and slumped down. He stared blankly into the dark forest, his eyes flooding with tears as his soul flooded with despair.

Will tended to the horses, and when they returned to the cabin, Mandy was pacing with Gregg at her shoulder. She studied their faces. Will could not look at her. Dakota, his eyes reddened and moist, could not take his eyes off Gregg.

"What is it?" she forced herself to ask.

Will walked slowly to her. "I'd like to examine him, if I may." He put his arms out but she clutched her son tighter.

Dakota crossed the room and wrapped his arms around her and their son. For several moments they remained embraced. With his eyes he asked Mandy to relinquish the baby, and with tears falling she reluctantly placed him in his father's arms.

He laid the smiling child on the bed. Will approached the bedside and observed his hands and feet. He felt the child's pulses, and finally listened to his heartbeat and lung sounds with an ear to his chest. He smiled back at the cherub-like face and brushed the pale cheek with his finger. "You're a happy little fella, aren't yeh?"

Dakota and Mandy came closer. Will stood straight to face them. "I can hear it clearly, even without a stethoscope."

"Hear what?" Mandy asked.

"He's got a defect, a hole between the chambers of his heart."

Mandy's hands flew to her mouth.

"Small ones often close on their own, but this one, I'm afraid, is quite large."

"How did this happen?" Dakota asked in a voice diminished by grief.

"No one knows, but you must not blame yourselves. It's nothing you did."

"What can we do about it?" Mandy asked.

Will walked to the hearth and placed one hand on the mantel. "I'm afraid there's nothing that can be done. I'm so very sorry."

Mandy and Dakota exchanged despairing glances. "But there must be *some*thing," Dakota said. "Some treatment? An operation?"

"Medicine has come a long way, John, and there have been great strides in surgery. But no one will ever be able to operate on the inside of a beating heart."

Mandy lifted her son into her arms. She cradled him close and kissed his head. His cheek caught her tears. Dakota stood stroking his son's arm. He looked at his friend despondently and forced out the dreaded words.

"How long?"

Will hung his head. How many times had he heard that question from a grieving father? How often had he watched a mother caress her child more endearingly? How could it be happening now, to his friends, in this place?

"As his heart tires he will grow progressively weaker, and his color will get worse. He will become more lethargic— sleepier." Watching the infant resting peacefully in his mother's arms, grabbing onto the wavy ends of her hair, made his next words almost unbearable to speak. "Perhaps two or three months."

Tears squeezed from Mandy's tightly shut eyes. Dakota enfolded his wife and son in his arms.

For several moments Will watched them, his heart aching with theirs. Then he moved to the door and put on his coat.

"I have no words to express how badly I feel." He lowered his gaze, unable to look his friend in the eye. "I…I know this sounds callous, but—God forgive me—I can't come back here."

"But, *Will*…"

The door closed behind him. The pervasive silence was broken by Gregg's baby gibber.

Dakota took his son and laid him on the bed. The boy smiled at the sight of his father's face and began to wriggle.

Mandy buried her face in her hands and wept.

Dakota's own tears fell unrestrained.

Baby Gregg waved his arms in the air and cooed.

CHAPTER 21

The next two and a half months passed too quickly as Dakota and Mandy spent their days doting over their baby and trying to comfort each other. The moments were fleeting, and so very fragile—each one treasured.

As Will predicted, Gregg grew weaker and paler, and his breathing became more difficult, but he never lost his bright smile at the recognition of his parents' faces. It was his smile that at times allowed Mandy the intercepting thought that somehow he would get better, or at least get no worse, and certainly not be lost to them. She had to fight down resentment toward Dakota because he did not share her dream.

All it took to kill that dream for him was to watch the infant as he slept. His lips were blue, his abdominal muscles worked with increasing effort to help him breathe.

Yet Mandy's heart revolted against what her mind insisted was fact. She could not comprehend how she could ever let him go.

Dakota struggled with overwhelming feelings of helplessness. His son, his own flesh, was dying and he was incapable of doing anything to stop it. It tore at his most basic instinct—that of protecting his offspring.

On one unusually warm morning the couple took Gregg outside to let him breathe some piney fresh air and experience the sights and sounds and smells of his mountain world. Dakota carried him tucked in one arm and pointed out the trees and the meadow and the sky. He placed his son's tiny hand on Lady's soft nose and let him feel her warm breath. He rode Chief slowly around the clearing in front of the cabin with Gregg safely secured in front of him.

Dakota passed the boy into Mandy's waiting arms and dismounted. He turned and saw Will standing at the edge of the clearing, leaning against an aspen tree.

An uncomfortable moment passed. Finally Will straightened and walked to where they stood. "I've had no peace since the day I left here."

There was no need to ask them how they were holding up. Their countenances spoke plainly of their agony, of sleepless nights, of the desperate clinging to the life of their child.

He came by every day thereafter, helping with the chores and just listening as his friends confided their deepest feelings to him. His being there held a value for them beyond price.

With each passing day Gregg continued to weaken and grow more listless, until it became an effort for him even to smile. Mandy was pale with purplish half moons under her eyes. She ate little and lay awake most of every night listening for the sound of his breathing or stirring. Sleep was a thief who robbed her of precious time with her son, and she fought it until she was overtaken by exhaustion.

After sleeping several hours one night for the first time in months, she awoke with a start. Her heart skipped, then pounded. She lay unmoving in the stillness, listening for her son's breathing. She heard none.

Throwing back the covers, she bolted upright and swung her legs off the bed. In the dim light she barely saw Gregg's little head in his cradle. She could not tell if he was breathing, and the fear of finding that he was not left her paralyzed.

But slowly she forced herself off the bed, took up her crutch and limped the few steps to the cradle. She removed the hide blanket.

He was breathing still, although each breath was labored and shallow. She lifted her son into her arm and carried him back to the bed. Placing him between herself and Dakota, she laid her hand on her husband's arm and squeezed it gently.

"Dakota," she whispered with a strangled voice. "It's time."

The irony struck like a spear. She had spoken those same words once before upon wakening her husband—on the day Gregg was born.

He instantly turned over. His eyes took in the form of his infant son.

They laid beside their baby, stroking him and kissing him and whispering to him. Dakota placed his finger in Gregg's palm and felt the faint movement of his wee fingers.

Gregg struggled in the effort to open his eyes, and upon seeing the faces of his ma and pa before him, the tiny corners of his mouth turned up weakly. Then he closed his eyes.

A few minutes later, in the silent stillness that precedes the dawn, his breathing ceased.

Dakota and Mandy remained for a time in bed with their son, caressing him and holding his little hands. Then Dakota rose and dressed.

"I'll be at the spot we picked out."

Mandy tenderly washed her baby and wrapped him in a snowy white coverlet made of elk hide she had treated. She sat by the hearth and held him close, humming. She gazed toward the cradle Dakota had made. Inside lay the yucca seed rattle he had so lovingly created at Christmas. She crossed to the cradle and reached for the rattle just as Will arrived on the doorstop.

His eyes took in the scene, and his heart shattered.

He walked with Mandy to the meadow in silence. Dakota was finishing the task of digging his son's grave. A small pine coffin waited nearby.

The couple stood holding their son and each other as Will recited the Twenty-third Psalm. In a strained voice he added, "Normally at a time such as this we mention a person's accomplishments and virtues. What do you say about a boy who is not even six months old? His greatest accomplishment was the joy he brought his parents, and he gave that with each breath he took."

The time had come for them to face the inevitable—they must lay their son in the ground. No physical pain they ever suffered exceeded this. No words were worthy of their anguish.

His eyes drowning in tears, Dakota took one final look at his son's precious face, then covered it with the hide. He took the boy from Mandy's trembling arms and placed him in the pine box.

Mandy laid the rattle atop the still form, then turned away, shutting her eyes and raising her hands to her ears to shut out the sound of the nails being hammered into the coffin that held her son.

Once it was lowered into the grave, Dakota lifted the shovel, but Will stayed his arm. "Let me do this."

Will finished burying Gregg.

The pain—his own and that of his friends—was not soon buried.

CHAPTER 22

*U*pon returning to the cabin, Will found Mandy sitting at the table and Dakota slowly pacing. They had not even had time for the reality of their loss to sink in, yet their separation from their infant was now complete. He would have paid any price for them to not have to endure the anguish ahead. But they must, just as he must relive his once again.

He sat down opposite Mandy. She looked at him, but her red-rimmed eyes were unfocused.

"Can you feel the emptiness?" She wrapped her arms across her chest. "I want to hold him again, even just once." She began to move back and forth in a rocking motion.

Will looked at Dakota who was standing by the hearth not even noticing his wife's actions. The doctor feared that these bereaved parents, like too many others he had observed, might require, even demand, comfort from each other, and receive none. He was no prophet, only painfully aware that one cannot lean on something that will crumble under the weight. He hoped he was wrong, that this grief would bind them ever closer.

But once again, his prognosis proved accurate.

The hours that had passed so quickly only a short time ago now dragged on. Some days Dakota and Mandy were numb; other days they spent engulfed in sorrow. Dakota had to be occupied all the time, exhausting himself with outdoor work. Mandy spent most of her time in bed. One morning he begged her to get up and walk with him outside, but she rebuffed him, and he left feeling further defeated.

He went to Will's place to help him fix his roof, but they accomplished little. Will had watched his friends drift apart over the weeks, and mourned their shattering relationship as much as he mourned their dead son.

"She doesn't even get out of bed till long after noon anymore," Dakota lamented. "And she thinks because I leave the cabin that I don't feel this as deeply as she does. It just isn't so. I've *got* to be out here fixing roofs and chopping wood and hunting and preparing hides 'cause…oh, Will…I'm afraid of what will happen if I give in to the emptiness inside of me." He threw himself on his friend's shoulder and wept. "I'm so lost!"

Will held him for the time it took to regain his composure, then let him continue.

"She won't let me near her. Not once in the weeks since Gregg died has she let me so much as touch her."

"Her way of coping is different from yours, John. You both need to understand that about each other." After a moment he asked, "Do you want me to talk to her?"

He shrugged despondently. "God knows I can't reach her."

When Will arrived at their cabin, he looked through the open door and saw Mandy standing at the hearth, stirring the fire. She wore the baggy, faded lavender calico she'd let out at the seams during her pregnancy. Her hair was unkempt, her shoulders sagged.

He knocked on the doorframe. "May I come in?"

"I was going to lie down and rest, Will."

"I won't stay long." He let himself in before she could protest, closed the door, and sat at the table. Pulling the chair adjacent to his away from the table, he patted the seat.

"I'm not up to making conversation."

"C'mon," he urged, "sit with me."

She complied with obvious reluctance.

"You look like you just got up."

"I did."

"But you just said you were going to rest."

She didn't respond.

"Mandy, I'm not one to tell a person how to deal with this kind of loss, but staying in bed isn't the answer."

"I have no reason to get up anymore."

"You have a husband."

"Yeah, one who gets up every morning and without breaking stride goes out to cut down a tree and chop up kindling we don't need. Or he rides off on his horse for hours on end. I don't know where he goes or what he does."

"Did you ever ask him?"

She didn't answer.

"Have you thought of riding along with him?"

Again, silence.

He slipped out of his chair and knelt on one knee next to her. He turned her face toward his and looked straight into her

141

eyes.

"John has told me of your great reserve of courage and how much you have sacrificed for others. I know you have the strength to live on, Mandy."

She shook her head. "I don't know how to begin again, Will. How to face even one more day."

"Maybe you could begin by, say…brushing your hair."

She looked away from him and stared vacantly into the fire.

"It's a small thing, I know, but don't expect any more from yourself just now."

He rose and stepped behind her chair, placing his hands on her shoulders. "I wish I could prescribe for you a way out of this. But the truth is, the only way out…is through. And you two *will* get through this. You'll either get through it separately, or together. I know that precious little baby of yours would never want you two to drift apart because he had to leave you. *He'd* want you *together*."

After giving her shoulders a long, gentle squeeze, he kissed the top of her head and departed.

Mandy sat at the table for several minutes after he left. Then she went back to bed.

Her longing for her baby overwhelmed her as she lay on her side. The discomfort remained in her breasts from her dwindled milk supply, and she yearned to renew the bond she had with him when she nursed him. Her arms ached to hold her son, to feel his head rest in the crook of her elbow.

A thought came to her unbidden. Dakota had carried Gregg in his arms much of the time, too. How he must long for the feel of baby flesh against his bare chest again, to rub his face into that round belly, to feel those tiny fingers grasp his large one. Her eyes fell to the cradle that remained in its place near the bed. A piece of Dakota's soul had gone into each whittle of the wood. His pain was truly as deep as her own.

She raised herself up and sat on the side of the bed. Her friend had told her she possessed the courage to survive this. She wasn't sure she had the will to.

Her eyes cast to the night table next to the bed. Laying in a patch of sunlight were the candle, her hairbrush and the .44 revolver.

Her fingers twitched. Her breathing became shallow. Her

hand slowly reached out, then returned to her side. She wiped sweat from her palm. Again she reached toward the table—each inch along the course a decision in itself.

Her fingers touched, then grasped, the handle of her hairbrush.

* * *

When Dakota returned to the cabin later that day the aroma of coffee startled him.

Mandy rose from the table as he hung the Spencer. He turned, and their gazes held for several heartbeats.

"Would you like some?" she asked.

He studied her a moment longer. She wore the white doeskin dress she'd worn at their Arapaho wedding ceremony. Her hair was brushed smooth.

He nodded. "I'd like some very much."

She poured him a cup and set it on the table opposite her tea. They sipped their drinks in silence. Mandy was the first to break it.

"Will was here today. He said some things…"

He offered her the time she needed to gather her thoughts and emotions.

"He said Gregg would want us together, wouldn't want us to drift apart because he was gone."

His misted eyes cast downward. "I don't want that either."

"I will try, Dakota. I will get up from my bed and try to get through each day *with* you."

His hand moved to the center of the table. Hers did the same.

A few days later Mandy accepted his invitation to walk outside. It was her first time out since Gregg's death.

She felt a strange detachment from the surroundings that once seemed a part of her. Could the sun have been shining down and melting the snow all this time? Were the animals really still seeking out the quiet and safe places to bear their young? Had life around them continued on as it always had before Gregg died? She had come to feel as if time had frozen around her.

Dakota was acquainted with her wonder of such things. He had experienced the same benumbing realizations weeks earlier.

They walked for half an hour through the woods and back toward the meadow. Mandy's steps slowed as they neared the place where their son was laid to rest.

"I don't think I can bear to go there."

"You don't have to. But there is something I'd like you to see when you feel you can go."

The decision was hers to make, and he waited with patience. Taking a tight hold of his arm, she allowed him to lead her.

At the head of their son's grave was a cross. Dakota had carved it from aspen wood and etched into it the words:

GREGG STARBUCK 1866-1867

It was otherwise unadorned. So simplistic, yet a beautiful token of his love.

"I...I had no idea. I should have come here sooner. I just couldn't...I..."

He put his arm around her. "You came when you could."

They stood silently for several minutes before their son's resting place. They prayed together, then moved on.

Upon reaching the top of a rise, they scanned the expanse before them. The greening meadow merged into a mountain laden with pines, which in turn shot upward, piercing an azure sky. But it held less of a magnificence than it had previously— back when they were whole. It was nonetheless a reminder that a world awaited their return.

"We have to leave here soon," Dakota said. "I must get you to your family."

"I know," she whispered. Even her torment over her family had numbed during the months of Gregg's illness and the weeks since his death. It was time to turn her thoughts and actions back to getting home, but...

"I don't want to leave him." New tears spilled over.

Neither did he know how they could leave their son behind. He turned her to face him.

"We'll come back here, Mandy. I promise you." With his thumb he caressed away her tears.

There was a spark of life in her eyes it seemed, or at least a glimmer of the hope of a future. His hand moved into her hair, and he lowered his lips to hers.

"Don't!" She turned her head sharply.

144

"What's wrong? I just wanted—"

"I know what it is you want." She took a step back.

"Mandy, I—"

"What I *don't* know is how you can seek such gratification for yourself. Your son is *dead*. He's lying in a grave not fifty yards from here."

He stood stunned, speechless. Shock over her scathing condemnation quickly evolved into resentment. He struggled to remain calm.

His recriminating expression as he turned and departed did not escape her.

She was left standing alone. Her eyes followed his retreating form, then turned toward her infant's grave.

He'd want you together, came Will's haunting words.

Glancing back, she saw her husband disappear into the woods. Losing sight of him left her with a sudden dread, as if he were gone for good.

He'd want you together.

"Dakota!" Contending with her crutch in the moist ground, she went after him. She cried out again, her eyes fixed on the spot where he had faded into the shadows of the trees.

"Dakota! Wait for me!"

No answer came. In despair, she floundered back to the cabin. He wasn't there. Chief was gone from the stable.

As the hours passed she felt crushed beneath the weight of her sorrows and fears. The longer he was gone, the more certain she was he was never coming back.

She took down her Bible from the mantel. After losing her son, she had neglected her relationship not only with her husband but also with her Creator and Savior. Opening to where the ribbon bookmark had lain undisturbed for…how long?…she read from the seventh chapter of Paul's letter to the Corinthians. It was as if the words were written about her: *without were fightings, within were fears.*

Her fears had conquered her. She feared her husband's touch, that it could lead to more, and they had no right to that kind of pleasure, not with their son lying in a grave. She feared getting pregnant, and she did not want that to happen now. Perhaps never. Wouldn't that mean they were trying to replace Gregg?

She wondered if she would ever come to know the peace

145

Paul expressed three chapters earlier: *We are troubled on every side, yet not distressed; we are perplexed, but not in despair; persecuted, but not forsaken; cast down, but not destroyed.*

Dakota rode in as the darkness grew thick. Mandy had forced the effort to cook a goose, and the aroma escaped through the open door of the cabin.

"How many times do I have to tell you to keep the door closed? The bears aren't hibernating in May, Mandy. And if a cougar or wolf got a whiff of what's coming out of this place…"

He slammed the door shut and set the latch.

"Sorry." Her eyes cast down.

With a strength she did not even know was left in her, she continued to try to mend what she had earlier rent.

"I roasted that goose you bagged this morning. Made some gravy, too. I know you must be starving."

"For a fact," he said coarsely as he brushed past her to wash at the basin. That was all it took to silence her.

Thus they ate yet another meal barren of conversation, Mandy redistributing the food on her plate more than eating it. After supper she washed the dishes. He cast bullets.

Later she took down her book of Longfellow's poems, the one he had given her when he returned from the government council. On that day he had snatched her into his arms and kissed her breathless. It seemed a lifetime ago.

She read "The Village Blacksmith," envisioning Dakota in the role of the smith, working at his forge while curious little faces peered in with awe.

Was it still his dream? He hadn't spoken of it in months. All their dreams disintegrated the day they learned of Gregg's prognosis.

The blacksmith in the poem was a widower. Was she making her husband feel like one now? Why couldn't she comfort him? Or receive it from him? They had been mourning separately, unable to lean on each other.

She turned to another story, "The Song of Hiawatha," and there read of the brave's thoughts about a man and a woman:

As unto the bow the cord is,
So unto the man is woman,
Though she bends him, she obeys him,

146

Though she draws him, yet she follows,
Useless each without the other!

That night as they lay in bed, Mandy turned to her side and watched Dakota, his back to her, as he breathed evenly in his sleep. He had once considered her the woman worth waiting half a lifetime for. She had hoped to prove worthy of that wait. She thought it would be easy. Indeed, it had been for a time. Not since they lost Gregg.

She couldn't change what happened to Gregg, but couldn't accept what was happening between her and her husband.

She reached her hand to his bare shoulder. She stroked it gently, stirring him into wakefulness.

"What is it?"

"Could you...will you hold me, Dakota?"

A long silence followed. The stillness pressed heavily upon her.

"Please, Dakota? I'm scared."

"There's no need to be. We're locked up tight. Nothing can get in."

Dejected, she entreated him again. "Please?"

He sighed deeply, then rolled over. He did not reach for her, but studied her careworn face in the dim light of the one chandelier lamp they'd always left burning at night during Gregg's illness. After his death, they could not bring themselves to leave it unlit.

She struggled for adequate words.

"Dakota, I can only hope that you will forgive me for the brutal things I said today. It's just that...I feel like we would somehow be...betraying Gregg by enjoying things, including each other, after losing him."

His countenance softened. His words came more gently than she had anticipated, than she felt she deserved.

"I feel that way, too, and it leaves me with monstrous guilt. I still have desires that I think should've died because Gregg did. I was enraged at you for saying what you did, but more so at myself because it was true. I think that's what I was running from today, not you."

"You didn't deserve it," she whispered sorrowfully.

He wiped a fallen tear. "Will has tried to explain to me

where some of these feelings may come from. He says that when we begin to enjoy life again, we feel like we're letting go of our grief. But that's the one thing we have left that still bonds us with our baby, so we don't want to let it go."

As the words settled in her soul, Mandy wept. Dakota caressed her, his own heart rent anew. For the first time, they grieved as one.

"When you left me today," she said, sobbing, "I was so afraid you were gone forever." She looked into his tear-filled eyes. "I want to be the woman you prayed for and built this cabin for. But I wonder if I can ever be that woman again."

His fingers pressed her lips. "You will always be that woman."

He lightly placed his arm around her and inched closer, gauging her reaction to his nearness. She was tense but not resistant. He drew her to his chest, feeling the tears on his skin and the trembling within his arms.

"I'll never leave you, Mandy. There's enough uncertainty in this world without your fearing I'll abandon you someday."

His gentle voice and soothing arms eased the tension in her body. They embraced for a long while.

As the lamp flickered its dying light, Mandy gave herself willingly to the one man whose love was deep enough, forgiving enough, enduring enough, to conquer her fears.

CHAPTER 23

*W*ill returned from a week-long trip down the mountain and went straightway to his friends' cabin.

"I got a good price for your pelts and hides." He held out a stack of currency to Dakota.

He handed Mandy a brown package. "I hope this comes close to what you were wanting. I'm not exactly an expert in such matters, you know."

She removed the wrapping and held up two dresses. One was a gray traveling suit with long sleeves and a gathered skirt. The other was red with a pleated bodice, fabric-covered buttons and a turned down collar.

"Oh, Will," she said as she admired the trimmings and styles. "These are simply—"

"*Exquisite!*" the men chimed in. She laughed with them, then shooed them outside so she could try on her new outfits.

As they waited, Dakota looked into his friend's eyes. "I don't know how to express my gratitude for all you've done for us, Will. If not for you..."

Will gripped Dakota's shoulders. "Just keep loving each other. That's all the thanks I ever want."

A few mornings later, it was with a heavy heart that Will helped his friends pack their belongings for the journey they were to have taken sixteen months earlier. The cabin was left clean and ready for the day they would return, or when a sojourner might need shelter.

Will had a going away present for Mandy and made her close her eyes. After retrieving something from outside, he took her crutch from under her arm and presented her with a cane he had fashioned from lodge pole pine wood.

Her eyes widened. "Do you think I'm ready for this?"

"As your personal family physician, I've determined that you are."

Dakota and Mandy made a final visit to Gregg's grave. Together they shed tears over their loss, and over the anguish of leaving him there alone.

"Only his body is here, Mandy. His spirit is in a realm higher even than eagles dare fly. He has beheld God, and he is happy. We'll meet him there one day."

These words of hope were all that made it bearable for Mandy to walk away.

Will was waiting at the cabin door. "I'll tend his grave," he promised.

"Thank you," Dakota said, his voice choking. "It means everything to us."

Will glanced around the clearing in front of the cabin. "It's going to be a mite lonesome around here until I get used to being by myself again." He grinned at Mandy. "Reckon you're the one I'll miss more. You're a whole lot cuter than he is."

She smiled. "You're not so bad yourself, Sawbones." Stepping into his outstretched arms, she hugged him and whispered, "Thank you, Will, for *everything*."

He moved to his long-time mountain companion, and their arms surrounded one another. "Remember, friend," Dakota said through a tight throat, "if you ever get to Denver..."

"Maybe I'll go there to trade next time. And don't you be strangers to this place, either."

"We've already pledged to return one day."

Will helped Mandy onto her mare as Dakota went inside the cabin to check for any forgotten items. Finding none, he started to leave, then paused in the doorway, turned, and took one long, final look around his mountain haven.

There, at the table, his friend from youth was hunched over a checkerboard figuring his next strategic move. In front of the hearth sat his wife, nursing his son and singing a lullaby. Over on the bed he made love to her, delivered their baby, and watched him die. His eyes lifted to the loft above the bed and settled on the cradle that now rested in the shadows.

After taking a renewing breath, he pulled out the latchstring, closed the door, and hung up the bell.

* * *

It was mid-June when they arrived in Colorado City.

They left the horses at the livery and eagerly checked into a hotel where they bathed and changed into clean clothes. Their next stop was the bank where Dakota deposited some of his pelt money. He also added Mandy's name to his account.

150

"I want you to have access to whatever's mine. We'll leave some money here for when we return to the cabin. After we're settled in Denver, I'll send for the rest of my funds in the other two banks, which ought to be enough to start up my shop."

Mandy was gratified to hear him speak of his plans for the future again.

They headed for a restaurant where they'd be able to enjoy a meal they didn't have to kill, skin and cook for themselves. They sat at a table by the front window, and as they waited for their meal, Dakota read aloud from the *Colorado City Journal*. Much had changed in the two years since they bumped into each other at his Arapaho village.

"Hey, from the way this article reads, they must've finally succeeded in laying a transatlantic cable. Can you imagine sending a message to Europe and it being received in only an hour?"

"It's bound to be a fast-paced and progressive world we've come back to. Any word on whether the railroad has gone to Denver yet?"

"I don't see anything about that. Looks like the push for statehood is still an ongoing issue, but President Johnson thinks Colorado isn't going anywhere. The population is down several thousand since the beginning of the decade. Oh, Nebraska got statehood earlier this year, though."

He further scanned the columns. "Oooh, the president may not think Colorado is going anywhere, but it looks like he might be."

"What do you mean?"

"There's talk of impeachment."

"Impeachment! What'd he do?"

But Dakota's eye had already caught another article. He squirmed in his seat.

"What is it?"

"They're working on another treaty with the Cheyenne and Arapaho to take effect this fall. The talks will be held at Fort Larned, in Kansas."

"That's near the Medicine Lodge reservation where your parents and the others went, isn't it?"

"It's about sixty miles northwest."

She saw the longing in him to know how they were faring.

151

"Maybe after we get settled we can take a trip over there."

"I sure would like to."

After eating a leisurely meal, Dakota rubbed his beard. "I guess I should head for the barber shop for a shave so I can look presentable to your folks. I'm thinking I should get my hair cut, too."

She leaned across the table. "You can get your hair and beard *trimmed*. Any more than that and you'll answer to me."

He leaned across, meeting her half way, and kissed her.

"While you're at the barber, I'd like to go by the mercantile and buy a sun bonnet. I could really use some shoes, too, ones that give my ankle more support now that Will's cane has freed me from that lousy ole crutch." Taking thought of just who it was who had fashioned that crutch for her, she said, "Uh, no offense intended."

He smiled. "None taken."

They decided to meet back at the hotel after they finished their individual errands. When Dakota returned to their room, Mandy noted his sober expression.

"What's wrong, Dakota?"

"I ran into an Arapaho who scouts for the army. I asked him about the upcoming treaty, and if he knew anything about the reservation at Medicine Lodge. He told me he was there two weeks ago. He knows of Wild Eagle and Long Hair." His expression revealed that the news was not good. "Wild Eagle is dying."

She let out her breath and put her arms around him, her own heart aching for the old man she had come to love dearly.

"Dakota, you need to go to them."

He held her at arm's length. "I need to get you to Denver. After that, if it's all right with you, I could leave you under the care of your father and then go see them."

"Of course it's all right, but...perhaps there's another way."

"What do you mean?"

"You could go to Kansas, and I can take the stage to Denver."

"Absolutely not!"

"It makes sense, Dakota. You may not have the time it will take to travel up there and then go back across the territory."

152

"I won't leave you alone like that."

"I won't be alone. There'll be—" She gathered his true meaning. He did not want to leave her without *his* protection. He had done that once before.

She looked into his anxious face. "Dakota, it could mean the difference between seeing Wild Eagle and getting there too late."

Early the next morning, they went to the stage office and learned that the coach to Denver left only once a week, on Sunday mornings. Five days away. Mandy did not want to wait that long to leave, so when they saw a train of supply wagons in the street preparing to head out for Denver the next day, she asked Dakota if she could go with them, provided they would accept a ride-a-long. He said he would have to speak to the wagonmaster.

"Already got some unescorted northbound ladies ridin' along." Bucksnort Bill Montana pointed to an oversized Conestoga wagon in the midst of the others. "It'd be crowded, but if they's willin', makes me no never mind. I'll check with 'em and get back to yeh."

Dakota ascertained that this was a respectable outfit, and that Bucksnort Bill had many years of experience and was considered trustworthy. Additionally, a dozen-man military escort would be riding along for this leg of the route since some of the supplies were destined for the headquarters in Denver. There were adequate provisions, and ample precautions were being taken.

Difficult as it was to accept her journeying home without him, and to separate for what they decided would be a month, he ultimately approved.

Her trip would take three days, twice the time the stage would've taken, but she'd still be arriving a couple of days sooner. Every day counted now.

The wagonmaster came to their table at supper that evening and told them the arrangements were made. "Thank you, Mr. Montana," Mandy told him. "We'll see you at six o'clock sharp."

"No need to be so formal, ma'am. Just call me Bucksnort."

In their room that evening Mandy stood in front of the dresser mirror, removed the comb Dakota made at Christmas and shook out her hair. She reached for her brush but Dakota stepped behind her, took it from her and brushed her silken strands. The task complete, he set the brush down and closed his arms around her waist. They beheld their images before them.

"How can I leave you?" he whispered.

"I'm wondering that, too. I know we're doing the right thing, but…" She turned in his arms. "I'm going to miss you so much!"

A month was a long time to be apart, and this last night together was passionate. The next morning they repeated their union, only with tenderness and a twinge of sadness, for it was their farewell.

At six o'clock they stood in front of the livery where the wagons gathered. Dakota tied Lady to the Conestoga in which Mandy would be riding. The other four female occupants were just arriving—not from the hotel, but from the saloon.

Two pairs of wide green eyes watched as the fallen angels threw their belongings into the wagon. They wore only camisoles and skirts, and their hair was uncombed, giving the appearance of having taken a quick leave. The eldest, apparently the madam, was fiftyish and had white hair. Of the others, one was blond, one brunette, and one a redhead. Black eyeliner made their eyes look wide and pretty, and each had a "birthmark" on her cheek.

The madam glanced at Mandy. "You the gal who's comin' along with us?"

"Uh…yes."

"Well, come on then before Bucksnort starts his rantin' and ravin'."

Forcing his fallen jaw closed, Dakota studied his wife's discomfited expression. "It's not too late to change our plans, honey."

"No. This'll be…fine."

They walked to the Conestoga where he set down her traveling case, swallowed her in his burly arms and planted a firm kiss.

When their lips parted she whispered, "Dakota, people are watching."

"Let 'em gawk," he said, and kissed her again.

One of the horses harnessed to the wagon behind them

began to jitter and tried to rear. A man tugged at the reins, cursing furiously at the horse. Dakota helped calm the animal, then looked the man in the eye. "I'd appreciate it if you'd watch your language around the ladies."

"Ladies? Them ain't ladies. Them're whores." Seeing the ire in Dakota's eyes, he was quick to add, "'Cept' your'n, of course."

"Just watch your mouth."

He assisted each woman into the wagon. Mandy sat near the rear and looked out as the wagons began to roll.

Dakota stood in the street and watched her be carried away from him. Not until the wagon headed onto the road north did he turn away.

"Now that's a fine specimen of a man," said one of Mandy's traveling companions. "Got some chivalrous sinew in him, too. Are you sure you want to leave him behind?"

Mandy looked around at the four women who would share space, provisions and conversation with her for the next three days.

"It's only for a month, then he's coming to join me in Denver."

"I don't think I'd let him go for that long," the brunette beauty said.

"How close are you?" asked the blonde.

"How close? Why, he's my husband."

"Kinda romantic for a husband," the redhead said.

"I noticed you don't wear a ring." It was the blonde again.

Mandy glanced down at her bare ring finger. "We've been living in a remote mountain cabin since we got married."

"Oh, I get it. No jewelry shops nearby. Well, I gotta give him credit. That's one I haven't heard before."

The madam entered the conversation. "A month is a long time for a man, sweetie. Any man. And that one of yours, well, when he lets out a stud horse whistle it'll pull the picket pin of every filly around. I could tell by the way he said his good-byes that he's stuck on you, but like I said, a month is a long time."

Mandy smiled in peaceful confidence.

"You think he's different, don't you?" accused the blonde.

"What's taking him away from you?" asked the brunette, without a qualm about intruding in the couple's business.

"He's going to an Indian reservation to visit his parents."

155

The redhead slapped her knee. "I knew it! Didn't I tell y'all that fella looked to be a 'breed? I tell you, girls, men with Indian blood in 'em...oh! just *imagine* bein' alone in a mountain cabin with that drop-dead good lookin' hunk o' man-flesh!"

And thus went Mandy's journey.

* * *

When her wagon turned onto the road and he could no longer see her, Dakota untied his horse from the post in front of the livery. As he took hold of the saddle, he glimpsed the *parfleche* she made for him at Christmas dangling from the horn. He ran his fingers across the beaded design of the mountains and the three intertwining circles, lingering at the yellow one that represented his son.

She had only just left, but he missed her deeply. He longed for the day they would be reunited, never to be separated again.

CHAPTER 24

*L*ong Hair steadied herself on a chair back.

"Dakota! I did not recognize you behind that hair on your face. How is it that you came here to us?"

Dakota walked across the room of the clapboard building that served as the reservation infirmary. He placed his hands on her shoulders and smiled as he leaned down to kiss her cheek. "On a horse."

She slapped him on the arm.

He glanced down at his father who lay asleep on a cot next to them. His appearance was sickly and his breathing labored.

"I heard he was ill, near death, from one of our tribesmen near the foothills. I came as fast as I could. What is wrong with him, Mother? Is he truly dying?"

Long Hair looked at her husband of almost thirty summers. "Yes, Dakota, soon he will join his fathers on the other side of the spirit world." She ran her hand gently along Wild Eagle's frail arm. "He has not much will to live."

The Arapaho chief roused at her touch. When he looked up and saw Dakota, he smiled weakly. "My son!"

"Hello, Father. It is good to see you."

"It is good for you to be here now. I will not be on this side for many more sunsets."

Dakota grasped his hand and held it tight. Wild Eagle studied his son's face intently with one eye narrowed.

"Woman Shot With Sun's Arrow—you two are married, yes?"

He smiled broadly. "Yes."

"Your eyes are bright, my son, as they were in the days she spent with us, before you two could no longer look at each other without pain. Yet, there is also a hint of something more. A loss?"

Dakota sat on his father's bed, in awe of the way he could correctly read so much in a face. He related the story of his and Mandy's life since he had last seen his parents. Long Hair shed tears as she listened to the details of Gregg's life and untimely death.

"Thunder Cloud has also given you a grandchild," he told

them. "We have not seen him or Blue Flower since we parted, but their child was to have been born before the last season of snow began."

Long Hair's tears fell along her cheek. "I have reached the age when I should be able to enjoy my sons' sons, but I am not even able to set my eyes on them." Dakota went to her and offered a comforting embrace.

Wild Eagle looked on with thankfulness for his son's presence, then drifted into unconsciousness.

"Dakota, I am so glad you are here. Your father can have peace now. He only wishes…"

He took her hands in his. "What is it?"

"He wants to go to his lodge, Dakota. They make him stay in this sick lodge made of wood, and he is unhappy here. It is his final wish to go back to his own tepee to pass over."

"I will see to it, Mother."

After some strongly worded parleying with reservation officials, Dakota carried his father to his tepee and gently laid him on his mat. Many of the chief's friends now felt free to visit him in the familiar surroundings of his home.

For several days Dakota helped Long Hair tend to his father's needs. The old chief seemed to perk up after his son's arrival, but his strength did not match his newly raised spirits. He gradually grew weaker.

One evening, while Long Hair was speaking to friends outside the lodge, Dakota bared his soul to his father, telling him of his pain in losing his son, and how he better understood what Wild Eagle had gone through when Dakota had been lost to him as a boy. He spoke of his regret at not having been able to return sooner to let him know he was alive, and to spare him the uncertainty of his first wife's loyalty.

"You returned to me as soon as was possible. I regret not having watched you grow, and not having the chance to raise you in my own ways. Yet I am grateful to the white parents who received you as their own and raised you to be the man you were when you came back to me. I am most proud of the man you are today."

The chief raised himself up and took hold of his son's arm. "And, my son, my heart soars because you have at last found the woman to complete you." He lowered his voice. "I wish it were permissible to see her again and speak to her face to face. I miss her very much. Will you tell her this for me?"

"I will, Father."

The simple effort of lifting himself took the strength out of Wild Eagle, and Dakota helped him lay his head back down. He never left his father's side until his spirit was released that night.

This grave new loss compounded that which his soul had known since his son died. He stayed a week longer to give and receive comfort from Long Hair, and tried unsuccessfully to convince her to come away and live with him and Mandy.

He also visited with the others from Wild Eagle's band and discussed the upcoming treaty with reservation officials.

As he hugged his mother good-bye, she told him, "You take care of the woman Man-Above sent you who was shot with the sun's arrow."

"I will take the best care of her."

"I hope it is going well with her family."

"I feel sure that it is. Her father is, like mine was, compassionate and loyal. He will rejoice over her as a treasure that was lost and now is found."

CHAPTER 25

The brick buildings of Denver inched closer. Elation filled Mandy's heart, but butterflies filled her stomach. Butterflies was understating it. She was downright tremulous. The wagons drove along the South Platte River, crossed Cherry Creek and pulled up in front of the merchants' shops on McGaa Street. They spread out in a circle across the entire width of the street.

Mandy eased herself down from the Conestoga and stretched out her muscles under the late afternoon sun. Her wagonmates also alighted and welcomed the circulation back into some numbed body parts.

"Guess this is where we say good-bye." The madam extended her hand to Mandy.

"Constance," she said as they shook hands, "it's been...an experience...getting to know all of you."

Mandy turned to K.C., the blonde who, at nineteen, was the youngest of the group yet seemed to have acquired vast worldly experience.

"So, you're the only one staying on here. I'd like to tell you I wish you luck with your new job, but..."

"So go ahead."

"I'm sure that being employed at Ada Lamont's Indian Row brothel is considered a coveted position by many of your...colleagues, but I hope for a better future for you, K.C."

"My future's looking just fine. You're the one who ought to be considering what you'll do when your man fails to show up next month. Come by Ada's, and I'll put in a good word for you." She turned and swished away.

Mandy turned to the other two soiled doves. "I don't envy you girls having another hundred miles to go."

"It beats stayin' in this ghost town," Stella replied. "Cheyenne's the up and comin' place to be, so we'll follow the wagon ruts up there."

"I still can't believe the railroad is going to Cheyenne instead of here."

Red-haired Alexandra shook Mandy's hand. "It's been real nice ridin' with you. Tell that 'breed of yours to look us up

160

if he gets up Cheyenne-way."

"Oh, I'll be *sure* to tell him."

Mandy tied Lady to a hitching post outside Keane's Dry Goods Store. Pulling her bonnet brim further forward so as not to be recognized by anyone before her family saw her, she turned and headed down McGaa to Fifteenth. There she turned left and walked a block to Larimer Street. A block and a half down the street was her father's law office.

Should she go there first, or to the house?

She headed northeast on Larimer, her heart pumping more erratically with each step. Finally she stood across from the office in which she had burned much midnight oil working for her father. Her eyes fixed on the sign hanging above the door:

SAMUELS & BERRINGER, ATTORNEYS-AT-LAW

She glimpsed the clock in the jewelry store behind her. Four fifteen. Pa would be in that office right now. After all this time, he now stood only yards from her. Her pulses raced frantically. She wiped her palms on her dress.

In her mind, she crossed the street, slowly opened the door and entered the front office. Looking beyond the large desk where she had pored over her father's briefs, she'd see him standing at his huge bookshelf in the back room, picking out the reference materials he'd need in researching a case. Then he'd turn and see her standing in the outer room. His face would turn as white as his hair when she pulled back her bonnet.

No, the office was no place for their reunion. She'd walk to the house a mile outside of town and send one of the twins for Pa. They would have more privacy there. She just hoped no one would notice her first.

She went back for Lady and started her trek home, catching her breath at each familiar face she passed. She felt devious in hiding her identity, but this reunion was going to be shocking enough without her family hearing secondhand that she was alive and in Denver.

Mrs. Newton, the seamstress, passed closer than comfortable. Andrew Bowman, the restaurant owner, crossed in front of her and looked back as she passed by him. Her palms grew slicker.

A weak gasp escaped her when Mr. Baswell tipped his hat as he strolled by. She reminded herself it was merely a common gesture.

Moving into the residential section, she delighted in how much prettier everything looked now that the homes were sprouting lawns and trees, a result of the new irrigation ditches she noticed had been put in place during her absence.

She could see her house now, the large, white, two-story structure with the enormous porch around the front and side, and the white picket fence that caught the sun's afternoon rays. Everything was just as it was the day she left for St. Joe.

One more familiar face approached her, and she nearly flung her bonnet and ran to meet Mercy Robinson, her best friend. Mercy's eyes were downcast and her bonnet half-shaded her face. She carried a basket on her arm. *You're right on time, Mercy, heading for the Friday afternoon quilting bee.* Mercy never looked up as she passed her friend.

Mandy's pace slowed as she drew near the house. Her throat felt parched and lumpy. Her heart raced. If only Dakota were there to lean on, to collapse upon. Every fiber in her reeled with excitement. Her family was only steps away. She was seconds from her long overdue reunion.

She tied Lady to the post and went to the front gate. Drawing a deep breath, she laid her hand on it and gave it shaky push.

The front door crashed open. An energetic lad of eighteen with wavy chestnut hair came forth. He took a wide bite out of a juicy red apple, then skipped down the front steps two at a time. When he reached the bottom step, he looked up and was surprised to see a woman standing at his gate. He eyed her curiously as he slowed his pace along the front path and used his sleeve to wipe juice from the corner of his mouth.

She pulled back her bonnet and let it dangle down her back.

His feet arrested. The apple fell to the earth like Isaac Newton's. His large brown eyes froze on her.

Mandy's eyes filled with tears at the sight of him. For two years she had thought about what she would say at this very moment. Nothing came.

"Ma...Mandy? Is...is it...it *can't* be you!"

Her voice was slow in returning, but she finally formed the words. "Yes, Jeffrey, it's really me."

"But you...we thought—"

"I know. There's so much to tell—"

He bolted for her, lifted her off the ground and hugged her tight. "Oh Mandy, this is too incredible!"

"I can't believe it either. I've dreamed of this moment for two long years."

He set her down, then stroked her face and hair and shoulders as he repeated her name, trying to rid himself of all doubt that it was anyone but his sister standing before him.

"Gracious, little brother, you used to be eye level with me. Now I have to look up a-ways at you. And when did you grow these?" She squeezed his formerly lanky arms. "Are Ma and Julie at home? I suppose Pa's at work. I almost went straight to his office but figured it would be best if one of you went for him."

Her gaze stretched past him toward the house, peering through the door and windows for a movement of any kind. Looking back at him, she repeated, "Well, are Ma and Julie at home?"

His face had lost its exuberance. Mandy's stomach knotted. "What…what is it, Jeff? What's wrong?"

He did not answer in words, but his eyes….

"Jeffrey? Tell me. Is it Ma? Her heart isn't strong, I know."

He couldn't look at her.

"Jeffrey, *tell me!* Is something wrong with Ma?"

He finally lifted his eyes to hers. "Ma's fine, Mandy. She and Julie are in town shopping."

Her hand went to her chest and she tried to slow her breathing. "Don't *do* that to me! I thought the worst."

He placed his hands on her shoulders. "Mandy, there's no easy way to tell you this. About two and a half months after you…after we *thought* you…" His voice broke. "Pa passed away."

His hands moved to her elbows as he felt her start to drop. "Let me get you inside."

He led her into the house and helped her sit on the red velvet couch in the parlor. She sat dazed with her brother's arm around her.

"I know what a shock this is for you. It was for us, too, when it happened. We were all so worried about Ma after you left, but it was Pa whose heart gave out."

Mandy stared vacantly across the room. "It's just not possible. All this time I've thought of him as alive. I pictured him in the courtroom, and here at home with all of you. I almost went to his office today."

Jeffrey laid his head against hers. "You can't believe he's gone, and I can't believe you're back. This is a day no one in this family will ever forget."

She wanted to go to her father's grave. Ma and Julie wouldn't be back for some time, so Jeff took her there.

"Sis, this is going to be...*very strange* for you. You see, we heard you stayed behind at a stage stop, and...there was this burned body and...they said it was you. So we had it sent back here and..."

She halted.

"We had a funeral for you, Mandy." He winced and added, "That body is buried next to Pa."

A shiver penetrated her spine. "But...you got a letter saying it wasn't me at that station, didn't you?"

His expression turned blank.

"A letter was sent a couple of months after that raid telling you it wasn't me who died there, and that I would be contacting you soon from Fort Lyon."

"We never got any letter. But I'm not surprised. A paltry amount of supplies and mail got through to here during those months because of all the Indian raids."

Her shoulders sagged and she let out a breath. "Or the government man never posted it, or... Oh, what does it matter? I never made it to the fort, and then I figured when you didn't hear from me, you'd go looking and not find me, and think I had died anyway. Oh, Jeff..." He offered her a supportive arm.

They continued walking until they reached the section of land a half mile from their present home that Pa had purchased in order to build a new house. He changed his mind when his daughter died, and wanted her buried there.

She looked down at where James Berringer was laid to rest, her grief insurmountable. As far as she was concerned, he had died that day, not on September 2, 1865, as the headstone displayed. Staring at the grave, a profound emptiness hemmed her in. The grievous wound left by Baby Gregg's death ripped open wider.

Her eyes drifted hesitantly to the grave next to Pa's.

164

Delicately carved roses adorned a rounded granite headstone that was set in neatly trimmed grass. Etched in it was the simple inscription:

AMANDA BERRINGER
BELOVED DAUGHTER AND SISTER
JANUARY 7, 1837
JUNE 19, 1865

Her mind was in mutiny. Her father's death was as unreal as her own.

"Ma and Julie should be home soon." Jeffrey gently touched her shoulder when she didn't respond to his words.

"Ma and Pa spent thirty-five years together and had remained so in love. How did she survive all of this?"

His answer was slow in forming. "Survive is a good word, Sis. With you gone, and then Pa… And with Pa's death came a lack of income, bills piling up, and Ma not used to handling those kinds of affairs. She was overwhelmed, mostly by the loneliness. Julie and I did all we could, tried to keep her busy, but she was inconsolable. We feared we were going to lose her, too. Then..."

She studied his uneasy expression. What could be worse to explain than Ma's deep heartache?

"This will be difficult for you, just as hearing of Pa's death was. If you had been here, though, you'd be better able to understand what I'm about to tell you."

"Understand what, Jeffrey?"

"Understand why Ma…this past spring… remarried."

She shook her head. "No, that's crazy! Ma would *never* do that! *None* of this can be happening!" She pushed him aside and turned back to her father's grave.

Jeffrey allowed her to absorb the impact of the dual shock she received this day. "Julie and I at least had time to heal and adjust to each situation. To be assaulted with such shattering news all at once is insufferable, I know."

She turned to her brother and clung to him, weeping. He held her head to his chest. "It's gonna take time, Mandy."

Again she was faced with leaving someone she loved dearly in a grave and returning home.

Walking at half speed, they returned to a still empty house. Jeffrey went to the kitchen to get her something to

165

drink. Mandy sat on the couch fingering the antimacassar and sensing an incredible paradox: so much had changed in the lives of her loved ones in the two years she was gone, yet not one piece of furniture was rearranged. The house gave the false impression that time had stood still.

The upright piano still set in the far corner of the living room where she had enjoyed making grand music for her family in the evenings. On the wall above it hung the Currier and Ives lithograph she had given her parents for their thirtieth anniversary. The two oil lamps with intricately painted glass shades, having survived the journey west, remained perched on their oaken pedestals on either side of the couch. She looked through the archway into the dining room at the familiar oak table, chairs, buffet and hutch. Mandy had picked out the light-blue flowered wallpaper that still brightened the living and dining rooms.

Jeffrey rounded the corner from the kitchen and came through the dining room holding two glasses of sugar-sweetened lemonade. He passed one to her and took a seat beside her.

"It shouldn't be long now before Ma and Julie get home. And George expects to return from Golden around seven. It's gonna be some family reunion."

Mandy's head lowered. Jeff apparently had no problem including this man in the framework of their "family." The lad noticed her disappointment.

"His name is George Barton. He co-owns a freight line that runs from Kansas City to San Francisco, and he operates the middle region from here."

She showed no interest in hearing more, but he continued. "Sis, Denver is on the decline. I don't know if you noticed, but there are few new businesses, and a lot of empty buildings. The Indians persistently cut the telegraph wires and raid westbound stages and freight wagons, keeping us isolated from eastern supply sources, and as you now know, even from the mail. And with fewer goods on hand, prices have soared. What gold they manage to bring out of the hills is worth half of what it was four years ago. One of the railroad officials checking out the town said it was 'too dead to bury,' and they laid tracks to Cheyenne instead."

"Are you telling me that Ma married this George Bacon

166

for financial security?"

"It's Barton. And don't jump to the wrong conclusions. She never would've married him for that reason alone. But things had gotten so bad after Pa died that we decided to pack up and move back to Pennsylvania, although none of our hearts was in it. Then George came along and was so kind and empathetic towards Ma. He's been widowed, too. He guided her out of our financial woes, and they found they really liked each other."

"Liking's one thing, but remarrying less than two years after your husband of thirty-five years dies…"

"He is good for her, Mandy, and she for him. I know it's hard for you to accept this news all at once. But in time you'll have to."

The sound of female voices came from the front yard. Mandy's heart skipped several beats.

"Oh Jeffrey, what'll we do? I mean, how should we handle this? If they just walk in here and see me—"

Jeff sprung from the sofa and raced out the door. Mandy heard him greet their mother and sister at the bottom of the porch steps.

She was unsure of what to do with herself. She couldn't stay seated. Her insides leapt about and forced her up. She went to the center of the room, replanted stray hairs and smoothed out her skirt. She stood facing the door, trying to keep a steady head, though the hand holding her cane was visibly trembling.

Jeff's voice was calm. The exchange of conversation outside was slow at first, in contrast with Mandy's sprinting heart.

A squeal from Julie.

A gasp from Ma.

Voices raised.

Footsteps pounded up the stairs.

Julie was first through the door. She froze in place, mouth agape. Ma followed, her shock equally apparent.

At long last, the wait was over.

"I made it home, Ma."

Julie dashed for her big sister and they fell into a firm embrace. Ma moved slower, still numb from the shock. Then the three women stood holding each other, shedding tears of joy coupled with those of painful memories.

"Mandy, this is too impossible to believe," Ma said. "A young man named Jim Fletcher told us you stayed behind at that way station. Then it was burned out. There were three bodies."

"I know, and I tried to get home, so many times. And a letter was sent but never arrived. There was always something to prevent me from getting here."

"And we want to hear every second of your story," Julie said, hugging her sister again. "Where have you been? What've you been doing? Who were you with?"

"Let her catch her breath, for heaven's sake," Jeff scolded his blond-haired, blue-eyed twin, whom he considered the impulsive one.

Ma couldn't take her eyes from Mandy's. "I cannot believe I'm beholding my little girl again. If only your Pa could have seen you back safe and—"

She threw a glance at Jeffrey and queried him with her eyes.

He nodded.

"And about...?"

Again, he nodded.

Ma's gaze returned to Mandy, searching for a reaction to the news, and finding fresh pain in her eyes.

Ma and her three children huddled close and mourned anew the loss of the strong and loyal husband and father, James Berringer.

When they dried their tears, Ma and her girls sat on the couch while Jeffrey sat on the coffee table facing them. Ma asked the question haunting all of them. "Mandy, *where were you?*"

She drew in a long breath. Memories flooded in. It seemed ages ago since she had left; it seemed like yesterday. She spoke of the Indian boy who wandered into the stage stop and the warriors who found her with him.

"And those Indians held you captive?" Julie inquired with excitement.

"Not once they learned what really happened." She related how she met Dakota and sustained her injury. She told them of Dakota's attempt to send them a letter, the smallpox and the breakup of the tribe.

"How'd you get along with only one person to speak

168

English with?" Julie asked. "I'd go crazy."

Jeff said, "The *Indians* would have gone crazy if *you* were the one stuck there."

"I eventually learned their language pretty well, especially during the epidemic. And some sign language, too."

"From this Dakota fella?" Julie asked.

Mandy nodded, her expression reflecting a certain rapture Ma had never seen before. She sat back and studied her daughter from under a raised brow.

"I could be mistaken, honey, but I get the distinct impression that 'this Dakota fella' came to mean something to you."

Mandy smiled. "You know me so well, Ma. He came to mean a great deal to me, and I to him."

She explained how they headed for Denver but the snowstorm precluded any travel north from Colorado City. "So we decided to go to the mountains and wait it out in a cabin he had built there."

Ma's disconcerting gaze did not escape Mandy.

"I know what you're thinking, Ma, but you need to know that before we went to the cabin…" She looked into each of their waiting expressions. "…we were married."

Mandy felt the weight of six eyes bearing down on her. "I really love him."

Ma let out a breath. "Well, I always looked forward to the day you'd tell me you found the right man, Mandy. But forgive me if I'm a little stunned by the announcement."

"*Stunned* seems to be the sole order on the menu today."

Mandy answered their questions but did not reveal all of what happened. Every time she started to tell them about Baby Gregg, her voice was lost to her. After all she had learned, and with all the sorrow saturating her being, she was unable to relive the loss of her baby, too. She explained merely that she had taken ill at the cabin and was unable to travel.

Nor did she tell them about the day she spent with Headless Jack and how his life ended.

"I'm looking forward to meeting this husband of yours," Ma said. "It's obvious he has won your heart, and he is a welcome addition to this family—as are *you*." She hugged her daughter.

"I only wish Pa could've met Dakota. But as much as I

miss him, I'm especially glad now that he went to Kansas. I hope he gets to see his father before it's too late, like it was for me."

Exhausted from the physical and emotional strain of the day, Mandy excused herself to go upstairs and lie down. Her mother and siblings again embraced her and expressed their utter disbelief, and relief, at her homecoming.

"We'll hold off on telling anyone about you until tomorrow," Ma said. "After you're rested, we'll have supper. George will be home by then."

Mandy tried hard not to show her dejection at the thought of another man in Pa's house, his place in this family, his place in Ma's bed. She would have to try to accept Ma's new husband, just as they would have to accept hers.

Her bedroom, like the rest of the house, remained unchanged. The four-poster bed, dresser and mirror were arranged as they had always been. The same porcelain pitcher and basin rested on the washstand. Her wooden jewelry box, glass vase and brass candle holder set in their places atop the lace doily on her dresser. The lavender drapes hung clean and wrinkle-free, framing the window that overlooked the street.

She removed her dusty traveling dress and lay down exhausted on her bed. The distant sound of voices awakened her some time later.

"Say that again!" came a deep male voice from the living room.

Ma's soft voice responded in words Mandy could not make out, but she knew how the conversation would go.

"She's *alive!* She's here now? Ardith, that's incredible! But, *how*? Where's she been all this time?"

After that she could only hear muffled sounds, and full wakefulness eluded her until Julie was at her side nudging her shoulder and calling her name.

"I'm sorry to wake you, but it's nearly eight thirty. Do you want supper, or should we let you sleep through the night? Ma says it's up to you, but I know she's anxious for you to meet George. Think you can make it?"

Her eyes not quite focused, Mandy answered, "I'll make it." For Ma's sake, she'd make it.

She steadied herself at the bedside. "Are any of my clothes still here? If not, I've got some packed—" She

170

suddenly remembered her horse. "Oh no! I forgot about Lady! I left her tied out there without a drop of water or a bite of food."

"Don't worry. Jeff put her up out back, curried her down, fed and watered her and tucked her in for the night. She's a beautiful animal, Mandy. A palomino, the kind of horse you always loved."

As she changed into one of the dresses that still hung in her closet, she told her sister about how Dakota had brought her gifts from the council he attended, including Lady. "He's got a palomino stallion named Chief."

"Hey, that reminds me. You said Dakota is the son of a chief. I guess that makes you a princess, right? Wow, just think—my sister, a princess!"

"Sorry, Julie, but it doesn't work that way. Chiefs aren't bluebloods, they're elected to a council, at least in Dakota's tribe. I'm no more a princess for marrying a chief's son than you would be if you married the mayor's son."

"Well, I say you're a princess, and that's that."

Mandy shook her head. Jeffrey seemed to have matured a great deal since she saw him last. Julie seemed the same flighty young girl she'd always been. Blue Flower Woman was the same age as Julie, yet was chosen to be the wife of an infamous warrior. The differences between the two were infinite. But her sister meant the world to her, especially after missing her for so long.

Julie filled the washing basin, and Mandy splashed the cold water on her face. Wanting to delay the inevitable, she took longer than necessary to dry off. Then, without much cheer inside, she went downstairs.

The stocky, balding man stood smiling as she rounded the corner from the stairwell into the living room.

"So, you're Mandy! You don't know how happy I am to meet you."

He opened his arms wide, but she felt too uncomfortable to move toward him. Sensing this, he put out his hand, and she shook it.

"I am pleased to meet you, too."

"We waited supper for you, Mandy," Ma said. "You two can get acquainted while we eat."

Ma seemed relieved and happy, so the pleasantries were worth the effort.

171

George sat in Pa's place at the head of the rectangular table. Mandy resumed her place kitty-corner to his left. Everyone else was seated in their traditional arrangement at the table—Julie sitting at Mandy's left, Jeff across from his twin, and Ma sitting opposite the head. Gregg's place, which had always been across from Mandy back in Pennsylvania, still left a noticeable void.

"Shall we pray?" George said, and they all held hands. Aside from thanking God for the food, he offered thanks for Mandy's safe return and for seeing them all through the trials of the last two years. He asked the Lord to smooth the way for an edifying reunion with others who had missed Mandy. She might have been impressed were it not for the fact he not once mentioned Dakota.

Throughout supper she revealed more about her husband, his Indian family and her life with them. George often changed the subject, asking how Colorado City looked these days, and which of her friends she was the most anxious to see.

During dessert the subject of her ankle was raised again, and George suggested she have a doctor examine it.

"A doctor did look at it. He said I was lucky to still have it attached, though the joint remains unstable. I'll probably never be able to go without a cane. The pain is always with me, but I've learned to bear it. And to prove just how truly independent I am, I'll serve us all another round of coffee." She got up and went to the kitchen.

Laying a hand on the counter next to the stove, she hung her head and sighed. The forced congeniality with George left her emotionally drained and yearning for her father. She could not believe he was gone. She had seen his grave, and there was a man in his place at the supper table who called her mother "darling." But she wished it was all a mistake, like her death and her grave. If Dakota were only here, at least she'd have the comfort of his arms.

The clatter of dishes as Julie gathered them from the table arrested her thoughts. She picked up the coffeepot, and as she reentered the dining room, she overheard George speak in a low voice.

"You all know, don't you, that that 'breed will never show. I'm just glad no children were born of that marriage. All we'd need is a half-breed's kid running around here."

172

"George!" Jeff warned sharply, seeing Mandy in the doorway.

The coffeepot shook in her hand. Setting it on the buffet, she hobbled speedily out of the dining room, through the parlor and up the stairs. Once in her room, she threw herself on her bed and wept.

After a few minutes she heard a faint rap on her door, but she made no answer. The door creaked opened and Ma entered, closing it gently behind her. She crossed the moonbeam-lit room and sat at the bottom of the bed.

"Was it a boy or a girl?"

Mandy lifted her head, studying her mother's wise and empathetic face.

"What I saw in your eyes wasn't anger, honey. I saw the pain of great loss. A kind of loss I have known, too, even though you and Gregg were both full grown when I lost you."

Mandy raised herself up and accepted the handkerchief her mother offered. New tears replaced the ones she wiped away.

"A boy. And he was *so beautiful*, Ma. He had soft brown hair that was just beginning to lighten. He had such a cherub face and he smiled nearly all the time. He'd laugh with his whole body when Dakota would rub his bearded face in his belly. But he had a hole between the chambers of his heart. That doctor I spoke of knew what it was, and told us he wouldn't live past six months of age." Her eyes lowered. "He didn't even make it that long."

Ma slid closer and placed her arm across her daughter's shoulder. "I'm so very sorry, honey."

"I wanted to tell you earlier. I tried to, but after all I learned today, I just couldn't bear to talk about my son's death."

"I understand. And I'm sorry about George's outspokenness. His family has a rather poor history with Indians, I'm afraid. That doesn't excuse what he said, though, and I wish he wouldn't speak out so without thinking."

"He speaks exactly what he's thinking, and what many people will think. Oh, how I wish Dakota were here with me now!"

"I'm sure you must, honey."

Mandy took her mother's hand and looked deeply into her

173

blue eyes. "Ma, we named him Gregg. It was Dakota's idea."

Ma's eyes sparkled, and a bittersweet smile crossed her face. "He sounds like quite a man."

Mandy dried her eyes as Ma rose to leave. She turned at the door. "Will you be coming back down?"

"In a few minutes." As the door opened, Mandy called, "Ma?"

She turned.

"There's bound to be talk about...you know...half-breeds and the son of a half-breed. I'm sorry if the family suffers because of it."

Ma looked upon her daughter with tenderness. "This family suffers because of the baby's loss, not his lineage. My son-in-law is obviously a man of honor who has a heart full of love for my daughter. Through him I have a grandson, who lives in heaven right now, and whom I am proud to claim as my own flesh and blood. And I know without question that his grandfather, who is with him now, feels the same way."

Mandy's heart was never more full of love for her mother than at that moment.

CHAPTER 26

*M*andy Berringer's return was the talk of the town. She spent much of the following weeks getting reacquainted with old friends and making new ones. Some of the rumors that floated back to her regarding her adventures were far more incredulous than any she had related. The *Rocky Mountain News* carried a feature article on her RETURN FROM THE GRAVE! She expressed her gratitude to Mr. Byers, the editor, for quoting her accurately and treating the events of her account with sensitivity.

Her headstone was removed and smashed to bits with axes by Jeff and Julie in celebration of their sister's resurrection. The body in the grave was exhumed, and as far as examiners could tell, Dakota's theory about it being an Indian youth was probably correct. It was reburied in the county cemetery.

Despite the strained atmosphere George's presence aroused, Mandy found that he truly was as good to Ma as Jeff had said. She may have even liked him had it not been for his bigotry toward the red man.

George's two sisters and a cousin were massacred by Sioux in Minnesota, and he was unable to see any Indian as anything but a savage. His loathing of them hadn't surfaced until Mandy presented the problem. He did agree to give Dakota the benefit of the doubt since Mandy spoke so highly of him and since he was, after all, half-white and had been raised for the most part in white society. George felt he was being very open minded to think thus.

His other great flaw was his propensity to speak his mind regardless of what impact his words may have on people. He had, however, apologized sincerely to Mandy for his remarks that first evening before he knew of her child.

She invited old friends over for tea and talk, learning in the process which ones were in reality true friends. They accepted her, her husband and the child she had borne without disputing background. There were others who made no effort to hide their contempt. Outwardly she tried to return their scorn with civility, but inside was bruised.

Her good friend Gretchen was now married to Harvey

Arlen, a tailor, and was the mother of a four-month-old girl. She visited almost daily, and Mandy soon knew of every birth, death, marriage, business opening and closing, arrival and departure of residents, and new and broken relationship that had taken place in the past two years. The most disturbing news was that of her former best friend, Mercy Robinson, who never came to see her nor returned her messages.

"I'm afraid you've lost her, Mandy," Gretchen said. "She's come to hate Indians these past couple of years because of all the hardship they've caused out here. She thinks you should've escaped from that village, or even killed yourself. She told me she'd have nothing to do with any woman who'd willingly join with an Indian or half-breed. Not even if that woman is you."

Mandy had expected to face the prejudice of certain self-righteous citizens, but Mercy's rejection wounded her deeply. The two had been the closest of friends since the day they met in church on the first Sunday after Mandy arrived in Denver six years earlier.

"Well, Gretchen, I'm glad at least you're the same sweet, lovable, brilliant and generous person you always were."

"Don't forget beautiful!"

The two friends laughed and reminisced further over tea. Esther, Gretchen's baby, grew hungry and Gretchen nursed her. A deep longing for that maternal bond was rekindled within Mandy as she watched the infant contentedly nurse, the tiny hand reaching upward and grasping her mother's hair. Dakota had been right when he described that bond as powerful.

For the first time since Baby Gregg died, the thought of having another child no longer seemed inconceivable. Mandy was beginning to realize that having and loving other children was not replacing Gregg, nor betraying him.

Gretchen finished nursing, and Mandy took the child and held her on her shoulder. "Be careful. She has a habit of—"

Gretchen's face screwed up as she watched her daughter upchuck down the back of Mandy's dress.

"Sorry," she squeaked as she finished buttoning her blouse.

"I don't mind a bit."

As the women walked to Mandy's front gate, Mercy Robinson was passing.

176

"Mercy!" Mandy called and stepped into the road. "I've tried to get in touch with you. You knew I was back, didn't you?"

Mercy appeared uncomfortable at this chance meeting, and her expression turned cold. "The whole town knows about the *princess* in our midst."

Her words stung. "I never claimed to be a princess. That's Julie talking. I really am glad to see you. I've missed you."

"You look none the worse for wear, Mandy, considering. But really, you need to get rid of that half-human buck you took up with and get on with your life." She turned her attention to Gretchen. "Surely you've been encouraging her likewise?"

"'Fraid not, Mercy."

She shrugged. "Suit yourselves." She turned and walked away, leaving Mandy stunned and dispirited.

After the town's Fourth of July celebration, Jeffrey left for the Midwest to look into several law schools. He had long ago decided to become an attorney, and thanks to George's successful freight business, he would be able to attend the university of his choosing without putting Ma into heavy debt. Mr. Samuels had left the sign above the door of his law office as it was—SAMUELS & BERRINGER—as a promise to Jeffrey that there would be a place for him when he finished his schooling. Jeff wanted to return to Denver after completing his education, but wasn't entirely sure the town would still be on the map.

Mandy missed him dearly, for she had just gotten reacquainted with him and now he was off to prepare for a new life. Julie noticed how blue her sister was feeling and suggested a stroll around the block to chat and lift her spirits.

"Julie, what ever happened to Jim Fletcher? Did he stay around long?"

"For a few weeks. He was wonderful, Mandy, helping all of us get through your loss. He went on to California then, much to my regret. I wrote him after Pa died, and he wrote back the most heartfelt sentiments. I still have the letter at home if you'd like to read it."

"Do I detect a note of heartfelt sentiments of your own, little sis?"

Her cheeks reddened. "I really hated to see him go. You

177

really must write him. He felt just awful about leaving you behind at that station."

"I'll write him the minute we get home. I've already written Cassie and the other relatives back East. I regret how the situation caused so much heartache for so many people."

"It all started with you doing a good deed for a little boy. And there's no sense dwelling on the might've-beens, as Gregg used to say."

On the following Sunday, thirty members of Mandy's church congregation traveled a few miles west of town for a picnic and games. Sack races, pie-tasting (and then eating) contests, relays and other rivalries played out under the hot summer sun. Mandy tucked her hair into her sunbonnet and enjoyed the feel of the occasional breeze on her neck. She walked among the thirsty competitors, refilling their rapidly emptying glasses with lemonade.

The big finale was a tug-of-war among all the males over eight years of age. It took a full twelve minutes of muscle-straining, heel-digging, jaw-clenching, palm-ripping effort before the red team finally pulled the blue team's flag across the marker.

Mandy applauded the winners, yet felt sorry for their unnecessary exertion. If Dakota were here, this would've been over quick.

Just as the contest ended and all the men collapsed in exhaustion, a woman screamed. As each person looked in the direction she pointed, gasps escaped them one by one.

The crowd's clamorous attention toward the struggling men had allowed a group of uninvited guests to approach unnoticed.

Seven Indians, some with bows and some with rifles drawn, were closing in a half-circle around the members of the congregation. Their sinister dark eyes measured the crowd.

By their dress and hair and weapons Mandy surmised that three were Arapaho, two were Cheyenne, and two were Sioux. The paint on their faces and horses was an announcement of war. Scalps hung from their saddles and lances. There was no question they had come to add more.

The Indians urged their mounts forward, herding their captives into a tighter circle. A man next to Mandy said, "How foolish of us to let our guard down so completely and be

178

separated from our guns!"

Another man stated, "We can still take these savages. There's only seven of 'em."

"I wouldn't do anything just yet, Mr. Packard," Mandy whispered, her hammering heart nearly in her throat. "You make any sudden moves and I assure you we're all dead."

"Well, I'm not going to stand for this. I have friends in the territorial legislature and they'll back up whatever we do here."

"Be quiet!" she retorted.

"Sure, listen to you! You're probably going to run off with them like you did the last time. My brother-in-law is a colonel in the army, and he'll track you all down."

"Shut up, Packard," said another man nearby, "before you get us all killed!"

Mandy hoped she was wrong and that after some minor harassing the Indians would leave. But that hope died quickly.

Three of the warriors slid off their horses while the mounted ones took aim with rifles. There was no doubt in her mind that despite their fewer numbers they intended to massacre this crowd. Any man, woman or child who moved to defend another would be the first to die.

Mandy shouted a word in Arapaho, then worked her way through the crowd using her cane as leverage when necessary. Packard slithered forward behind her.

She stopped in front of the Arapaho leader. "Please do not do this," she pleaded in his tongue, hoping the language would come back to her adequately enough to speak intelligently.

The Indians showed surprise at the words of the white woman. The four still on horseback continued to observe every motion of the crowd while the Arapaho leader confronted Mandy.

"How is it that you speak the tongue of my people?" The warrior's voice was not curious; it was demanding. His deadly visage had not changed.

"My husband is half-Arapaho."

His eyes surveyed the crowd.

"He is not here now. He is at the Medicine Lodge reservation to see his father who is dying." It couldn't hurt to drop a name. "His father is Chief Wild Eagle of the Southern Arapaho."

The warrior canted his head back and peered through

disbelieving eyes. He turned to his comrades for a discussion in Cheyenne. The men of the congregation began a discussion of their own behind Mandy.

"We can't just stand around doing nothing."

Mandy half-turned her head and whispered, "Please don't do anything yet."

Packard said, "She's the last person we oughta listen to. I say we—"

An elbow in the ribs from the preacher cut him off.

The brave turned around. "Silence!"

The crowd seemed to know what he meant. They stilled.

He moved to stand before Mandy. "By what name is your husband called?"

"He is called Dakota."

The braves looked at one another, shaking their heads.

"You lie, woman!" the leader growled. "We have heard of Wild Eagle, and he has a son, but he is not called Dakota."

Mandy fought crushing fear just to keep her eyes fixed on his. She must quickly earn his respect to even be allowed to continue.

"You are speaking of Thunder Cloud. He is the half-brother of my husband."

Another brief conference. One brave nodded. Another scrutinized Mandy's form, taking notice of the strands of hair straying from her bonnet and the cane she leaned on. Something registered in his eyes. He began to speak loudly, pointing and signing with enlivened gestures.

"I say we take 'em *now* while they're off guard," Packard urged.

"Somebody *shut him up!*" Mandy ordered through clenched teeth. "Don't think for one second that their guard is down."

"She's in it with 'em," Packard insisted. "My nephew is a judge and he'll show you no mercy for this, you squaw traitor!"

Two of the Arapaho glowered at the loud-mouthed man, then started for him.

"He is not a wise man," Mandy blurted out as they darted past her. She was careful not to touch them, having learned her lesson the day she grabbed Thunder Cloud's armband when he set out to avenge the massacre of the Cheyenne. "But must he die for it?"

The lead brave stopped and turned to her. His eyes burned into hers. Her heart thundered beneath her blouse. The frightful sobs of Ma, Julie and the other women filled her ears.

The warrior drew his knife and raised it to the side of her face, the bright sun reflecting a blinding glare into her eyes. The sobs around her became strangled gasps.

Ma screamed. "No! Mandy!"

Two churchmen started to rush toward her but were stopped by the points of knives in their own throats. Mandy could no longer keep up a facade of courage as cold panic gripped her. She shut her eyes and drew in her breath.

Cold metal glided across her jaw. She breathed a final prayer.

Please, God, give Dakota the strength to endure.

The knife slid beneath her ear. She felt a sharp tug on her bonnet and waited to feel the cutting pain in her neck and the warm flow of her blood.

Neither came.

With trepidation, she opened her eyes. The brave had not taken his eyes from hers. She risked a downward glance. The tie of her bonnet dangled from one side, the bow still intact.

He yanked her bonnet off and cast it to the ground. With obvious pleasure he watched her yellow hair tumble past her shoulders, the sunlight dancing upon it. His fingers captured a lock of soft strands, fondled the ends, then groped them by the handful with undisguised desire.

He pulled her by the hair, drawing her close. They stood toe-to-toe. She again forced her eyes to lift to his.

"By what name are you called?"

"M..." Her parched mouth could barely form the word. "Mandy."

He shook his head. "By what name are you called by the Arapaho?"

"I...am called...Woman Shot With Sun's Arrow."

He stared at her for a long moment, then released her hair.

"I am disappointed. I would have been the envy of many warriors to have had such a scalp hanging from my lance."

She couldn't make out his meaning. Did he intend to take her alive? What about the others?

"We have heard the story Thunder Cloud has passed on to the Plains tribes about the woman with sun-colored hair who risked her life to save our people from the vicious white man who removes heads. It is said she also cared for the tribe when the white man's disease claimed their village, and defended the wife of Wild Eagle from a vexing tribesman with her walking stick." He glimpsed her cane, then her hair. "You are this woman?"

Mandy stood mutely before him.

Others, too, will hear of the boldness of the white woman with the yellow hair who gave of herself more than once to save our people.

Thunder Cloud had spoken those words at their parting, but she could not conceive of it becoming a widespread tale.

Dumbfounded by the unforeseen *in absentia* intervention of her brother-in-law, she slowly nodded. "I am."

"You are a woman of great courage. You spared the lives of my people in Wild Eagle's village." His eyes took in the crowd. "We will therefore spare your life, and the lives of those in your village."

If not for her cane, she would have collapsed.

"I say we move in *now!*" Packard whispered. "She's probably bargaining with these savages, trying to save her own scalp."

"Don't move or say another word," Harv Arlen demanded, "or we're letting them have you, Packard."

"I do not know by what name *you* are called," Mandy said to the warrior.

"I am called Broken Timber." His countenance softened. "Friend of Woman Shot With Sun's Arrow."

He reached out and fondled shimmering strands of the golden hair that enchanted him so. They exchanged a long look, then Broken Timber turned quickly, went to his horse and swung up. The other braves followed suit.

Packard rushed forward, grabbed Mandy's arm and spun her hard. He opened his mouth, but never got the chance to utter his curses.

A whishing sound from the backs of the ponies drew all eyes toward them. Seven Indians had arrows drawn and notched in their bowstrings. All of the arrowheads were aimed directly at Packard's chest.

His jaw fell. His face blanched.

"I suggest you let go of me, Mr. Packard."

He instantly released her, but otherwise could not move.

"If I were you," Mandy warned, "I'd move away *reeeeal* slow-like. Because one word from me, and my pals here—the ones with the arrows?—will have you looking like a porcupine inside of a second." She leaned closer. "You see, I, too, have friends in high places."

The man's eyes rolled back and he dropped to the ground in a swoon.

When the Indians left, Mandy's trembling hand reached for Harv's arm for support. Her family and all the others gathered around her.

"What'd they say?"

"What'd *you* say?"

"What just happened?"

"They looked like they were gonna kill us!"

All she told the congregation was that it turned out those Indians held her brother-in-law in high regard. And that relationship had just saved all of their lives.

She also told them these warriors would not bother the citizens of Denver anymore. But others would, and they must remain vigilant.

Riding home in the wagon, Mandy felt the warmth of the setting sun on her back. Its rays, shining their impartial light throughout the territory, would know where Dakota was at this very moment. She wished they would reveal their secret to her. She wished they would tell her he was nearly home.

* * *

Saddle and bridle secured, Dakota swung onto his horse and guided him northwest. He was going home. Home was now a place he had never even set foot in, but it was where his wife was. His heart. His future.

He made good time to the Santa Fe Trail where he turned west. Although it was not the most direct route, it was the safest, being well traveled by freighters, emigrants and the military. There was safety in numbers. At the Kansas-Colorado border he met up with a six-man unit of cavalry heading for Fort Lyon.

Within a few miles of the fort, a sharp crack rang out behind them, and a soldier was felled. Before the men had a chance to react, another shot sounded. The riders dug their heels into their mounts, but an Apache war party gained on them, firing their rifles adeptly from the backs of their ponies and dropping the soldiers one by one.

The palomino, breathing hard through flared nostrils, outran the ponies but could not outrun the lead bullets piercing the air around him.

One struck Dakota.

He jerked to the side, hit the ground hard and rolled several times. Lying in the dust, he fought to remain conscious. Incredible pain shot down his right arm. Though sensing little else of what was going on around him, he was aware of the warm flow of his lifeblood spurting into his shredded buckskin sleeve and spilling onto the thirsty ground. He tried to move but could not.

The sound and vibration of hoof beats surrounded him. A brave came to his side with knife in hand. He felt the cold metal press against his forehead. The shrill cry of a victorious Apache warrior filled his head.

As his senses faded into oblivion, he conceived a final petition.

Oh, God, please...take care of Mandy.

"Oh, Ma, what shall I wear today?" Mandy picked through the dresses in her closet. "Today makes four weeks exactly, and I know he'll be here."

Every day that week Mandy had dressed herself up in her finest, most feminine frocks, awaiting her husband's return. She didn't know which moment of which day he'd show, so she had herself looking her best from awakening to retiring.

"How about this pretty bright yellow one, dear?"

"I hate that dress. It makes me look like a banana."

"Don't be ridiculous, Mandy."

"I guess I'll settle for this pale blue one." She slipped it on and studied herself from all sides in the mirror. The initialed comb Dakota made at Christmas adorned her hair.

"Heavens, Ma, I feel like a schoolgirl preparing to go courtin' my first beau. I just know he's coming today. Today makes four weeks exactly."

"You said that already."

Mandy could hardly eat, her nervous stomach unable to endure the work of digestion. Every noise outside sent her to the door. The late afternoon found her sitting on the porch swing, peering longingly down the street. At midnight Ma encouraged her to go to bed. They would leave a light burning in the front window.

As the empty days came and went, Mandy's concerns deepened. There were no letters, no wires, no word. He'd know how worried she'd be and get in touch if he could. She yearned for the moment he would burst through the front door, rush to her waiting arms, kiss her passionately right in front of everyone and say, "I'm so sorry, Mandy. I knew you'd be worried, but…" and explain away his absence and her fears.

Two weeks overdue. Ma and Julie offered reasonable excuses for such a delay. George made inferences that things might work out for the best if Dakota never did return.

She sent wires to Fort Larned. No, they had no information on her husband. And no, they could not spare any men to go to the reservation and investigate.

August's first week slipped by.

One evening at supper she said, "I met a family in town today. A Negro man by the name of Elijah Washington, his wife and four children. They've been here two years trying to make a go of running a dry goods store, but decided to cut their losses and head back East."

"That's too bad," George said, shaking his head. "But it's a common occurrence here these days, I'm afraid."

"Anyway, they're heading south to Pueblo, then east. They'll be passing through Fort Larned."

"Really?" Julie asked. "They could take a message there and have it sent down to the reservation for you. Did you ask them to?"

"No, I didn't ask them to take another message." She looked around at the faces at the table. "I asked them to take *me.*"

"Mandy, no!" Ma exclaimed. "I won't let you go."

"I have to find out what's happened. You must understand."

"I understand how heart rending this is for you, but you can't go off—"

"On a wild goose chase," George broke in.

"I don't agree, George. I believe Dakota really loves her and would come if he could. But Mandy," she added, turning to her daughter, "this isn't the answer."

Julie said, "He's probably just held up some place where there's no telegraph office. Or maybe he did send a letter that never got through, just like when he wrote us about you."

"If he ever really did write," George murmured.

"Mandy, you've got to give him more time," Ma insisted.

"He's three weeks late and well aware of what this silence would do to me. His father went years without knowing what happened to him and his mother, and it tormented him. He would do *whatever* it took to get in touch. I've *got* to find out what's happened to him, even if..." She could not finish the thought.

"And just how do you expect to finance this trip?" George asked.

"The Washingtons have been kind enough to not charge me for riding along with them. I'm sure there's more than enough money to cover my other expenses in that account Pa started for me."

Ma and Julie exchanged discomfited glances. Ma explained, "Honey, after your pa died, I used that money on necessities. I'm afraid there's nothing left."

The news pressed heavily on Mandy. She had counted on that money, but told her mother, "That's okay, Ma. I'm glad it was there when you needed it."

"Well, I guess that settles the issue," George stated.

Ma did not like the look on her daughter's face. "Mandy, what are you thinking?"

"I only need money enough to get as far as Colorado City where my name is on Dakota's bank account. I'll find a way to get that far."

"Mandy," Ma said, "please consider the anxiety you'd be bringing on this family."

"Believe me, Ma, for that reason, as well as all the others you and Julie have mentioned, I've waited as long as I have." She looked deep into her mother's troubled eyes. "Tell me something, Ma. If you hadn't received word of my death, and I had just disappeared from that stage station, how long would you and Pa have sat at home and just waited for me to show up?"

Ma's eyes lowered. A prolonged silence followed.

Finally, Ma said, "George, I want to pay Mandy the money I took from her account."

"You can't be serious, Ardith!"

"She's going, George. With or without our help, she *will* go. If not with our blessing exactly, at least I want it to be with our help."

The next morning while George went to the Colorado National Bank, Mandy went to her father's grave. For several silent minutes she stared at the patch of long grass beneath which lay the man she loved and missed so much.

"The arrow that flieth by day…" she said softly. "I think it has found its mark, Pa. It has buried itself in the deepest reaches of my heart, and left me precious little to hope for."

After a few more minutes of silent prayer, she returned home to collect her things, and the family drove to town in the buggy.

Elijah Washington loaded Mandy's brocade satchel into the back of his Conestoga. Her belongings included some travel dresses, her blue cloak, her Bible, Longfellow's

Evangeline, and the Remington .44. She would be sharing the back of the wagon with three children, ages four to twelve. Elijah's wife, Charlene, carried their eight-month-old daughter in her arms on the wagon seat next to her husband.

Ma hugged her daughter, tears in her eyes. "Do you have any idea how hard it is for me to let you go again after what happened the last time?"

"I think I do, Ma. And I thank you for understanding enough to help me go."

George stepped next to her and touched her arm. "I have only had your happiness in mind, Mandy. I know you probably don't believe that." He kissed her forehead. "And remember, if you ever get stuck or run out of money, you wire me from anywhere, and I'll send you the money for a stage home." He locked his eyes onto hers. "But *only* for a stage home."

She understood, and nodded in agreement.

As George assisted her into the wagon, a voice from behind called, "Going looking for your man, are you, Mandy?" It was K.C., her wagonmate on her trip from Colorado City. How quickly the news of her departure had spread.

"I warned you he was no different, didn't I?" the painted lips asked. "You're on a fool's mission."

Mandy climbed into the wagon without offering any defense to the taunting fallen angel. She waved good-bye to her family and friends who stood watching her leave, her heart aching for her mother.

The trip was too slow for Mandy's restless soul. But the Washingtons were friendly and generous, and their singing along the way made for lively entertainment. They were cheerful despite their misfortunes of recent years. "The Lawd giveth and the Lawd taketh away," Elijah would say. "Blessed be the name of the Lawd!"

They stopped in small towns and at ranches along the route where Mandy asked if anyone had seen a man who fit Dakota's description. None had. She made rounds of the businesses in Colorado City. No one had seen him.

They trekked south through the hot August days. Stopping in Pueblo for provisions, she wired her family that she was safe. Each proprietor there gave the same response to her query: "Sorry, haven't seen him."

Until a young man at a blacksmith shop offered a spark of

hope.

"Yeah, just a couple of hours ago a man was here who *sorta* fit that description. Rode a palomino, too, but—"

"Oh, it *must* be him! Did he give his name?"

"We never did get around to names. But ma'am, I don't think he's the one you're looking for."

"Why not?"

"Because you left something out of your otherwise detailed description that I don't think you'd be likely to if you had this fella in mind."

Her eyes questioned him.

"You see, the man who was here this morning…was missing an arm."

Mandy's spirits fell.

For a brief moment, she had been so sure…

CHAPTER 28

*D*akota rode northeast into the plains, but knew not where his future lay. Once he was headed for Denver, but not now. Perhaps the cabin. No, she'd find him there. He did not want to be found.

He passed wagons of argonauts and emigrants headed in both directions on the trail. Some had stopped him and asked about the weather ahead, or how far to the next town. One wagon had a broken axle, and he helped the man with the repairs as best he could.

He hailed a Negro couple who waved at him as their Conestoga passed, unaware of the three children sleeping in the back and the white woman traveling with them reading the melancholic words of her favorite poet:

Art thou so near unto me, and yet I cannot behold thee?
Art thou so near unto me, and yet thy voice does not reach me?
When shall these eyes behold, these arms be folded about thee?

As he trotted along the flat, dry road without a destination, he retraced in his mind the events of the past several weeks—events that changed his life forever.

* * *

He awoke on a cot next to a white plaster wall. His sheets were drenched with sweat. Fever had raged for many days. He felt a searing pain in his right arm all the way down to his fingertips. He didn't remain conscious long.

Each time he came around, his mind cleared a little more and he realized he was in an army hospital ward. A steward informed him he was at Fort Lyon and recounted for him the Apache attack. Only two of the seven men made it back alive to the fort that day, and only because a platoon dispatched from the fort had come upon them and chased the Indians off while they were in the process of scalping. Dakota's was to be the next. The warrior's knife was in place at Dakota's head, ready to slice, when a well-aimed bullet from a cavalryman's Colt robbed the savage of his victory. A tourniquet was applied to Dakota's profusely bleeding arm, and he was immediately brought to the fort. The palomino was found and secured, too.

For five days he remained either unconscious or delusional. Now his mind was clearing, but his body was profoundly weak.

A doctor making ward rounds stopped at the bottom of Dakota's cot. "Welcome back. We weren't at all sure you were ever going to make it back."

Dakota moistened his parched lips. His voice was barely above a whisper as he made the effort to speak. "Takes more than a piece of Apache lead to keep a good man down."

"Ah-ha! A man with a sense of humor." He moved to his patient's bedside. "You're going to need it now that you're well enough to eat the food here."

Dakota's mind was filled with more serious concerns. "Doc, my wife is expecting me and will be sorely worried. You've got to get word to her. Her name is Mandy Starbuck, and you can reach her in care of attorney James Berringer in Denver."

"Sure thing, John." He wrote the information on a piece of paper.

"You know my name?"

"A few of the shopkeepers here in the fort recognized you from your past visits here. There seems to be some discrepancy about your name, though. Some say you go by the name Dakota."

"Either will do."

The middle-aged yet still freckled physician with strawberry-blond hair introduced himself as Major Coleman McDonald. He pulled a three-legged stool over to Dakota's cot. "Now, tell me how you're feeling."

"Well, considering what they tell me I've been through, I guess I shouldn't complain. But since you asked, my arm's killin' me, Doc."

The surgeon hesitated. "Which one?"

"My right one—the one that took the bullet, remember?" The corners of his mouth crooked up. "They did teach you right from left in medical college, didn't they?"

"I was sick a lot. Missed some classes."

"So, do you medicine men have any painkillers or do I

have to whip up some of my Indian grandmother's potions?"

"You've been receiving laudanum, and you can continue to get it as you need it. Just let the steward know." His eyes cast down and he bit his lower lip. "There's something I need to tell you. It's about your arm."

Dakota studied the Irishman's sober expression. A gnawing sensation gripped his stomach. "It looks that bad?"

"Starbuck, I hate to have to tell you this…but it's gone."

"What's gone?"

"Your right arm. I had to amputate it."

The words struck with the force of a tornado leveling a feeble shanty. His mind shunned what his ears just heard.

"You…you're kidding, right, Doc? That warped Irish humor?"

The surgeon looked at him sympathetically and slowly shook his head.

Dakota cast his eyes down to his arm, for he knew it was there, but the sheet covered him up to his shoulders.

"But Doc, it hurts. My whole arm, even my fingers. It hurts a lot, and it burns."

"They're called ghost pains. It's a common reaction."

The doctor spoke as if he was serious. Dakota refused to believe it. He looked at his arm again. He reached across his chest, and with a quaking left hand took hold of the end of the sheet and slowly peeled it back.

Eight inches below his shoulder a bulky white bandage was wrapped around what was now the end of his arm.

Horror seized him. He became tremulous, then frenzied. "*No! No!* Don't *do* this!"

Two stewards came running. The surgeon sent one for a sedative while he and the other fought to keep the patient down, his strength suddenly renewed through shock.

Dakota's rapidly pounding heart aided the sedative in its work. Within ten minutes he was controllable again, though still assaulted by the hideous sight of his missing arm.

"How could you do this to me?" he demanded of the one responsible.

"The bullet nicked an artery. You lost an enormous amount of blood out there. If those soldiers hadn't reached you the very minute they did, or hadn't the sense to tie off your arm, you'd have died lying in a pool of your own blood. With

192

the blood supply cut off to the rest of your arm, there was no way I could save it. Please believe that I did everything I could. It was either lose your arm or lose your life."

"My arms *are* my life! The work I do with my hands is my livelihood. I'm going to open my own blacksmi…"

No. The dream was now severed along with his arm.

"It will take time, but you will learn to get by. Your wife can help you—"

"No! Leave her out of this. And *don't* send that message."

"But—"

"I *forbid* it. *Do you understand?*"

Reluctantly, the doctor agreed.

With Dakota's refusal to speak further, the officer rose from the stool and went on to complete his rounds.

Dakota turned his face to the wall. What he just witnessed was inconceivable. Reprehensible. He had lost his arm, and felt as if he was losing his mind.

The sedative finally accomplished its task, and he drifted into a deep sleep.

After completing his ward rounds, Dr. McDonald returned to Dakota's cot and watched him as he slept. "I'm sorry, my friend," he whispered. "I truly am." As a man who also depended entirely on his hands to make his living and give him a sense of significance, he empathized with the Herculean task his patient now faced, and envied him not one bit.

In the days that followed, Dakota slept little, and when he did it was restlessly. The sensation of pain still plagued him.

The agony within was even greater, and he slipped deeper into depression. And Depression's companion was Anger, which grew until it consumed him. He'd always been exceptionally strong and capable. How could he do what he believed he was meant to do with only one arm? His *left* arm. How could he provide for his wife?

Mandy. How many times had she snuggled into his arms, telling him how safe they made her feel? How often had she squeezed them and called them exquisite?

His thoughts were interrupted when the doctor appeared at his cot. "I hear you're not eating much, Starbuck. You need to build up your strength."

He turned his head away.

The surgeon sat on the stool and began unwrapping the

193

bandages. "How's the stump feel?"

Dakota recoiled at the sound of the word. *Stump.*

"Starbuck, *talk* to me."

"I have nothing to say to the butcher who did this to me."

"I'm too thick-skinned to take that personally. So, tell me what you're thinking. I'm guessing it's about her. How you'll do for her? How she'll feel about you? These questions are not new to me. During the war I had to amputate more limbs than I care to recall, and the same fears arose in those men. You're not alone."

"Those other men—did any of them build their wives a cabin before they even knew her? Did they fashion a pair of crutches out of cottonwood when her ankle was crushed? With *two* strong arms I provided our food. I built a cradle for our son. I even delivered him myself with my *two* scared but sturdy hands." He paused and closed his eyes. "And then I dug his grave."

The doctor sat in silence.

"Could you see me doing *any* of those things now? What am I supposed to do *now?*"

"You'll learn to get along in a different manner." The surgeon's voice was not without compassion, but the bitter truth must be faced. "Just give yourself a chance. From what I've heard from the people here who know you, your dual bloodline has offered you a life that makes you twice the man most of us could be. Don't let your pride break you, Starbuck. Don't let it!"

Dakota again turned his head toward the wall.

McDonald knew he would get no further with him this day, so when the wound was cleaned and redressed, he left his patient to his own thoughts.

Twice the man. No. He was *half* a man now, just like he was a half-breed. He wasn't a whole anything.

His left hand is under my head, and his right hand doth embrace me...just like King Solomon and his queen.

He buried his face in his pillow and grit his teeth as sorrow yielded once again to rage.

For three more weeks he stayed at Fort Lyon, keeping close to his cot. When forced to go outside by the stewards for summer sunshine he avoided people, especially those he knew from past layovers at the fort. When confronted by anyone, familiar or not, he unconsciously turned his right side away from them in a weak attempt to conceal his incompleteness.

One day he walked past his surgeon's office and overheard a conversation between the doctor and a trapper with whom Dakota was acquainted.

"I heard about the 'breed losin' his arm. Musta been some kinda nightmare out there."

"To be sure."

"How long afore he gets outta here?"

"That's up to him. He lost a lot of blood, but I think he could travel if his strength weren't additionally sapped from refusing to eat and his overall refusal to fight."

"Ain't like him to give up."

"I only wish he would allow me to at least notify his wife." He paused. "Of course, if someone else were to take to intervening in the situation and send off a message on their own…"

Another pause.

"Why Doc, even if you was t' accidentally drop that piece of paper with her name on it, and I was t' find it and pick it up, I'd never give a thought to go interferin' in another man's business."

Dakota snuck around the corner of the building, waited for the trapper to leave, then followed him at an easy pace across the quadrangle. He lingered outside the gunsmith's while the man took care of some business, then "accidentally" bumped into him as he exited.

The big man turned in anger, but when he saw it was Dakota he held his tongue. "I'm sorry, man, real sorry. I didn't hurt yeh, did I?"

Such coddling sickened him, but he forced a smile. "I'm fine. It was my own fault for not looking where I was going. Hey, you're Rasmussen, aren't you? We've met before."

"Sure, I remember you, breed." He nodded toward Dakota's arm that was now turned away from the Dane's burly form. "Sorry to hear 'bout your turn of bad luck."

"Thanks, but it's not feeling too bad anymore. I'll be headin' home in a day or two."

"You will?"

"Yeah. I'm overdue as it is. It took me a while to get things settled in my mind, but now I'm just lookin' forward to

195

gettin' on with my life, with my woman at my side."

"But I thought...er, I mean, I'd think that's just what you oughta do."

"For a fact. I feel a mite guilty for havin' let her fret over me for this long, but now I'm thinkin' about the kind of reception that'll be waitin' for me when I finally get home." He arched a brow. "You a married man, Rasmussen?"

"Outlived three wives."

"Whoa! Then you know how they hug the stuffin' out of you when you first get home after months away."

"Yeah!" He smiled broadly, his eyes twinkling.

"Then I figure she'll rant at me for a good half hour for not gettin' in touch. But then, after all that frenzy is spent, we'll...well, I don't need to explain to a man such as yourself what comes next, do I?"

The trapper's face could've lit up a moonless night.

"So, I figure sendin' her word ahead of time would spoil my fun. Besides, we need to keep 'em on their toes, don't we? Keeps 'em from takin' us for granted."

"You got that right, breed." Before turning to leave, he gave Dakota a gentle slap on the left shoulder. "I wish you luck, all of it good."

Dakota thanked him and watched as he walked away.

The Dane slowed his pace, reached into his shirt pocket and pulled out a piece of white paper. He studied it for a few seconds, then crumpled it, threw it to the ground, and strolled on.

Dakota walked over and picked up the paper. He fumbled at opening it, then set it against his chest and smoothed out the wrinkles. Holding it in front of him, he read:

Mandy Starbuck, c/o James Berringer, attorney, Denver.

He put one edge of the paper between his teeth, then yanked on the other edge, ripping it in half, then quarters...until it was in tiny pieces.

As he walked back to the infirmary, a trail of irretrievable fragments of the paper—and his life—mingled with the dust and was carried away by the wind.

When he finally left the fort, he headed west but with no sense of direction or purpose. Sometimes he stopped in small towns where he could eat in a restaurant and sleep in a bed. At other times he'd go off the trail and sleep under the stars.

196

He tried hunting with the rifle, but shooting left-handed and without a second hand to steady it left him hungry and the animals redeemed. He lived off the plant life for two days before finally managing to bag his first wildlife—a rabbit. To skin it, he used his feet to hold the carcass steady while cutting from neck to tail with his awkward left hand. Then he clumsily cut away the hide and carved out some meat. It took him thirty minutes to do poorly what used to take him five to do adeptly. For a paltry amount of meat. Fortunately he had the forethought to acquire a good supply of matches to save him the task of fumbling with a fire.

Moonless nights on the prairie were his worst times. Beyond the light of the fire was a thick, black emptiness—a void that equaled the one inside him. He had blankets to keep warm, but yearned for Mandy's soft body to snuggle against his. Instead, he lay alone in the stillness, conflicting emotions warring within him.

Would it have been better never to love her than to hurt this much now? For many years he had known loneliness, but had the nights ever felt so heavy, or lasted so long?

I'll never leave you, Mandy. There's enough uncertainty in this world without your fearing I'll abandon you someday.

He shut out such thoughts lest they vanquish him.

He entered the town of Pueblo late one afternoon, choosing again to have his meals served to him and a roof to sleep under. The next morning, while leading his horse from the livery, he stopped outside a blacksmith shop next door.

Through the open double door he watched a young man, no more than twenty years old, struggle with a plow beam. Although he looked the part of a smith—his shirt sleeves rolled high, a Levi Strauss denim apron over dark pants, his skin moist with sweat and blackened from soot—he seemed uncomfortable in his task. He worked in obvious frustration for several minutes without noticing Dakota's scrutiny.

"Your fire's not hot enough, lad," Dakota said, startling the young smith.

"Huh? What'd you say?"

"Your fire—it's not hot enough. The flame's not concentrated."

The smith looked at the fire beneath the beam on which he was working, then back at Dakota.

"Do you have more fuel?"

"In the back," the lad answered with a toss of his head toward a room behind the shop.

"Bring it on out here and heap it on to what you've got. Don't spare your fuel if you want a good day's work from your fire."

Dakota helped the young man pack the fuel into the forge and showed him how to arrange it for maximum heat. As they worked, the smith told his tutor that he was the son of a blacksmith and took over the shop when his father died last winter. He had never found smithing to his liking.

"I'm good at ciphering, not welding and molding and shoeing. I'd like to be an accountant and keep people's books for them, not reshape their plow beams."

"You've got to heat it here—in the arch. It'll be easier now with a good fire." Dakota studied the beam the smith had come to loathe. "Ran on its nose, did it? Shoved itself into the dirt?"

"How'd you know?"

He shrugged. "Seen it before."

Under Dakota's direction, the smith got the beam reshaped and had a secure, sturdy plow that would run straight. His strong arms along with Dakota's expertise made short order of a difficult task.

"I don't know how to thank you, mister," the young man said as his much-welcomed visitor was about to leave.

Dakota looked around the shop in contemplation. "You can thank me by selling this place to someone who is suited to this work. Then go out and keep people's books for them. Accomplish whatever it is you want in life before you're no longer able."

* * *

As he rode along the trail, words out of time continued to haunt him.

It just goes to show what a man can do with a good fire, the right tools, and two strong arms.

I'll never leave you, Mandy.

His head spun from the invading voices, and he forced them out.

198

Leaving the trail once again, he headed for a small watering hole where he could slake his thirst. As he slid from his horse he stumbled, landing with his full weight on his stump. He cried out from the deep pain in the arm and fingers that were only phantoms now. He cursed his body for the tricks it played on him.

Pulling himself to the water, he placed the injured part in the cool ripples. He felt the vibration of approaching hooves before he heard their sound. He was relieved to see that the thirsty men were Cheyenne.

They spoke to him in sign language. He made the effort to communicate back using his left hand. It was like speaking every third or fourth word in a sentence and expecting them to comprehend his meaning.

They understood enough to invite him to their camp. They did not need hand signals to read the pain in his arm, nor the loneliness in his eyes.

CHAPTER 29

*D*akota was ridden with fever again. The blow to his stump caused it to hemorrhage under the skin and get reinfected. For a week he stayed in a tepee in the small Cheyenne camp, sometimes overtaken with the delusions his fever brought.

Cool cloths against his hot, sweat-drenched body soothed him. Throughout the day and even the night poultice compresses were applied to his stump. Thus the infection did not consume his entire system, but merely produced what Major McDonald had referred to as laudable pus—a necessary adjunct to proper healing.

A soft, cool cheek pressed against his fiery one.

"Mandy, you found me."

The infection and its assailing fever were finally fought down during the eighth night, and the enemy inside him was once again subdued. Cool compresses in tender hands washed away the beads of perspiration from his once-strong body. The infections, the lack of sustaining food, and having had virtually no strenuous activity for weeks had erased several pounds of muscle from him. But he knew he would be all right. Mandy was there.

Opening his eyes, he looked around the tepee. The morning light shone through the open flaps at the top. He saw a young Cheyenne woman enter with a steaming pot and place it at the opposite side of the lodge.

"Where is Mandy?" he asked in his Indian tongue as he turned onto his side.

She looked over and smiled, glad to see him well enough to speak to her. She did not understand his words, but at least he was speaking them to her and not to some vision occupying his feverish mind.

She brought him a clay cup filled with broth and gestured for him to drink. He sat upright and took the cup from her, but she kept her hand over his to steady it.

She was the most beautiful woman he had ever seen. Her eyes were dark and exotic; her hair was black and luxuriously shiny. Her doeskin dress hugged a shapely figure.

She appeared to be of mixed heritage like himself, and he took a stab at asking her in English, French and German if she spoke those languages. She understood none of them, though she could speak to him in sign.

Her name was Dawn. She asked his, and he told her.

"Dakota," she repeated, then signed, "The land from where the forefathers of our tribes came."

The mere effort of sitting up caused tiny beads to form once again on his forehead, and his strength was sapped. Dawn wiped his face with a cool cloth.

A startling thought took hold of him. This woman's hands and voice, even her smell, were those he had sensed during the time his mind was turbid from fever.

Mandy was not there.

His mind had played new tricks on him. But the gentle voice…the soothing strokes on his stump…the cool cheek next to his… He couldn't be sure, but once he thought he felt Mandy's soft lips press his.

He looked at Dawn and studied her face—her finely sculptured cheeks, her firm mouth. No, it had all been another trick of his mind. The women of the camp had probably spelled each other in caring for him. The rest was hallucination.

Dawn offered him some thickened soup. He forced the effort of raising himself up again and tried to take the cup from her to feed himself, but she wouldn't allow it.

He rallied a little each day. He learned he was in the lodge of Dawn and her father, and only occasionally did any woman other than Dawn attend to his needs—always with the tepee flap wide open. He began to relax with her, but frustrated that he could not communicate. Only now did he realize just how shackled Mandy must have felt when she lay injured among strange-speaking people. Although he had sympathized, he hadn't given her nearly enough credit for getting through with her sanity intact. He wished he could tell her now.

One day Dawn entered the lodge with news of an Arapaho visitor in the camp. Her father would bring him by shortly.

"You must look presentable," she signed, and gave him some freshly washed buckskins. She left the tepee and closed the flap to allow him to struggle into his pants, then came back in to help him into his shirt. She shaved his face and was in the process of combing his hair as she did every day when the

201

black-eyed Arapaho brave entered the lodge.

Dakota nearly choked when he looked up into the face of Thunder Cloud.

The warrior's eyes took in the scene—an incredibly beautiful woman combing Dakota's hair, and by her manner and his acceptance of it, obviously not for the first time.

"What are you doing here?" the warrior demanded.

"Thunder Cloud!" Dakota rose slowly, still weak in the limbs. He noticed his brother eyeing his stump, and he turned his right side away.

"I do not know how you found me, but I am so glad you are here, my brother." He reached out and placed his hand on the warrior's shoulder, wondering at his brother's slowness to reciprocate. Perhaps the shock of seeing his missing arm.

"We must talk," Thunder Cloud said. He glimpsed Dawn from the corner of his eye. "*Alone.*"

"You can speak freely. No one here understands our language. You cannot know how frustrating it has been."

"Yes, you looked very frustrated when I came in."

Dakota's brow wrinkled as he studied his brother's face, questioning his tone.

"I want to speak alone," Thunder Cloud repeated.

"All right. I am sure Dawn will not mind leaving us for—"

"Not here. I was told you have been in this lodge for nearly a half moon. But now you will come outside. The sun still shines, Dakota. There is life out there, although it seems you have chosen to ignore it."

A twinge of discomforting guilt stabbed the elder brother. A familiar twinge he'd been suppressing for the last several days.

"As you say, my young brother, we will walk under the sun and talk."

The sun glared brightly into the eyes accustomed to the dimness of the lodge. Climbing a small rise, the warrior slowed his pace.

"Why are you here? Where is Man-dee?"

Dakota explained the happenings of the past year and a half since the brothers had last seen each other, and how he and Mandy had decided to go separately to their families. Thunder Cloud was greatly saddened by the news of his father, and of his nephew, but insisted on settling another matter.

202

"While hunting today I met a Cheyenne, and he told me of the Arapaho brave his daughter was caring for who had reinjured his amputated arm. I thought it was another named Dakota, but as he described you, I became convinced it was you. But then he told me of the plans, and I was again convinced it was another. Had we not already been so close to this camp, and hungry, I would have turned back and gone home to my Blue Flower."

"What plans are you talking about?"

Thunder Cloud spun on his heel and faced his brother. "You stir contempt in me, Dakota! You bring shame on yourself and your family. And what of Man-dee? How can you live with this infidelity?"

"Infidelity?"

"Perhaps your white half has another word for it that allows your conscience to go unchallenged."

"I do not know what you are talking about. It is true I have not been to see Mandy since my arm was cut off, but I never…" He turned and looked out across the plain. "You misinterpreted what you saw. She is just being kind."

"Hah! Did you lose your sight as well as your arm?" He came alongside Dakota. "Can you not see how she looks at you, feel how she touches you, this strange woman you cannot even speak to? I have been told that striking beauty washes you and feeds you every day. I saw her grooming you. These are things you are obviously well enough to do for yourself."

Dakota again turned away and ran his fingers through his hair. "You do not understand—"

"I understand you better than you do yourself." He stepped around him for a face-to-face encounter. "You do not think of yourself as a proud man, do you? Others, too, would be surprised to learn that the 'strong but gentle half-breed son of Wild Eagle' depended so much on his own natural strength that he could not bear to lose even a measure of it. You have spoken so boldly of your faith in Man-Above, and the Jesus you claim is His Son who died on man's behalf, yet you do not even acknowledge that your strength always came from *Him*, not *this*—"

He slapped Dakota's left arm away from his side.

"Are you so defeated by the loss of one arm that you would throw away everything that has been given you?"

Dakota tried to turnabout again but was held in place by his brother's strong hand.

"You spoke vows, Dakota, to remain with your wife always."

"That was before I was mutilated, and could still provide for her and—"

"You see yourself as mutilated?"

Dakota exhaled sharply. "Now who is the blind one?"

Thunder Cloud shook his head. "Then perhaps it is best that you stay and marry that alluring, raven-haired woman."

"I never considered anything like that!"

"She has asked her father to arrange it. And if she takes such good care of you, then you are better off with her, because I guarantee Man-dee would not treat you so. She would not wash you. She would not dress you or groom you. She would not feed you or even hunt for your food. She would help you learn to do all those things skillfully for yourself. Now, you tell me—which woman of the two will be more requiring of your manhood?"

Dakota hung his head. "There was never any thought of my staying here. I swear it, Thunder Cloud. There has never been any woman in my life other than Mandy, and never will be."

"Will such noble sentiments satisfy her throughout the lonely years ahead? Will they keep her warm on winter nights as she lies alone in her bed?"

Dakota's eyes misted.

"You are a fortunate man, Dakota, for I am confident that when you decide to return to her, she will be waiting for you."

A sardonic snicker escaped from Dakota's lips. "If our father had waited for my mother to return, *you* would not be standing here now, would you?"

"Man-dee will wait."

Dakota's eyes gazed toward the western sky, where Denver was. Where she was. Waiting.

Glancing back to the camp, Dakota noticed Dawn looking anxiously toward them. "You speak some of their tongue. Tell her for me that I must go, and that I am sorry if I allowed her to think I would stay."

"I will tell her, with you standing at my side, so she will interpret in your face the words of my mouth."

Dawn was visibly dejected when the warrior gave his brother's message.

"I am sorry," Dakota said, hoping she would understand his heart if not his words. He went into the lodge to gather his belongings.

Outside the lodge, Dawn told Thunder Cloud that if Dakota's wife refused him, he could come back to her, for she would gladly have him.

"She will not refuse him. He will not be back."

The brothers rode out together, and when they came to the lake where Dakota had injured himself, they stopped before parting company. The elder wished his brother well and sent his regards to Blue Flower and their child.

"We are expecting another in the almost-summer. Perhaps this one will be a man-child."

Dakota lowered his eyes to the *parfleche* hanging from his saddle. As he had done so often, he fingered the yellow circle of beads.

"Be happy for whatever is sent. Just pray that it is strong."

"I will, my brother. And I am grieved to hear of the nephew I lost. He was the first of Chief Wild Eagle's grandsons. My children shall regard him with the honor he deserves."

They grasped shoulders and said a final good-bye. Thunder Cloud turned his horse and galloped away.

Dakota dismounted to fill his canteen from the cool, clear lake. Squatting at the water's edge, he glimpsed his reflection. He shot to his feet and stepped back in dread. Then, with fearful hesitation, he forced himself to return. He slowly leaned forward to behold his body—or what was left of it.

His face came into view. His shoulders. He paused. He turned his left side forward and leaned further into his reflection. By degrees, he straightened.

He appeared more whole than he expected. In his mind's eye, he had lost so much more.

His right hand doth embrace me.

His eyes squeezed shut.

You spoke vows, Dakota.

He turned away from his reflection, but the voices were not so easily obliterated.

You have spoken so boldly of your faith in Man-Above.

205

Not lately, he hadn't. And he'd given up wondering what God was exacting from him anymore. He had lost so much in such a short time. His tribal home. His son. His father. His inordinate strength, and with that his ability to provide for his wife and fulfill his dream.

Are you so defeated by the loss of one arm that you would throw away everything that has been given you?

He spun and hastened toward his horse.

You do not even acknowledge that your strength always came from Him, not this.

He slowed, then stopped, his head bowed. He could not deny his brother's potent words. He dropped to his knees. His eyes, brimming with tears, lifted to heaven in humble surrender to his Creator.

And, my son, my heart soars because you have at last found the woman to complete you. You take care of the woman Man-Above sent to you who was shot with the sun's arrow.

When it came to him, it was like a thunderstorm that cleanses the parched and gritty air following a long drought.

He had always believed that his Father provides the way to endure trials, and realized now He had not allowed these to befall him without first having given him Mandy.

She was his gift from God.

After a time on his knees, he wiped his tears with his sleeve and rose, his soul broken free of the bondage of fear, and yes, what he now acknowledged as sinful *pride.*

The wind blew on his face and through his hair. He drew deep of the refreshing, renewing, life-giving air.

He may never have the answers to his many questions, but now knew a peace that surpassed understanding. A peace whose source was the only One who could make his life what it was meant to be.

He stepped to his waiting horse. There he paused to caress the three intertwining circles on his *parfleche.*

He raised his eyes again, and whispered, "*Hahou.*"

He was going home.

Home was where Mandy was.

CHAPTER 30

*F*ort Lyon was a busy place, much more so than Mandy expected. She had never been to an army fort, and had no idea of the amount of non-military activities that took place. There were shops and outdoor markets, white and Indian traders, and even a hospital.

She accompanied Elijah to a shop where they bought provisions before continuing their journey eastward, and she sought information about Dakota.

"Pardon me, ma'am, but I couldn't help overhearing. Are you by any chance Mandy Starbuck?"

She turned to face a freckled man with strawberry-blond hair who held a large brown carton in his arms.

"Yes. Do you have information about my husband?"

"I'm Major Coleman McDonald. I'd like to speak to you about John, or Dakota, or whatever you call him. Would you follow me to my office?"

"What do you know about him?" she asked along the way.

"Let me drop off these supplies and then we'll talk."

Hefting the carton to one arm, he opened his office door and allowed her to enter first. Once inside, he unloaded his burden in a back room and returned to his desk where she stood.

"I must say, your husband was an enigma."

"*Was?*"

"I want you to know I did all I could for him."

Her hand flew to her mouth and she gasped in a breath.

"Oh no, I don't mean he died! I'm so sorry."

She collapsed into the captain's chair opposite him and let out the breath.

"How'd you get here so fast, anyway?" he asked.

"What do you mean? You couldn't have been expecting me."

"Actually, I was. I don't mind saying that I had a part in Rasmussen sending that telegram."

"Who? What telegram?"

"So, you didn't get word from Rasmussen?" Her blank expression gave him his answer. "Of course, you didn't. It's too soon for you to have received his message and traveled from Denver. He left here just a few days ago." His visage became decidedly darker. "Which means…you don't know."

"As long as he's alive, no other explanation matters to me right now."

"Actually, Mrs. Starbuck, it does matter. To *him*. You see…he was badly injured from a gunshot wound."

Her breath caught. "But he got well, right? Well enough to go home?"

"He recovered physically, but full recovery…is going to take some time."

"What do you mean? Is he recovered or isn't he?"

The doctor hung his head and wet his lips. "This is as difficult telling you as it was to tell him." He moved a chair next to hers and sat down. "When your husband was brought here he had already lost a lot of blood. Even as a surgeon with battlefront experience, I wasn't able to salvage his arm. In order to save his life, I had to amputate."

Every fragment of her being was cast into shock.

"I swear I did all I could."

She did not blame the doctor and told him so. "But he's always been so strong, and so skilled with his hands. This must be unbearable for him."

"Mrs. Starbuck, there's something else you probably don't know yet, and I'm sorry to be the one to have to tell you. Your father-in-law passed away while your husband was visiting him."

Her head hung low.

"In addition to the consummate losses he's suffered in the recent past, now he believes he'll never be able to provide for you in the future. He was here for several weeks, deeply depressed. I tried to get him to at least contact you. He's not ready to confront life, or you, I'm afraid. He's a man with a great deal of pride."

She got up and paced in front of the desk. "And I fed it, always making such a big thing out of his muscles and his strength. Now look what it's done. He can't even face me."

"In time, he will. It's obvious he loves you very much."

"Did he give any indication of where he was going?"

"He rode west, but I have no idea where. I don't think he even knew."

208

She pounded her cane into the floor, the skin over her knuckles blanched from the pressure of her grip. "Pueblo! It *was* him in that blacksmith shop. I missed him by only a couple of hours!"

She paced frantically, her words coming nearly as fast as the ideas that raced through her head.

"I've got to go back that way. But how? My ride is going east. And where would he have gone? The cabin, maybe? No, he knows I'd go there looking for him."

He rose and stepped in front of her, halting her forward motion. "I'll look into some travel arrangements for you. You just calm down and take things one at a time. The strain of this is showing on you. You look entirely depleted."

"Doctor, could I impose on you for…a professional opinion?"

"Surely."

He listened to her history and symptoms and performed a brief examination.

"Would you say about two months?"

She nodded. "Am I likely to have trouble this time, too?"

"Not based solely on what happened during your last pregnancy, but it would be prudent for you to get home and take it easy."

"But I've got to find Dakota."

"Go home and take care of yourself, Mrs. Starbuck. Let *him* find *you*."

Mandy thanked the Washingtons for their kindness and hospitality. Before parting, they prayed together, asking the Lord's blessing on each of their journeys. She then joined an Army family Dr. McDonald knew who were moving west and rode with them as far as Pueblo. There she sent a wire telling her family only that she had made it as far as Fort Lyon but was on her way home. Imagining what George would do with the knowledge that Dakota was alive but his whereabouts unknown, she left that part out.

She went to the blacksmith shop, which now had a For Sale sign hanging.

"He sure knew his trade," the smith said as he pumped bellows of air into his fire. "Just the little he showed me that day helped me out a great deal. But it's what he said when he left that meant more to me than all of what he did."

"What was that?"

He paused in his task and turned to her. "He told me I ought to accomplish what I want in life before I'm not able. I kind of felt sorry for him, like he was really talking about himself. But it gave me the notion to put this place up for sale, and I sat down and wrote to some companies in California who have advertised for accountants. That's what I do best. Don't know that I ever would've taken that step if it hadn't been for your husband. I'd appreciate your telling him that for me when you see him again."

She arranged to ride north with a Bureau of Indian Affairs agent and his wife who were taking a wagonload of orphaned children to the Sioux reservation in Wyoming. They insisted the children communicate only in English, for it would now be their primary tongue. But when alone with the children, Mandy carried on rousing conversations with them in sign language, and they became fast friends.

In Colorado City, she again asked the merchants if they had seen Dakota since she had passed through.

"No, I haven't seen 'im," said one of the storekeepers. "But, one arm, yeh say? I did hear 'bout a fella with one arm who fell ill and was holin' up with some Cheyenne southeast of here. It might just be an Indian tale, but that's what I heard."

In her hotel room that night, she stood in front of the mirror brushing her hair. Memories of a similar image came to her, and she could almost see Dakota's reflection as he came behind her and brushed her hair.

How can I leave you?

Her eyes cast to her waist, which had not yet begun to swell.

If Dakota knew of the baby, would it make a difference? Could he abandon the child as he had her? He told her once he would never abandon her. What did he call *this*?

She flung the brush onto the dresser, threw herself on the bed, and wept.

CHAPTER 31

"*T*he Berringer house is down that street on the left, with the white fence in front." The black-haired, energetic lad ran off to chase his dog.

Dakota dismounted and walked the rest of the way, submerged in apprehension.

He should have gotten a shave. With a few days of scruff on his face he imagined his appearance was rather unkempt, but Mandy liked it, so the scruff stayed. Letting go of the rein, he hastily combed his hair with his fingers and straightened some wrinkles out of his store-bought clothes he determined would be more appropriate to wear when meeting Mandy's family.

Stopping in front of the two-story white house, he looped the rein around the hitching post. He stared at the front door.

Father, help her accept this. Help us do this together.

From the corner of his eye he caught a movement. He looked to his right. She was there, squatted down, pulling weeds in the garden at the corner of the house. A breath of wind blew tendrils of fair hair that had strayed from her sunbonnet across the back of her dark blue dress.

For once she did not hear his quiet Indian approach, even as he stood directly behind her. Overcoming the stricture in his throat, he called her name.

At the sudden close voice she sucked in her breath. Rising quickly, she whirled around.

A stranger faced him.

"Oh, I-I'm sorry, miss. I thought you were Mandy."

"I'm sorry, too." The blond girl removed her bonnet and studied the handsome stranger before her who seemed to show forth his left side. After a head-to-toe assessment, she said, "For the first time in my life, I'm sorry I'm not Mandy."

She could not have been more than eighteen, but her scrutiny made him uncomfortable nonetheless.

"Are you a friend of hers?" she asked.

"Well, I hope she's still feeling friendly toward me."

"She's a fool if she isn't."

His eyes narrowed. "You *must* be Julie."

"That's right. And you still haven't said who you are. I don't ever remember her bringing you home, and believe me, I'd've remembered."

"Is she at home now?"

"'Fraid not."

"What time to you expect her?"

"Don't know exactly. She's away."

"What do you mean by 'away'?"

"Out of town."

"Out of...? Where did she go?"

"Uh, some places around."

"Places around where?"

"The territory."

"Julie, *where is she*?"

She set her hands firmly on her hips. "Why should I tell you about my sister? I don't even know who you are. For all I know you could be some—"

"I'm Dakota."

Julie's mouth froze wide open. He again asked her regarding Mandy's whereabouts, but her only response was to fly to him and throw her arms around his neck.

"Oh, Dakota, I knew you would come. I just knew it!"

He slowly slipped his arm around her back, grateful for the enlivened welcome. He had not known what to expect from her family.

After releasing him, she studied him again, and his right side turned.

"She never mentioned—"

"She doesn't know."

Her blue eyes widened. "Is *that* what took you so long getting here?" He nodded. "We knew it had to be something awfully serious. I'm really sorry."

"Where did she go?" he asked anxiously.

"Looking for you."

"What?"

"'Fraid so."

"But she couldn't have known where I was."

"She headed out for the Medicine Lodge reservation, but only got as far as Fort Lyon. Last we heard she was back in Pueblo and heading home, although she didn't say why."

"If she turned back from Fort Lyon, it must mean she

212

knows about… She may have even talked to the doc." He straightened and added, "and if she did, she thinks I've forsaken her!"

The front door opened. George crossed the porch and descended the steps. He glanced across the yard and slowed.

"Hello there, young man." He walked to them, a protective eye on Julie. "Are you a friend of Julie's?"

"I'm—"

"His name is John," Julie hastily interrupted. "He's an old friend of Mandy's."

Dakota's eyes cut to Julie's. Her expression pled with him to go along.

"I'm George Barton." He put out his hand, and Dakota shook it with his left hand. "Unfortunately, Mandy is not at home."

"Yes, Julie told me." His uneasy gaze returned to her.

"She had some matter she felt she had to attend to in another part of the territory, but I think she's about finished with all that." He eyed the stranger discreetly, wondering if he would be any more suited to Mandy than the noxious half-breed who abandoned her.

"I was just going to invite him to supper," Julie said.

"Fine. Fine. I'll see you in a few hours then. I have some business in town, then I'll be meeting Jeffrey's stage."

Dakota watched the stout man go through the gate and start for town.

"Who *was* that? He acts like he owns the place."

"Essentially, he does."

"What do you mean? Isn't this your parents' home?"

"Yes. It belongs to my ma and George. He's my stepfather."

"*Stepfather?*"

"Mandy never knew till she got home in June. Our pa died shortly after she disappeared. Ma married George a year and a half later."

Dakota glanced at George's retreating form. He envisioned Mandy coming home, expecting her father's joyful welcome, and finding out he was dead. She had been dealt as crushing a blow as he had by losing her father so soon after Baby Gregg.

"I *never* should have let her come home alone. For a lot of reasons."

"You couldn't have known, Dakota." She took his arm and coaxed him toward the front door. "C'mon. We've got things to talk about. Let's not waste time on the might've-beens. Now, about George…"

Ma was helping clean a sick friend's house, so they had a few hours alone. Julie had much to tell him, including the facts about George's consummate hatred of Indians, including half-breeds, and his insistence that Dakota was Mandy's greatest mistake. She tried to convince him to continue withholding his identity for the time being.

"No, I can't deceive your family like that."

"It's only until George gets to know you a bit better. He'll only accept you as a decent, peaceful and trustworthy man if he gets to know you first as a white man. Then he'll be more willing to accept…your other half."

"How can he ever consider me decent and trustworthy if I lie about my very identity?"

"Please, Dakota, just for today. We've been planning this welcome-home supper for Jeffrey. I'd hate to see the day spoiled by a big argument with George. Please?"

Dakota shook his head. "I don't have to stay here. I can get a room in town."

"No, you belong here with us. But I know what I'm talking about. Trust me, Dakota. *Pleeeease?*"

He rolled his eyes and wondered why he said, "All right."

Julie breathed a sigh of relief and smiled at the man with the heavenly eyes. She made coffee while Dakota tended to his horse. When he returned from the stable out back, the rest of the family was filtering home.

Julie introduced him as "Mandy's friend John." He hated it, and wondered if Julie could dodge the question of his last name as skillfully as she diverted the conversation from other revealing issues. He would not lie about his name, or withhold it if asked.

While the women prepared supper, men-talk took place on the front porch. Hunting. The economy. Statehood. The railroad. Jeffrey spoke of law school, George of the freight business. Dakota mentioned that he had been a blacksmith, though now had to give it up.

"A blacksmith?" Jeff asked. "That's interesting, because

214

Mandy's hus—"

"Jeffrey," George interrupted, "why don't you go see if you can help your mother and sister?"

"With the *cooking*?"

"Go and see if they need any more wood for the fire."

"If they did, they'd call."

"Jeffrey…"

The lad went reluctantly.

"So, John, how long have you known my stepdaughter?"

Dakota rested his hand on his abdomen, where a stick of dynamite with a slow fuse burned inside his gut.

"Well, sir, uh…a couple of years." His face grew warm and his palm sweaty. He momentarily wished his parents hadn't raised him so well. He wished he were a better liar.

"She'd been away for two years, you know."

"I know."

"Yes, I suppose Julie caught you up on a lot today."

"For a fact." He squirmed in his chair.

"Somehow I'm still sort of vague on just how it is you knew Mandy."

"Supper's on the table, fellas," Julie called from the dining room window, and smiled at the look of relief her words brought to Dakota's face.

He took her aside when the others went to wash up in the kitchen. "I can't go through with this anymore. I'm going to tell them."

"After supper. Cross my heart. I'll break the news then."

His shoulders sank and he let out a sigh. "You Berringer women really are somethin', you know that?"

"For a fact!" She wrapped her arms around his, escorted him to the table, and sat him down next to her in Mandy's place.

Supper went well, most of the talk revolving around Jeffrey's trip and the law colleges he visited. Whenever the conversation got back around to Dakota, Julie would steer it away again. But even she ran out of superficial things to say, and eventually George got to speak.

"So, John, did you lose your arm in the war?" he asked in his usual blunt manner.

Dakota's gaze lowered.

"I'm sorry, John. Is it hard to talk about?"

215

"The answers to your questions are no and yes. No, I didn't lose it in the war. It's more recent. And yes…it's difficult."

"I'm sorry," George said. Wishing to move away from the uncomfortable subject, he asked, "Speaking of the war—which side did you fight for?"

"Neither."

"Oh?"

"I spent the war years here in Colorado."

"Did you have no heart to join the fight for either side?"

"I had no heart to go back there and fight *against* either side. In my mind I knew the North was right in trying to keep the Union together and abolish slavery, but I was raised in the South and had no desire to take up arms against it. But more importantly, my family was here in Colorado, and with both the North and the South vying for this territory to be added to their domains, there was imminent danger of war being waged on *this* soil, and they were vulnerable. I felt I belonged here with them."

"I see. So, where about in the South were you born?"

"I said I was *raised* in the South. Virginia. I was *born* here."

"Uh-oh." Julie sank slowly into her chair.

Silence followed as those at the table performed some mental arithmetic. The figures didn't seem to add up.

"But how is that possible? You look to be in your mid-thirties, which means you would've been born..."

"Probably sometime in early '32."

"Probably?" Jeff queried.

"Uh-oh." Julie slunk further in her seat.

"Julie, will you please refrain from making strange noises at the table?" her mother scolded. "And sit up straight!"

George persisted. "How did it come about that you were born in Colorado in 1832? The only white people here then were trappers, traders and trailblazers."

"There were Indians. Plenty of them."

The sound of George's knife crashing on his china plate echoed through the dining room.

Ardith's stunned gaze fell sharply on Dakota.

Jeffrey's fork was suspended before his open mouth.

Julie's eyes squinted shut and her face grimaced as she

216

waited for the earth to open and swallow them all up with Dakota's next words.

"I'm half-Arapaho."

For Julie, being swallowed up in the earth would have been far more preferable to the tomblike silence that followed.

After a long half minute, Jeff concluded, "You're Mandy's husband, aren't you?"

Dakota couldn't discern if the excitement in the youth's voice came from pleasure or indignation.

"Excuse me." Julie timidly raised herself up from her chair. "I'm going to get some more water."

Dakota took hold of her elbow and gently but firmly sat her back down.

"Julie, you knew?" Jeff cried.

"Julie!" George raged. "How could you do this to your family?"

"Now wait just a minute, Mr. Barton," Dakota objected. "She only tried to keep peace in the house, thinking it best if you got to know me before I set the match to the gunpowder. Don't be blaming her."

"You stay out of our family's business."

"Like it or not, sir, I *am* family."

Julie said, "If you weren't so fired up against Indians, George, I wouldn't have—"

"Julie, dally your tongue!" Ma commanded. She turned cool eyes on Dakota. "We don't take well to deception in our home."

"Nor do I, Mrs. Berrin…Barton. I had no intention of deceiving anyone when I came here today. I came to get Mandy and to meet all of you at last. I apologize for the mess I made of it."

Dakota regretted the fretful lines on her face that were his to claim.

He rose from the table. "I'll stay in town to await Mandy's return."

"Don't go!" Julie pled as he walked through the kitchen to the back door.

He proceeded to the stable and grabbed the saddle blanket. As he settled it on Chief, he confided, "I didn't know what to expect here today, fella, but this sure beats all."

"Wait, young man!" George called as he crossed to the

stable.

Dakota lifted the saddle and positioned it on the horse's back.

"Please, wait."

Dakota stopped and slowly turned toward the man who was Mandy's stepfather.

"I realize…it's just that…" The man sighed and blurted out, "I'm sorry."

Dakota looked at him guardedly.

"Your chicanery in there was out of line, but I admit my attitude helped make the situation difficult. To be honest, I didn't think you'd ever show. But Ardith and the twins never lost faith in you. Needless to say, neither did Mandy. Julie told us just now what held you up. I can't tell you how sorry I am. I'd like you to remain here with us."

Dakota glanced past George to the back porch where Ma, Jeff and Julie stood watching. He walked to the bottom of the steps and looked up at Ardith. Mandy had her mother's eyes— kind and forgiving. She was a good woman, had raised Mandy well, and he regarded her with tremendous admiration. He cared what she thought.

"My daughter loves you, Dakota," she said, "and I understand why. You cared for her when she was injured and far from home. You named your son after the brother she misses so much, and suffered through that greatest of losses with her, the loss of your child. You found in her what you found lacking in all other women, and even built a cabin with her in mind. Won't you stay and wait for her with us?"

He looked long into her blue-gray eyes.

"I'll stay."

CHAPTER 32

"Come warm yourself by the fire, Mandy. There's nothing to see in that vast blackness."

Lady Samantha Chamberlain spoke from her place by the small fire where her brother Charles and her cousins Simon and Katherine also huddled.

Their guide, Guy Clairborne, spoke without looking up from his task of cutting rabbit meat away from the bone to serve up to his tourist-clients.

"Lady Samantha's right, Miz Starbuck. Ain't nothin' out there tonight. The only Cheyenne camp I heared of is prob'ly a good twenty miles. And like I already done told yeh, iffen that's where yer mind's set on goin', then yer goin' in on yer own. Some Cheyenne are friendly still, but I don't trust any of 'em these days."

Mandy returned to the fire and wrapped her blue cloak snugly around herself.

She had met up with the British cousins in Colorado City. When she heard they were traveling into the plains, she "reworked" her plans, as she had done once before in that town, and asked to join them. The resentment she had borne toward Dakota had made her feel wretched. Setting aside emotions, she determined again to find him. If he was too proud to come to her, she would do whatever it took to find him and convince him they would make it—the *three* of them—and Dakota would learn to provide for them somehow. But they needed to be together.

The idea of having a true pioneer woman in their midst excited the cousins. Mandy rejected the notion that she was a pioneer, but that's how it went down in Lady Samantha's journal.

A former trapper who had once made his living trading pelts back when there were beavers to be found, Clairborne now received exceptional recompense for taking adventure-seeking foreigners through the mountains and prairies of Colorado. He considered it a lifestyle far inferior to that of his younger days, but it was easy money and it kept him outdoors. So he put up with the snobbery and ignorance of those who wanted to "rough it" in the Wild West of the American continent.

These four bluebloods would go home with stories of having "lived off the land" when in truth they had only shot an occasional deer. Although they possessed reasonable hunting skills, they sorely lacked the knack for skinning and preparing the meat. They also lacked any desire to learn.

The women, who had ridden horseback in the mountains, insisted on a sturdy buggy with extra springs and lush padding for their plains excursion. Thus Mandy had a comfortable and less jarring ride, which was more suitable for her condition. Her pregnancy had gone flawlessly so far, and she did not feel at risk by changing course to a direction that may lead her to her husband in a matter of days.

What did make her a bit nervous was the thought of wandering the plains while there were ongoing hostilities around the territory. But she was emboldened by the thought that should they be confronted by any of the Plains tribes, she could sign to them who she was—the sister-in-law of the infamous Thunder Cloud.

"I say we *should* go to the Indian camp, Mr. Clairborne," Simon said.

"So do I," Samantha agreed. "The only Indians we've seen have been in towns, dressed in woven shirts and wearing an occasional feather. I want to be able to write firsthand about their appearance and their customs and their living arrangements in their natural habitat."

"My word, cousin," Katherine said, "you make it sound as though you're researching animals."

"I didn't mean to. I think they're marvelous, really. Have you read Longfellow's 'The Song of Hiawatha'? It's truly a touching and romantic story."

"Yeah, real touchin'," Clairborne said, dishing out their portions. "Just like any people, there's good and there's rotten Injuns, but don't ever git the notion there's anything romantic about 'em."

"May I quote you, Mr. Clairborne?" Samantha asked, reaching for her journal.

"Go ahead. And y'can quote me on this, too: I ain't goin' near no Cheyenne camp, *no how*!"

And he was right, for the next morning he took a careless

step near the warm rocks around the fire's embers and was dead within an hour of being bitten by a rattlesnake.

Mandy and her companions were shocked and fearful. Although they had never gotten close to Clairborne—he was not the friendliest of men—it was with sadness that they buried him in an unmarked grave out on the lonely prairie.

Then they sat down and discussed their options.

"I suppose we need to return the way we came," Charles said. "Did anyone observe the landmarks and such on the way?"

Mandy had, thanks to Dakota's tutoring. But she was hoping to head in a different direction. "I thought you wanted to see some Indians close up. Let's try to find that Cheyenne camp."

The cousins looked at each other warily. "No," Charles said. "Without Clairborne, we'd better get back to civilization as soon as possible."

She had to admit it was the most rational thing to do. But it meant giving up hope of finding Dakota at that village. Difficult as it was, she went along with the majority. "We'll head south until we pick up the main trail."

"Which way is south?" asked Simon.

"That way," Katherine answered, pointing east.

Mandy tried to veil her astonishment at how little they had learned in their wilderness trek. "Keep in mind that the mountains are west."

As they packed their belongings, the foreign visitors voiced further misgivings about traveling without a guide.

"You can shoot, can't you?" Mandy asked.

"We shoot very well," Simon answered. "Finding the little beasts is the problem."

"What have you been doing for the past three months?"

"Following Clairborne."

"He didn't teach you how to hunt and track?"

"We paid him to *guide* us."

Mandy looked into the four lost faces of the English cousins. They were all in their twenties, all dark-haired and nicely complexioned. Intelligent and well spoken they were, but ignorant of the wilderness, even more so than she had been before her lessons with Dakota began.

They headed south and west. Before long, Mandy noticed

the tracks of unshod ponies. By the looks of an arrowhead left behind at the place where the Indians had stopped to eat their kill, she presumed they were Kiowa. They had come from the northeast and now headed directly west at a slow pace. She steered the group farther south.

That night they supped on a goose Mandy shot with Clairborne's Hartford sporting rifle. "There must be water nearby for them to have been flying so low. Tomorrow we should try to find it."

When daylight came Mandy checked a snare she had built and set the night before and found a rabbit. They were set for breakfast.

Riding out in the early morning, she gave the surrey horse its head and he took them to a small lake where they replenished their supply of water. It was delightfully cold, so they removed their shoes and splashed in it like children, allowing themselves a momentary respite from their troubles. It took Mandy back to Pennsylvania, to the times she and Gregg had water fights with their cousins Cassie and Hannah and Erik while visiting them at their farms near Harrisburg as youngsters. Visits with those cousins provided some of the best memories in her life, and she envied these four their nearness to one another.

As the others returned to the buggy and horses, Mandy remained at the water's edge and scanned the landscape around her to the horizon. Other, more recent memories came to her, memories of the months she spent living on these plains. Its vastness was exhilarating.

"*Hanea' kaa*," she said aloud. *As far as the eye can reach.*

The next morning they awoke to find the horses gone, having broken free from the tether lines Katherine and Samantha had tied. The men were furious with their scatterbrained sisters. Mandy defused their explosive tempers and insisted they just keep moving. No might've-beens.

It was Mandy who tracked the game every day, and every night she set her snares. Every morning there was food for them. Bearing the responsibility for the group's survival taxed her.

Ten weeks into her pregnancy, she was feeling the effects. Although she had no morning sickness, she had little appetite for what she had to kill and clean and cook herself. Her energy was sapped, and she wished for relief.

Charles offered to help and went hunting with her for supper one evening. He spied a rabbit and sighted him in with Mandy's .44.

"No!" she shouted as she turned and saw him preparing to shoot, but was too late. "Are you crazy?"

"What do you mean? I bloody well got him!"

"You got him all right, and with that gun, you got him so good there'll be nothing left of him to eat. Why didn't you use the Hartford?"

"Oh, I didn't realize—"

"Yes, yes, I know. You didn't realize the gun was so powerful. Just like Simon didn't realize those berries he picked for our dinner yesterday were poisonous. Just like the girls didn't realize that horses' tethers won't hold to a branch thinner than my little finger. I'm constantly amazed by how much you people don't realize!" She stormed away.

But later that evening she was penitent. As they sat around the fire, she apologized for her outburst, telling them that it wasn't so very long ago that she, too, had been quite ignorant, and only learned what she had under compulsion.

"Until then I barely knew a cow chip from a sunflower, and am still a mite dunderheaded when it comes to wilderness ways."

"That is quite obvious." A French-accented voice materialized from the darkness outside the fire's circle of light. They all jerked around but could not tell from which direction it came.

A short, lean man in a red capote coat showed himself at his own leisure. "If I had chosen it, you would all be dead now."

He remained several feet back from the fire, and they could not make out his features.

"On a night such as this, your noises have carried far. You all foolishly faced the fire and could not have seen me even if you had heard me."

"We're cold!" Simon protested.

Mandy was disgusted with herself. "We're also night-blinded."

"You knew that, mademoiselle, yet you allowed yourself to do it?"

She lowered her eyes. "I didn't think about it."

"Your thoughtlessness could have cost you your hair."

She knew it without being told, and felt further remorse over having been so short-tempered and presumptuous with Charles earlier in the day.

The visitor sneered at Katherine's offer of rabbit as well as a place to sit next to Simon. He instead walked outside the circle of fire, picking a spot of his own choosing to lower himself to the ground.

Drawing him into a conversation took an intense and unabated effort, but the cousins, especially Samantha, were more than up to the task.

His name was Jean Hebert. He was French-Canadian, in his fifties, and like Clairborne, had once made a living trapping along the Platte, the Arkansas and the Colorado Rivers. Unlike Clairborne, however, he wanted nothing to do with "people who come from abroad, abuse the resources of this land, then leave it for a more sedentary life." He left no question that he had taken an instant dislike to these ignorant vagrants and to the inane American woman with them.

Mandy knew this frontiersman could see them safely and swiftly back. Although she was bone weary and would welcome his experience, she hesitated to ask for his help.

Katherine, on the other hand, was not the slightest bit reticent. She asked him outright to lead them back to Colorado City and offered a substantial sum to do it. He didn't need the money and didn't need the annoyance, and said as much.

"We really could use your expertise, Monsieur Hebert, especially Mandy here. She's been carrying the load for all of us."

He glanced at Mandy. "Her? If you are in her hands, I pity you all. Perhaps I should indeed accompany you to town."

Mandy stood. "Do what you want, mister. We'll manage with or without your help." She lifted one of the torches from the fire and left to set her snares.

The next morning Hebert went with her—uninvited—to check her snares. She was shocked and embarrassed to find the trap had come apart and the animal had wriggled free.

Later that day she fired at and missed an antelope.

"*Sacre bleu!*" Hebert grabbed the rifle from her and nabbed the now running animal with one shot. They ate very well that night.

The Frenchman shook his head as he ate. "I do not know how you people have survived, considering your total lack of *savoir-faire*." He turned to Mandy. "Where did you learn such fantastic skills as making snares that cannot hold a small creature and missing an antelope at fifty yards?"

Her humiliation was worsened by the thought she was casting a poor reflection on Dakota's competence.

Katherine spoke up. "Mandy was doing quite well before you came along, Monsieur Hebert."

"*Oui,* I could see that." His jovial laugh further shamed her.

"Relax, Mandy," Samantha told her the next day as the women walked behind the men. "As long as we depended on you, you were superb. Now that Hebert's come along, you unconsciously are relinquishing that responsibility that you never wanted in the first place."

Mandy marveled at how someone so dimwitted in the ways of the world could be so savvy about the workings of the mind.

Samantha also concluded that Hebert, for all his nagging and complaining, was enjoying the fact he was needed. She was certain he'd see them through to Colorado City.

At supper that evening, Hebert's mood lightened and he told intriguing stories of his adventurous life on the frontier to the group's eager ears and Samantha's quick pencil. Some of the people he spoke of were as fascinating as he was, and she intended to immortalize them all.

"Who is the most notorious character you ever encountered?" she asked.

"Male or female?" They all laughed.

"Either-or."

"Well, mademoiselle, there was one man whose reputation for violence and evil spanned several territories. I had one brief encounter with him, and it was one too many."

"Who was he?"

"He was called by the name Headless Jack."

The crash of Mandy's tin plate and utensils hitting the ground snatched their attention. The group looked at her questioningly. She picked up the mess, but her supper was no longer edible.

Charles urged Hebert to continue his story. He started to speak, then stole a glance at Mandy. Her eyes were fixed on the fire.

"On second thought, he's best forgotten. He's not fit to take up space in your journal, Lady Samantha."

A day from their destination, the group's spirits lifted and their pace quickened. All the cousins spoke fluent French, and when they held conversations with Hebert she couldn't understand, Mandy rode his horse ahead of them and thought through what she should do next.

Despite her current fatigue, she felt stronger overall than she did during her last pregnancy. But should she continue her search? For how long? Or should she, as the good doctor had put it, let Dakota find *her*?

In the afternoon, she and Hebert went hunting. Several times she noticed him eyeing her curiously. When she called him on it, he told her it was her imagination. Or perhaps, wishful thinking. She rolled her eyes and walked on.

Spotting some antelope heading toward a riverbed, the two hunters stealthily approached through the thick cover of cottonwoods along the bank.

Mandy stood close behind the Frenchman as he raised his rifle and took aim. She caught movement from the corner of her eye and glanced to her right. Two Indians sprang from behind trees and streaked toward them, knives raised.

"Hebert!" She raised her Remington and fired. One Indian went down, a bullet in his heart.

Hebert turned, paused but an instant, aimed at the second Indian and pulled the trigger.

Click.

Mandy fired again. The second Indian fell dead at the Frenchman's feet.

The shock of his gun misfiring and nearly costing him his life left Hebert momentarily stunned. He gaped at the two bodies, then at Mandy. Her face was ashen. He set the rifle against a tree, placed a steadying hand on her shoulder, and removed the Remington from her uncontrollably shaking hand.

"It seems I have misjudged you, *madame*. Your quick wits and sure aim saved us both."

She couldn't answer. Sixty seconds ago she was patiently waiting for him to shoot their supper. Now two men were dead by her hand.

"There's bound to be more of these around," he said. "We'll have to forget about eating and move away from here. But first…"

He walked to the second Indian's body, lifted the head by a braid, and set his knife next to the hairline.

Mandy's scream bolted him upright. His eyes cut in every direction. He could see no Indians or any other danger. He looked at her, baffled.

"Do not scalp them!"

He stared at her in disbelief. "Are you crazy, screaming like that? What is wrong with you?"

"Don't scalp them, Hebert. Please!"

He oozed a breath of frustration. "They would have done the same to us. Fresh Indian scalps on my belt will make others hesitate." He bent over the Indian again.

"*Please*. Leave them."

Reluctantly, angrily, he complied. "They are your kill," he spat, and walked away.

When they returned to the English, Simon said, "Mandy, you're shaking like an aspen leaf, as you Westerners say."

Hebert was the one who gave answer. "We had a run-in with some Indians and have to get out of here *now*, so get your things together."

They reached Colorado City late the next morning. The first thing each did after checking in at the hotel was to take a luxurious bath. Later they dined together at a restaurant. The foreigners proposed toasts to their companion-guides who saw them through what could have been a disastrous adventure. Mandy raised her glass of milk as they drank a special toast in memory of the trustworthy guide, Clairborne.

After the meal, the cousins bid Hebert good-bye and headed back to the hotel. While he traded for provisions to see him through to Santa Fe, Mandy again asked the storekeeper and the customers if they had seen Dakota in recent days. Their replies took the form of the usual shaking of heads.

In front of the mercantile, she stood by the voyageur as he secured his belongings to his horse.

"The one who taught you how to survive out there…he is the husband you search for, *n'est-ce pas?*"

"*Oui*. But I would not want you to think less of him

227

because of my failures."

"*Au contraire*. You have reflected his great skill, as well as his great love for you. He cares enough about you to teach you how to survive without him."

She inwardly acknowledged that this man understood Dakota's need to teach her better than she ever had. Those skills had saved her life, and in turn the lives of the Chamberlains.

He studied her with the same curious eye he had the previous day. "You remind me of a woman in a story the Indians of the plains tell. They speak of a white woman with hair the color of the sun and a broken foot. She saved the people in their camp by facing Headless Jack alone and leading him away."

She avoided his gaze.

"She made her Arapaho rescuers promise not to peel off the man's hairless scalp."

Perceiving that he had penetrated a sheltered part of her soul where he had no right to be, he said no more.

She untied his horse and handed him the rein. Hebert took her hand and kissed it. "*Au revoir*," he said softly. He mounted his horse and rode away.

That night as they gathered in the Englishwomen's hotel suite, Charles asked, "So, Mandy, what are you going to do now?"

"I'm not entirely certain. I don't know whether Dakota would be more inclined to stay out on the plains or head up into the mountains. Either way, I won't be able to keep this up much longer."

"Perhaps you could write me and let me know how things turn out," Samantha said, patting the journal on her lap. "My story of the Colorado pioneer woman is thus far incomplete."

Mandy smiled. She hoped one day to send them the good news that she and Dakota and their child were living happily ever after.

CHAPTER 33

*H*arv Arlen slid the wooden bowl across the table to Dakota. "More fried potatoes, my friend?"

"Oh, please, no Harv. I'm 'bout ready to bust." He turned to his hostess. "This sure was a fine meal, Gretchen. I thank you both for inviting me."

"Our pleasure. I'm sure that before long we'll be doing this as a foursome. Now, if you'll excuse me, I believe I hear a tiny someone calling my name."

The men rose from their seats when she did and sat again after she left. Harv poured more coffee.

"Have you given any more thought to our conversation of the other day, Dakota? With my tailoring business expanding to take in orders from the mountain communities, I'm in need of a trustworthy man to be in charge of delivering the goods up there and bringing back the proceeds."

"I've given it a lot of thought. Your offer is tempting, but it would mean spending weeks at a time away from Mandy. I don't think either of us wants that right now." He stared at the brown ripples in his cup. "I swear, Harv, every hour that goes by is an exercise in patience. It's been too long since she's sent word."

"Seems to me there was a young lady here for supper not too long ago who spoke those same words about some fella she was waiting for."

Dakota smiled. "Anyone I know?"

"Naw, you wouldn't know her, nor care for her much. She's not your type. She's impulsive. Bull-headed. And she has some crazy habits, like inviting seven rabid Indian braves to a church picnic."

The two friends laughed, but then Harv reminisced soberly. "You know, I thought we were all goners that day. But she went forward and spoke up to those warriors, looking them straight in the eye. Then that one raised his knife to her neck and…" He shuddered. "I get chillblains just thinking about it."

Dakota chuckled, but only because he knew the outcome of the story. The first time he heard it, he nearly choked on his heart.

"I think you're wrong, Harv."

"What about?"

"I think that girl sounds to be just my type."

"What girl?" Gretchen entered the room carrying Esther.

"Why, this one right here." Dakota stretched out his arm so Gretchen could place her daughter in its cradling welcome. He smiled down at the sweet face whose large, blue eyes quickly fastened on the fringe of his buckskin shirt.

The first time Gretchen placed Esther in his arm he nearly panicked. But each time thereafter he grew more confident, and she was always content when tucked away there. He didn't even mind the episodes of her upchucking on his shirt, for these times with her created in him a renewed yearning to father children. Perhaps someday, if Mandy came to feel the same way...

The following day, with George and Jeffrey in Fort Collins, Ardith enlisted Dakota's help in moving some of the upstairs furniture so the end-of-summer cleaning could get under way. It was gratifying to him to be called upon to use his returning strength to help move dressers, beds and chests of drawers.

After the noon meal, they took on the parlor.

"Mandy said you were strong," Ardith grunted as they moved the divan back against the wall. "She wasn't joking."

"It's your good cooking that's given me back some of what I'd lost."

"Always the gentleman." They plopped down together on the divan and took a breather. "Quick with the compliments."

"They're well deserved."

For a long moment she studied the face of the man her eldest daughter loved. The man who clearly regretted having stayed away so long.

"You're leaving soon."

His mother-in-law was the most perceptive woman he had ever known. Much like his father.

"Yes."

"You do realize she could come home, and you'd miss her, and she'd go out after you again, and you two could spend the rest of your lives chasing each other's shadows."

He shook his head. "I'll find her."

His confidence was assuring. "I believe you will."

After the supper dishes were cleared away, Dakota sat at the dining table and worked on improving his penmanship using his awkward left hand.

"Your cursive is coming along nicely," Julie said, peering over his shoulder. "A couple of weeks ago your letters looked like turkey tracks."

He smiled. "Always the lady. Quick with the compliments."

She sat down next to him. "Ma says you're leaving to find Mandy."

"It's been too long."

"That's just what she said."

"So I've heard."

She watched in silence for several minutes as he wrote his signature over and over. In a quivering voice she said, "You're like a brother to me, Dakota."

His hand stopped mid-stroke. He set the pencil down and turned to see her blue eyes filling with tears. Placing his hand on hers, he leaned over and kissed her cheek.

"You Berringer women…"

She dabbed a tear at the corner of her eye. "Mandy said she became quite fond of your brother, too."

"True, although they had a bit of a go-around before they discovered any endearing qualities in one another." He brushed her chin with his finger. "Unlike us."

She blushed. "Well, she certainly speaks affectionately of Cloudburst now."

His head rolled back in laughter. "It's Thunder Cloud. And yes, they…ironed things out."

He smiled in reminiscence of his wife's and his brother's topsy-turvy relationship.

"But any time the two of them are together, you can count on it being a memorable experience."

* * *

Walking timorously down the main street of a small plains community, Mandy's stomach churned. While in a mercantile asking about Dakota, she overheard snatches of a conversation about a much sought after Arapaho warrior who had been captured and confined.

231

Her eyes fixed on the brick jailhouse down the block.
The "little guy" was to hang at dawn.

CHAPTER 34

Shuffling along the boardwalk, still two doors away from the jail, Mandy stopped cold. The door of the jailhouse opened and two men emerged. One was a lean, graying man with a star on his vest.

The other was Travis Haines.

Mandy stiffened, then spun and stepped toward the storefront window nearest her. She pulled her bonnet forward and concealed her cane in the folds of her dress. She stared at the items in the window display but was blind to the things her eyes rested upon. Her ears, however, seemed crushed by the sounds of the approaching footsteps and the voices of the two men drawing nearer.

"I reckon this means you can get on with your life now, eh, son?"

"There are no words to describe the feeling of release I have, Sheriff. Tomorrow I'll be going home for good."

Mandy's breath held as the voices closed in behind her. Her desire was not to be hiding from Travis but to greet him.

"You've got a little girl, right?"

"Sure do. Her name's Mollie. She's gorgeous, just like her ma. And this time when I get back to her, I'm not leaving till she's off and married. Even then, I might just tag along."

The men's laughter blended with the other sounds of the town as they sauntered away. Mandy peeked from under her bonnet and made sure they were well on their way before she dared move.

She hesitated at the door of the jail as her chaotic thoughts wove themselves into quiet resolve. She didn't know whether to ask for God's help for what she was about to do, or for His forgiveness.

She entered the building and faced three men in the front room. She introduced herself merely as the daughter of a Denver lawyer. The man sitting on the corner of a desk with one leg dangling off said he was the deputy. Two town councilmen sat in straight-backed chairs on either side of the desk. None were amused by the reason for her coming.

"Ma'am, he ain't takin' callers. And to be honest, I can't

figure on why you'd want to visit a thievin', murderin' redskin."

"I'm aware of the charges against him, Deputy Ames, although I don't recall hearing the details of his trial."

The men burst into spontaneous laughter. The lawman recovered first. "He got all the trial he's gonna get, ma'am."

"How could the sheriff—and you as a deputy—perpetuate such a miscarriage of justice?"

"T'ain't no such thing. The law don't apply to Indians."

"I am quite versed in the law, sir. He has the right to counsel. I speak a bit of his tongue, and demand time alone with him."

"You're kiddin', right?" one of the councilmen asked.

"By no means."

"Lady, you don't know who you're dealin' with here."

"He is Thunder Cloud, is he not? I know of him."

"Ma'am, I can't let you go in there with that savage," Ames said.

"He's behind bars, isn't he?"

"Yeah, but—"

"Then there is nothing to fear from him. On the other hand, you three should be in fear of what the Bureau of Indian Affairs will do when they hear of this. As a federal authority, they—"

"All right, all right!" Deputy Ames lifted his hands in the air. "I've heard enough."

Enough? Enough to let her in or to throw her out?

The deputy rose from his desk. "I'll give you five minutes with him, not a second more. But I'll be right there the whole time so's he can't try nothin'."

"Agreed." She followed him to the door of the cell area and waited while he unlocked it. "By the way, do you speak any of the Arapaho language yourself?"

He threw her a look that communicated the absurdity of the question.

There were two cells in the back room, one on each side. It was dimly lit and depressing. As Ames relocked the door behind them, Mandy's hand moved to pat the hard but unnoticeable bulge in her dress pocket.

Her heart skipped at the thought of seeing her brother-in-law again. But if the deputy perceived a familiarity between them, it would be disastrous.

Mandy and the deputy stood at the warrior's cell, but he ignored their presence. He sat cross-legged and motionless on the cot under the window, his back leaning against the brick wall but his face turned toward the adjacent one.

"There's someone here wants to talk to you, red man. Wants to give you some counsel."

The brave's only movement was that of his bare chest as he took slow, tense breaths. The bear claw necklace that had once pierced Mandy's back the day he confronted her in the corral was missing. Confiscated, she assumed.

"He's a real chin-flapper, ain't he?"

"You promised me five minutes," she whispered.

"And not a second more."

She worked moisture into her dry mouth and shifted her brain into Arapaho speech.

"Do not show any sign of knowing me, my brother."

His eyes darted to the side. He otherwise remained expressionless.

"This lawman does not understand what we say, and we must not let him know we are acquainted."

He slowly turned his head, his coal black eyes rising to meet hers. Those eyes—once they had terrified her beyond reason. No longer.

"Do you understand?"

He slowly nodded once.

"Don't them eyes just give yeh the creeps?" the deputy said. "If them ain't killin' eyes, then I never seen none."

"Thunder Cloud, I have only a short time." Her hand slipped again to her dress pocket, and his eye caught the movement. He stood, then walked to the cell door.

Ames pulled Mandy back. "Step away, ma'am. Don't get within arm's reach of that badger."

She complied, not wanting to do anything to make Ames rescind the small amount of time allotted her.

"My heart is happy at seeing you, Man-dee. Many times I have thought of you and Dakota, and wished for us all to be together."

"I have as well. But we have no time for such dreams now. There is something I must ask you. In the moon cycles before that day you found me on the prairie with Little Dog,

235

how far from your village had you gone to hunt?"

He questioned her with his eyes.

"I must know."

"For whatever reason you must know, know this. Those days were the brightest of my life. My heart was full of love for Little Fawn, and we were to be married. Though game was scarce, I never traveled more than one day's ride to find sufficient food."

"You never went far to the north, close to where the tribes of your northern brothers dwell?"

"Never."

Her shoulders fell with her sigh. "Prepare yourself, my brother. I am going to give you a knife."

He almost let a smile slip out but caught himself. He sent an intense glare to the lawman, then glanced back at Mandy, making sure his gaze did not soften when he looked at her.

"No, Man-dee."

"But—"

"Where is Dakota?" Her distressed expression gave him his answer. "He has not yet returned to you?"

"What? How…how did you know—"

"I have seen him."

She let out a breath and stepped toward the cell. Ames grabbed her arm and pulled her back.

"You saw him? When? Where?"

"It has been perhaps a half moon. He was at a Cheyenne camp recovering from…a wound."

"I know about his arm."

"You know? He said he sent you no word."

"And when I could no longer live without knowing what happened to him, I set out to look for him. I spoke to the Army medicine man who cared for him, and have searched for him since."

"You have been wandering this land searching for him? Alone? While he allowed that…?"

"While he allowed what?"

The brave's jaw tensed. "My brother does not always show the wisdom of his father."

"How was he when you left him?"

"His body is weak but well enough. His heart is still heavy. He has left that village, but his pride keeps him from returning to you."

"I try to understand what he is going through. But it is hard to be patient." She paused. "I carry his child."

His fist tightened around the bar. "He did not mention this to me."

"He does not know. And did Dakota speak to you of our son? And your father?"

"Yes, and I grieve for you."

"And I for you."

Their eyes locked. Her hand moved to her pocket.

"What you are planning is foolishness. If I escape with a knife, they will know where I got it. I will not risk any harm coming to you."

"They will think you have been keeping it hidden, waiting for the right time."

"Man-dee, where would I keep a knife hidden?"

Her eyes scanned his form. She blushed and averted her gaze. He wore only a breechcloth.

"Promise me one thing, Thunder Cloud. Promise me you will use the knife only to threaten and not to harm."

"I will *not* take it from you. If the man who trapped me and brought me here suspects you have helped me, he will take vengeance on you. His eyes are full of hate. I do not want you to face such a man."

Travis. He was not like that with her. His eyes were gentle, and always a little sad. She had no doubt, though, that Thunder Cloud described him exactly as he saw him.

"The man who brought you here is a friend of Dakota's and of mine. But he is convinced you murdered his wife."

The warrior was visibly stunned. "How could such a man be a friend to you? He is cold and venomous."

"He believes you to be the same way. But I know both of you better."

"Ma'am," Ames cut in, "your time's 'bout up. Git this over with."

"Deputy, is there *any way possible* this man will get a fair trial in this town? He says he's innocent."

"Not according to the victim's husband, who says an eyewitness got a good look at the savage."

"That's hearsay evidence. No judge would consider it admissible in court."

"If we had a judge. And them Indian Affairs people can do what they want later, but it won't change anythin' tonight."

Mandy looked back at her brother-in-law. "I must leave now. Take this knife as I—"

"No, Man-dee! Go from here. Go to the north and find my Blue Flower. Tell her I was killed when I fell from my horse, or while fighting the Kiowa. Do not tell her I died at the end of a rope while the white men and women and children cheered. Allow her to live with honor, though I shall die without it."

Her hand grasped the handle of the camp knife she had removed from Clairborne's waist belt after the guide's untimely death. Thunder Cloud's eyes noticed the furtive movement. His gaze held an ominous declaration of warning.

She grinned in return. "There is something you should know about me. Even after all this time, I still have not learned how to keep my place."

She turned toward Deputy Ames. "I've done all I can here." As she stepped away she lost her balance and fell toward the cell. Initially taken off guard, Ames moved quickly to steady her and pull her away from the proximity of the dangerous prisoner.

"That was close!" he said as he caught his breath.

"It certainly was. Sometimes I forget how unstable my ankle is. Thank you for your assistance, Deputy. Your reactions are quite quick."

"Gotta be in this job, ma'am."

He preceded her to the door, and as he stopped to unlock it, she turned, imparting a long last glance at her brother-in-law.

Thunder Cloud, his dark eyes firmly fixed her hers, nodded once.

* * *

A loud banging on the door of her hotel room woke Mandy from a fitful sleep. There was not even a hint of gray in the sky as she lit the bedside oil lamp. Slipping into a robe, she took up her cane and went to the door.

"Who is it?" she asked through the door, thinking *I believe you already know, even though you ask.*

"It's Sheriff Branham, ma'am. I need to talk to you."

238

The foreknowledge that this moment would come did nothing to prevent the gnawing feeling from heightening.

She unlocked the door and stepped aside as she opened it. After the sheriff entered, she attempted to close it, but someone pushed hard against it. Deputy Ames entered. And after him, Travis Haines.

"Mandy! What are you…?"

"You two know each other?" Sheriff Branham asked.

Ames pushed Travis aside to confront Mandy. He spoke with impatience, almost frenzy.

"Ma'am, did that Indian you talked to today give you any hint he was fixin' to escape?"

"Escape?" Her voice faltered.

"You heard me."

"W-was anyone hurt?"

"You'd better believe someone was hurt, and hurt bad," Branham answered. Mandy's heart drummed in alarm.

The sheriff gestured toward Travis. "This man here has spent over two years looking for the animal that murdered his wife. He was to have his revenge tomorrow, but now the savage is long gone. That kind of hurt ain't easily done away with."

Mandy's relief that no one had been physically harmed did not show outwardly, for she remained enshrouded by the tension in the room. She dared not look at Travis, but could feel his onerous gaze.

Ames continued, "Did he mention anything about where he was headin' at the time he got captured?"

"No."

"Did he—"

"Save your breath, Deputy," Travis cut in. "I can spare you a lot of wasted time."

Travis pushed Ames aside and stood before her. "I know this woman," he said through clenched teeth. "It was her husband's brother who—"

Her breath caught as she awaited the words that would seal her fate.

A painfully long silence followed.

"Who what?" Branham asked.

"Who…"

More silence.

239

"Mr. Haines?"

His eyes remained fixed on Mandy.

"I suggest you conduct your investigation elsewhere, Sheriff."

"Are you sure, Haines? She was the only person outside of my deputies who had any contact with that Indian."

Travis nodded.

The lawman moved toward the door but turned as he opened it. "I'm really sorry, Haines. I know what this means for you."

The sheriff and deputy let themselves out. Travis remained, his eyes impaling her.

"Look at me, Mandy."

She did not stir.

"I said *look at me!*"

Her head jerked up.

"The sheriff said he was sorry, that he knew what this meant for me. Do *you* have any idea what this means to me? *Do you*, Mandy? Do you know what you have done to me?"

"I did it *for* Thunder Cloud. I have done nothing *against* you."

"Spare me your legal constructs! You have seen to it that two years out of my life have been *laid waste*. You have kept me from burying the one thing that has been eating away at me like Herod's worms, keeping me from my daughter and any chance for peace."

"Your own bitterness brought that on you, Travis."

"Don't you dare lecture me!"

Gone was the sadness in his eyes. Now there was only the rage Dakota alluded to during Travis' visit to the mountains. She yearned for the friendly smile and endearing wink he so freely offered that night they met in front of her hearth.

"You had a lot of nerve back at the cabin telling me about my duty to Mollie. Why aren't you at home with your husband and child instead of in this godforsaken town breaking murderers out of jail?"

She brushed past him to the dresser and leaned against it, eyeing the image of her accuser in the mirror.

"My son is dead, and Dakota has deserted me."

He straightened and stared back into her reflection. "*What?*"

240

She turned to him and recounted the events that had taken place since he had left the mountain without saying good-bye. He was stunned at the revelations of what his friends had been through.

"Mandy, I-I don't know what to say."

"There's nothing you can say. But what I can assure you is that Thunder Cloud is *not* the one who killed Becky. There's no question of that now. He wasn't even close to your home when it happened. I couldn't let him hang for it."

He let out a long sigh, then walked to the window and pulled aside the curtain. He stared out into the night, the emptiness without matching that within him.

"My reason for living these past two years has just disappeared into the vast, black void of the prairie."

"You have a better reason to live, and she's waiting for her father to come home."

He hung his head in surrender. "What about you?" he asked.

"I don't want *my* child to grow up without a father either."

He turned toward her. "You're...?"

Her hand went to her abdomen. "I have to find him."

"He doesn't know?"

She shook her head.

He gazed outward again into the early morning stillness. "Go home, Mandy." Releasing the curtain, he turned to her. "It's time we both went home."

At noon that day they dined at the hotel, then Travis accompanied her to the stage depot.

Mandy took the window seat and smiled at him as he stood on the boardwalk, hat in hand.

"Maybe next summer Mollie and me will take a trip out to see you two. Except, I guess by then it'll be three."

"I'd like that very much."

As the stage pulled away, she was warmed inside, for as she glanced back to say good-bye, Travis winked at her.

241

CHAPTER 35

*G*eorge paced the parlor, his hands locked behind his back.

"I'm afraid I have to agree with you, Dakota. Too much time has passed. We need to go and find her."

"I'll make better time tracking her, Mr. Barton, if there are fewer distractions."

"And *I* would be a distraction?"

"Yes, sir."

George's brows raised. "Well, it appears you have learned your lesson about holding back on the truth." He grinned. "I have no doubt you'll do just fine without me."

Ardith and Julie spent the evening making jerky and gathering provisions for Dakota's trip. He showed them how to make Indian pemmican, which Julie found most interesting.

"I'm afraid I've lost another daughter to the ways of the wild, and I have you to thank for both, Dakota," Ardith chided. When he leaned down and planted a kiss on her cheek, all was forgiven. "You sure have a way about you, young man."

"Mandy always said you'd like me."

"You wipe that foolish grin off your face. You look like a jackass eating cactus."

When the work was completed, their moods dampened, for only then did they let themselves think about why it was all necessary.

"Are you sure you don't need any money?" George asked.

"I've got enough and can get more if needs be."

"You keep in touch," Ardith said.

"As best as I'm able, Mrs. Barton."

George and Ardith retired early that night. Jeff went to Mr. Samuel's law office in town to study some of his father's books. Julie sat at the piano and aimlessly pressed a few keys. Dakota sat next to her and studied her face.

"What's on your mind, sis?"

"How worried should we be, Dakota?"

"There's any number of reasons why we haven't heard from her. The Indians are sabotaging the telegraph lines all the time. We don't even know if she's gone to places that have an office."

"She could write."

"Maybe she has, and the mail just hasn't gotten through yet."

The same excuses Julie offered Mandy for Dakota's belated return. "So, you're not worried?"

"I know she can take care of herself. But yeah, I'm worried."

"I guess you'll be leaving at daybreak?"

"No, there's one item of business I have to take care of first in town."

"Anything I can help you with?"

"Not in that regard, but there is another way you could help me."

"Name it."

"I need to send a letter, but I'd like it to be legible. Would you mind?"

"Not at all. Who's it to?"

He sighed. "I acted ungraciously toward the doctor who tended me at Fort Lyon. I owe him an apology."

"Tell you what. I'll write what you dictate, but you sign it yourself, to show him how far you've come."

"I'm indebted to you, Julie."

"For a fact, you are." She flashed him a smile.

The next morning, Dakota left the Lawrence Street store pleased with his purchase. He placed the small package wrapped in lavender paper inside his *parfleche*. After packing his supplies, he said difficult farewells to his new family and set out.

He arrived in Colorado City late the next evening, having made only brief rest stops along the way. His first stop was the hotel where he and Mandy stayed after coming down from the cabin.

Yes, the clerk had seen her recently. "She met up with a group of English tourists and their guide and headed out onto the plains."

"Tourists? What was she doing with them?"

"No idea. But the way the Englanders told the story, their guide got killed by a rattler, and she and them was left afoot when their horses run off. It was your wife who kept them all alive until some French trapper come upon them and

243

accompanied them back into town, but not before she killed two Indians who tried to ambush them."

"*What!*"

"That's how the story goes."

He shut his eyes and raked his hair with his fingers.

"I guess it's been about a week since she left last."

"Did she leave by stage?"

"Best check at the depot."

The clerk there was of little help. He remembered her but had too many people passin' through to recall where they all headed.

"What are the destinations from here?"

"I got one goin' north, one goin' south, and one that goes east."

He ruled out north since he had come on that route and checked the stages he passed. She'd already been south. He headed east.

Stopping at each town along the stage route, he found he was on the right course.

"Yes, she was here asking about a fella—sounded like you."

In each town there was someone, usually several people, who remembered her in their shop. "Sure was a determined gal."

One town left him baffled. Several people said they knew of the woman he described, but he was certain it was the wrong woman. The one they spoke of had been under suspicion for busting some murderous Indian out of jail.

He changed direction after speaking to a depot agent who recalled her heading north. But after the next town, he lost her. Nobody to the east or west knew of her either. He grew frustrated at losing so much ground after having been so close.

Added to this, his energy reserves were sapped. The surgeon had told him it would take months to build up his strength due to the amount of blood he'd lost. Although his stay in Denver helped him recoup some of his vigor, expending so much of it now was taking its toll.

Tired though he was, he ventured on. An old fear clung like a leech, struggling to take rule. He had never felt so painfully helpless or terrified as on the day she was taken from him.

No, he could not allow his fears to reign if he was to be of any use to her. Her trail was no longer easy to follow, but she would leave one nonetheless.

A friend once told him, "I swear you could track a whisper in a cyclone." Now he could not manage to find his own beloved who, until that last town, left blatant indications of her whereabouts.

Yet he determined that if he had to crisscross the entire territory to do it, *he would find her.*

CHAPTER 36

*M*andy had taken the stage to many towns along the eastern plains, but wished for a way to investigate the smaller communities off the main stage routes where Dakota may be more willing to show himself. Then she saw a freight wagon, and on its side was written in bold red letters:

BARTON & KEIFFER
KANSAS CITY—DENVER—SAN FRANCISCO

Introducing herself to the driver—a burly woman she initially mistook for a man—she explained that George Barton was her stepfather and that she was in desperate need of a ride through the Front Range communities.

"We're not supposed to take on passengers, but if you're the boss's daughter, I reckon it'll be okay."

"*Step*daughter. When do we leave?"

Four hours into their journey, one of the wagon's axles loosened. They had to divert south to the nearest town with a blacksmith. Her purpose in searching the smaller communities was now defeated as Mandy found herself in this town with a population of a thousand.

The instant the driver alighted from the wagon she insisted that Mandy, as the boss's daughter, front the money to pay for the needed repairs.

"*Step*daughter." She handed over the money.

While the driver spoke to the smith, Mandy witnessed two separate bouts of fisticuffs, heard a gunshot and a woman scream, and watched a man get thrown through a storefront window. And this is where she would be spending the night.

Thus when the hotel clerk suggested she leave any valuables in the lobby safe, she readily agreed. After paying for the room, she deposited all but two dollars, which she'd need for that night's supper, in the safe. She immediately went to the Main Street businesses to inquire about Dakota.

It was with trepidation that she went about her usual pattern of questioning shopkeepers, one of whom recalled his name and thought he might've done some smithing there at one time. Upon returning to the hotel, her stomach was so capsized from the stress of her wanderings through this exceptionally violent and unsympathetic town that she skipped supper.

Once in her room, she sat on her bed and withdrew *Evangeline* from her satchel. The heroine's search for her beloved Gabriel could not be thwarted by the insistence of others.

> *Whither my heart has gone, there follows my hand, and not elsewhere.*
> *For when the heart goes before, like a lamp, and illumines the pathway,*
> *Many things are made clear, that else lie hidden in darkness.*

Her heart was with Dakota, and she must follow there and not elsewhere. It lit her path to him. It is what kept her going on such days and nights as these.

When she came downstairs the next morning, there was a clamor in the lobby. A dozen guests were milling about, arguing with the hotel manager. Mandy asked a well-dressed, heavyset woman about the cause of the commotion.

"That no-good lying weasel of a clerk got everyone to put their money and valuables in the safe and then ran off with all of it last night. I had jewels and a thousand dollars in there. And now they're gone. Gone!"

Mandy was dumbstruck. All of her money, save two dollars, was in that safe.

"Hold on now, everyone." The manager motioned for the guests to quiet down. "I've spoken with our insurance representative here, and you're all covered. You will all be paid back *in full*. There will be extra paperwork for those of you who left non-monetary possessions with us, but present your receipts to our agent, and I'm sure everything will be worked out amicably."

"When can we expect our money?" asked a young man in the crowd.

"As soon as the claims are processed. It shouldn't take longer than sixty days."

"Sixty days! You must be joking! You'd better cough up my money now, mister."

Stunned and in fear of a riot, Mandy quickly filled out the claim form and headed for the smithy. She had to get out of this town with what little she had left. She was equally saddened and relieved that she had no choice but to continue on to Denver with the freighter.

The smith told her that the man-sized female driver had staggered by the evening before, all liquored up, belching out that she wasn't waiting for the wagon to be repaired to leave this miserable town, and didn't care what became of the wagon, the supplies, or the boss's *step*daughter. She had bought herself a horse, apparently with the money Mandy gave her to pay the smith, and left town. Furthermore, neither the wagon nor its supplies would be released until full payment was made.

Mandy returned to the hotel in a stupor.

"How much did you lose, miss?" asked a woman in the still-gathered crowd of irate victims.

"Not nearly so much as many of you, ma'am, but it was all I had."

The woman walked away shaking her head.

"Excuse me, miss."

Mandy turned to face a tall, extremely attractive and well-dressed man.

"I couldn't help overhearing about your quandary."

The man oozed masculine charm. His hair and eyes were dark brown. He had a finely trimmed moustache, and held within a perfect set of teeth was a thin, pleasant smelling cigar of a cherry blend tobacco. His silver-buttoned black suit coat covered a brocade vest, and a black string tie bloomed from under the collar of a white shirt.

"Perhaps I can be of some assistance to you, Miss…"

She had been raised smarter than to trust such a stranger, even one who just might have a solution to her calamity.

"Who are you?" she asked.

His hand went to his chest. "Forgive me for not introducing myself. I am Preston Patterson, a man who simply cannot bear to see a damsel in distress. And you, my dear lady, have all the symptoms."

"But how can you help?"

"I own a large ranch eight miles outside of town. I offer you food and shelter and anything else you require to make you

248

comfortable until your situation reverses."

"Forgive me, but I don't understand. Why would you do this for strangers? And I can't speak for the others, but I've been left short of cash and couldn't pay you."

"There are no 'others', miss. Just you. And as for payment, well, you don't fall short in that area whatsoever."

Her jaw fell. She didn't know whether to be more appalled by his turpitude or her own naivete. She spun in contempt and started for the front desk.

"Don't make any hasty decisions, Miss... What was your name?"

She turned to him. "Starbuck. And it's *Mrs.* Starbuck."

Patterson's brow raised.

"That's right. Though my finger lacks a ring to display it, the fact is, you have just propositioned a married woman."

He shifted his weight and looked at her through pensive eyes. She proceeded to the desk where the frazzled hotel manager sorted claim forms.

"Mr. Turner, I can't wait sixty days for my money. I need it now, at least some of it. Even I can't make two dollars stretch back to Denver."

"Sorry ma'am. Our insurance agent says sixty days. No exceptions."

"Haven't you been listening to me? I *can't* wait!"

"It's you who hasn't been listening. I can't give you any money. If you're destitute, try the bank. Maybe they'll give you a loan."

"A stranger in town with no money and no collateral?"

"Take them this notice of settlement due and tell them you'll pledge it to the bank." He wrote on an official looking form. "It's all I can do for you now."

Seething with frustration, Mandy snatched the paper from him and sidled her way across the lobby through the throng of wrought-up guests. Her only hope now was the bank. Surely they'd accept an official insurance pledge to be repaid in sixty days. Surely they would.

Just outside the door of the hotel, leaning against the building with his arms crossed in front of him and a cigar wedged in the corner of his mouth, was Preston Patterson.

"My offer still stands, *Mrs.* Starbuck."

Mandy subdued the urge to thrust her cane into his chest.

249

She breezed past him and on to the bank.

The teller couldn't have appeared more indifferent as Mandy explained her dilemma and presented her offer.

"Well, Mrs. Starbuck, your request is highly irregular. You need to speak to the loan officer. His desk is right over there."

Her stomach growled as she waited half an hour before the man was free to see her. She repeated her offer as he massaged his temple with his index finger.

"Well now, Mrs. Starbuck, your request is highly irregular."

"So I've been told. Will you do it?"

"I'm really not at liberty to make this sort of decision. You'd have to discuss this with the bank manager since the circumstances are so unusual."

"Is he here?"

"He's with a customer, but if you'll wait in that chair over there, I'm sure he'll see you as soon as he's through."

Forty-five minutes this time before she was facing the manager with another round of explanations and pleas.

"Well now, Mrs. Starbuck, you're request—"

"Is highly irregular, I know. My situation is irregular, sir."

"I really think this is something our president will have to deal with."

In a voice only slightly lower than a scream she said, "And who's he going to refer me to? Governor Hunt?"

"I assure you, our president will give you your answer."

"Can I see him now?"

"He comes in an hour before closing on Wednesdays. The rest of his time is taken up with mid-week meetings."

"So that means I have to wait until—"

"Four o'clock."

She glanced at a grandfather clock across the room. Nine fifty-five.

She left the bank with six hours to kill in this miserable excuse for a town and hardly knew how to spend it. Even window-shopping was dangerous. One never knew when a body might come flying through the glass.

Walking along the street, she considered her situation. She had two dollars. If she spent it on food, she'd have nothing left. Another night in the hotel would cost three dollars, and she had

250

already been informed that payment had to be made up front. No exceptions.

Somehow she felt more secure with the pittance in her pocket than in her stomach, although her stomach was arguing that point. Having not eaten in nearly twenty-four hours, she did not want to go much longer without food. She had the baby to consider.

Without the loan, there'd be only one solution to this nightmarish predicament. She was in a town that had a telegraph office, and George had offered to wire her money. But he had made it clear it was for a stage home. He would not fund a "ridiculous search for a half-breed who doesn't want you anyway."

Like Evangeline, Longfellow's heroine, Mandy at some point must give up her search for her husband. She may have reached that point today.

Checkout time at the hotel wasn't until noon, so she returned there. The penetrating aroma of fried ham and sizzling hash browns wafting from the restaurant drove her rumbling stomach into cramping.

In her room she lay across the bed and tried to rest, but to no avail. She sat up again, anxiety not permitting her the posture of one who relaxes. Her eyes fell to her book on the nightstand—Longfellow's tragic poem. Her heart was in the same place as Evangeline's. She picked up the book and began to read.

Patience! came the voice of the priest to the heroine, and to Mandy.

> *Accomplish thy labor; Accomplish thy work of affection!*
> *Sorrow and silence are strong, and patient endurance is godlike.*
> *Therefore accomplish thy labor of love, till the heart is made godlike,*
> *Purified, strengthened, perfected and rendered more worthy of heaven!*

She could *not* give up. Her sorrow was indeed strong, and his silence unbearable, but she must be stronger still. Yet it would take a strength she lacked on her own. She fell to her knees beside the bed and asked God for His strength and His intervention.

After checking out at noon, she walked the streets several times, cane in one hand and satchel in the other. She looked at the clock in the town square a dozen times. She reflected on the months she had spent with the Arapaho where passage of time was something to flow with, not contend with. Staring at hands on a dial was a tormenting method in which to thread one's way through time.

At three thirty, tired and profoundly hungry, she went to the bank in hopes of being granted an early appointment. She sat for half an hour.

At precisely four o'clock the manager told her she could see the president. He led her to an office behind the teller cages and gave the door two quick raps before opening it. "Your four o'clock is here to see you, sir." He turned and gestured for Mandy to enter.

She stepped into another world. Whereas the décor of the bank lobby was austere and unimaginative, this office was luxurious on the scale of royalty. The thick pile carpet was deep red. The wallpaper had a gold and red spiral design. The glass-enclosed bookcases were made of mahogany, as was the oversized desk Mandy approached. A high-back, brown leather chair faced away from her toward a multi-paned window framed by heavy velvet red drapes with gold fringe.

The manager left, closing the door behind him. The room was as silent as the sunbeams shining through the windows.

Mandy felt like a church mouse in a cathedral—small and insignificant. Her fate was in the hands of a man who did not even have the courtesy to turn his chair around and acknowledge her presence.

She wondered if perhaps the old geezer had died and no one had even noticed. He could've been there for days, no one daring to enter his habitation to disturb him.

A puff of smoke rose from behind the chair. So, he was alive. Too bad. It probably would've been easier to secure the loan from a corpse.

He sent up another smoke signal, and the swivel chair began to turn. Before she ever saw his face, the aroma of cherry blend tobacco reached her nostrils. She held her breath and stared in disbelief.

252

He removed the cigar and smiled up at her. "Why, hello, *Mrs.* Starbuck."

Preston Patterson placed his cigar in an ashtray and settled leisurely into the soft leather cushion. "I have been informed that you have requested a loan with only the promise of an insurance draft as collateral."

She couldn't even answer.

He rose and walked around the side of his desk. "Well, was I informed correctly?"

She nodded.

"I'm not sure how I should deal with this. Your re—"

"quest is highly irregular."

He gave her half a smile. "What would you do if I didn't give you the money?"

She remained silent.

"I'm just curious. How would you get by?"

"Will you permit me the loan? Yes or no."

He studied her face impudently. "No."

Fury rivaled the desperation in her. Would he truly refuse her out of spite?

She turned and stamped toward the door. She jerked it open part way when Patterson's hand encompassed hers and forced the door closed. Every inch of her tensed.

"My earlier offer still stands, Mrs. Starbuck. Won't you reconsider?"

She pulled away from him.

"What's the matter? I'm not going to harm you." He backed away and half-sat on his desk, folding his arms across his chest. "That's not my style."

"I'm well aware of your style, Mr. Patterson. Loitering in hotel lobbies, seeking out destitute women you can manipulate into—"

"I've never had to seek out any woman. *They* seek *me* out."

"Not *this* woman." She exited the room, then the bank, slamming both doors behind her.

She looked woefully down the street toward the telegraph office. Having George wire her money was her only recourse now. It may work out for the best after all. Perhaps along with the money she'd receive good news—news that Dakota had gone there.

253

Yet more incredible tidings greeted her at the telegraph office.

"There's no messages goin' west, ma'am. Indians again."

She left the office in a daze. Standing on the boardwalk, she glanced heavenward. *This is how You answer my prayer for intervention, Lord?*

She looked to her left, then to her right. She literally did not know which way to turn. No direction offered any hope. Out on the prairie or in the mountains she could take care of herself. But in town one could not survive on one's wits. It took money, and she had almost none. She was now weakened to the point of feeling unsteady from her keen hunger, and she worried about her baby.

She headed back in the direction she'd come. As she passed the door of the bank, Patterson stepped out, hindering her path. She tried to step around him, but he took hold of her arm.

"Wait."

"Leave me alone!" She was too downcast and spent to go another round with this man.

"Your perseverance and fidelity are admirable, Mrs. Starbuck, but they'll not put food in your stomach nor a roof over your head tonight. You don't really want to sleep in an alley and feed on whatever scraps the grimy restaurants discard, do you? I'll have my cook prepare you a feast worthy of your noble virtues. Succulent roasted pork. Butter-dipped corn on the cob. Mashed potatoes and flaky biscuits, both shrouded in gravy. Chilled melons with whipped cream."

Her dry lips pressed together as moisture flowed into her parched mouth.

"You can already *taste* it, can't you?" Leaning close, he spoke softly in her ear. "A luxuriously comfortable room with a soft bed of down awaits you. And I assure you, Mandy, that if you should so desire, you can sleep in it alone tonight. You have nothing to fear from me."

There was a realm within her that cried out for such deliverance from hunger and fatigue. She looked up into his alluring brown eyes.

"You *deserve* that kind of comfort. Come with me."

She shut her eyes against his quixotic countenance. "No," she whispered half-heartedly.

"Come with me. You need not go hungry any longer."

From a deeper realm within her, the strength of her convictions and her sensibilities surfaced and overruled all of her immediate desires.

"No," she said, this time with both halves of her heart.

"Don't let some timeworn notion of dignity keep you from satisfying your needs."

"All I have left is my dignity."

He lifted her chin with his fingers. "It's all there for the taking, awaiting you." He lowered his lips toward hers. "Come with me."

Their lips were nearly touching.

"I'd rather starve."

His movements halted. Seduction faded into contempt. He shoved her against the iron security bars shielding the window.

"Go ahead, then. Beg for money and scavenge for food. Let the rats keep you warm tonight!"

He yanked open the door of the bank and disappeared inside.

Mandy grasped one of the bars for support, breathing heavily, disturbed by the thought of how frighteningly vulnerable she had become.

She tried to shake off the feeling as she walked away from the bank. She also tried to cast out the lingering vision of that steaming, succulent pork, that buttery corn, those gravy-smothered biscuits and that whipped cream-topped melon.

Something else lingered in her mind. How did Patterson know her first name? She didn't recall having told it to anyone, and she had signed into the hotel as Mrs. John Starbuck, the same name she had printed on her insurance voucher.

.

Thoughts of food and the hotel gave her an idea. Earlier that day as she passed the hotel's dining room, wishing she could go in and have a meal, she noticed the sole waitress running ragged waiting ten tables. Perhaps, if despite her weariness and the condition of her foot, she could handle that kind of work and earn even one dollar, she could spend the night in the hotel. She headed there.

Mr. Kelsey, the dining room manager, was one of the few men of sympathy in the town. "But Miz Starbuck, I just can't afford to hire you on. If I could, I'd've hired someone long ago

255

to give Bridget some relief with the supper crowd. Wish I could help. I really do."

As she turned to leave, she saw Bridget, the red-haired, blue-eyed waitress, busily clearing a table. Almost unconsciously, the woman picked up a coin and slipped it into her apron pocket. Mandy turned again to the manager.

"Mr. Kelsey, if you would let me work here tonight, I wouldn't ask for any wages. Just let me work for tips, and perhaps a meal after the work is done?"

"Now, Miz Starbuck, it just don't set right with me, havin' someone work for me without payin' them a fair wage. That's akin to slavery."

"But I'm the one who offered to do it. Please, I've got to earn a dollar to be able to stay here tonight."

"Well, if you put it that way…"

"Oh, thank you, Mr. Kelsey. Thank you!"

Donning an apron and listening to a quick lesson in the art of waiting tables from Bridget, Mandy took on three tables while Bridget took the other seven. Despite Mandy's inexperience and having to work with a cane, the waitress was most grateful for the help.

For the next four hours Mandy hustled as she never had in her life. Her ankle grew more painful, and twice she had to loosen the laces on her shoe because of the swelling. She tried to keep track of her tips, but her mind was too busy doing the figuring on the numerous order slips she wrote out.

While she was back in the kitchen area late in the evening, her stomach pleading for a morsel of the juicy steak, puffy mashed potatoes and simmering brown gravy the cook was preparing, Bridget entered in a dither, her brogue thick with excitement. "Oh, Mandy, you did it! Yer ship has come in!"

"What do you mean?"

"Yeh said yeh needed a dollar? I guarantee yeh'll get at least that much from the man who just sat down at table number one. The last time he came in here he left me two whole dollars. And he's at your table!"

"Really?" Mandy cracked open the door and peeked into the seating area. She turned back to Bridget. "Would you do me a favor? Take that table for me, and I'll take number four for you."

"Are yeh daft, girl? Has this cookin' smoke done addled

your brain? Didn't yeh hear what I just told yeh?"

"I can't explain now, but I don't want to serve that man. You keep his tip. I don't want anything from him."

"But…I…at least let me split it with yeh."

Mandy shook her head. "You keep it all."

She avoided Patterson's gaze for the hour he spent there. It was closing time when he finally got up to leave. Mandy carried an armful of plates into the kitchen, and was grateful to find him gone when she returned.

"Look, Mandy, he left five dollars!" Bridget exclaimed as she cleared his table. "Can yeh believe it? That's as much as I usually get in a week, and he was only here one hour. Please, yeh've got to take half."

"Keep it. You're the one trying to support three kids and a sick husband. Besides, I think I made my dollar."

Bridget reluctantly slipped the money in her pocket. "Do yeh think yeh'll be back tomorrah?"

"The way things are going, I may be here for sixty tomorrows."

After they finished cleaning up, Bridget went home and an exhausted Mandy finally sat down to her long awaited meal— her first in a day and a half. She chose a booth with a padded seat and lifted her painfully swollen foot onto it. Her eyes were wide with anticipation as she cut through the thick, tender, and sinfully juicy T-bone steak. Her taste buds screamed in satisfaction as her mouth closed around it. She formed a crater on top of a huge pile of mashed potatoes and poured thick, spicy brown gravy on it until it overflowed like a volcano. Eating had never been such an exuberant experience.

When she had eaten enough to satisfy her grouchy stomach, she took out her tip money. She had put off counting it for fear of finding she'd come up short, and she wanted nothing to ruin this exquisite meal.

As she finished the count, a tall, dark figure came to stand next to the table. His voice and sardonic tone almost ruined her appetite.

"Did you make your dollar?"

She held up a shiny coin and beamed. "With a dime to spare."

"It could have been so easy. But now look at you. You look haggard. Used up."

Her jaded eyes held his arrogant gaze. "Better to be used up…than *used*."

He shook his head, his face reflecting pure repugnance.

"Why are you traveling alone? Where is *Mr.* Starbuck?"

The situation hardly called for the entire truth. "I anticipate rejoining him any day now."

His stance shifted uncomfortably. "Is that so?"

Reaching into the inside pocket of his suit coat, he withdrew a long brown envelope and threw it on the table.

"I'm not interested in any more of your propositions, Mr. Patterson."

He was already walking away.

She continued to partake of her banquet. Her eyes frequently glimpsed the envelope, but the hand that held the fork would not be thwarted from its mission. Upon completing her meal, she eyed the envelope again. She was certain it wasn't a loan draft. Patterson would be more likely to keep pressing until she was starved into submission.

Reluctantly, she picked it up, opened the tucked in flap and removed a piece of white paper folded in thirds. After another moment's hesitation, she unfolded it. It was a letter addressed to Preston Patterson.

And it was written in Dakota's handwriting!

Her eyes sped to the bottom of the page. She wasn't mistaken. The letter was signed John Starbuck. She read the words that shook in her hands.

Mr. Patterson:

In compliance with your regulations, I am hereby submitting in writing on this 18th day of June 1867, my authorization to release to my wife, Amanda (Mandy) Starbuck, any or all of the funds available in my account. You are also hereby authorized to act without further inquiry in accordance with writings bearing her signature, supplying any endorsement for her on any draft or other instrument rendered for this account. You are hereby released of any liability in connection with her use of the account.

Thank you for your services.

John Starbuck

Acknowledged by Preston Patterson, President

Mandy stared at the quivering paper. Based on the date, Dakota must have stopped in this town on his way to the reservation. He told her in Colorado City that he wanted her to have access to what was his, and had added her name to this account, too. His forethought just saved her from an indeterminate fate. She kissed the paper as relief flooded her soul.

Patterson had known all along. She had misconstrued his startled expression upon hearing her name as being caused by her marital status. But it was never the *Mrs.* that bothered him, it was the *Starbuck.* And that's how he knew her given name.

Preston Patterson played dirty pool.

She fondled Dakota's letter, her fingers caressing the words formed by the hand that was no longer a part of him.

Gazing out the window into the night sky, she offered a prayer of humble apology for her faithless presumption regarding His lack of intervention outside the telegraph office. And one of thanksgiving for the way God had long ago intervened in what would happen here today. How many times must He prove His faithfulness before she would trust Him even when she couldn't trace the workings of His hand?

The next morning, she went to the bank, withdrew two hundred dollars, and offered the president a gracious "thank you for your cooperation" in handling the Starbuck account.

After paying the blacksmith for the repair work on George's freight wagon, she approached a man she knew had also lost all his money to the hotel thief and had spent the night curled up in an alley. Judging him as trustworthy, she offered him a job driving the wagon to Denver, paying half of a generous wage now and promising half upon delivery. He readily accepted. Along with the money, she gave him a letter to deliver to George explaining what had happened.

Catching a ride with a midwife who was going to make calls on her patients in sparsely settled towns to the east, Mandy set out for what she hoped would be the turning point in her quest.

259

The signature on the page of the hotel register read John Starbuck, but the handwriting still seemed foreign to the one who penned it. Would he ever get used to the current result of taking pen in hand and signing his name?

Upon entering the small dark room, he threw the key on the dresser and his *parfleche* on the chair. He lay on the bed fully clothed, deciding it wasn't worth the effort to undress. By the time he worked his way out of his buckskins it would be nearly time to work his way back into them. He pulled the bedspread across himself, settled into the soft mattress, and closed his eyes. But sleep would not come.

She kept him awake this night as she did every night. No matter how hard he drove himself every day in his search for her, he never was so exhausted that he could fall asleep without thinking about her, yearning for her, praying for her.

He turned to his side and pulled the cover up higher. He repositioned the pillow, then punched it a couple of times. Finding it impossible to get comfortable, he sat up, leaned back against the pine headboard, and gave free rein to the thoughts that would not be forced away.

Here he was in a single bed in a dank hotel room in a vulgar town. Alone. How he longed to lie with her once again, to feel her soft skin as he traced the contours of her face, to snuggle against her and share his body warmth when she complained of the chilly morning air. For a time after losing his arm, he spurned the idea of making love to her. *His left hand is under my head, and his right hand doth embrace me.* Now he yearned for her deeply.

He got up from the bed, crossed to the window and looked out into the darkness. So much could happen to a woman alone out there: bad weather, bad roads, and his greatest fear—bad men.

At least he knew where she had been as of two weeks ago. After wiring her family, he received a return telegram from George offering new hope. They had received a letter from her by way of a freight driver she had hired in this very town. Dakota knew the town well. He had spent some time here as a blacksmith and had made an extremely good wage. But he hated its bawdiness and came to realize that the corporate character of the town reflected the individual nature of most of its citizens. With few exceptions, they were cheap, inconsiderate and uncaring, and he hated to think that Mandy had spent any time with them. But at least he could get a solid lead on where she had gone from here.

He returned to the drab, unwelcoming bed as the sky was beginning to lighten. After a couple of hours of distressed sleep, his search continued.

The morning desk clerk remembered her. "She's the one with the gimpy leg, right?" Dakota's contemptuous glare had the man clearing his throat before adding, "I, uh, think she went to the bank to see about a loan after the robbery we had here. I don't think they gave her any money, though, 'cause I heard she waited tables in the restaurant that night so she could earn an extra dollar to pay for a room."

Dakota's voice rose with his anger. "You mean you wouldn't rent her a room because she was a dollar short?"

The clerk raised his hands in innocent surrender. "Hey, it weren't me. And the other guy was just followin' the rules, mister. Nobody gets a room without payin' up front. No exceptions."

Dakota fought down the urge to choke the varmint, but he needed him to answer a question. "You say she went to the bank for a loan, and *then* came back here to work?"

"That's right."

Dakota's wrath heightened when he confronted the loan officer at the bank.

"Her request was highly irregular, and I sent her to the manager."

"Did Patterson know anything about this?"

"Well, I wouldn't know about that, sir."

Dakota reached across the desk, grabbed the man by the shirt collar and twisted hard. "*Did he know?*"

"She got in to see him in the afternoon!" the man choked.

Dakota released him and stormed for the office behind the teller cages.

"You can't go in there!" one of the tellers called out.

"So stop me."

Preston Patterson was replacing a book in the massive

261

bookcase when the door flew open. He turned suddenly, startled. "What's all the commotion? Who are—" He stopped short as recognition came to him.

"Oh, it's Mr. Starbuck, isn't it?" A malevolent smile appeared as he surveyed the steadfast figure before him. "You've...*changed* since we last met."

Dakota faced him full front, no longer turning his right side away from any man. His eyes never left those of the pariah standing across the mahogany desk.

"My wife came here requesting a loan. Why didn't you give her the money from my account?"

"She asked for a loan and didn't qualify. She didn't mention wanting money from your account."

"She wasn't aware of the account and you *knew* that, you pus-sucking maggot! And you knew the reason I wrote up all that stupid legal double-talk was so the money would be available to her in case something ever happened to me."

That stupid grin again. "It appears something *has* happened."

"You were bound by your own regulation to give her that money."

"True, but..." Patterson stepped to his desk, picked out a cheroot, bit off its end, and placed it between his teeth. "I was having far too much fun with her."

Dakota raced to the man, grabbed him by the throat and forced him against the bookcase.

Two men charged through the door and across the room. They wrenched Dakota off the bank president.

"We got word there was trouble here, boss," one of the brawny men said. "Want us to handle him in the usual way?"

"No, we've not finished our business yet, boys." Patterson straightened and readjusted his suit. He gestured for the men to wait by the door.

"I'm not an uncaring man, Starbuck." He picked up the cigar that had fallen onto the desk and struck a match to light it. "I offered to help your wife."

"I can imagine what you offered. But she met your challenge, didn't she, Patterson, choosing to wait tables on a broken foot over any favor you had to offer."

Patterson's eyes narrowed. "I never liked you, Starbuck. Not since the day you were hired to forge the security bars for the bank's windows. You'd come here to take measurements, the townswomen would be all aflutter, and I could never conceive of why they were so attracted to a lowly, filthy blacksmith. And you never gave a single one of them so much as a second glance, which made them all the more crazy." He made an exaggerated study of Dakota's empty sleeve. "But I don't suppose you have a problem with doting women any longer, do you?"

"As I recall, you were never seen without a fine-looking woman on your arm, Mr. Bank President. What possible interest could you have had in what women thought of a 'lowly blacksmith'? Could it be that you had to *buy* your women?"

"Get out, Starbuck!"

"But you found in my wife a woman who wouldn't be bought. And that plagues you, doesn't it, Patterson?"

Patterson bared his teeth. "Take your measly six hundred dollars and *get out of my bank!*"

"*Six* hundred? I had *eight* hundred dollars here when I came through in June."

Patterson became noticeably uneasy. "It's like you said, I was bound by my own regulation, so I informed your wife of the money after…"

Dakota grinned. "After she made mincemeat out of you." He leaned closer to the banker. "And after you gave thought to what would happen once I got wind of your withholding the money." He shoved the man back a step, turned and strode out of the office, his head high and his smile wide.

After withdrawing his remaining funds from the bank, Dakota spoke to the blacksmith Mandy paid to repair the wagon. But he did not know where she went after leaving town, and neither did anyone else. He went to the livery to get his horse.

He scratched his steed behind the ears. "She's been a busy girl, Chief, but no one seems to know where she went or how she got there. So, we're back to where we started. At least I know she's got money, and as of two weeks ago she was all right."

He smiled again with pride over his wife's matchless fortitude.

"She's *better* than all right."

CHAPTER 38

The stage station's chimney smoke was visible through the crisp October air from a mile away. Supper would be cooking beneath that smoke, and Dakota hoped he'd be able to share in some of the spread.

The attendant led the last of the lathered horses into the stable where they would rest up and continue the journey west the next day. As he scattered hay, he looked out over the paddock fence and noticed a stranger riding in from the south. Always cautious, he walked to the gate where his rifle rested and waited for the stranger to approach. "Howdy!" he called as the palomino stopped a few yards from the gate.

"Howdy." Dakota's eyes turned toward the door of the large wooden building where the aroma of frying meat escaped through an open window. "I was wondering if I could get a meal here."

"It'll cost yeh."

He dismounted slowly, his exhaustion even more acute than his hunger. Tying the rein to the fence post, he gestured toward his horse. "Could you get him something, too, and maybe brush him down?"

"It'll cost yeh extra."

He nodded his consent and went into the station.

The passengers had finished freshening up and were gathering in the middle of the large room. Dakota struck a deal with the station agent, then washed up in the cold water in the basin.

Bone weary, he sat in a chair where the heat from the stove had a further sedating effect. He set his elbow on the arm of the chair, rested his head in the palm of his hand and closed his eyes.

"Tomorrow evening we'll be in Denver," a female voice said in anticipation. "I can hardly wait."

The voices in the room grew distant as his body yielded to the demand for sleep.

"Supper's served up, folks," the stationmaster was saying, "so y'all all take a seat and dig in. I'll go round up that stray that wandered off to the creek."

The stage driver offered to go instead. "She's my passenger, my responsibility. And a real puzzler at that."

"She's an odd one, all right," said another female traveler. "She hardly spoke a word on the stage, just kept reading that book that made her all teary-eyed."

"Then when we get here," a male passenger added, "she spouts on and on about the old stage stop that used to stand here, and its managers. As if we cared to hear about it."

"Why, this place is a lot bigger and far better fortified than the one that burnt down here a coupla years back," the stationmaster said.

"She never even told us her name," one of the women stated, "so we started calling her by the name of that ridiculous book—*Evangeline*."

Dakota's eyes shot open.

* * *

She sat on a rock by the bank of the creek, her blue cloak draped around her, an open book on her lap. She gazed out on the water whose level was much lower than the last time she was there. Not far from the spot where she now sat was the place where she'd helped the stationmistress draw water, an Indian boy close to her side.

The pages on her lap rustled in the wind. She held them in place and read:

Fair was she and young, when in hope began the long journey;
Faded was she and old, when in disappointment it ended.
Each succeeding year stole something away from her beauty,
Leaving behind it, broader and deeper, the gloom and the shadow.

It had been a little over four months of first waiting and then searching, but to Mandy it seemed a lifetime, as it had been for Evangeline. Mandy's journey, her search, was over. It ended here in disappointment. She could go on no longer. She was almost halfway through her pregnancy, and the quest had taken its toll.

How she longed for him, to hold him, to see his warm smile, to hear her name flow softly from his lips.

Mandy.

She could hear it carried on the wind as if it were real. It was eerie.

"Mandy."

Her heart skipped. The voice sounded *too* real. She raised her head and stared across the creek into the prairie, listening. The only sounds were those of the water babbling its way past her and the creaking of the nearly bare branches under the force of the rising wind.

Yet she sensed more. Her heart dared to believe there was more, and it began to beat faster. Slowly she turned her head, fearing her imagination had once more reacted to the yearnings of her heart.

Then she saw him.

Neither moved or spoke.

Her glance shifted to his right side. Then she studied his face again, her soul crying for the things he had suffered. She raised herself from the rock and turned to face him, unable to believe in the reality of his presence.

Twice he started to speak, but the words died on his lips.

She breathed his name.

He walked to her, slowly at first, then each stride lengthened and quickened until he reached her and snatched her into his arm. Her arms surrounded his neck, and they cleaved to each other with a renewed strength neither had known for a long time. Both had dreamed of this moment, and both feared it was another illusion that would end with a painful awakening. They could not let go.

Dakota found his voice first, but still could not find adequate words to explain.

"There's so much I want to say, but all of my languages failed me the moment I saw you sitting there."

"You don't have to say anything. Just hold me."

Hold her he did, long and tight.

"I'm so sorry for what I put you through, Mandy. I went crazy. And it cost you so much sadness and suffering."

She pressed her fingers to his lips. "None of that matters at this moment. I'm just so glad I found you."

He had to chuckle. "I think *I'm* the one who found *you*,

darlin'."

"But I've been searching—"

"I know. I know where you've been and what you've been doing."

"But how could you know?"

"I went to Denver."

"Oh, Dakota! You went there? I should've stayed like everyone told me to. But I just couldn't go another day without knowing what had happened to you."

"I know. *Believe me*, I know!"

"What matters is that we found *each other*. Oh, Dakota, I love you so much."

He called on all of his senses to help convince him she was truly with him at last. He felt the softness of her skin as he pressed his cheek to hers. He drank in the scent of her hair as he buried his face in its welcoming thickness. All he had longed for was his at this moment. He drew her closer.

Something pressed against him. The present he bought before leaving Denver was inside his shirt.

"I have something for you." He stepped back and retrieved the small package.

With a questioning expression, she took it from his hand and slowly removed the lavender wrapping paper, exposing a brown felt box. She lifted back the lid on its hinge. Her eyes beheld the treasure inside, and her breath held.

Removing the glimmering gold band from the box, he showed her the inscription inside:

Perfect love casteth out fear 2-14-66

Her eyes brimmed with tears.

He took her left hand and held it out. "Hold it steady now." He placed the ring on her third finger. "It's long overdue, just as this reunion is."

She raised her hand in the air, fancying how the sun's rays dazzled the ring. The sparkles in her eyes matched the ones dancing on the gold band, and he knew what she was about to say.

"Oh, Dakota, it's simply—"

"*Exquisite!*" they exclaimed together.

He drew her to him again. She felt another little "package" between them.

"I have something to share with you, too." She took a

267

backward step. "I hope...oh, Dakota, I hope you'll be happy with it."

She unclasped her cloak and let it fall to the ground. She placed her hand with the shiny gold ring on her abdomen. He took notice of its increased size and roundness.

"Are you...does this mean...what are you telling me?"

In her most articulate Arapaho, she replied, "I think you already know, even though you ask."

His face outshone the late afternoon sun. He rested his hand on top of hers. "You have made me the happiest man alive."

"Truthfully, I wasn't sure how you'd feel about it. I was afraid it would make you even more concerned about how you'll provide for three instead of just the two of us."

"I *am* concerned. A thorny road lies ahead of us. I don't yet know how I'll make a good life for you and our child, but I do know that we *will* make it. *Together.* And we'll be a growing family again, and I want that more than anything." His hand moved along the contours of her abdomen. "How far along are we here?"

She smiled in reminiscence. "I can't be certain, but remember that last night we spent in Colorado City? Or perhaps the next morning?"

His expression altered. "It was one of my best memories, until I found myself languishing on an army cot, believing that night was to be our last together."

She reached to touch his face. "Let's go forth and make new best memories."

Their kiss was fervent and lingering. Their lips parted reluctantly.

Mandy glanced down at her well-worn book, lifted it from the rock and leafed through the pages a final time, resolving never to read it again.

"I'm glad ours was a happier ending than that of Evangeline and her Gabriel. They found each other too late."

Dakota reached over and closed the book. "Our story's not over, my love."

She smiled at him. "Let's go home."

They slipped their arms around each other and Mandy took a step, but Dakota held back. "What's wrong?" she asked.

"Not a thing. In fact, in light of all the changes that have

268

taken place in our lives, it's satisfying to know some things will never change."

Her brow crinkled.

He stepped around the rock and bent to the ground.

Their laughter carried west with the wind when Dakota extended his arm and offered Mandy her royal blue cloak.

EPILOGUE

April, 1868

Dear Cassie,

I was so glad to receive your letter, my dear cousin, and can hardly wait for you to arrive this summer. I am as anxious to hear the particulars of your experiences as a nurse during the war—and especially your secret confinement in that Southern prison camp—as you are to hear the details of my goings-on. We four will be burning gallons of midnight oil!

Much has changed since I wrote you last. George's freight line is closing its Denver office due to the poor economy here. He and Ma will be moving to Kansas City next month. I don't need to tell you how much I will miss my mother. I've even begun to get along with George of late. Dakota is buying the house from them, and Julie is staying on with us. Jeff will soon be leaving for Illinois where he will settle in before beginning his law studies at Northwestern University in the fall.

I have made mention to you of a dear friend, a former doctor, who lived near us in the mountains. Well, he surprised us one day by showing up at the house when he came to Denver to do winter trading. As it turned out, his timing could not have been more perfect, which leads me to the happiest news of all.

About six weeks ago—on Valentine's Day, and our second wedding anniversary—it became apparent that our baby would wait no longer to be born despite it being a full month before I was due. We sent for the doctor, but he was tied up. So Will, who had seen us through the death of our first child, was pressed into service—albeit with a tincture of apprehension—to see us through the birth of our TWIN boys. They were small, weighing only about four pounds each, but are healthy and doing well, as am I. Needless to say, Dakota and I are most grateful for the way God has doubly blessed us, and Will has experienced again the very thing that brought him the most pleasure in his former profession.

As you can imagine, our honey-blond twins, whom we named David and Jonathan, keep us busy day and night. But

Dakota is in his glory with his sons, although at times is troubled by his inability to do things with them as he did with Baby Gregg. (Julie tells him he should be thankful he doesn't have to change diapers). But despite his restrictions—or perhaps in part due to them, for his reliance on God has never been deeper—the twins could not have a more capable or loving father. His abilities, and not his disability, are what define the man I love and trust wholeheartedly.

We had some concerns when he opened his blacksmith shop earlier this year that there might be an element of prejudice, and it has turned out that way, but not so much in the form we assumed. For many people it is his handicap—more so than his heritage—that makes them hesitant to do business at his smithy. But time has proven to be on his side. People are beginning to realize that he is perfectly capable of putting in a full day, and that the workmanship he and his apprentice Cody North produce is unsurpassed in Denver, and indeed, the entire Front Range. Cody is an extremely talented and ambitious young smith whose sole drawback is his inexperience, and he and Dakota have a wonderful working relationship. (Julie is working on a relationship of her own with the charming Mr. North). So, business is still a bit slow, but growing, and we are thankful.

With so much empty space in the house, there is plenty of room for you and that enigmatic husband of yours to stay right here with us until you get yourselves settled in your own home. And you will get to meet our very good friend, Travis Haines, who will be visiting us this summer with his daughter, Mollie. We are excited about having a full and joy-filled home.

Suffice it to say that Dakota and I have come to know a joy given us by no one on this earth, and no one on this earth can take it away. We appreciate more than ever the deep-rooted friendships we have made, the family bonds that hold us together, and the confidence of God's workmanship in our lives—whether we recognize it at the time or not. Secure in these relationships, we need not fear any terror by night, nor arrow that flieth by day.

Take care, and we will see you soon.

> *Love,*
> *Mandy*

Read Cassie's thrilling story of love and intrigue in
Erin Rainwater's

True Colors

You can contact Erin via her website at
www.erinrainwater.com

Discussion Questions
The Arrow That Flieth By Day

1. Psalm 91:5-7 reads: *"Thou shalt not be afraid for the terror by night; nor for the arrow that flieth by day; nor for the pestilence that walketh at noonday. A thousand shall fall at thy side, and ten thousand at thy right hand; but it shall not come nigh thee."* (KJV)
~What are some examples of how this verse is used as a recurring point of focus throughout the book?

2. After the smallpox epidemic, Mandy feels her efforts were fruitless.
~What strategy does Dakota use to convince her she's wrong?
~Have you ever tried a similar strategy, and if so, did it help?

3. Dakota's friend Travis Haines is on a mission of revenge for the death of his wife.
~Have you ever known anyone with a deeply ingrained need for revenge in his or her heart?
~What attempts to talk them out of their objective tried but failed? Did any succeed?
~Besides the fact that Mandy prevented him from satisfying his revenge, what ultimately sends Travis home to his daughter without achieving his goal?

4. Will Bowden knows from experience that a couple's grief can either draw them closer together or split them apart.
~What are some of the reasons Dakota and Mandy drifted from one another?
~What virtues in them made them hang on despite their grieving separately and growing animosity?

5. It took a traumatic experience, followed by a time of introspection and a confrontation with Thunder Cloud for Dakota to see what negative attribute he'd been harboring in his heart all along.
~What did he discover there?
~What has it taken for you to discover less than virtuous qualities in your heart?

6. Books have been written about why bad things happen to good people. Despite Mandy being a woman of faith, some pretty bad things happen to her.

~What types of reactions, both good and bad, does she manifest in her difficult circumstances?

~How do you think you might have responded in similar circumstances?

~How do you answer people who question why God allows evil in the world?

7. Temptations abound when Dakota and Mandy are separated.

~What are some of Dakota's temptations while recuperating at the Cheyenne camp?

~How is Mandy tempted when she ends up nearly penniless in a strange town?

~How does each overcome their trials?

8. I had a pastor who once said that Christians can sometimes learn some of their greatest lessons from unbelievers.

~What are some examples of that happening in this story?

~Can you share examples of it happening in your life?

9. Recall the following predicaments the characters faced in the story and consider what you might have done in their place.

~Mandy thinks her only way of escape is to steal a horse.

~Mandy holds Headless Jack's ultimate fate in her hands.

~Dakota believes his wife is better off without him as he now is.

~Julie begs Dakota to withhold his identity from her family.

~Mandy learns that Thunder Cloud is going to be hung for something he didn't do.

10. Mandy and Dakota often did not see God's hand working in their lives until much later, in retrospect.

~What are some of the incidents they experienced, unaware of God's perspective at the time?

~Share occasions when it has taken 20/20 hindsight for you to see God's workmanship in your life.

Made in the USA
Monee, IL
15 March 2023

29496624R00166